three
daughters

three
daughters

•

letty cottin pogrebin

FARRAR, STRAUS AND GIROUX

NEW YORK

Farrar, Straus and Giroux
19 Union Square West, New York 10003

Distributed in Canada by Douglas & McIntyre Ltd.
Printed in the United States of America
First edition, 2002

Library of Congress Cataloging-in-Publication Data
Pogrebin, Letty Cottin.
    Three daughters / Letty Cottin Pogrebin.— 1st ed.
      p.   cm.
    ISBN 0-374-27660-9 (alk. paper):
    1. Parent and adult child—Fiction.   2. Fathers and daughters—Fiction.
  3. Jewish families—Fiction.   4. Married women—Fiction.   5. Sisters—Fiction.
  6. Rabbis—Fiction.   I. Title.
  PS3616.O35 T47 2002
  813'.54—dc21   2002023432

Designed by Abby Kagan

www.fsgbooks.com

1   3   5   7   9   10   8   6   4   2

for ethan, benjamin, maya, molly,

zev, and arlo

I learned to speak among the pains.

—*Yehuda Amichai*

three daughters

one

THE DRIVER OF THE DODGE CARAVAN gave Shoshanna the finger, gesticulating furiously through his windshield like the villain in a silent movie.

You couldn't blame the guy. She was a horrific sight—a wild-eyed middle-aged virago in a mud-splattered coat racing across the Henry Hudson Parkway to snatch a piece of paper from the pavement. She rammed the paper into her pocket and ran back to the shoulder of the road, unflustered by her close call, then dropped to her haunches and studied the oncoming traffic. That was the nerve-racking part, waiting for the right conditions, the perfect moment to lunge. A station wagon roared past, revving up the wind. In its wake, a momentary lull, an open space, plenty of time to sprint out, snatch up another scrap, and fly back to her redoubt at the edge of the highway before the next car rounding the bend in the distance could reach her. She'd timed it perfectly, her road dance.

Wait. Run. Retreat.

Wait. Run. Retreat.

Shoshanna might have passed for a litter-phobic environmentalist but for her periodically emptying her overstuffed pockets onto the back seat of her Volvo and smoothing each bedraggled sheet with the tenderness of a poet saving love letters from the flames. The salvage from the highway was, however, unromantic—the tattered remains of her Filofax, which, despite manifestly hazardous working conditions, she'd succeeded over the course of the afternoon in repossessing piece by piece. More surprising to her than the virtuosity of her performance was the fact that it was necessary at all. That she herself had triggered this paper chase, this anarchy in the afternoon, made no sense. Such things happened to other people, not to the archenemy of disorder, the ultra-organized Shoshanna Wasserman Safer, for whom chaos was anathema and mindfulness next to godliness. Losing track of something as important as her Filofax was consistent with neither her sense of self nor the profession she practiced with a rare blend of doggedness and delight. Shoshanna made a living straightening out other people's messes. She systematized, organized, solved problems, averted crises. Keeping Things Under Control was both her obsession and her job. She tamed the wildness, knowing better than most how quickly chaos can overtake one's life when given the slightest opportunity.

Thirty years ago, on a California beach, she'd seen a joyful day turn tragic simply because she and her best friend had not been paying attention. The Evil Eye—that stalker for whom human contentment is an affront and bliss an incitement to riot—had leapt into the breach and the worst had happened. Ever since, she'd been keeping an eye on the Eye, studying its wily ways, noting how effortlessly it could transform a carefree walk in the woods into a deadly struggle against nature, a marshmallow roast into a conflagration, or a healthy pregnancy into a nightmare of loss. She knew its habits: laughter was its lure, pleasure its call to action, good fortune its invitation to havoc. The Eye could sneak up from behind and give a person a hard shove into chaos as easily as a car might stray across the white line on this highway. Because she understood this, Shoshanna had become a stalker of the stalker, guarding against the fall of its shadow across her path, tuned to its footsteps in the dark.

This compulsion, she'd learned to her dismay, she shared with Charles Lindbergh. The renowned aviator, WASP avatar and Nazi sympathizer, was hardly the soul mate she'd have chosen had she not read in his daughter's memoir that he was "ever on the alert for dangers, though the dangers were unspecified. 'It's the unforseen . . .' he would warn us. 'It's always the unforeseen.'" Shoshanna Safer had become a watchdog of the unforeseen, an expert on preventable chaos, and because nothing dire had happened in her orbit since that desolating day on the California beach, she'd come to believe that the only force capable of defeating her was divine whimsy—a flash flood, a letter bomb, the freak accident like the one that sent a construction crane plummeting forty stories to land on her neighbor's leg. Random strikes were beyond her capacity to predict or prevent. But today's accident couldn't be blamed on God's caprice or the stalker. This was a mess of her own making.

Wait. Run. Retreat.

Whirling on and off the highway, scavenging pages, she struggled to reconstruct how she'd lost track of the datebook in the first place. Remembered having it at the breakfast table that morning when she'd flipped through it in search of a free weekend. (She and Daniel had been trying to get away togther since New Year's.) And when she went downstairs to her office, coffee cup in one hand, datebook in the other, always a two-fisted journey. (Running a business from the garden floor of their brownstone had greatly increased her productivity once she'd figured out how to keep work and family separate, with the help of the Filofax.) Had it when she'd called her cousin Warren to congratulate him on his promotion (thanks to the reminder her secretary, Fiona, London's gift to a Jewish compulsive, had written in the 10 a.m. slot). And when she'd grabbed a peanut-butter-and-jelly sandwich at her desk and a dollop of strawberry jam dripped on today's page—Wednesday, February 17, 1999. Ash Wednesday. The day she lost control. The day order turned to ashes.

Could have left the book behind on her desk, its sticky spot drying in the sun; but no, she remembered it lying on the passenger seat exactly where it belonged, open to the route directions Fiona had clipped to the calendar page to facilitate the drive to Riverdale. The new client had been waiting on his porch when Shoshanna swung into his driveway.

Blue jeans, cashmere V-neck the color of moss, moccasins with no socks, though it was about 30 degrees out. His jeans, she'd noted, were pressed. An ashy smudge marked the center of his forehead. Perversely, it reminded Shoshanna of the Star of David her sister Rachel wore on a chain around her neck as proudly as if it were the Croix de Guerre. Rachel's trademarks were the Jewish star and the double strand of pearls she wore virtually every day of her life, though the pearls came off now and then—say at the beach or on the treadmill—while the Magen David never left her chest. Shoshanna, discomfited by public displays of religion, had a mezuzah tacked to her doorpost, but that was it. Why stir up the anti-Semites? The smudge on the client's face seemed to shout "Catholic! Catholic!" and she'd wondered if her naked forehead was shouting back "Jew! Jew!"

In his wood-paneled study, Venetian blinds sliced the winter sun into gauzy slats. Dust motes floated lazily on bars of afternoon light. Fresh-squeezed orange juice glowed in crystal goblets. A woman notices when a man does something like that. Then again, after years of monitoring the stalker, Shoshanna noticed everything. She'd registered how neat he was, how orderly, and his study even more so. Tidy stacks of magazines squared off on the coffee table like troops on review. Diverse interests—*Time* in one pile, *Men's Health* in another, *The New York Review of Books, Travel & Leisure, Foreign Affairs*. A pyramid of green apples rose from a wooden bowl. Beside an upholstered wing chair stood a small table bearing a phone and a notepad with the words *Milk, Eggs, Brillo, Post Office* written in a fine hand. Clearly, he wasn't one of those newly divorced men who need help stocking their pantries, a task she'd been called upon to perform more than once. So what *did* he want her to do? Test-drive his Viagra?

"Retired this year. Widowed. Wanna join a gym," he'd announced in a flat staccato, and handed her a sheet headed *Health Clubs*. "Check these out, would you? And be exacting." He wanted her to evaluate six local gyms—compare their facilities (state-of-the-art equipment? climbing wall? pool?) and their classes (varied? crowded? good hours?); interview personal trainers (low-key? hyper? motivating body types?);

survey the locker rooms (clean carpets? thick towels? wide lockers?); and sample the fruit smoothies.

"Details under each category, please," he'd added, pointing to his ruled columns. "I'll review your findings and join the best one. Clear?"

"Yes, sir!" She'd felt an impulse to salute.

He'd risen from his chair, a client after her own heart, a man who knew when to end a meeting. (If hell existed, Shoshanna was sure it would turn out to be a meeting.) Still in the moss sweater, no coat, he had accompanied her out to the Volvo, and as they'd stood there on the passenger side, she'd extended her hand and said, "Looking forward to working with you." Stock line, only this time she'd meant it. Being spectacularly sedentary, she might even shape up on his dime. "So, when do you need this?"

"How's six weeks hence?"

Hence? Who'd he think he was—Alistair Cooke? She'd flipped the pages of the Filofax to March 31 and, bracing the book against her fender, had written *Health club report due* (in perfect penmanship, in case he was watching). She was about to open the passenger door and toss the Filofax on the front seat as usual, the way she *always* did, when he'd tugged at her arm like an excited kid.

"Hey! Before you go, come see the view."

Shoshanna had interrupted herself mid-gesture and—because she always indulged her clients—set the book on the car roof, and followed the man around to the back of his house, where a wide lawn, pockmarked with old snow, sloped to the banks of the Hudson River. Dried poufs of hydrangea blossoms clung to bare branches. Tall pines swayed with the breeze. It was hard to believe they were only minutes from Times Square; the Edenic hush, the water gleaming like molten glass in the glow of the late-afternoon sun. Even the dour outlines of New Jersey seemed incandescent.

"Nice, huh?" he'd asked, his pale eyes watering. He'd wiped his face with his sleeve. The mossy sweater came away streaked with ash. The mark on his forehead had faded to a ghost image in shadowy taupe; he was a neat man with a dirty face. He was thinking of his wife, he said, the sunsets he now had to watch without her. Something throbbed in Shoshanna's throat. A presentiment that her beloved Daniel would die someday, most likely before she did, and she would be alone.

"Amazing! And to think we're in the Bronx!" she'd said quickly, blotting out the thought.

"*Riverdale,*" he'd corrected. As they ambled back to her car, the man began reminiscing about his wife, how she brought out hot cider in a thermos for their winter sunsets, how the light played on her face, how she died eighteen months after they learned she had a brain tumor. Shoshanna, fearing the chaos of her own empathy, finessed a gentle farewell, hastily jumped behind the wheel, and took off, never noticing the Filofax on the roof on the passenger side. After all these years, the stalker had found its opening and pounced.

Squatting now at the edge of the highway waiting for her next dash, she could imagine what must have happened. The datebook, heavy in its leather binder, had stayed put as the car snaked through Riverdale's quiet, tree-lined streets. But once she'd pulled onto the highway and picked up speed, the wind had whipped open its cover and sheared through its pages, carrying away her telephone directory in the downdrafts of winter, ripping her calendar from its rings, sheet by sheet, the way old movies show the passage of time, yanking attachments from their staples and paper clips. In minutes, the tidiness of a lifetime was torn from its moorings and set adrift.

She could visualize all that now, after the fact, but hours ago, when she'd first started driving home from Riverdale with her new work assignment and a slice of the widower's sorrow, she hadn't known anything was amiss until her cell phone rang.

"Hi, Mom. Any chance you could babysit Saturday night?" Nelly always cut to the chase, a habit that doubtless contributed to her competence as a horseback-riding instructor, though it made for rather perfunctory conversation.

"Love to, Nell. One sec, I'll see if we're free." She'd reached for the Filofax and had nearly run off the road when the seat beside her yielded only upholstery buttons and a flaccid safety strap. Impossible. It had to be there. It was *always* there. The minute she got in the car, reflexively, even before turning the key in the ignition, she would prop the date-book on the passenger seat like a companion riding shotgun. Where else could it be? "Call you back, Nell," she'd gulped into the phone and hit the Off button before her daughter could ask what was wrong.

A signpost announced FOR EMERGENCIES ONLY. Surely a missing Filofax qualifies. She'd piloted the car into the rest stop and searched the floor, between the seats, the gearshift well, the rear seat, even the glove compartment, though the bulging book couldn't have fit in on a bet. She'd rummaged in her satchel for the organizer's familiar contours, then, ever more frantically, combed each crevice of the car a second time. Coming up empty, she'd burst into tears. Ten miles from home, yet she'd felt cosmically dislocated, as if she'd lost her footing on the planet. Her gravitational pull, her grounding, the finely meshed gears of her life, depended on her Filofax. The fat black book was the curator of her commitments, the repository of every appointment, address, phone, and fax number, plus an uncountable number of items she'd clipped, wedged, shoved, stapled, tucked, or pressed between its scuffed leather covers—not just credit cards and business cards but restaurant reviews, expense slips, snapshots, theater tickets, fabric swatches, poems, aphorisms, and a zillion memory joggers. Shoshanna's much-admired capacity to remember not only her friends' birthdays and anniversaries but their food allergies, wine preferences, favorite flowers, kids' names, the gifts she'd given them in the past, and the food they'd eaten at her dinner table (so she wouldn't duplicate a menu) had been made possible by the record-keeping systems in her Filofax. She'd never bothered to memorize her schedule; that's what the calendar section was for. It told her what she had to do, where she had to go, what she had to look forward to, or dread. Without it, she couldn't function. Without it, her nexts would be nevers. Clients would be waiting for projects she'd forgotten were due. There would be empty seats in concert halls, angry hosts at dinner parties. She would disappoint, offend, irritate. Great chunks of her life would vanish; her time would be ungovernable, her world would turn upside down. Without it, she wouldn't show up in her own future.

Energized by a billowing panic, she'd gunned the Volvo out of the rest stop and retraced her route to where she'd first entered the highway and there had found the stuff of her life blanketing the southbound lanes like the after-trash of a ticker-tape parade. Everything was everywhere: calendar pages and address sheets tattooed by tire marks, flapping against the concrete divider, lodged in the slush, impaled on bare branches, snared by the chain-link fence. A wedding invitation plastered to a speed-limit sign like a Lost Dog notice. A memo wrapped around a lamppost. Receipts fluttering in the brush. The asphalt looked like a hundred bulletin boards run over by a Mack truck.

At first, she'd just stared, her mouth dry as wool, until she'd reminded herself that this was a problem and she was a problem-solver, and if she could clean up other people's messes, she ought to be able to clean up her own. She would "accentuate the positive," as the old song had it, "and eliminate the negative." And there were plenty of positives—things to be grateful for—another hour of daylight, no rain, no snow, warm clothes, sturdy rubber-soled shoes, no appointments for the rest of the afternoon. Her plan took shape. She would begin with the easy stuff, the detritus caught in the shrubs and trees. Walking along the shoulder of the road, she picked up everything she could reach, loaded her pockets, then ran to the Volvo and dumped her gleanings on the back seat. No sweat so far, except that this simple harvest took longer than she'd anticipated and the sun was sinking fast. Next phase: on-site research. She'd studied the flow of vehicles, calculating how long it took most drivers to travel from the bend in the road where they first came into view to the spot where her quarry lay. Though the cars bore down like buffalo, they seemed less menacing once she'd noticed that, like cattle, they often traveled in herds, with enough space in between for her to scoot out, grab a sheet or two from the pavement, and zoom back to the shoulder before the next batch barreled toward her, horns blaring.

Wait (for the spaces).

Run (and seize a page or two or three).

Retreat (even faster).

Her first foray was as terrifying as a sky diver's maiden jump, but once she was back on the sidelines with spoils in hand, the adrenaline rush sent her down to her haunches again, ready for the next sprint. Fear gave way to pride as she perfected her routine, spurred by thoughts of what remained amid the roadkill. The twenty-five-year-old newspaper clipping announcing the engagement of Shoshanna Wasserman and Daniel Safer, her version of a rabbit's foot. The Bloomingdale's gift certificate her sister Rachel had given her for Hanukkah that she'd had no time to spend. A "Buy Ten, Get One Free" card from Starbucks with eight holes punched out. Her father's letter.

When it arrived a week ago, she'd stuck the aerogram in the inside flap of the Filofax and left it there moldering, for the news that Sam Wasserman would be coming to New York was not without its complications. Since he'd made aliyah in 1987, he'd been back only once, in '90, when Shoshanna and Rachel talked him into flying home to celebrate his eightieth birthday.

"Home is Jerusalem," he'd objected, but he came nonetheless and thoroughly enjoyed the fuss made over him by his family, who, after three years, had forgotten his sullen side—the frequently harsh critic, the brooding silences—and remembered only the sweet Sam.

"Dear Shoshie," he'd written in his shaky hand,

Given your oft-stated and presumably still-fond memories of my visit to New York nine years ago, you'll be pleased to learn that another important occasion seems to justify my journeying to the States. I've been asked to accept a Lifetime Achievement Award from Rodeph Tzedek. High time, too. I was beginning to wonder if my 30 years with the shul added up to a hill of beans. But now that

*they've seen fit to remember their old rabbi and give me this honor,
I'm sure as hell going to take it. Though I'm writing this letter in
February and won't be arriving until next December, I wanted to
give you fair notice, because I'm told the last weekend of this year is
going to be a big megillah due to the millennium. Since people seem
to be making plans very far in advance, I'm asking you now to save
the date: Friday night, December 31. I'm hoping everyone—and I
mean* everyone, *including the* great-grandkids—*will come and
share my* BIG NIGHT. *Until then,*

> *Shalom and love.*
> *Your Dad.*

Shoshanna knew he didn't really mean *everyone*. Nothing was that
simple in the Wasserman family, starting with the fact that Sam had
three daughters—Rachel, Leah, and Shoshanna—one of whom hadn't
spoken to him for nearly thirty-five years, and the other two, to their
enduring frustration, had no idea why. Whatever its cause, the cata-
clysm that blew Sam and Leah apart had left behind nothing but a
tense, truculent silence, and the clear message that Shoshanna and
Rachel were not to broach the subject with either party. But lately,
maybe because she was facing her fiftieth birthday and suffering new
intimations of mortality, Shoshanna had become determined to help
her father and sister heal their breach before it was too late. For their
sakes, of course, but also to assuage her own guilt, the years having convinced her that she must have contributed *something* to their estrange-
ment, perhaps just by being born. ("As a pawn can change a chess game,
a baby can change a life." The aphorism was clipped to one of the Filofax pages that hadn't turned up yet on the highway.)

Since the family's Leah Problem was said to date back to the year
after Shoshanna's birth, she could only assume that she had been at least
a partial cause of her sister's discontent, just as her sister was, in some
unspoken sense, the source of the unrest Shoshanna felt within herself.
Even when everything in her life was humming along, Shoshanna's personal Leah Problem disrupted the harmony she craved. Motivated by

that vague disquiet, the fixer of brokenness hoped to mastermind a cease-fire between her father and his exiled daughter—and, by reconciling them, to bring about her own relief. At eighty-nine, Sam had to know this trip could be his last. But, like his adopted country, he wasn't the type to make a unilateral peace move. If he and Leah were ever going to reconcile, someone—namely Shoshanna—would have to broker their reunion, find a way to engineer it without raising the hackles of a proud old man or setting off the choleric Leah, or, for that matter, infuriating their third sister, Rachel, who had received the identical letter from their father (Xeroxed) and saw no reason, as she put it, "to stir up stagnant waters." Unsentimental, pragmatic, at peace with the status quo, Rachel dismissed the notion of a pre-millennial reconciliation as hopeless.

"Give it up," she'd told Shoshanna. "They're both old mules. They'll never change."

But Shoshanna was sure Sam's upcoming visit could lead to a rapprochement if only she could figure out how to get the process rolling. Maybe emotional blackmail—she'd tell her father the present she wanted most for her fiftieth birthday was a truce between him and Leah; beg him to make the first move. Maybe give him an ultimatum: "Invite Leah to your award night, or I won't come." ("Don't do me any favors," he'd say. "Stay home.' Then what would she do?) Or maybe approach it the other way—tell Leah about the letter and ask *her* to take the initiative, or at least be open-minded if Sam reaches out. Guilt-trip *her* with the birthday present request. Or maybe leave both of them out of it and cook up something that would bring them together once Sam arrived in New York. In other words, trick them into wanting to make up. Ruminating on her options, Shoshanna had stirred up stagnant waters of her own and, thoroughly confused, had shoved Sam's letter in the Filofax along with everything else that mattered. And now it was gone, swallowed by the wind.

Wait (the wind was growing colder by the minute). *Run* (scoop up Blockbuster video card, one theater ticket—where was the other?—two bedraggled "D" pages from her phone directory). *Retreat*. Shoshanna hiked up her coat collar, trudged to the Volvo, and emptied her pockets for what must have been the hundredth time, then returned to her crouch. Her thighs ached. Her fingers had frozen into claws. Her frenzied hair—an auburn thatch her father had once dubbed "the burning bush"—looked more like a copper pot-scrubber flecked with twigs and litter. Her knees pushed through her trouser legs, raw potatoes grating against the stony roadside patch where she was kneeling now, as if in prayer, waiting for the next lull, the next mad dash that would restore order to her universe, one page at a time.

Night falls fast in February. Illuminated now by the oncoming headlamps, Shoshanna darted smoothly in and out of traffic, on and off the road, running, bending, grabbing, reaping, goaded in her labors by the sight of the sodden papers rising to new heights on the back seat. Why, one might ask, would a rational woman risk her life for a lousy datebook? Not risking—saving it, she'd have answered. Which is not to say she didn't recognize the lunacy of her road dance, as well as her dependence on her calendar and her overreaction to its loss. What, after all, was a datebook in the scheme of things? Nothing. Less than nothing compared to the tragedies in the daily papers that she'd made it her business to memorize.

TEENAGERS TRAMPLED AT ROCK CONCERT. SIX DEAD
MOVIE STAR PARALYZED IN HORSE ACCIDENT
TOURISTS KILLED IN COPTER CRASH
BOATING TRAGEDY CLAIMS FAMILY OF 4

It wasn't voyeurism that drew her to morbid news stories, but rather the hope of extracting from each a cautionary message, a clue, a survival technique, or an emergency plan that might someday come in handy to safeguard those she loved. To that end, she deconstructed every cave-in and crack-up, every washout and shipwreck, on the chance that what might appear random or accidental was actually attributable to human error and thus preventable. Once, having watched the aftermath of an earthquake on TV, she'd devised an evacuation plan from the brownstone and foolishly shared it with her sister Leah during one of their annual lunches. Greatly amused, the incorrigibly alliterative Leah had accused Shoshanna of being "a maven of misery, a connoisseur of catastrophe, a diva of disaster."

"I'm just preemptively prudent," Shoshanna had said, playing along, though she'd regretted giving her sister more ammunition for her mockery.

"What nareshkeit, Shoshie. For Chrissake, you live in Greenwich Village. The San Andreas fault doesn't run down fucking Bleecker Street. Besides, you ought to know it's futile to strategize about chaos."

On the contrary; for the last thirty years Shoshanna had been doing just that. Outsmarting the stalker. Outstaring the Eye. Perfecting her strategies. At the movies, she checked the location of the emergency exits. (Other people did the same, but how many also made sure that the exit doors were unlocked and the fire escapes unobstructed?) At the theater, she was a human smoke alarm, monitoring the burning candle at stage left or the cigarette an actor meant to stub out but missed. When Nelly and Jake lived at home, she wouldn't let them attend big-ticket soccer matches or rock concerts where the crowds might riot and crush them. She made her children carry hypothermia blankets when hiking, even if it was 90 degrees out (this precaution gleaned from the headlined calamity: FOUR DIE STRANDED ON MOUNTAIN IN FREAK SUMMER BLIZZARD). At home, she kept bike helmets, life jackets, freeze-dried meals, ipecac to induce vomiting, salves for burns, Benadryl for allergic reactions, and antidotes for poisons, bee stings, and convulsions. Other parents also stocked first-aid supplies, but how many bothered to take their fire extinguishers to the fire house to have them tested?

Better safe than scorched, she'd say, having picked up the alliteration tic from Leah.

Shoshanna wished her children were as judicious. But in that curious way that offspring often become dialectics of their parents, Jake was into helicopter skiing and white-water rafting (she often suspected he'd chosen the University of Colorado for its proximity to extreme terrain) and Nelly, passionate about horses from the time she was a tot, had always been hell-bent on galloping where the rest of the world feared to trot, and often did it bareback. Though Shoshanna allowed that this outcome was preferable to their having gone the other way and become more fearful than their mother, living with daredevil children was not easy for her. As soon as Nelly was old enough to travel alone, she had insisted on taking the Saturday-morning train up to Westchester, where she'd apprenticed herself to a horse trainer who gave her broad responsibilities in the stables and unlimited riding privileges. Claremont, Manhattan's only riding academy, hired her as an instructor right out of college, and at the end of every workday, Nelly saddled one of the horses and gave it free rein in Central Park, churning up the bridle paths as if she were tearing across the plains of the Wild West. One evening, her horse whinnied, reared, and skidded to a halt inches from a jogger in blue satin shorts who'd materialized in the middle of the dirt track. The young man was hunched over, writhing in pain.

"Achilles tendon," he moaned.

"Hop aboard," said Nelly. She hoisted him up behind her and, like a cavalry officer bringing in the wounded, rode him to Roosevelt Hospital's emergency room entrance.

"You're not going to disappear into the sunset before I can thank you?" he called as a white-suited orderly rolled him away. "Ditch the horse, and the minute I'm out of here, I'll buy you dinner."

That was how Nelly met Ezra. Six months later, they were married, and a year after that, Pearl and Ruby were born. Despite having survived a kick-in-the-head accident as a child, Nelly put the twins on ponies well before they were three, and they loved it to the point where Shoshanna feared the Evil Eye might take notice. The other day, while she and Nelly sat on a bench in Adventure Playground watching Ruby climb the miniature pyramids, Shoshanna exercised a grandmother's prerogative. "Isn't that kind of high for her?"

"She's fine, Ma," replied Nelly as Pearl scampered up the wooden structure to join her sister.

"It scares me the way you let the girls take chances."

"They wouldn't be up there if they couldn't handle it. You've got to stop worrying so much."

"There's a lot to worry *about* with little children. I just read this terrible story—you keep an eye on the twins; I'll read it to you." Shoshanna extracted a newspaper clipping from her purse. " 'A toddler sightseeing with her parents fell to her death from the Golden Gate Bridge despite her father's desperate rescue attempt. Witnesses said the father tried to grab the two-year-old as she slipped through a gap between the walkway and traffic lanes.' "

"How awful!" said Nelly.

"You can learn something from that."

"Like what?"

"Like, bridges aren't safe for kids. Like, when you're in an unfamiliar situation, you might want to keep the girls on a leash."

Nelly groaned and rolled her eyes.

"Better leashed than lost," said Shoshanna.

"You're nuts, Ma!" Nelly hugged her and changed the subject, but Shoshanna couldn't shake the image of her precious granddaughters slipping through the cracks.

The world according to Shoshanna was divided into two kinds of people—those like her daughter Nelly who took their well-being for granted and those like Shoshanna who knew something horrible could happen because it already had. Her job was to stay alert on behalf of both breeds. Contented now—sometimes even flagrantly so—she knew she was a tempting target for the stalker. Yet she also knew that paying the Eye too much mind could sour her joy and make her an overcautious pain in the ass, as she'd often been to her children. Most of the time, though, she managed to strike a balance between pleasure and vigilance, keeping her worries to herself and enjoying life to the fullest without letting the stalker get the better of her. Not for nothing did a plaque on her desk say DYBBUK STOPS HERE.

Now, scuttering across the highway, Shoshanna vowed never again to be distracted by a Hudson River sunset.

Her friends would be as surprised to eavesdrop on her thoughts as to catch sight of her in the middle of the southbound lanes. "That couldn't be our Shoshanna!" they'd exclaim. "She's the most put-together person we know." They'd point to her famously neat files, her shipshape household, the clockworks of her busy life. They'd describe her as a detail person, someone who checks the gas jets on the stove before going to bed and never locks herself out of the house, who makes lists and keeps a pair of reading glasses in every purse. Someone who, were she a man, would be wearing a belt *and* suspenders. As proof of the pudding, her friends would say, just look at her business. The brochure said it all:

Overworked? Harried? Stressed-out? Let us simplify your life! Give us your To Do list, we'll give you back the one asset that is irreplaceable: Time. My Time Is Your Time *makes your time your own.*

The company's founding director sounded like a cross between the concierge at the Plaza and the Flying Nun:

Licensed as a paralegal, EMS practitioner, real estate broker, and Notary Public, Shoshanna Wasserman Safer also holds a B.A. in Political Science and a Master's in Organizational Dynamics. A professional problem-solver catering to the needs of the overburdened, she has, among other things:
- *written speeches for a steel company president*
- *organized a clown convention*
- *helped an infertile couple locate a surrogate mother*
- *served as an anonymous bidder at art auctions*
- *run book tours for authors*
- *located natural-looking prostheses for a breast cancer survivor*
- *researched dunking stools for a documentary on witchcraft*
- *collected fabric and tile samples for a top designer*
- *handled logistics for weddings and funerals*
- *transported a valuable pet parrot to Philadelphia*

Her newest client, the neatnik in Riverdale, had been referred by a woman who'd hired My Time Is Your Time to organize a photo safari for her husband's fortieth birthday, and that client in turn had been referred by a man who'd used Shoshanna to screen responses to his personals ad.

"I want the fun of a new relationship," he'd explained, "not the work." He'd left it to Shoshanna to interview applicants and set him up on dates, a task she'd found nearly impossible to fulfill without warning every prospect that the guy was a turd. (She'd charged double for the effort.) Compared to such smarmy assignments, she preferred the grunt-and-grind stuff—making travel arrangements, waiting for deliveries, dog-walking, house-sitting, packing for a move, keeping people's tax records, balancing checkbooks, filing insurance claims, updating frequent-flier accounts, cleaning out closets, organizing clutter, waiting in line at government offices. The jobs most of us avoid or procrastinate about Shoshanna undertook with relish, savoring the rewards of instant gratification, client gratitude, and the sense that she was contributing to a more orderly universe.

Finally, her friends might say, to understand how in control this woman is, get your hands on her Filofax. Which is exactly what Shoshanna had been trying to do for the last several hours while a question stuck in her head like a nail: How could *this* happen to *me*? There had to be a reason. Nothing happens without a reason.

Bingo! She'd almost missed the blue onionskin aerogram under the 246th Street overpass—Sam's letter, damp, limp, stained, but readable.

With this she lumbered back to the Volvo, sank behind the wheel, and encountered her face in the rearview mirror. Future shock! She'd be fifty in June. Bad time to cop a glimpse of where her looks were headed. Not a pretty sight—green eyes suspended in a net of red mesh, lips cracked and caked, cheeks like dried apricots. Her skin showed in its furrows the disappointment she felt in herself. If not for Daniel bucking her up whenever she found a gray hair or a wrinkle, the depredations of age might have been too much to bear. But as soon as she began to grouse about this or that, he'd always say something reassuring (the other day, he called her "a man's idea of an interesting woman," quoting Henry James), or he'd run his fingers through her hair and rhapsodize on her "cherub head," her "sweet-potato soufflé," her "fountain of russet ringlets." Someday he would stop raving about her looks, and then what?

She gunned the car into the southbound traffic. The dashboard clock glowed 8:10. By now, Daniel would be frantic. In their twenty-five years together, certain acts had become ritualized, among them the "What-are-we-doing-tonight?" phone call. No matter how many times they might have touched base during the day, this rite of reconnection was sacrosanct. The call usually came around five o'clock, rarely later than six, sometimes from his end, sometimes hers, nothing formalized, except that it happened, this checkpoint of intimacy, every day of their lives. Now it was after eight and they hadn't talked since breakfast. She knew he'd be relieved to hear her voice; then, having established she was safe, he'd be colossally pissed. She felt for the cell phone and punched their home number.

"For God's sake, Shoshe, where are you!!" he shouted above the static. "Are you all right?!"

"I'm fine, love." She tried to sound fine while digging pebbles out of her bloodied knees. "My Filofax blew all over the road. I've been recapturing it."

"Filofax? What road?!"

"I'll explain later, it's a bad connection."

"Shoshanna, where *are* you?"

"West Side Highway. Almost home, I promise."

"Well, take your time," he drawled sardonically. "Maestro Mazur will wait."

Dammit! She'd stapled the Philharmonic tickets to today's calendar page so they'd never get lost. What a joke! Back at the office, once she'd got her gleanings spread out on the floor, she would collect the remaining concert and theater tickets and deposit them in a desk drawer. She would organize the dirty pages into categories and figure out what was missing, and hope next Saturday's page turned up so she could phone Nelly back about babysitting the twins, and she'd look for the "W" page with Wasserman on it and call Leah about booking their annual lunch at Mamaleh's, on March 8. Just imagining these tasks on the drive down the highway drained her last gram of strength. She'd also have to answer her father's letter. For now, she would limit herself to the innocuous: congratulate him on the synagogue honor, and tell him how excited everyone was at the thought of seeing him after all this time. In the next few weeks, though, she'd have to decide what to do about Leah.

two

MARCH 8 WAS THE LOGICAL TIME to tell Leah about Sam's visit and discuss how the two of them might break their impasse. Shoshanna had suggested that date for their lunch as part of an overall strategy to ingratiate herself with her crusty, cantankerous sister because March 8 was International Women's Day, and Leah, who considered herself the mother of the movement (which she sort of *was*), observed the date as a major holiday. Though it was more than two weeks off, Shoshanna had already decided to spring for a bottle of champagne so they could toast the working women of the world. And since she was planning to raise the subject of Sam, a touch of midday inebriation couldn't hurt.

Lunches with Leah were often difficult. No, that was mealymouthed; lunches with Leah were always an ordeal. Some of the tension no doubt stemmed from their history, from their being half sisters and absent from each other's lives for so long. Nevertheless, grown women who meet only once a year ought to be able to cobble together ninety minutes' worth of non-explosive subject matter. Normal people talked about their families, about books, cultural events, and world affairs. For normal people, just catching up on twelve months of one another's lives could grease the conversational gears. But as Leah would be the first to admit, she wasn't normal. For one thing, she was a certifiable genius—

Summa, Phi Bet, Mensa, with an IQ off the charts. For another, she was a self-diagnosed "mercurial, moderately manic meshuggener," an outspoken, irascible woman who heard insults where none were intended; who, without warning, might let loose a scatological stream or slide into a sulk; who zigzagged so precipitously between affability and insolence that Shoshanna experienced their most casual exchange as the verbal equivalent of whiplash. She was never sure which Leah she was going to encounter from one year to the next or how to behave. Nor did it help that her sister felt free to correct her vocabulary, pronunciation, and grammar, as Leah did with anyone who happened to misspeak within earshot. No wonder that, long after kicking the habit, Shoshanna often found herself biting her nails rather than hazarding a defective sentence. Regardless of how careful she was in Leah's presence, something always went wrong, be it syntax or subject matter, and it always seemed to be her fault. The pressure could be crushing.

"Eleanor Roosevelt said, 'Small minds discuss people, average minds discuss events, great minds discuss ideas,'" Leah once declared over a Bloody Mary. Under her scrutiny, Shoshanna talked of people and events but feared her ideas too pedestrian. More than that, she was afraid of pressing Leah's hot buttons, which rivaled in number and complexity the instrument panel of a 747.

Button One was Sam. Shoshanna dared not speak his name in front of her sister, which wasn't easy, since he was her father, too, and as it happened, Shoshanna adored him. To Leah, however, he was the "Archangel of Abandonment," "the father from hell," "the man who wasn't there."

Button Two was their older sister, Rachel, who like the third leg on a milking stool stood between Shoshanna and Leah whether they spoke of her or not.

Health was a powder keg because Shoshanna couldn't help badgering Leah to give up cigarettes, a suggestion that invariably met with cataracts of profanity and militant chain-smoking, especially in nonsmoking restaurants.

Anything to do with Leo was a nonstarter since last year, when Leah announced that her husband was in a slump but wouldn't say why. A fine artist, often called promising in his youth, Leo Rose had lately been painting children's portraits-to-order. Which made art a conversational minefield as well.

Kids were a sensitive topic, but unavoidable given that Shoshanna and Leah each had two and Rachel, the earth mother, had four (five counting the long-deceased Gideon). Shoshanna was careful to soft-pedal the accomplishments of her offspring: Nelly, the blue-ribbon horse-woman who, with her husband, Ezra, was raising blue-ribbon twins; and Jake, the honor student in Boulder, Colorado. The contrast with Leah's sons, though unspoken, was self-evident: Freddy, twenty-eight, was serving five years to life on a narcotics conviction, and Henry, unemployed at twenty-six, was, at last report, living at home.

No wonder Shoshanna often left their lunches feeling guilty for her many blessings and sorry for her Job-like sister. Leah, however, indulged in self-pity only when it moved her to new flights of alliterative fancy. After cataloguing her burdens, she would twirl her long braid as if tempting a naughty boy in the vicinity of an inkwell and declare her lot in life "a surfeit of shit," "a deluge of dreck," "a cornucopia of crap," "a miasmic mess," and "a fucking fiasco." What order was to Shoshanna and fitness was to Rachel, language was to Leah. The self-proclaimed Venus of Vocabulary liked to flex her "sinewy similes and muscular metaphors" and limber up on puns and rhymes. As likely to talk over a person's head as in his face, she insisted every word in the dictionary was there to be used whether or not it was understood by others. There was no such thing as an ugly word, she said, only words that described ugly behavior. In America, where vulgarity and vitality are often the same drug, Leah offered a double dose. Everything was "sayable." Protocol was "invented by those in power to squelch unconventional thought." Propriety was "a euphemism for the socially constructed inhibition of free expression." The concepts of community standard, etiquette, decency, and public decorum were impotent against her untempered speech. To Leah, "rogue" and "asshole," "scalawag" and "shithead" were equally utilitarian expletives. She lived in Frost's "cave of the mouth."

Which was why Shoshanna always booked their lunch dates in the caves of Manhattan. Past humiliations had taught her the importance of location, location, location, and driven her search for out-of-the way restaurants where their inevitable dustups would not be witnessed by anyone she knew. She'd learned her lesson years before in a theater district trattoria when two friends of hers who happened to be lunching in the next booth overheard the tirade that began when Shoshanna had ordered scampi.

"I still feel guilty eating shellfish, don't you?" she'd remarked, altogether innocently.

"What's to be guilty about?" Leah's bark was loud enough to herd sheep.

"You know, all those years we ate only kosher." She'd meant it as filler, small talk. Turned out to be small like the pin in a hand grenade.

Leah shot her a look that would tarnish silver. "May I remind you, dear sister, I wasn't around *all those years*."

"Oh, right." Shoshanna stared at her plate. For most of her childhood she'd never even known Leah existed.

"Whilst you were being served hot pastrami on rye on Manhattan's fashionable Upper West Side, I was scrounging ham and cheese on stale Wonder bread. And your fucking father couldn't care less. The great Rabbi Wasserman kept kosher to the letter but managed to lose track of a daughter."

"Sorry! I wasn't thinking. I didn't mean anything." She couldn't place a lunch order for years afterward without first subjecting herself to self-censorship. Where Leah was concerned, Shoshanna measured everything in years. Off years and On years, years when Leah wasn't in her life at all, years when Leah adored her, years when Leah barely tolerated her, and great blocks of time when they made do with the sort of tepid relationship that would shortchange a third cousin. Shoshanna was fourteen before they'd ever met, so the first fourteen years she called the Big Blank; then came the Big Bang, when Leah showed up unannounced and moved into her life, lock, stock, and barreling over everyone in her path. Next came the period when they were as inseparable as a pair of shoes; how many years was that? Three, maybe four, followed by a long arid stretch when they hardly spoke at all. Since the truce (in a battle Shoshanna had never consciously joined), they'd maintained sporadic contact—an occasional phone call, the rarest encounter at a large family event that Leah would deign to grace with her presence, an exchange of High Holy Day cards, and their annual lunches, usually in the dead of winter. Shoshanna was determined that the next one, on March 8, be cordial and conflict-free, and she had hit upon a plan to ensure that outcome. If it worked, she might actually eat more of her food this year than her fingernails.

Weeks before the actual event, having read that Olympic divers dramatically improve their performance by visualizing the perfect dive while still in the locker room, Shoshanna had started visualizing the perfect lunch. She'd conjured Leah's appearance—which, after a year apart, could be quite a shock—her leathery skin, the gift of a lifetime of sun and cigarette smoke, both unfiltered; the liver spots dotting the backs of her hands and dappling her broad cheeks; the fleshy pouches softening the prow of her jaw. Though barely sixty-two, Leah had aged badly and didn't give a damn. "Troubles that don't show on your face lie on your heart," she'd say, a Yiddish proverb. Shoshanna knew she would arrive, as always, dressed in black from top to toe and carrying a knapsack, like a hump on her back, stuffed with books and papers. Her limp, the result of a horrific boarding-school experience, alluded to but never explained, would be forthright and unapologetic. Her thick, woolly hair—more salt than pepper now—would be trussed in a long "Pocahontas pigtail," the style she'd worn since childhood and saw no reason to change. Her darkly husky voice, minus its mellow top tones, would still resonate. A permanent squint would crinkle her yellow-speckled brown eyes. "Too many books, too little light," she'd explain glibly, though it hadn't stopped her from wearing prescription sunglasses indoors. Purple-tinted.

Observing Leah in her shaded specs for the first time, their older sister Rachel (whom Leah called "the fact fetishist") volunteered one of her inimitable trivia nuggets: "Did you know dark glasses were invented by the Chinese in the fifteenth century?"

"I didn't," said Leah, with an off-handedness bordering on disdain.

"It's true. And they weren't invented to protect people against the sun but to stop them from seeing a judge's expression in court."

"That's why I wear them," Leah had replied, deadpan.

"You'll ruin your eyes," Rachel said.

"Worth it. In the interest of judicial integrity."

As always, Leah skewered anyone who came too close. Rather than be made sport of, Rachel had learned to back off, but Shoshanna, eager for a deeper connection, kept reaching out and paid the price in puncture wounds. That her thoughts had been invaded by her prickly sister during the drive down the West Side Highway wasn't all that surprising. Lately, Leah had been horning in far more frequently than her role in Shoshanna's life merited. Her uniqueness, the sheer memorability of her, went a long way toward explaining the vividness of Leah's image and the metallic clarity of their mutual past. Then again, it might have something to do with the confluence of Sam's visit and Shoshanna's fiftieth birthday, both of which weighed heavily upon her mind, though at the moment her legs weighed more. Knee joints throbbing, thighs numb, right foot straining to control the brake and accelerator, she wondered if those hours of squatting and gallivanting on the highway had left her permanently disabled, like Leah.

One year, watching her sister list to the left en route to their lunch table, Shoshanna had felt genuine concern. "Surgery might fix that," she'd ventured gently.

"Ah so! Fräulein Doktor Safer prescribes hip replacement surgery. What are you, a shill for the AMA?"

Shoshanna had persisted. "I'm serious."

"Me, too. Bodies needn't be perfect, you know." Was that a dig? Leah had disapproved mightily when Nelly had a nose job in high school after a fall from a horse, though it was the plastic surgeon's idea to lop off a slight bump while he was attending to the injury anyway.

"I'm not talking vanity now, I'm talking health," said Shoshanna.

"Some people pop pills and act hip. I'm a pill who popped a hip." Behind the purple lenses, Leah's eyes twinkled.

"Not funny. Keep walking like that, you'll end up a cripple."

"Everyone's crippled somehow. My affliction just happens to fucking show."

For all her physical disrepair, there was something ineffably youthful about Leah, a quality that trumped her looks, erased her years, and put her students at ease. Shoshanna attributed the magic to her bohemian black wardrobe and her affinity for junk food, but Leah insisted it was her potty mouth that charmed the young. She was probably right. Never had Shoshanna known a woman as militantly profane, nor could she understand how this English professor—a prominent public intellectual and editor of an academic journal—got away with using four-letter words in every context including the classroom. Yet, somehow, Leah managed to be inoffensively obscene. An equal-opportunity vulgarian, she was foul-mouthed with colleagues and strangers, men and women, the chattering classes and the proletariat. Raunch rolled off her tongue, sometimes in ribald English, sometimes piquant Yiddish. Fanny Hill meets Sophie Tucker via Mae West.

"I'm an aficionada of Anglo-Saxon but an amorista of Yiddish," Leah said once, emphasizing the feminine endings. "Don't you just love shtetl eloquence? It ought have a word of its own—shteloquence!"

Shoshanna remembered the scene. They were in Murray the Sturgeon King's restaurant, standing at the appetizer counter studying an impressive display of fish, including a species neither of them recognized. Leah pointed at it through the glass and asked the man next to her if he knew what it was.

"Some kind of Jewish fish," he said.

"You mean it's circumcised?" asked Leah, straight-faced.

"No, it's smoked."

The fish turned out to be sable. Leah ordered it with a toasted bagel and a schmear. "Putz," she'd said, when they'd found a table.

"Al D'Amato lost his Senate seat over that word," said Shoshanna, pleased she'd remembered

"It served the bastard right. He thought it was just another put-down, but any Jew worth his kosher salt knows putz means prick."

"Even me."

"Even *I*," Leah corrected firmly. "In New York City, you can't call a candidate a putz, especially a Jewish candidate, and expect to be elected to public office. Anyway, to paraphrase Casey Stengel, he coulda looked it up."

"In an *English* dictionary?"

"Webster's Third. It's chock-full of Yiddishisms—golem, schnorrer, schlemiel, kibbitz, kreplach, they're all there, putz included, though Webster got it wrong. By him, it's a Christmas decoration."

By Leah, Yiddish was mamaloshen, her mother tongue by adoption. American-born, Ivy-educated, she prided herself on speaking "pitch-perfect, polished English prose." But she also championed Yiddish, "the spicy tongue that puckered Jewish mouths for eight hundred years until the Nazis slaughtered most of its speakers and assimilation seduced the rest." Were Leah running the Department of Jewish Heritage, Yiddish, not Hebrew, would be the official language and Ashkenazic culture the coin of the realm.

At lunch a few years later, in a quiet little French bistro, Leah worked herself into a lather on the subject. She began with a put-down of French cuisine—the goose-liver pâté was "utterly oomph-less" compared to chopped liver with schmaltz; the *coq au vin* was a "wan version of Jewish chicken"—then segued to the general superiority of Eastern European Jewish culture to its Israeli and American counterparts.

"Why eat falafel," she asked, "if you can have flanken? Why settle for a kibbutznik's recorder if you can get a klezmer's clarinet? Why dance the hora when you can do the kazatzka? The hora has no heart, Shoshie; no kishkes. There's a reason why the goyim cried at *Fiddler on the Roof*—because it was reminiscent of the Yiddish theater. Most of what you see today on Broadway is gazz and gornischt compared to the golden age of

Second Avenue; same with the comics on *Saturday Night Live*. They haven't earned the right to kiss the hem of the lowliest Borscht Belt tummuler in some cockamamie kuchaleyn in the mountains.

"And literature? Don't ask! Most American Jewish writing is a pale imitation of the writing of the Pale. Now *there* was a Weltanschauung worthy of the name. Isaac Bashevis Singer! A genius! Those Nobel nudniks knew what they were doing when they picked him. Ever wonder why Yiddish writers became socialists and Hebrew writers became Zionists, Shoshanna?" Leah waited expectantly, as if the question had been plaguing her sister for years.

Shoshanna shook her head.

"Because Yiddish loves *others*, while Hebrew loves itself!" She closed with a mournful rendition of "Oyfn Pripetshik" that didn't scan with her *crème brûlée*.

It happens that Leah spoke a quite respectable Hebrew—had learned it as a child when she still lived under her father's roof and the language came with the territory. However, since Sam rejected her, she'd rejected his modern Sephardic pronunciation in favor of an Ashkenazic accent, a small rebellion that she refused to acknowledge as such but explained by saying, "It makes Hebrew sound more like Yiddish." When Leah wasn't criticizing the biblical tongue, she was bad-mouthing the Promised Land. In 1987, at the start of the Palestinian Intifada, Shoshanna made the mistake of booking their lunch at Falafel-à-Go-Go, an Israeli restaurant on the East Side of town. Leah arrived in a fury, having just learned of Prime Minister Rabin's order for IDF soldiers to break the arms of the Palestinian stone throwers. The minute she heard the wait staff speaking Hebrew, Leah lit into them.

"So what do you think of your government now?"

The waiter, a knitted yarmulke hugging his close-cropped hair, looked at her blankly.

"Come on, man! Isn't it obvious Israel is suffering terminal machismo? It's related to the cult of the Hebrew tongue; can't you see that?!" When her booming voice drew the cook out of the kitchen, Leah responded to her enlarged audience by upping the decibels even more.

"Hebrew is the language of right-wing triumphalism and Zionist hegemony! What makes you people so cocksure of yourselves, anyway? You're occupying another people's territory, you've spawned the worst kind of religious fanaticism, and let's be honest, you've produced little notable literature. Yet the average Israeli is as arrogant as a cactus!" When the cook opened his mouth to protest, Leah nearly jumped down his throat. "Name ten timeless works written in Hebrew, not counting the Tanach. Oh, Hebrew's clever, I'll give you that, the way it starts with a root, then tacks on all sorts of prefixes and suffixes to make its meanings. But it has no neshamah. If any language has the right to speak for the Jewish soul and carry our traditions on its shoulders, it's Yiddish!"

This fiery speech wasn't delivered to an international convention of linguists but over hummus and pita at a hole-in-the-wall restaurant where two guys in white aprons, to the chagrin of a dozen neglected customers, spent the next fifteen minutes defending their culture. Midway through the argument, not realizing she'd done it, Leah slipped into Hebrew herself, though that didn't convert the Israeli staff to her views, either.

The following year, with the Intifada still raging and American Jews at odds over Israeli policy, Shoshanna booked their lunch in a Japanese restaurant just to be safe. Then, without thinking, she made the mistake of telling Leah that their sister, Rachel, was in Tel Aviv, attending her first Hadassah conference (and, implicitly, visiting Sam in Jerusalem).

"You have to talk sense into Rachel, Shoshie," Leah said, building up steam. "I can't believe she would belong to an organization that supports civil liberties for Jews in the U.S. but pays no attention to how Israel treats its Arabs. What has to happen over there before the ladies' auxiliaries wake up? What'll it take for Hadassah to protest the occupation? It's bad enough that the so-called American Jewish leadership is 99 percent male, but it's a fucking shondeh that your sister supports those namby-pamby groups that dare to call themselves *women's* organizations when all they do is rubber-stamp the guys!"

"Wait a minute, Leah. Not every Jewish group has to take a position on Israeli policies. Hadassah supports health care and hospitals. Go join Peace Now if you can't stop your krechtzing."

"I don't krechtz, woman. I *kvetch*."

"There's a difference?"

"Big difference! If you're gonna use the sacred tongue, you gotta be precise. A krechtz is a sorrowful moan, a sigh of resignation or misery. A kvetch is more whiny and cranky, more crabby and bitchy. You must never confuse a krechtz with a kvetch or, for that matter, a geshrei."

"Lesson learned," said Shoshanna. But Leah wasn't finished.

"A geshrei is a full-throated cry. Refinements matter here. The krechtz is utterly unique—as involuntary as a yawn or a sneeze. It emanates from deep inside the body, from a place over which one has little control. The krechtz *proves* that the soul exists. Anyone can kvetch, dear sister, but only an old Jew can krechtz."

Maddening, that didactic tone, but always leavened with so much wit and erudition that a tribe of sycophants regularly risked humiliation in return for the pleasure of Leah's company.

"They'll follow me anywhere, if only out of morbid curiosity," said the professor of her adoring fans, a revolving cadre of admirers—whom she'd long ago dubbed the Schmendriks (after expounding on the difference between a schmendrik, schlemiel, shmeggegi, schnook, schmuck, and schmo, as well as the larger significance of Yiddish having developed such particularized variations on the Fool). Schmendriks were graduate students, political junkies, unreconstructed hippies, and women's studies majors, who wandered into Professor Wasserman's office at all hours to unbosom themselves on every subject from post-structuralism to the Zen of physics, from the films of Jim Jarmusch to the current political situation in Bosnia or Botswana, though their experience in foreign affairs, Leah avowed, "stems mainly from their having breakfasted at the International House of Pancakes." Schmendriks read their poetry aloud and critiqued one another's work. Debated the merits of meritocracy and the effects of urban anomie. Served as sounding boards for Leah's nascent theories and early readers of her work, all the while sustaining themselves from her bottomless cache of Ring Dings, Snickers, Mounds bars, and Baby Ruths.

Witnessing one such chocolate debauch, Shoshanna remarked, "When you go on a diet, the Schmendriks are going to suffer sugar withdrawal."

"No fear of that; I never diet."

"Everyone dies *sometimes*."

"*Pas moi.* I have no desire to be perfect. When you're perfect, people feel they have to find something wrong with you. Let your flaws hang out and everyone roots for you."

The Schmendriks didn't just root for Leah, they worshipped her. Shoshanna remembered a different group being similarly besotted when, as a teenager, she volunteered at *The Feminist Freethinker*, the quarterly Leah founded in the 1960s and still served as "editor emerita." Having been her sister's sidekick back then, Shoshanna knew the original Schmendriks—now referred to as the Golden Oldies—Leah's women's movement colleagues, who, thirty-odd years later, were still "in struggle," still turning out for demonstrations, still circulating petitions and debating feminism's philosophical fine points. Since then, Shoshanna watched as each new generation rushed to sit at Leah's feet, eager to endure her Tabasco tongue and the stench of her Gauloises cigarettes in return for a chance to help her put out the magazine. Around Leah, people felt the urge to be helpful.

Except when they felt the urge to scream. Shoshanna remembered searching for words to describe her relationship with her middle sister, as if defining it might make it easier. Neurotic? Galvanic? Knotty? Ambivalent? Combative? Nothing seemed exactly right. Bogged down, she'd settled for "the opposite of my relationship with Rachel." Fourteen years her senior as opposed to Leah's twelve, Rachel called forth an entirely different vocabulary: Accepting. Supportive. Genial. Sustaining. Effortless. The "Good Sister" (as Leah had dubbed her) was easy to be with no matter how often they got together, while with the "Bad Sister," an annual reunion was enough, more than enough: too much, even. Yet Shoshanna felt about her lunches with Leah the way she felt about her period: it gave her cramps but she'd be miserable if she missed one.

March 8 was going to be cramp-free, the perfect dive. No nail-biting, no yelling, no scenes. Having visualized her sister, braid to Birkenstocks, Shoshanna had gone on to imagine in advance every step of this year's meeting. The bustling exchange of greetings as they hung up their coats and settled at their table. Leah kvetching about the long subway trip from Brooklyn. Shoshanna complaining about her sore throat. (After cavorting for hours on the highway, she was bound to come down with something.) She would launch the body of their conversation by commenting on the presidential primaries. Though Shoshanna wasn't yet sure whether to support Bradley or Nader, Leah would surely have a strong preference to which she could defer until she actually made up her mind. They both would take aim at McCain, Bush, and Gore, then gleefully eviscerate Rudy Giuliani and reaffirm their mutual support of Hillary for the Senate until, with a seamless sidestep, Shoshanna would say something breezy about My Time Is Your Time ("Would you believe this guy actually wanted me to find a taxidermist for his hamster!?") and Leah would offer a trenchant academic anecdote or a riff on some current feminist feud. The professor could dish the dirt with the best of them, though this turf, too, was mined. Responding to one of her convoluted tales of movement backbiting, Shoshanna had joked, "Leave it to women to form a firing squad in a circle."

Instantly, Leah's eyes grew dark. "Are you suggesting women have to be nice? For Chrissake, if the fucking founding dads had waited around to like each other during the American Revolution, we'd still be at Bunker Hill."

"I was *kidding!*" Shoshanna protested, but on certain days on certain subjects only Leah could be funny.

This year, she would steer clear of feminist topics and concentrate on trivia. Maybe start with her kitchen renovation, an unmitigated disaster the mere recounting of which could amount to a comedy sketch. Then again, any mention of home improvement could trigger Leah's grievances about her place, which, by her own description, was straight out of Charles Addams, haunted by despair, if not by ghouls. Shoshanna had never seen Leah's house in Brooklyn, nor had Leah ever visited the brownstone Shoshanna and Daniel owned in the Village. The sisters always met on neutral ground, in restaurants.

This year, Shoshanna was going to suggest Mamaleh's, a mama-owned Jewish deli on Avenue C. Since it wasn't exactly famous for its wine list, she'd bag the champagne idea and toast the working women of the world with celery tonic. Given Leah's Judeo-feminist passions, the combination of Old World cuisine and a bona fide women's holiday was too good to resist. Shoshanna would call Leah when she got home. Or maybe she wouldn't.

three

MAINE. March 1961. The sun seemed permanently lost to the tan-gray coastline where three figures made their way along a deserted beach, lashed by the wind—Sam and Esther Wasserman in their bar mitzvah finery, and their shoulder-high daughter, Shoshanna, who had trouble remaining upright as she slogged through the sand. Much as the gluttonous try to walk off a heavy meal, the Wassermans were out for a stroll at the ass-end of winter, trying to shed the weight of a family secret. Esther, pink-skinned, freckled, buttoned to the chin in her Persian-lamb topper, was teetering on high-heeled pumps that left pterodactyl footprints on the hard brown berm. Sam was wearing a double-breasted camel's-hair coat and wing-tipped cordovans that seemed vaguely incompatible with his full beard. Shoshanna, the object of their attentions, trembled in the loden parka that used to make her feel like a college girl but now hung from her shoulders, limp and sad as an outsized hand-me-down. She was twelve years old.

Like hostile locals scoping out a car with New York plates, a cloud of flapping gulls squawked and cawed, affronted by the off-season interlopers. Sam and Esther, oblivious to the birds, were talking to their daughter incessantly, as if without constant encouragement she would fall into a faint. Indeed, unconscious was how they'd found her less than an hour ago, when their niece Emily, panic-stricken, had summoned them to the parlor. Now, trudging down the beach, Shoshanna recollected in soft focus everything that had happened before the world went dark—the bar mitzvah, the card game, her cousin's crazy revelation, everything up to the moment when her brain, unable to absorb another word, had shut down, dragging her body with it. She wished they'd never come to Maine.

"Who schleps all day in a car for a bar mitzvah?" Esther had protested when Sam first announced the trip. It was important to him, he said. Sid was his youngest brother, Warren was his favorite nephew, and while he didn't live near enough to coach the boy, the least he could do was attend the ceremony and honor Sid's request that he deliver the sermon. To arrive Friday night before sundown at Sid and Anna's seaside village in Maine required a dawn departure from West End Avenue. Shoshanna, prone to carsickness, hadn't thrown up once, but the drive seemed interminable despite her parents' willingness to play Geography, Twenty Questions, State Capitals, and Name That Tune, and to stop four times for bathroom breaks. Once in Maine, of course, Shabbat dinner, especially Aunt Anna's yummy noodle kugel, and singing zmirot with the family made it worth the trip.

The next morning, the two Wasserman families, aided by a howling tailwind, walked the half mile to the tiny synagogue (whose entire congregation could probably fit in five rows at Rodeph Tzedek). After Warren acquitted himself admirably chanting the Torah and Haftarah, and Sam gave a talk on the responsibilities of a son of the Commandments, and everyone joined a community kiddush in the social hall, they returned to Sid and Anna's house, an old fishing shack, lovingly restored and furnished with early-American pieces straight out of Shoshanna's history unit on the Shakers. The air smelled of the coffee that had brewed itself automatically in a preset electric percolator. When the adults gathered in the kitchen to prepare lunch and Warren disappeared into his room with an armload of bar mitzvah gifts, his big sister, Emily, challenged Shoshanna to a game of gin rummy. She'd leapt at the offer; it wasn't every day that someone twice her age was willing to play cards with her. They sat across from one another in ladder-back chairs at the long pine table in the front parlor. A kaleidoscope of jeweled colors, reflecting off the stained-glass chandelier, shimmered on the ceiling as if compensating for the wan gray day. Sea spray coated the windows like glaze on a cake. The coffee aroma drifted down the hall on a crest of adult voices discussing whether it was right for President Kennedy to name his brother Attorney General. Later, Shoshanna would remember her great anticipation for the gin game and her profoundly satisfying, and increasingly rare, sense of preadolescent contentment. Independent yet secure, on her own yet within earshot of her parents, she shivered with excitement when Emily pulled a score pad from a drawer and shuffled the cards like a pro. This was serious. This was Shoshanna's chance to put all Sam's strategies to the test.

He loved cards, her father—gin, bridge, hearts, poker, pinochle, canasta, anything with a deck and a score pad and a "worthy opponent." Since she was six or seven, Shoshanna had aspired to that role. She'd watched him teach her mother five-card stud and remembered how frustrated he'd become when Esther had messed up the point values. She knew he was hungry for a live-in poker partner; had watched him beat every relative in an impromptu family gin tournament, then instantly ask for a rematch; had stood over his shoulder during the monthly bridge parties in her parents' living room, two tables in play, and corned-beef sandwiches and sour pickles on the sideboard, and the clatter of nonstop kibitzing. When the other couples left, he'd make Esther revisit every one of her bids and browbeat her into promising to read the *New York Times* bridge column. Esther would insist no game was worth all that effort. Besides, it wasn't fitting for a rabbi to be so competitive. Sam would disagree. Card games are like Jewish law, he'd tell her. You have to know the rules, consider the alternatives, reason intelligently, remember every card—the way the great sages kept centuries of precedent in their heads—anticipate the consequences, then act decisively. He loved to win, but more than that, Sam appreciated a well-played game and would go to great lengths to find one. Shoshanna was determined to become his "worthy opponent," having learned long ago that her father's undivided attention was not free for the taking but could be earned in three ways: engage him in Talmud talk, the more convoluted the question the better; be irresistibly adorable; or ask him to play cards. Because she'd shown great interest in playing with him, he'd taught her everything she knew about gin rummy, which was everything *he* knew, which was virtually all a person *could* know about the game.

"What are you waiting for?" asked Emily. "Discard already, come on!"

"Shh, I'm calculating," she said, keeping her cards in a tight fan. Only three cards had been played, yet, unbelievably, she was holding a knockable hand—four jacks, four nines, a six, ace, and two. She spread her two lays faceup on the table, discarded the six, and slapped the ace and deuce off to the side. "Knock with three," she said, positive she'd caught her cousin with a slew of points but careful not to gloat.

Emily studied Shoshanna's cards, then glared across the table, her face reddening, its expression weirdly agitated. "You think you're so smart, you little twerp! Well, I've had it with you and your whole damn family!" Suddenly Emily gripped the table and shoved it forward against Shoshanna's chest, sending the cards skittering to the floor like loose razor blades. The girl's instinct was to flee, but there was no air in her lungs and her breastbone hurt too much to move. She didn't understand what was happening. Could a grown-up be this distraught about losing a hand of gin? Had Emily also lost her mind? Shoshanna drew a painful breath and summoned the most insulting words known to the seventh grade.

"You're just *jealous!*"

"Of you? Don't make me laugh!"

She rubbed her chest but stood up like a worthy opponent. "You're jealous of . . . of my sister. 'Cause she's prettier than you. And good at everything. And everybody loves her." It was true; Rachel was all those things—cute, kind, nice, a terrific athlete. She really *was* the family favorite.

Emily's mouth opened like a sinkhole. "I couldn't care less about your fabulous *sister*," she hissed, and jabbed a finger into the child's chest, setting off new shock waves. "I'm the senior grandchild in this family and I'm sick of hearing about Rachel."

What was Emily thinking? This wasn't physics, it was simple arithmetic: She was twenty-two, Rachel was nearly twenty-six. "My sister's four years older than you!" said Shoshanna. "Can't you count?"

"Your *sister* isn't even your real sister!"

Out of nowhere, dots and squiggles rolled in at the edges of Shoshanna's vision like a fog of black atoms; the dots swirled and connected until they threatened to blot out her cousin's face, the chairs, the table, the light. She tried to anchor herself in the stripes of Aunt Anna's braided rug. "That's crazy, Emily. What are you saying?"

"I'm the oldest cousin, Shoshanna. Rachel wasn't even *in* this family until your father adopted her. Shows how much you know, you little snit!"

Snit was the last thing she'd heard.

Fade to black.

Until today, everything bad that had ever happened to Shoshanna had happened in a dream, and when the action got too scary, she'd always awakened in her own bed under her white organdy canopy, safe and warm beneath her flowered sheets. This time she found herself lying on the braided rug, looking up at the chandelier in Aunt Anna's and Uncle Sidney's parlor. This time it wasn't a dream. Esther was pressing a damp washcloth to her forehead, rocking and weeping, her dimples deflated, her freckles white with fear. Sam was feeling for her pulse. "Everything's going to be all right, ketzeleh; everything's going to be fine," he kept murmuring over and over in a singsong chant that sounded like davening. But all the prayers in the world couldn't make things right again.

Rachel *adopted*.

Esther folded the washcloth in half, quarters, eighths, then dipped it in cool water, squeezed out the excess, and started folding again. Like a Boy Scout trying to coax a spark from dry twigs, Sam rubbed his daughter's arms. He slid his warm hands behind her neck and lifted her up from the floor. "Come, tateleh, let's go for a walk. Mommy and I will explain everything." Shoshanna let herself be raised, toggled into her loden coat, and led, weak-kneed and light-headed, out the door and down to the harbor. Like mobile bookends, her parents propped her up on either side and guided her along the quay, across cobblestones slick with fish scales, past docks littered with nets and lobster traps, past clam boats and sailing skiffs tethered to moon-white buoys bobbing tipsy with the tides, until they reached the open sea and the broad, barren beach where the three of them were inching along now, slow as crabs.

Her parents had been talking nonstop since they'd left the house, pouring paragraphs into her like cups of black coffee.

"I just wanted us to be a normal family," Esther began, through lips bitten bare of Pond's Honey.

"Our lives were complicated, so we left a few things blank," said Sam.

"Nobody needed to know all the details." Esther tilted her head toward Shoshanna, mingling their copper hair. The daughter's unruly mane might have been the Before picture, her mother's coiffed upsweep the After.

"We should have told you, Shoshaleh. I always said we should, didn't I, Esther?"

"I thought you were too young," said her mother. "A child can't be expected to keep such a secret."

Their voices broke over each other's in the rhythm of the waves. "Anyway, we're telling you now," said Sam, who began filling in the blanks shorthand-style, as if dictating a résumé. "Your mother got married the first time in '33, had Rachel in '35, got divorced in '38, and married me in '47. I adopted Rachel that same year. We lived in my old apartment in Brooklyn. You were born in '49. In '50, we moved to Manhattan, to West End Avenue, when I got the job at Rodeph Tzedek, and . . ."

Esther interrupted: "And that's when we decided to backdate our wedding. No one knew us from before. New friends, new congregation—we said we were married seventeen years instead of three, who'd be hurt. But with a 1933 wedding, he could be Rachel's daddy, and we could be a normal American family like everyone else."

Shoshanna shook her head. Too much information. Too many numbers.

"Forget the all-American-family stuff, Esther; keep it simple," said Sam. He held Shoshanna by the shoulders. His widow's peak took dead aim at the frown line between his brows. "Listen, zeesaleh, all you have to remember is this: I adopted Rachel. I love her like I love you. Supported her from twelve on—until Jeremy took over. Emily was dead wrong, bubbeleh. Rachel's your *sister*. Legally, she's as much my daughter as you are."

His Yiddish pet names, usually so endearing, sounded hollow now. Shoshanna could sense how badly he wanted to get this over with. She pulled out of his grasp. The wind whipped at her stockinged legs and stung her face. The damp, cold sand penetrated the thin soles of her patent-leather shoes. She stared at the horizon, a sharp line between sea and sky that reminded her of the carpenter's level in wood shop. If only she had a tool to set things straight. If only everything were as simple as centering a bubble between two lines.

"Sam, please; let me talk." Esther's voice rustled like silk after his muslin. "When your daddy got the pulpit at Rodeph Tzedek, we figured new place, new people, why not make a fresh start. Everyone's always judging a rebbitzin anyway, wanting to know her business . . ."

"You're confusing her, Esther. Just the basics. Please."

Fighting the gulls and the wind, her mother pressed on. "So we decided to tell a little white lie; let the congregation think we were each other's only marriage and your daddy was always Rachel's father. We erased the divorce part, that's all. What harm in that?" She reached out a gloved hand and stroked Shoshanna's hair. "The relatives went along with it; they understood."

So they'd all been in on it—aunts, uncles, Emily, Rachel herself—in cahoots all these years. The whole family was a fraud, slippery as that jellyfish beached on a bed of shells, slimy with phony dates, bogus anniversaries, flimflam answers. How could she have been so stupid? There must have been clues. Her mind dug back until it dredged up a conversation with her father a few years ago, when she'd noticed that Sam wasn't in any of Rachel's baby pictures. How come? she'd asked. His answer, she remembered, was delivered with the soft smile of embarrassment: he was young-looking for his age and needed the beard to give him rabbinic authority, but in pictures he thought it made him look like a greenhorn right off the boat, so he used to decline being photographed. "Luckily," he said, "I got over my foolishness in time to show up in *your* baby pictures." She'd actually swallowed that.

Also Rachel's reminiscences—all the great times she had as a kid with Daddy Sam—pure fiction. And the stock answer Esther gave to friends who asked about the fourteen-year spread between Rachel and Shoshanna: "Sam and I had trouble conceiving," she'd whisper, suggesting *that* was the secret. Falsehood piled upon falsehood, as if every two lies made a truth. Shoshanna's head was throbbing. Distill the essence, her father used to say when a math problem seemed overwhelming or a poem beyond her grasp. Focus on the big picture. Don't let the details derail you. Okay, Daddy; here's what I learned today on the beach in Maine: Nothing is as it seems. Facts are a mirage. Mothers and fathers can't be trusted. A sister can turn out to be a half sister and a liar. Distilled to its essence, the message was: Betrayal is everywhere.

She remembered in the third grade telling her best friend about her crush on their teacher, only to have the friend spread it around the whole class. When Shoshanna thought she would die of shame, Sam had comforted her with advice she'd never forgotten: "Learn from it, maideleh. If someone betrays you once, it's their fault. If they do it twice, it's yours." Her family would get no second chance. From now on, she'd be vigilant, never take anything at face value, never let anyone else control the information she needed to make sense of her own life. She would read between the commas and check for concealed motives. She would grow into a woman who hates surprises. Shoshanna wished she didn't know now what she didn't know then. But secrets, once told, can't be stuffed back in their box. Revelation feeds on itself, and ravenous for detail, the eyes and ears suck up more than the heart can hold.

"Who was Rachel's father?" she asked, her voice as gritty as the sand.

"A nobody from nowhere." Esther cleared her throat and made a few false starts before she could talk about her first husband, Martin, alias Lucky, a cigar roller in a factory on the Lower East Side. Terrible temper, possessive, violent. Forced her to quit her job, even though they needed the money. Beat her if she so much as smiled at another man—a neighbor, the milkman, the butcher. Even during her pregnancy, Lucky hit her for not polishing his shoes, and once for burning the latkes. Only when he yanked off his belt and went after the baby did Esther grab Rachel and the Sabbath candlesticks that had belonged to her grandmother, and run away, leaving everything else behind.

"We stayed with my parents for a week or two but I couldn't ask them to mind Rachel permanently, them with four of their own still at home. Besides, they hardly spoke English. She'd have picked up their accent, and I wanted her to be a real American and a lady, so I got a job in a blouse factory and used my wages to pay for this wonderful boarding school, Blue Spruce, where the uptown people sent their daughters. Lucky never gave us a dime." Esther stopped to mop her eyes and shake the wet sand off her suede shoes.

That was where Esther and Sam had met, at Rachel's school. They had a lot in common, what with their divorces and all. "Back then, it was a shondeh for a Jew to be divorced, a terrible, terrible disgrace." Gazing down the beach, Esther recalled her ostracism, then blinked it away. "That's why your dad and I decided not to tell the new congregation about our first marriages."

The story kept spiraling into wider circles, spinning new strands, like a web. Distill the essence, Shoshanna told herself. *Divorces. Marriages.* The essence was the plurals. "How many marriages?" she asked.

They'd stopped moving now, like a funeral procession waiting for the coffin to pass. Wisps of dried seaweed fluttered across the beach. Far out to sea, a long black tanker glided against the steely sky. Shoshanna wished she were on it.

"I was married before, too," Sam said finally, his eyes riveted to the boat. "To a woman named Dena."

The receding tide left a starfish writhing at their feet, its points folding, coiling, seeking water as desperately as Shoshanna was sucking air into her lungs. She bent to pick it up.

"Don't!" her father commanded. "It might sting!"

44

She peeled the starfish off the wet sand, watched it wriggle in her palm, stroked its puckered surface, then hurled it in an arc above the waves—a falling star. Her parents exchanged glances.

Her father once had another wife. Another life. Esther had another husband, a life before this one. Rachel, too; a different father, a secret life. Who *were* these people? Shoshanna shut her ears against the keening of the gulls but she couldn't drown out her mother's drone.

"So our new friends got to know us as an ordinary family with two wonderful daughters . . ." (*She said this already. Why was she repeating herself? Why didn't she stop?*) ". . . and in case Dena ever let Leah visit on weekends again, we decided we'd introduce her as a cousin."

"Introduce who?"

"Leah," said Esther.

Her father shot her mother a look of raw rage. "Fuck you, Esther." The word flopped from his mouth like a dead fish. Rabbis didn't say fuck. Sam Wasserman never even said damn or hell. Esther collapsed inside her fur coat as if she'd been punched. She dabbed her eyes with a shredded tissue and buried her face in her gloved hands. When she looked up, the whites of her eyes were gray. "Tell her, Sam. You have to tell her!"

Still as driftwood, the classic tableau: women waiting for a man to speak.

Sam tucked his chin into his collar. "My daughter by my first wife. Her name is Leah."

"Your *daughter?* You have another *daughter!!!?*"

"Tateleh, please. Let me explain." One of his wingtips kicked the sand and brought up a rusty toy spade. Shoshanna wanted to dig a hole to China. She grabbed the spade and bent the corroded handle until it snapped.

She let her father explain. When his first marriage broke up, Dena got custody and he got visitation rights—one day every weekend. He would pick Leah up on Friday afternoons and bring her with him to shul, and they'd spend all of Shabbat together until Saturday night, after havdalah and after they had dinner, just the two of them, when he'd return her to her mother. This arrangement worked well as long as they all lived in Brooklyn. But when Dena decided to send the girl to Blue Spruce boarding school—which was more than an hour away—it was hard for him to drive upstate and back to the city in time for Friday-night services, so sometimes he'd spend Sunday with Leah up at school instead.

"That's how your mother and I met. She was visiting Rachel. I was visiting Leah." (Shoshanna concentrated hard, afraid she might miss something, as she had when Esther first said they'd met at Blue Spruce and it hadn't even occurred to Shoshanna to ask what Sam was doing at a girls' school in the first place.) "Well, we got friendly and eventually we got married and I adopted Rachel and"—he was rushing now, as if he had to leave—"and instead of one day every week, I talked Dena into letting Leah spent the whole weekend with us, twice a month. Our apartment in Brooklyn was small, but Rachel's bedroom had a double-decker. She let Leah sleep on the top bunk. They were good friends then . . ."

"*Best* friends!" corrected Esther.

Sam began stroking his beard, a sure sign of distress. The cleft between his eyebrows deepened. "That visitation arrangement lasted until Leah was twelve, almost thirteen. The summer of 1950, Dena suddenly went nuts. Made crazy threats. Said she'd kill Leah rather than let me have her, even for a day; I had to stop seeing her . . ." There was something wet on his cheeks. Sea spray? "I had to give her up." Shoshanna felt herself splitting, doubling. One part of her sat on the sand listening to Sam's spectral story, the other floated above it all, observing this incredible phenomenon—*tears* on her father's face. Fuck and tears the same day. Next would come the Messiah.

He closed his eyes and placed his hands on Shoshanna's head, broad hands with palms like bowls. How rabbinic, thought the floating cynic; he's going to give me the priestly benediction. *Y'verechecha adonai v'yishmerecha.* But the earthbound Shoshanna pulled away from him and buried her face in Esther's coat, inhaling a gamey infusion of wet fur and expensive perfume, her mother's fragrance—Joy.

"*Now* do you understand, darling?" Esther whispered into her hair.

Both Shoshannas remained silent.

"Bubbeleh, wait! Let me draw you a diagram. A family tree! That'll explain everything." Sam truly believed that human beings were created in the image of God and thus were capable of limitless cognitive feats and, if given sufficient information in an age-appropriate and intellectually creative manner, could understand anything. This worldview made him a passionate teacher though an oddly emotionless father whose interactions with his daughters were most intimate when they were pedagogical. Not that he couldn't be warm. Not that he wasn't affectionate with his family, or sensitive to his congregation's pastoral needs, or sympathetic to those in pain. It was simply easier for him to relate to people through *subject matter*. The more complex a discussion—the harder he worked at learning from someone, or teaching them something—the closer he felt to them. The shortest route to Sam's heart was through his mind.

A brace of seagulls swooped and swirled overhead as his soles tamped down the sand until its surface was flat as a slate. From a heap of rotted boards he extracted a long stick with a sharp point and drew two circles a yard apart, each the size of a large dinner plate. He carved an *S* in one, an *E* in the other. "That's your mother and me," he said. Joining the rings with a horizontal line, he added a vertical line that ended in another circle. At its center, he scratched an *S*. "That's you, tateleh." The tension released between his brows. Everything was under control. The three spheres reminded Shoshanna of a pawnshop. On the other side of Esther's circle he drew a horizontal line ending in another circle and inserted an *M* for Martin, alias Lucky. Down from the Martin-Esther axis, he drew Rachel's circle and, off on an angle, a line connecting her circle to his—the adoption. Working more quickly now, he carved a disk to the right of his *S*—"the deranged Dena"—and from the *S-D* axis dropped a sphere so flawless it might have been traced with a compass. He labeled it *L*. Shoshanna fixated on how beautiful Leah's circle was compared to hers. Sam stepped back and admired his completed diagram, the spheres and rings, the lines and linkages joining the known to the unknown. It was a relationship map, a divorce map, the story of three marriages, four adults, and three offspring—R(achel).

L(eah). S(hoshanna)—three daughters on an equal plane. He was right: now she understood.

"Does Leah know about me?"

"Know about you? She was with us the day you were born. She . . ." Sam's voice cracked. His Adam's apple rolled beneath his beard.

Esther continued, "She adored you, darling. She loved to bathe you and feed you. Rachel and Leah actually fought over who could diaper you."

Together, the two names had a mythic echo. "Rachel and Leah," Shoshanna repeated. "Like in the Bible."

"Exactly!" said Esther, smiling for the first time. "When your father and I met, we couldn't believe we'd given our daughters those names and they were the ones who'd brought us together. Rachel and Leah. Some coincidence, huh?"

"Coincidences are God's way of remaining anonymous," said Sam.

Esther hoisted herself to her feet, but Shoshanna stayed down, studying the diagram. No longer the ravings of a mad scientist, Sam's family tree had become a divining rod pointing toward buried truths. Since she shared a mother with Rachel and a father with Leah, both were obviously her half sisters (though Rachel had been close as skin, Leah nonexistent). But what were Rachel and Leah to each other— stepsisters, because their parents were married? Or full sisters, since both had the same father, by blood or by law? And if they were full sisters, then, strictly speaking, weren't they closer to each other than either was to Shoshanna? Ridiculous! Rachel was her *sister*, period; the only sibling she'd ever known. Could she suddenly be demoted by half? What did these new relationships mean? Knowing the secret, would Shoshanna feel differently toward Rachel from now on? Toward her parents? Who was Esther, really? Could this mother who had hovered over Shoshanna since infancy be the same woman who sent Rachel away to school as a toddler? And if this mother could part with a daughter at three, why not at twelve? Sam, too, seemed suddenly a stranger. At twelve, Leah probably believed herself to be as precious to him as Shoshanna thought *she* was now. But that hadn't stopped him from deserting her, and not, like some absent fathers, at her birth when she was an unknown quantity, but when she was almost fully grown. If he could abandon one flesh-and-blood daughter at twelve, why not another? The twelves nagged at her. Rachel, twelve when she gained a father; Leah, twelve when she lost one; Shoshanna, twelve now, orphaned by her parents' lies.

The family tree was fading with the light. She pushed up off her knees and turned to the horizon, but sea and sky had merged and the tanker had disappeared, taking a piece of her with it.

Her childhood ended on that beach in Maine.

four

RACHEL HATED PUCE. Not the color; the dark red pleased her, especially when she used it for barns in her "Country Needlepoint" line. What she hated was the word, the ridiculous *p'yoose*. Rex the decorator had ordered a pillow with an aphorism surrounded by a floral pattern in "green, gold, and puce." Give me a break, she thought. She'd have said brick. Brick red was something a person could understand, but ask a hundred people to define puce and she'd bet not five of them could even tell you it's a color.

Same for mauve. She had eight different shades of purple stuffed into the yarn baskets in her workroom—skeins of violet, lavender, orchid, amethyst. But *mauve*? How could "mauve" communicate the intensity of an elusive hue whose range spanned pale violet to purplish red? Mauve choked on its own marbles-in-the-mouth pretension. Mauve, schmauve. Actually, Rachel couldn't care less what name a manufacturer put on the yarn label so long as her assistants knew which purple to use for a stand of lilacs and which for a summer sky. When Rex told her the colors he wanted—saying "*mohh-ve*" in the faux-British accent affected by half the decorators on Long Island—all she could say was *puhleese*. (To herself, of course.)

Not that she had anything against precision. On the contrary, she was a stickler for it—"assiduously accurate," "fanatically finicky," "maddeningly meticulous," according to Leah. This was obvious in Rachel's needlepointing, a hobby she'd turned into a lucrative vocation, but also in the gazillion facts she'd committed to memory. She knew not only what puce and mauve look like but where they fall on the spectrum. She could rattle off the seven spectral bands in their proper order—red, orange, yellow, green, blue, indigo, and violet, and just for the hell of it elucidate the difference between hue ("pure color"), tint ("color desaturated by white"), and shade ("luminosity or brightness").

So it wasn't disdain for precision that explained her impatience with Rex but rather her loathing of affectation. "Strip it down," she'd say. "Nothing's so complicated that it can't be simplified." As such, she was her adoptive father's daughter, sharing Sam's view that any body of knowledge could be taught if explained clearly enough. The difference was, Sam's curiosity led him to explore intellectual, philosophical, and religious questions, while Rachel's led her to memorize poll results, statistics, mini-biographies, Believe-It-or-Nots, and other such "factoids" that she filed away to recite at the appropriate time, not for conversational upmanship but to feel in command of a speck of the cosmos. Her mind could be engaged by all sorts of eclectic tidbits as long as each was delivered in a tidy package, neatly framed, like a needlepoint picture. Having absorbed reams of dubiously useful trivia, Rachel, generous with her wisdom, willingly shared her factoids with others. Just yesterday, for instance, she'd informed Rex the decorator that mauve was the name given to the color accidentally invented in the mid-nineteenth century by a Londoner named William Henry Perkin (no *s*) while he was attempting to synthesize quinine from coal tar. The other night at a dinner party, after her litigator husband, Jeremy, finished describing a witness's testimony, Rachel had capped his story with a quintessential Rachelism: "Did you know the verb 'to testify' comes from ancient times when Roman men had to swear on their testicles?" Everyone roared.

During one of her lunches with Shoshanna, Leah advanced the theory that Rachel's "fact fetishism" had its roots in the dislocations of her childhood. "A girl whose father vanished, whose mother struggled to provide for her, and whose fate for nine years was in the hands of a revolving teaching staff might naturally gravitate to what is secure, i.e., facts," said Leah. "That may explain why our older sister has a fondness for firmness. Also, someone raised institutionally and vying with dozens of little girls for affection would have reason to lack confidence in her intrinsic worth, or her ability to hold the attention of others, and, to compensate, might become a walking *Information Please Almanac*." Had Rachel heard this, she doubtless would have replied (parodying Leah's alliterative style), "Freudian folderol!" Though she and Leah shared AWOL fathers and the Blue Spruce experience (Rachel for nine years, Leah for only three), Rachel's interpretation of her own behavior was characteristically commonsensical: "Have five children and the facts find you." She saw herself as a woman of simple passions: family and home, God and Judaism, sex and sports. An uncommonly fit and gifted athlete, her love of all things physical followed logically from her penchant for all things factual; either you ran a mile in six minutes or you didn't, a ball was fair or foul, you gained weight or stayed trim. As for sex, you either had orgasms or struck out. (Until recently, she'd always homered.) Rachel could relate to Shoshanna's problem-solving but not to Jeremy's legal hairsplitting or Leah's appetite for ambiguity. Abstract questions made Rachel nauseous. Critical inquiry and literary symbol-chasing gave her hives. Moral dilemmas and psychoanalytic concepts glazed her eyes. All this notwithstanding, she had infinite patience, curiosity, and ardor, plus a great capacity for engrossment when it came to Judaism.

Others who'd suffered her losses might have rejected religion altogether, but Rachel remained a believer because the alternative was *sohu va'vohu*, emptiness and nothingness. Torah explained the unexplainable; it constituted a legal and ethical system and her people's history. She cherished it not because she accepted every biblical story as fact or factoid but because it gave her spiritual comfort, an agenda for social action, and a path to the divine. She often quoted the sage with the unlikeliest of names, Rabbi Ben Bahg Bahg (Rachel was always careful to credit the authors of her aphorisms): " 'Turn it and turn it for all is in it, and in it you shall find all.' " She'd been turning the sacred texts inside out for years. " 'When I pray, I speak to God; when I study, God speaks to me' (Rabbi Louis Finkelstein)," she said, and kept up her end of the conversation by attending her Long Island synagogue services regularly and taking adult education classes at the Jewish community center, and courses in Jewish history at SUNY Old Westbury or Adelphi College. God spoke to Rachel most clearly through the Hebrew Bible, its spare prose suiting her temperament better than the dizzying disputations of the Talmud. "On the one hand, on the other hand" made her nervous. She liked her answers single-handed.

Living within Judaism's confines came as easily to her as working within the frame of a needlepoint composition. She took direction well: in class; on paper; in wool; in halachah, Jewish law. She lit her Shabbat candles and kept kosher, and though one mitzvah, the hallah ritual, struck her as primitive, she threw a piece of dough into the fire anyway, to remember the Temple sacrifices. Rituals, like other clear-cut obligations, appealed to Rachel Brent. You nursed because a baby was hungry, sponged a counter because it was sticky, flung your dough into the oven because God commanded it. You delivered a needlepoint pillow on time because you said you would. Rachel preferred to follow a pattern, even if, as with Rex's pillow, the design was her own. After drawing a sketch on graph paper, she would transfer the design—every monogram, numeral, and leaf—secure in the certainty that a square on the page corresponded to a stitch on the canvas. A needlepointer could bank on measured mesh and counted threads and the rightness of each stitch for its purpose. Turkey stitch for flowers, hair, beards, or clouds, but never for sky or skin. Moorish stitch for mountains and cobblestones. Cashmere Diagonal or Gobelin for finer textures. Never substitute Fern when the instructions call for the more subtle Herringbone. For dramatic effects, use Crossed Roads or Diamond Squares. Backgrounds: Hungarian or Encroaching Oblique. Brick stitch for buildings and fences, Jacquard for zigzags. Initials, ropes, and straps were best done in the Couching stitch, while the French Knot was right for accents and polka dots.

Needlepoint, like Judaism, was codified, its rules to be followed to the letter. Miss a stitch and ruin the canvas. Use the wrong stitch, you'll regret it later. Each stitch, like every ritual, had its place in the grand design. Simplicity and accuracy were Rachel's core values. Give her a rule, a recipe, a single-celled organism. A haiku poem, a mathematical formula, the solidity of a statistic. Rachel was a tiny woman. She wanted tiny truths.

The pillow she was making for Rex the decorator bore a slogan that proclaimed one such truth: A PROMISCUOUS PERSON IS ANYONE WHO HAS MORE SEX THAN YOU DO. He'd ordered it as a surprise for his lover. The pillow was due March 1, and though the needlepoint panel was done and blocked, she'd miscalculated the time, forgotten that February was a short month, and had yet to attach the backing, sew on the piping and fringe, and stuff it. Tomorrow was March 1. Tonight, she would finish the job.

It was one of those rare evenings when Jeremy was at home. They were sitting by the fire listening to music, she sewing away like mad while he did the *Times* crossword puzzle.

"Let's see," he said, peering at the pillow over the top of his newspaper. She held it up so he could read the message. "Hmmm. That would make the whole world promiscuous." A sour expression wrinkled his face but ironed itself out an instant later.

Rachel winced. They hadn't had sex in months. She'd begun menopause relatively late, but its symptoms had not only persisted but worsened. Hot flashes had made a wreck of her, cooling her libido even as they drenched her body in raging sweats and left her dry and parched inside. Intercourse had become excruciating, like sandpaper or ground glass in the eye. More than most people, Rachel Brent knew there was more to sex than fucking; but lately, every variety of lovemaking had lost its appeal. Hormone replacement therapy might have put things right except that there was breast cancer in the family—Esther had died of it—and for Rachel, the doctor said, taking estrogen was risky. So she'd gone the holistic route—motherwort, meditation, herbal teas, biofeedback, yoga. Nothing helped.

"I would if I could, Jer; you know that."

He raised an eyebrow and returned to the puzzle.

All her life Rachel had been sexually charged, autoerotic since the crib, that is, for as long as she could remember, and orgasmic to the tune of four or five rolls of thunder for every crack of lightning. Despite the puritanical ethos of the fifties, she'd spent her youth being led around by her loins in search of a lover as fired-up and skilled as herself. Jeremy—a Clark Gable look-alike, only taller, with magic fingers and a prick that never quit—more than filled the bill. Not only did he pursue her like a hot wind, he was also a year out of law school and practicing with a large Manhattan firm, which found favor in the eyes of her parents. He had "good prospects," said Sam. Esther declared him "a provider *and* a looker." For her part, Rachel fell in love with Jeremy at first sight, slept with him on their first date (and every day thereafter), and agreed to marry him before he asked her.

He dropped his bombshell a week before their wedding. They were in bed at his apartment in London Terrace on West Twenty-third Street. She was tracing every vertebra on his back with her fingers and basking in the afterglow of their lovemaking. "How many guys have you had?" he asked, rolling over to face her.

She untangled their postcoital sheets, surprised by the question. "Why do you want to know?"

"Just curious."

"Five," she said. "Or nine." He looked at her quizzically. Rachel laughed. "Okay, a baker's dozen at most. Does it matter?"

"Nope. I like my women experienced."

"How many women are we talking about here, Jer?" She was beginning to feel uncomfortable.

"Eleventy-nine." He tweaked her nipple.

"Seriously," said Rachel. "I told you, now you tell me."

"Too many to count, honey. I practiced on them to get good enough for you."

He was more than good enough. Satisfying many women had added up to one hell of a Sex Ed course. "Practice makes perfect," she said, trying to make light of her growing unease. "Now that you've got it down, no more fooling around, right?"

"Right," he said, and kissed her, then rose onto an elbow, lit a cigarette, and, with a grin clearly meant to disarm, asked casually, "Ever made it with a woman?"

"Don't be ridiculous!" Rachel flashed on Miss Cardwell, instantly blotting out the memory. Coerced sex didn't count. She gathered the bedsheet up to her neck. "Have *you*? With a man?"

He took a long drag and exhaled slowly. "Yeah," he said.

The smoke obscured his face. She waited until it dissipated, until she could see his expression. "What are you saying?" She felt afraid.

"Relax, babe . . ." He reached for her.

She recoiled, grabbed the headboard, and pulled herself upright. "You've had sex with a man!?"

"Once. An experiment. Just wanted to see what it was like."

She didn't want him to tell her what it was like. In a pornographic novel, a homosexual interlude might have aroused her, but as a chapter in her fiancé's autobiography, it made her sick. She felt as if she'd fallen in love with a new Porsche that turned out to have a hundred thousand miles on it. She got dressed quickly and started to leave.

Naked, he jumped off the bed and, spewing remorse and self-reproach, said how meaningless it had been. A lark. A high school thing. Didn't enjoy it. Hadn't meant to shock her—just thought they should be honest with each other, start their lives together with a clean slate. He tried to take her in his arms. She backed away, shoved a hand through the strap of her purse, and reached for the doorknob. He heaved up more apologies. He loved her so much. Wanted her to be the mother of his children. *Needed* her. She heard a catch in his voice. "Don't let this be a deal-breaker," he implored. Then came the oaths.

He would never sleep with anyone else, ever. Promised to reclaim his dignity in her eyes, become a great lawyer, a big success, support her in comfort. If she went through with the wedding, he swore he'd spend the rest of his life working to earn her respect.

She stood in the doorway, cupping the knob, swiveling it until her palm slipped on her own perspiration. He seemed so vulnerable, standing there naked. It was almost as if he'd slid back into his past and become the small, insecure boy whose widowed mother never protected him from the fact that she had no strength and few resources, and Rachel, knowing how brittle was his grown-up bravado, watched it break apart now before her eyes. "I have to think," she said. In the end, she deposited his revelation in the same box where she stashed the other secrets she kept from herself—the father who'd hit her, the Blue Spruce misery, the shameful games with Miss Cardwell. And that Saturday night, she walked down the aisle, smiling radiantly.

Professionally, Jeremy more than made good on his promises. He became a personal-injury lawyer with an income that sent five kids to college and afforded Rachel the life of a wealthy suburban matron, whose home included a needlepoint studio and workout gym, and two cars in the garage. But, like his sexual precocity, this, too, had come at a price: his weird moods and driving ambition, his long hours and frequent absences, which she'd accepted, just as she'd accepted his erotic history, because of the pact she'd made with herself. A simple quid pro quo. She got reliably satisfying sex, financial security, and the big family she'd fantasized about in boarding school. He got a girl so eager to put down roots that she would provide the seeds, irrigation, and labor herself. Not only did she mother his children with a devotion that was wholehearted and domestically creative, but she made their home into a showplace that burnished his reputation and wowed his clients. Rachel, having long ago forgiven Jeremy the false front that he never forgave her for seeing through, had recognized, behind his brash self-confidence, the kid on the run from his early circumstances, the boy haunted by his absent father (as she was by hers), the only child of a woman who couldn't cope. God's puppet strings were in plain view: Rachel, a woman of a thousand talents, was the antidote to her husband's past. Jeremy, a hunk with a six-figure income, was the antidote to hers.

For years, their pact held largely because the sex, however sporadic, had been surefire. But now she was more interested in her needlepoint business and Torah classes, more excited by a new addition to her clock collection than by the husband whose key in the lock used to turn her to clotted cream. Since menopause, she'd curdled.

Unwrapping the fringe she'd ordered for Rex's pillow, Rachel was upset to find it was the wrong shade, more purple than puce. "Think I can get away with this or should I just do the piping?" she asked, but Jeremy, who could have been an Armani model in his soft flannel shirt and corduroy trousers, had nodded off in his chair with the newspaper spread across his chest like a Linus blanket. She visualized the body beneath her husband's clothes—the flat belly, the hollows of his but-tocks, his sex, which she'd always found to be a thing of beauty, flaccid or hard. But tonight all she felt was an aesthetic appreciation, the sort one might feel for a fashion model or a sculpture, nothing more. How could the drives of a lifetime disappear? she wondered, discarding the fringe and pinning the piping in place. Where had her sexual energy gone? What had doused her Eternal Light?

Equating physical lust with spiritual ardor didn't strike Rachel as heretical, since both, in her view, were gifts from the Almighty. She made love the way she made kiddush—with kavvanah, a holy inten-tionality, and a conscious gratitude for her blessings. The fire she stoked in the bedroom and the fervor of her prayers emanated from the same torch, though the first was inborn, the second a product of Sam's influ-ence in her life. When he became her new father, he'd refused to put her, a twelve-year-old, with the five-year-olds at Hebrew school, the level for which she qualified, but had insisted on teaching her at the dining-room table, for an hour or so after supper, three times a week: Tuesdays, Hebrew; Wednesdays, Jewish history; Thursdays, the Torah portion of the week. So quickly did he bring her up to speed that she'd been able to celebrate her bat mitzvah at thirteen, same as her friends. The leather-bound Hebrew dictionary Sam gave her was the first object she'd ever owned with her name embossed on it, her new name, Rachel Wasserman.

Rodeph Tzedek was Rachel's second home, the institution that cured her of her hatred of institutions. Everything about the sanctuary awed her, from its soaring dome to the smell of its holy books. She loved the rock and sway of the liturgical chants and the wordless lyricism of the niggunim, the textures on the bimah—satin, velvet, gilt—the Torah scrolls, cloaked in royal-blue vestments and crowned with silver bells, the bronze menorahs flanking the ark. Most of all, she loved the stained-glass windows, one for each of Jacob's sons. It took her years to notice that Jacob's daughter had no window.

Since the change of life, what was missing was the first thing Rachel noticed, what she thought about incessantly. More palpable than everything she had was everything she'd lost—Esther, her mother, dead for nearly thirty-five years; her son Gideon, for twenty; her libido gone. She'd begun seriously ruminating on disappearance when Daniel called a week or so ago, frantic because Shoshanna was missing, which, to Daniel, meant he hadn't seen or heard from her since breakfast. Rachel remembered glancing at one of her clocks—there were six in the living room, about a fifth of her collection. It was 7:30, half-past house wren on the clock face with different bird pictures where the numbers should be. For the Safers, a twelve-hour lapse in communication was unusual enough to justify Daniel's alarm. It was a family joke how compulsively he and Shoshanna kept in touch. He came home for lunch just to hang out with her, or, when the excuse of a research assignment brought her to the NYU library, she'd drop by his faculty office and chat him up. They talked on the phone twice or three times a day, schmoozed like teenagers, nuzzled like puppies, opened each other's mail without permission, refused to see a movie unless they could see it together. Even at the height of the women's movement, when her radical colleagues were touting the superiority of sisterhood to heterosexual love and wives were dumping their husbands for leaving the toilet seat up, Shoshanna said Daniel was her best friend. Some thought the Safers' marriage close-knit, while others (Leah, for one) called it impacted, but since they'd been together for a quarter of a century and were still setting off sparks, it was hard to fault the formula.

Rachel, a frequent witness to their idiosyncratic intimacies, had never forgotten the time when she and Shoshanna were trying on bathing suits at Loehmann's and Shoshie rang Daniel on her cell phone to see what he thought about her buying a bikini the color of Cheez Whiz. (He said it was fine—no surprise, virtually everything she did was fine with him.) Rachel thought orange wrong for her sister's skin tone, though the three strategic triangles were fetching on Shoshanna, whose breasts defied gravity, who never exercised and paid scant attention to her diet, yet somehow stayed firm as a peach. Shoshanna looked great in triangles and everything else. Height makes the woman, concluded Rachel, from whose 5-foot vantage point her sister's 5'7" was towering.

"You two may as well be joined at the hip," Rachel said as she wriggled into a one-piece spandex and patted her own hips for emphasis. A size 2, she was well proportioned, a greyhound not a Pekingese, and pretty in a well-scrubbed, outdoorsy way. "How does Shoshanna love him? Let me count the ways: mash notes in his desk drawer, candlelight at breakfast, a consultation from the dressing room at Loehmann's. Leah's right; it's 'totemic togetherness.'"

"What's wrong with a wife wanting to please her husband?" Shoshanna peeled off the bikini and stepped into a tank suit.

"Nothing, honey, it's great," replied Rachel, though she couldn't fathom how any two people could be so enmeshed in each other's lives, and certainly couldn't imagine giving Jeremy a veto on her wardrobe. First he'd have to notice what she wore. Then he'd have to care. In fact, he was too busy to do either and more interested in dressing himself in designer suits, monogrammed shirts, and cashmere coats from Paul Stuart, having turned his back on discount shopping when he got a full scholarship to law school, and all but forgetting his premarital, post-coital pledge. What little attention he paid to Rachel and the home front was directed to the creation of an image that confirmed his professional prestige, one requiring a large house on Long Island, children who reflected well on him, and a wife who knew how to stay fit and entertain elegantly. His task, as he saw it, was to win high-profile cases, and he always said he would rather be envied than liked, though, with his blue-sky eyes and a smile that stretched from one Clark Gable ear to the other, he'd always managed to *appear* likable. If anything, Rachel thought his face had grown more appealing with age, which only proved that looks are deceiving, since he'd actually matured into humorless workaholic, serious bordering on dour, a formal man who came to life only in bed. Rachel gave him an A in erotics, but flunked him at intimacy.

Married since the flood, the Brents, as opposed to the Safers, were strangers to each other's worlds. Friday, for instance, Jeremy hadn't a clue that Rachel had been in a customer's apartment, fitting a needlepoint slipcover onto his piano bench, while the guy, who happened to be rather a stud, sat around in his boxer shorts (which might have been a problem for her premenopausally, when her furnace was still running full blast). By the same token, if the Chief Justice of the Supreme Court needed him this minute, she couldn't have located Jeremy were he not sitting across from her asleep in his chair. And she couldn't have said whether he was arguing a case last Friday or talking his way into some woman's skivvies. Though she rarely asked and didn't really want to know where he was, during her darker moments Rachel wondered about all the times he "couldn't be reached," was "in a meeting," "at a conference," "caught in traffic," "seeing clients," "still at lunch," "researching a case," or "taking depositions." Challenged to account for their time, missing persons always seem to produce a plausible explanation. Anyone can get away with anything in New York; the city lends itself to stealth.

Though Jeremy's absences never amounted to a full-fledged, reportable disappearance, his business trips and late nights at the office added up to an aggregated vanishment. He was a cumulative missing person, more erasure than text. He behaved as if home was a nice place to visit but he didn't necessarily want to live there. Most of the time, Rachel tried not to think about where he might be, or why he felt absent to her even when he was in the room. She didn't question why she'd been willing to travel through life on tires with a slow leak, patching them, pumping them up with her own enthusiasm, pretending she wasn't riding on the rims. That her marriage was seriously deflated was the one factoid she couldn't or wouldn't acknowledge. She had too much to lose.

But her sister's marriage was a pumped-up, living organism. In twenty-five years, Shoshanna and Daniel had never spent a day out of touch, so last week, when he didn't know where she was, Rachel was sure something terrible must have happened to her. When there was still no word after the bird clock struck 8 (the dove), then 8:30, fear pierced Rachel's heart like a needle in the pad of a thumb.

Englishtown, New Jersey. 1951. An outdoor flea market spread across acres of fallow fields. Vendors hawking World War II surplus, second-hand furniture, used tractors, chipped dishes, toys, tools, and all manner of livestock. Esther and Sam, who were shopping for a desk chair for the rabbi's den, left Shoshanna in the care of Rachel, who, at sixteen, was old enough to be responsible for a toddler but young enough to be distracted by a display of old *Life* magazines, in particular, an issue from 1935, the year she was born. The ads were incredible: women's dresses, $3.98; cereals she'd never heard of; bearlike sedans, all of them black and none as spiffy as her boyfriend's two-toned Chevy or the convertible belonging to Sam's pulpit colleague, Cantor Levy, who loved to put the top down on his silver gray Olds and sing, "Come away with me, Lucille, in my merry Oldsmobile." When the Wassermans joined him for a Sunday ride, Shoshanna sang along at the top of her two-year-old lungs.

Shoshanna!!

Rachel snapped out of her reverie and, in one heart-hammering instant, realized her charge had wandered off and been swallowed by the crowds.

"Shoshie!! Shoshie!!" she cried, zooming up one muddy aisle and down another, every peril multiplying her panic. She hadn't noticed the rocky stream before; the displays of hoes and rakes, picks and knives, scythes and saws, all within reach; the farm trucks backing up without honking; the grizzled men with motor oil under their fingernails, each a potential kidnapper. "Have you seen a red-headed baby?" she asked the man selling galvanized washtubs, the thick-armed woman sifting powdered sugar on a tray of fresh doughnuts, the couple demonstrating a miracle cleaner. A small plane droned overhead. Above the din Rachel screamed her sister's name so urgently that other shoppers joined in the search.

"She's wearing heart-shaped barrettes! Blue leggings, white blouse, brown shoes with plaid laces. She had a lollipop, a yellow one!" Even then, Rachel was a careful observer, though not careful enough. Waited fourteen years for a baby sister, adored Shoshanna from the instant Esther brought her home from the hospital wrapped in white fleece, her face a tiny rosebud in the snow. And now she was gone. Shoshie, so small; flesh, bone, beating heart. Please, God, don't let her die. Please, please, please . . . A vow formed in Rachel's head. What sacrifice was great enough to warrant divine intervention? Let her be all right and I'll . . . I'll never touch myself down there again.

From three aisles away, a man in a hunting cap whooped, "Found her!" and hoisted Shoshanna over his head like an umbrella. "She was squattin' by the chicken pens, tryin' to push this yeller lollipop into their beaks," he said, and deposited the baby in Rachel's arms.

She never told her parents what had happened that day in the flatlands of New Jersey, and her vow of abstinence lasted less than a month. But until she left home in 1956 to marry Jeremy, she watched over her little sister as if the child might vanish at any moment, and loved her fiercely. After the wedding—with Shoshie as flower girl—they went their separate ways, Rachel to the suburbs, Shoshanna to second grade. Despite the age difference and despite Leah's having come between them in the sixties, when Shoshanna was an impressionable adolescent and Rachel an overextended mother of five—and despite the awkwardness she felt when Shoshanna married Daniel and he and Jeremy never quite clicked—Rachel had done her best to stay close to her sister. How close were they if she couldn't help Daniel figure out where his wife might be last week when Shoshanna disappeared? As with Jeremy, there was a great deal Rachel didn't know about her sister if knowing is measured by the whens, wheres, and what-are-you-up-to's.

On his second phone call (after the wren and the dove), Daniel had said he was feeling "tremendous anxiety," and something totally inappropriate—doubtless propelled by her nervousness—had popped out of Rachel's mouth before she could squelch it: "Only four words in the English language end in *d-o-u-s*: Tremendous, horrendous, stupendous, and hazardous." Usually, her factoids were silent until summoned, say at parties, where she might feel pressure to be clever, but occasionally they arrived unannounced and refused to be muzzled.

"I'll have her call you the minute she gets home," Daniel had replied, ignoring Rachel's inanity but picking up on her underlying anxiety, something Jeremy never seemed able to do. When they hung up, she was nearly undone by her fears. With Shoshanna unaccounted for, the "dous" words seemed like an omen spelled out on a Ouija board. Horrendous. Hazardous . . .

HAZARDOUS WHEN WET. The sign was cruelly redundant. Flashing lights, wet pavement, broken glass, crushed metal—these things speak for themselves. Rachel had been alone in the house when the police called. "There's been an accident, a serious one involving Gideon Brent . . ." Jeremy was in Chicago at a legal seminar, so Rachel had left eighteen-year-old Simon in charge of the younger kids and driven herself to the location the police had described, just beyond the Route 110 overpass. Rain battered her windshield, the rhythm of the wipers almost drowning out her "Adonai, Adonai, God of mercy, God of kindness, be Thou merciful. In your hands is the power of life . . ." But her prayer had been in vain, a *tefillat shav*, a waste of words.

Orange cones marked the accident scene. A squad car with whirling lights. A body stretched out on the rain-slicked pavement, covered to the ankles by a police tarp. Two feet stuck out, one in a bloody white athletic sock, one in a sneaker. Gideon's Adidas. "I'm his mother," she said. A soft-spoken officer wearing a thin mustache removed his cap and lowered his eyes. "Sorry, ma'am. He was killed on impact, EMS told us. Black ice." The cop pointed to a gouged elm. The car had spun out of control, slammed head-on into the tree, ricocheted back, and hit a sign stanchion. That's why it was so banged up. This time, she didn't want to hear about the properties of black ice or the hydroplane effect or the percentage of accidents that happen in the rain. The crushed tangle of chrome and steel that was once her son's red coupe said enough. Gideon, twenty-one tomorrow and on his way home from college to celebrate, had died in that twisted tomb, his body no match for a rainstorm and a ninety-year-old elm.

Her lips moved silently. *Baruch dayan ha'emet*, Blessed is the Righteous Judge. She remembered the right blessing. the one Jews are supposed to say upon first learning of a death. She said it. But she didn't believe it. That night, something dead-ended in Rachel—the optimism that had carried her through at Blue Spruce, the belief that if you make the best of things, life will keep getting better. Until the black ice, life had. She'd been on an upward journey since Leah Wasserman arrived at school and they became friends, and in no time at all, Leah's dad married Rachel's mom, and Rachel had a home, a room of her own, a baby sister, and a new father who filled her head with miracles as amazing as her own. Life got even better when her body flowered and its pleasures increased, and she found a husband with whom she'd had five healthy babies—Gideon, Simon, Zelda, Dalia, and Tamara—the perfect family; two boys, three girls, all born with seed-pearl fingernails and full heads of hair. With each child's birth, she added another candle to her Sabbath ritual and chanted, "*Or hadash al tzion ta'ir*. A new light shines for Zion." Including her candle and Jeremy's, she kindled seven flames every Friday night. Her life was full of light.

Things got better still when Jeremy won a six-million-dollar verdict against a beverage company whose soda bottle exploded in a woman's face and disfigured her horribly. His one-third share of the judgment bought them the big house on Long Island—a sun-yellow colonial with white window trim and black shutters, six bedrooms, an eat-in kitchen, and an atrium that she transformed into her needlepoint studio. In this house, Rachel spun her world, made beautiful things and made everything beautiful; put fresh flowers in every room, roses on their bed table, daisies on the children's windowsills, freesia in a bud vase on Jeremy's desk whether or not he noticed. She sewed, knitted, crocheted, needlepointed, and tended her garden. She harvested plum tomatoes, purple eggplant (not mauve), zucchini as thick as a baby's thigh. She taught her children the sports she excelled at herself, helped them with their schoolwork, and recited the Sh'ma with them at bedtime. Saturday, she went to synagogue. Sunday, she shopped the garage sales, adding to her collection of clocks and mirrors, or stopped by the plant nursery, or baked brownies with her children. The rest of the week, she furnished and decorated, neatened and polished, cooked and baked— all from scratch, even gefilte fish—made dinner parties for her husband's clients and tried to please him, to keep him home. Home was sacred space to Rachel, her body a vessel of delight, and the work of her hands her art.

When the youngest went off to elementary school, she began to sell her needlepoint pillows and tapestries and soon was putting away money of her own, her knipl. "Progress is my most important product," she'd say, but never felt complacent about her blessings. In shul, she sang songs of praise, not supplication. She made the best of her disappointments, overlooked Jeremy's shortcomings and concentrated on his good points—the important work he did representing victims, his financial generosity, his lovemaking. She believed life would keep getting better and God's countenance would always shine upon her and be gracious unto her.

After Gideon was killed, her other blessings seemed suddenly provisional. She tried to remember *before*—all those years of escalating pleasures—but the happy times became a blur as the poet Yehuda Amichai warned they would. He'd done a reading at Rachel's temple, and one of his poems had stayed with her, the title a poem in itself— "The Precision of Pain and the Blurriness of Joy"—and so true. People tend to be exquisitely precise when describing pain. We don't just say it hurts, we say it throbs or aches; it's a burning, wrenching, gnawing sensation; it's sharp or dull; it chafes, it stings. But where pain specifies, joy generalizes. It was great! we say. Terrific! Beautiful! Fantastic! We are too immersed in our pleasure to record its nuances; too distracted by joy to itemize it on memory's ledger. Twenty years later, staring into her fireplace with Jeremy snoring in his chair, the good times blurred, but everything associated with her son's death was as clear as black ice. Like Amichai, Rachel had "learned to speak among the pains."

There could be no taharah, the men in the black suits told her at the funeral home. She protested. No ritual purification? She wanted Gideon made ready for the Olam Ha-Ba, the world to come. Why couldn't his body be cleansed and swathed in white linen like every other dead Jew? she asked her father.

"Because of the accident." Sam's face was a mask of self-control.

"Wasn't it enough he lost his life? Does he have to lose his dignity, too?"

"Just the opposite, tateleh. Blood is the essence of human dignity. It's a person's elemental life force, that's why Jews don't embalm a body. Or wash an accident victim. We bury people *with* their blood, *in* their blood-soaked clothes, so as not to lose a drop." Sam's voice cracked like a china cup, his tears disappeared in the thatch of his beard. Rachel gathered him in her arms. Everything was upside down: a laywoman ministering to a rabbi, a daughter comforting her father, a grandfather outliving his grandson. Gideon's dying was perverse, absurd. Parents are supposed to predecease their children. Children are not supposed to die.

From Esther's passing, Rachel remembered the prayers, the rhythms of bereavement, how each stage of mourning was designed not just to memorialize the deceased but to nudge the survivors back to life. Though knowing didn't make it easier, she found herself grateful for the wisdom of halachah—a text for every trauma, a reason for every rule. She was grateful that Jews don't prettify the corpse, that Gideon's blood would not be hosed down the drain, that his casket was closed, out of respect, and no one would cringe at the sight of her precious boy in his sticky garments. She knew that his body would not be left alone until his burial, and the people from the hevra kadisha, the fellowship of holiness, would be watching over him, reading psalms, and she was glad about that, too. Though his soul was with God, she wanted his body guarded. Living or dead, no one should have to be alone, she thought, as she had been alone so many nights when it counted: When the police called about Gideon. When she identified his body. When Esther died. When Daniel called last week, worried about Shoshanna. And now, finishing the St. Patrick's Day pillow, alone again, with Jeremy a few yards away, snoring. The difference between solitude and loneliness is the difference between chosen isolation and abandonment. Last week, as she awaited news of her sister, the pain triggered by her fear had been precise enough to resurrect the terror she'd felt when she'd lost Shoshie in Englishtown. Tonight, with the precision of pain, she was reliving her son's funeral.

Standing room only in the chapel. Sam's fingertips lightly brushed the coffin as he walked to the podium and, in a voice like a rusty hinge, intoned, "Gideon Nathaniel Brent was an extraordinary young man. As many of you know, he headed our synagogue's delegation to Israel last summer. I asked him to take on this important role—though he was only twenty at the time—not because he was my grandson but because he was a natural leader, a young Moses—modest, caring, intuitive, wiser than his years. Why was a boy like Gideon taken from us?" Shoulders stooped, Sam hesitated, and seemed to give up trying to understand. "I have no answer. We will miss him always. Mysterious are the ways of the Lord. Amen."

More eulogies, friends, teachers, teammates, more psalms, El Maleh Rachamim. Rachel read in the prayer book, "Grant perfect peace beneath your protective wings to the soul of my son . . ." Fill in the blank. Scripted sorrow, one size fits all, which was as it should be, she thought. Death, the great equalizer. There are no lesser losses. Every Jew, regardless of station, was memorialized with simple words and laid to rest in a plain pine box. But Sam was wrong about the Moses part. Unlike Moshe Rabeinu, Gideon did get to see the Promised Land, but also unlike Moses, Gideon would never live to be 120.

In the hearse on the way to the cemetery, she told her other children how to mourn their brother properly and what to expect in the week to come. Jewish mourning rituals are brought to you by the number seven, she said. Focusing on the number helped her make things understandable, even to Tamara, who was nine at the time. "It's all about sevens," she explained. "Seven categories of relatives count as official mourners. We're the ones who do k'riah." (Before the funeral she had recited the words of Job—the Lord giveth and the Lord taketh away—and then ripped the lapel of her blazer and pinned a torn black ribbon to each of her children's shirts.) "We do this because our patriarch tore his garments after seeing the blood on his son Joseph's many-colored coat. The torn fabric symbolizes our broken hearts." She gazed out the back window of the hearse at the line of slow-moving cars behind them, headlights aglow at midday, then back to her children's faces. "We're going to sit shiva for seven days. You know what shiva means?"

Tamara rolled her eyes. "Who doesn't, Ma? Seven."

"We'll burn a memorial candle for seven days to light the void in our lives. For seven days we'll cover our mirrors to show we have no use for vanity. And with my mirror collection, that's a pretty big job." None of the children cracked a smile. "We'll sit on low benches for seven days, and we won't watch TV or talk on the phone." (She shot a knowing glance at the adolescents, Dalia and Zelda.) "No one will play sports" (a nudge for Tamara, the tomboy). "Men won't shave" (a nod to Simon, now her only son, who'd sprouted five facial hairs yet started shaving when Gideon did). "We won't wear leather shoes, only sneakers or slippers. The front door will be unlocked so people won't have to ring the bell when they make a shiva call to keep us company or help out with the cooking, laundry, and everything else we can't do this week." She left out the fact that, for seven days, mourners can't have sex, though who would want to?

The sides of the open grave were polished to a glossy sheen by the diggers' spades, the scooped-out earth rising like a hillock to one side of the grave. Someone had spread green sod over the mound as if it needed a modest covering—upholstery for "the lone couch of his ever-lasting sleep." (Shelley, or was it Keats?) The mourners surrounded the grave in a haphazard circle. Everyone said kaddish. Everyone cried, though the traditional prayer for the dead contained no mention of death, only lavish praise of the Almighty and a plea for peace. It's a test, Rachel decided; God is asking, "Can you praise me even after I've taken your child? Can you still bless me?"

She wasn't sure.

Workmen in gray uniforms grabbed hold of the straps under the casket, positioned the box over the opening, and slowly lowered it until it struck the ground with a sickening thud. One worker rolled up the grassy sod and jammed a long-handled shovel into the mound of dirt. Jeremy pulled the shovel out and, according to custom, inverted its bowl—upside down, unnatural, absurd, like the death of a child. He scraped up a clump of earth and tipped it into the grave. Pebbles skittered across the coffin lid like hail on a roof. Following Sam's instructions, Jeremy returned the shovel to the mound rather than handing it directly to Rachel, lest he seem in a hurry to bury his loved one. She hefted some dirt and threw it into the cavity, feeling her son's death in her shoulders, grateful (again, grateful) for a chance to physicalize her loss and make it real. Next the children, one by one, ladled out their small scoops of sorrow. Watching them do their part to bury their brother, she remembered how, every summer at the beach, Gideon would let the little girls bury him, all but his head; how he'd play dead while they decorated his mummy shape with seaweed and shells, and tickled his face with beach grass, until just as they'd despaired of his ever moving again, he rose up, barking like a sea lion, and dove into the surf with his squealing sisters running in his wake. This time, it was no game. The plain pine box disappeared beneath the earth.

At home, a consolation meal awaited them. Hard-boiled eggs, lentils, bagels, doughnuts, raisins, grapes—round foods to reaffirm the circle of life. Rachel ate nothing; she had not yet decided to go on living. All week long, the countertops groaned with cheeses, noodle puddings in aluminum pans. platters of pink lox and brassy whitefish, baskets of bread and fresh fruit. Bakery boxes tied with red string poured forth strudel, cookies, babka. Someone located her party urn and put up coffee. Everyone was trying to be helpful, but nothing helped. Yet somehow she managed to rise from the mourners' bench to embrace friends, to thank them for their food and receive their sympathy. "May his memory be for a blessing." ". . . a blessing." ". . . blessing." Day brought the chaos of visitors. Morning and evening, she said her kaddish—"*Yiskadal, v'yiskadash, sh'may rabbah*"—trying to find it in her heart to sanctify a God who would destroy a boy of such promise and devastate a Jewish mother who lived by the rules. Well, not *all* the rules. Knowing herself incapable of abstaining from sex for two weeks a month, and unwilling to be a hypocrite about it, Rachel never went to the ritual bath. Was that her sin? Avoiding mikvah? Hadn't she made up for it with tikkun olam, doing her part to repair the world? What more should she have done?

At night, after the last visitor was gone, her anguish burst its bonds and the mirrors shook with her wailing, and only when she sat at Gideon's desk warmed by the light of his study lamp, only then could she find peace.

When the seven days were over, she threw the family's torn black ribbons in the garbage, sent the benches back to the funeral home, and asked Jeremy and the children to walk around the block with her to mark their reentry into the world. Jeremy refused, pronouncing the custom "silly."

"Not silly, symbolic," she said. " 'Yea, though I walk through the valley of the shadow of death' means we must walk *through* our grief. It'll help, Jeremy."

"No, it won't," he replied, and went to the office as if it were a day like any other.

Rachel didn't hold his resistance against him. She knew that his mother, an Orthodox Jew, had tried to keep the rituals while he was growing up, but was defeated by widowhood and poverty, by overwork and fatigue. Judaism became yet another set of expectations she couldn't fulfill, another of the many shortfalls that made her feel like a failure. Jeremy had relieved her of her guilt by rejecting religion altogether and insisting she give up her "silly" practices. When she died, he continued to do nothing, perhaps in his mother's honor, perhaps to assure himself that he hadn't been disappointed in her and had never wanted more. At least that was Rachel's theory. Because he wouldn't mourn the Jewish way, Rachel was convinced his despair was more intransigent; it stuck to him, a thin, cold veneer on top of his other layers of self-protection.

They made love during shloshim, the first thirty days after the shiva, since sex is permitted. Her body responded, but her heart wasn't in it. She mourned her son for eleven months. Though halachah dictates a period of one month for a child—eleven for a parent—eleven seemed right for Gideon, who would never become anyone's parent. On the first anniversary of his death, at sundown, Rachel lit a yahrzeit candle to symbolize his ongoing presence in her life, and the next day, when the wick flickered out, she made a sketch of Gideon sitting at his desk in a pool of light, a still life for a life stilled. She transferred the drawing to graph paper, then to mesh, and made her needle her paintbrush and cried into the wool, and, when the needlepoint picture was framed, hung it over the fireplace and willed herself, for the sake of her remaining children, to choose life.

Last week, as she waited for news of Shoshanna, the picture, which had been hanging above the fireplace these last twenty years, suddenly seemed ominous. The ship's clock on the mantel struck its brassy gong, the first of a cacophony of dings, dongs, bells, and tweets proclaiming 9 p.m. How could she not watch the time in a room full of clocks? Surveying their expectant faces, what might have been obvious to a more introspective mind struck Rachel with the clarity of a chime. She'd begun collecting clocks after Gideon died. She'd been hoarding time.

That night, waiting, she'd walked along the wall of mirrors and caught sight of her anxious eyes framed in squares and ovals, edged in silver, gold filigree, Deco brass, schoolhouse oak. She combed her fingers through her bangs, which immediately settled back across her brow as if they'd never been disturbed. Hair was one of her blessings. Thick, straight, and shiny, it could have been barbered with a bowl and needed no coddling. It had always been the envy of Shoshanna, whose unruly mane was her only out-of-control feature. Rachel shivered. Not *was*—is.

She'd stopped in front of a cloisonné mirror, the one she'd been standing before during the party for Sam's eightieth when Leah came up behind her trolling, "Mirror, mirror on the wall, who's the most fucked up of all?" She'd been amused until Leah added, "Is it narcissism or inadequacy, this need to reproduce yourself ad infinitum? What's your demon, Rachel?"

"Neither," she'd replied quietly. "I love how mirrors reflect the light, that's all."

Having Leah in her home that day was a first for Rachel, and not an easy debut. Shoshanna had warned her it might be dicey, that Leah could be thin-skinned as a grape one minute, a ten-ton truck the next. At Sam's party, she was a Sherman tank, rolling over Rachel's every statement and making a ruckus. It seemed impossible to Rachel that she and Leah had ever been friends, let alone inseparable. Yet without Leah, Rachel knew she would have lost her sanity. Not only had they been best friends at Blue Spruce and co-conspirators in the plot to get Esther and Sam to the altar, but it was Leah who'd insisted the two girls make their relationship even closer. Stepsisters wasn't good enough; Leah demanded they be blood sisters and had them sneak into the Bride's Room, where they pricked their fingers with the pin from Esther's corsage and swore "fealty forever." After the adoption, Leah took to calling Rachel "sister," "because that's what we are now, *real* sisters." And when Shoshanna was born, it was Leah who focused on solidifying the three sisters' relationship. "Now that my father is your father, we're *full* sisters, but Shoshie's only our half sister. It doesn't seem fair, does it?"

"Uh-uh," agreed Rachel, though Leah's logic was a bit beyond her.

"So since two halves make a whole, whenever we're together we constitute Shoshie's FULL sister! But," she added, hugging Rachel, "we need each other for the calculus to work." (Even at twelve, Leah had a way with words.) She decided another blood-sister ceremony was in order. She sterilized one of Esther's sewing needles, drew blood from her finger and Rachel's, then pricked the baby's pinky. To the tune of Shoshanna's wailing, she rubbed their three fingers together until the blood co-mingled. "Now everything's copacetic!"

Then, suddenly, she was gone. Rachel remembered the Friday when Sam came home without her. That weekend was unbearably boring and drab. Even Shoshanna seemed to sense something was wrong; she cried most of the night. When Rachel badgered him for an explanation, Sam said Dena had taken Leah away and there was nothing he could do about it.

"You mean we'll never see her again?"

"Never."

"Not even on Passover or Hanukkah or Yom Kippur?"

"Not ever," said Sam, his face clenched so tight his widow's peak dipped down almost to his nose. He refused to discuss Leah and forbade Rachel to even speak her name, said it would hurt him too much to hear it. Rachel had sulked at first, but after a few months, the wonder of having Shoshie all to herself, of being the baby's full sister without Leah's calculus, eclipsed her sadness. After a year or so, she even stopped missing Leah. No one ever told her what had happened to banish her sister and best friend from the family, but as long as it wasn't her fault—she hadn't caused it, didn't ask for it, couldn't fix it—she decided not to feel guilty about supplanting Leah in a life she couldn't have had anyway. Before they moved to Manhattan, Esther quizzed Rachel on the made-up family history, the new marriage date, and the make-believe anecdotes that she was instructed to casually drop into conversations in order to establish in a natural way that Sam was her father—always had been. She parroted the lies with ease. Why not? They'd been lifted straight from her prayers.

Fifteen years later, when Leah showed up at the Wassermans' apartment and wooed Shoshanna away, Rachel, who had moved well past guilt or remorse, felt only resentment. Even now, she remembered the precise pain—an aching, desolating emptiness—she felt when Shoshanna began making excuses and canceling her weekly visits to Long Island. In a way, that was the second time Rachel lost her little sister. Not at a crowded country flea market but in a stealth attack by a newly minted Ph.D. whose life was far more exciting than Rachel's six-bedroom baby farm in the suburbs where the only diversions were some funny clocks and a stroll down looking-glass lane.

Standing before the cloisonné mirror, awaiting word from Daniel, she remembered how the young Shoshie used to peer into every eye-level frame before choosing one that pleased her well enough to station herself before it, humming and preening while Rachel brushed her hair. When, finally, the bloom was off Leah's rose, Shoshie had re-entered Rachel's life ready to resume their relationship as if it had never been interrupted. But, the other night, with her sister missing again, Rachel recalled all too easily what life without Shoshie felt like. She would not survive if she lost her little sister for good. After Gideon, she'd willed herself to stay alive; for her children's sake, she'd given God a second chance. If Shoshanna died, God would die with her.

At ten past nine that nerve-racking night last week, the phone rang, a shriek that made it seem radioactive. Rachel stayed in her chair, unwilling to hear a policeman's voice stuttering "serious accident involving your sister." The answering machine clicked on:

> "Your call's important, thanks a heap;
> But I have promises to keep,
> And miles to go before I sleep;
> So leave your message at the beep."

That greeting would have to go. She leapt for the receiver.
"Hello! I'm here. Hello!"
"Hi, Rache, it's me."

"Oh God, Shoshie!"

"I'm okay, don't worry! I'm okay. Sorry if Daniel got you worried. But you'll never believe what happened! My Filofax blew all over the road."

It was after midnight when Rachel finished Rex's pillow. The hearth was a carpet of glowing coals. "Ready for bed, hon?" she asked, looking up.

Jeremy's chair was empty. So totally had she zoned out on her losses that she hadn't even noticed him leave the room. She had a headache. The chills. Felt drained and depressed. What she wanted more than anything else right now was to crawl into Jeremy's arms and be held. Would he do that for her without expecting a fuck? She turned out the lights and climbed the stairs.

"Are you asleep?" she called softly into the darkness of their bedroom.

Nothing. She would get undressed, slip under the covers beside him, and snuggle. That would help a lot, even if he was dead to the world. She felt her way to the small lamp on her dressing table. In its peachy glow she could see the bed, its coverlet undisturbed. He must be in the bathroom, then—but the door to the john was open and the lights were off. She backtracked into the upstairs hall, calling his name as she hurried past each of the rooms that had once contained her children's lives, their music, their wet towels, their laughter. All was dark and still. Maybe he'd had a heart attack. Maybe he'd gotten up from his chair, staggered around, and never made it past the first floor. Now she was running, down the stairs, through the living room, into the library, dining room, kitchen, family room, his den, her studio, flipping light switches, checking behind couches, under the tables, half expecting to find him sprawled out and gasping for air. But the house was empty. She doubled back to the kitchen and pushed at the door leading to the garage. Her Lexus was there. His Mercedes was gone.

five

BLACK WAS LEAH'S COLOR, her only color. The day she turned up on the Wassermans' doorstep in 1964, everything on her body was black—leather jacket, T-shirt, jeans, high-top sneakers, even the duffel bag, huge as a hassock, slung across her back, and the shoelace that secured her waist-length braid.

"Hi, Esther. Remember me?" A crooked grin crackled through her face.

Remember her!? Esther had thought of her almost daily, hounded by a collaborator's guilt. She'd never forgiven herself for standing by while Sam forsook his daughter and adopted hers, for protesting too little, for letting well enough alone when it wasn't well enough at all and she knew it. "How could I forget you, darling! Come *in*, sweetheart! Come in! Come in!" Her first impulse had been to embrace Leah, but fearing rejection, she'd stuck out her hand and pulled the visitor inside.

Shoshanna rushed down the hall, attracted by her mother's exclamations, and studied the stranger, a tall young woman, wearing a smoother, softer version of her father's face. Widow's peak, earth-toned eyes, thick hair. Its texture was woolly like Shoshanna's, though Shoshie's hair was Esther's color, the deep red of an Irish setter (Sam called it Jewish setter) while this woman's hair was Doberman brown, like Sam's. *"Omigod!"* she bellowed. "You're Leah!!!" Who else could it be?

"Yeah, the prodigal daughter returns. Long-lost but not forgotten, I hope."

"I don't believe it! Mom! She looks *exactly* like Daddy!"

"And like *you*," said Esther. "But so . . . so grown-up."

Leah dropped her duffel to the floor. "Bad form to barge in like this, I know, but Dena flipped out completely last night. Tried to kill herself. Third time."

"What happened!?" Esther and Shoshanna asked in unison.

"She took a flying leap into the Boston Harbor. Made for one hell of a tea party, let me tell you—scuba divers, helicopters, TV cameras, rubberneckers. They fished her out and took her to the emergency room. One of these days, the meshuggener's going to get it right and it'll be my fault for not stopping her. Unless she kills *me*, first."

"Pooh, pooh, pooh," said Esther. "God forbid."

"What about *you*?" asked Shoshanna.

"Me?"

"Last night."

"Once she was safely strapped to a hospital bed, I packed the basics"—she pointed to the duffel bag—"bid adieu to the scene of my tragic youth, and hopped the first train to New York. Trouble is, I don't know a soul here and I'm flat broke; life with Dena was a study in incessant insolvency." She faced Esther. "I need your husband to loan me enough for a room at the Y, just till I find a job and a place of my own."

"What's with the 'your husband' business? He's your dad. He'll be thrilled to see you."

"Oh, sure." Leah shook her head. "Believe me, if I had anywhere else to go, I wouldn't be here." She touched an index finger to the tip of Shoshanna's nose. "Not that he doesn't owe me, your father; he owes me big."

"*Our* father," corrected Shoshanna.

Leah replied with a snort.

Esther led her to the kitchen and pulled out a chair, all the while clucking like a chicken. "Don't worry, darling. Everything'll be okay. Sit. Sit. You'll relax. You'll rest yourself. Take off a load. Make yourself comfy. We'll have tea. We'll talk."

Shoshanna had known about Leah for three years, since Sam drew the "circle" in the sand. But seeing her, touching her—actually having her in the apartment drinking tea with lemon and honey the way Sam took it, and twirling the tassel of her braid the way Sam worried the fringes of his beard—was a kind of enchantment. Zorro had landed in Marjorie Morningstar's kitchen, a vision in black, silver rings on all ten fingers (including the thumb), a woman unlike any Shoshanna had ever seen. Her sister.

"You'll stay for supper, angel." Esther mewed, even as she plied Leah with tea, stewed fruit, golden bricks of mandelbroit.

"If *you're* cooking, Esther—absolutely."

Leah *likes* my mother! Shoshanna realized in disbelief. How can that be? Poor thing was totally eclipsed soon after Esther entered Sam's life, bringing one daughter with her and giving birth to another, yet here Leah was fourteen years later smiling at the evil stepmother and the stepsister who'd displaced her, and signing on for dinner. It made no sense.

Later that day, Shoshanna, unable to intercept her violin teacher in time to cancel her lesson, found herself in the living room sawing away at a Mozart sonata when Sam came home from shul. By repositioning the instrument and craning her neck, she could see through the French doors to the vestibule, where, to the accompaniment of her grating, cup-rattling bow strokes, the reunion between her father and his all-but-forgotten daughter unfolded like a silent movie. He hung his coat in the hall closet, then froze in his own footsteps as Leah came into view with Esther close behind. The stunned patriarch and the woman in black scrutinized each other, neither of them moving a muscle, until simultaneously, as if a switch had been thrown, he began stroking his beard and she twirling her braid hard enough to drill a hole in her skull. Sam opened his arms. Leah backed away. With a few muddy-sounding words, Esther shepherded them to the threshold of Sam's study, where, to Shoshanna's dismay, the melodrama ended enigmatically behind a closed door.

No one told Shoshanna what had transpired that day; she'd had to figure it out for herself, as children often do, deducing from boundaries drawn and measured words how a mess gets papered over and order is restored. Like so much else that matters, the truth about her father and his other daughter was shrouded in secrecy. She was used to that by now and wasn't sure she cared. The important thing was, she had a new sister! Zorro moved in that afternoon. Shoshanna helped her unload the contents of her duffel bag into Rachel's old drawers (even her socks and underwear were black), and squeeze her books—all with intimidating titles—onto Rachel's shelves.

At dinner that night, the family seemed pleasantly symmetrical with four around the table, more like the families she saw on TV, except that Leah never once addressed her father directly but spoke only to Esther or Shoshanna, who, flattered by the attention, responded garrulously with details about her schoolwork, favorite books, movies, hobbies, friends—and how much she despised taking violin. When Sam tried to join the conversation, which was often, Shoshanna, following her big sister's lead, let his comments float about the room unacknowledged, like a foul odor in an elevator. The tension in the room was as thick as the mashed potatoes on their plates as Esther announced in her cheeriest voice, "Leah will be staying with us for a while, till she finds her own place. I've made up one of the beds in Rachel's room."

"Fine," said Sam. "That's fine."

Apologetically, as if she'd just remembered Rachel's room was originally supposed to be Leah's, too, Esther added, "Rachel got married eight years ago and moved to Long Island, but we still call it her room. Funny how people put a label on a room that stays stuck long after its original inhabitant is gone." When they finished eating, Esther scraped and stacked the dirty dishes, plopped the empty breadbasket on top, and, balancing the pile under her chin, backed through the swinging door to the kitchen while Sam retreated, empty-handed, in the other direction, to his study.

"Your father's a man who brings joy when he leaves a room," Leah commented, watching him go. "Your mother deserves better."

Less than a month after Leah arrived, she had parlayed her Ph.D. in English Lit. and two years experience as a TA at Radcliffe into a visiting professorship at Barnard, though her real work, she told Shoshanna, was "fomenting revolution." To that end, she immediately hooked up with a few like-minded rabble-rousers and started a consciousness-raising group that explored the impact of male supremacy on their lives, formulated feminist theory, and organized future actions. They called themselves Wednesday's Women, a name derived from the nursery rhyme, but only after the members had debated which line was more relevant to their struggle—"Wednesday's child is full of woe" or "Thursday's child has far to go." Woe won. WW met weekly (on Wednesday nights, obviously) in Leah's—formerly Rachel's—room.

Leah also founded a magazine, *The Feminist Freethinker: A Journal for Pro-Women Progressives (and Tentative Fellow Travelers)*. The parenthetical phrase tickled her immensely, but when she said it aloud, anyone could sense the disdain Leah felt for all things timid, for shilly-shallying, for the cautious, hesitant, or uncommitted. To avoid being lumped in that pathetic category, Shoshanna resolved to apprentice herself to her new sister—to watch closely, listen hard, read a lot, and become a bona fide intellectual with opinions as bold as Leah's and the vocabulary with which to express them.

There was a confidence in Leah that dazzled, a fearless certainty to her convictions, a willingness to issue sweeping, declaratory statements without so much as an introductory "I think." In the mid-sixties, the force that would soon become known as the Women's Liberation Movement could boast but a few hundred adherents across the country, yet Leah had already declared it "more transformational than the Industrial Revolution." She called Mary Wollstonecraft "the Tom Paine of womankind," and said Martin Luther King, Jr., couldn't exist had Harriet Tubman not been his "precursor." She declared Margaret Sanger's contributions to the twentieth century "seismic," Emma Goldman "more radical than Chairman Mao," Simone de Beauvoir an "ovular"—not seminal—thinker, and Colette "the apotheotic sexual libertine." Having never heard of these women, or half the words her sister used to describe them, Shoshanna, realizing how much she had to learn, took every opportunity to observe her idol. She eavesdropped on Leah's phone calls, discussions with friends that went on into the night. She looked up words like "phallocentric" and "gynocracy," and tried to use them in conversation. She memorized the lyrics to "Union Maid," "Which Side Are You On?," "Brother, Can You Spare a Dime?," and a dozen other protest anthems of the Left. She plowed through the "slush pile," unsolicited manuscripts submitted to *The Feminist Freethinker*, most of them essays on male privilege or class struggle or profiles of obscure women vying for a place in the magazine's "Forgotten Heroines" department. She learned line-editing symbols—squiggles that stood for delete, insert, capitalize, transpose, new paragraph—and after volunteering to cut and shape a sprawling memoir by an incest survivor (an effort her sister pronounced "creditable"), Shoshanna began editing manuscripts on a regular basis, most of which Leah published with relatively few additional revisions.

Afternoons, the sisters stretched out together on the window seat facing the George Washington Bridge and watched the boats chug up the Hudson, or Leah graded papers while Shoshanna did her homework with an occasional assist from her personal professor. Whenever Leah appeared to be upset, Shoshanna spent her allowance on the junk food her sister loved (and Esther refused to permit in the house). No one else had a grown-up best friend whose idea of a balanced diet was an Oreo in each hand. No one else had a sister who talked like a thesaurus. Shoshanna had never been happier.

As for Leah, while scrupulously avoiding all interaction with Sam, she behaved as if she'd always lived there, leaving her apple cores on the coffee table and her Birkenstocks wherever they'd been kicked off. She clipped her toenails on the living-room couch and let the cuttings fall between the cushions. She chain-smoked Gauloises (which stank up the house something fierce), dropping more ashes on her chest than in the ashtray. Her sloppiness was something of a shock in a family that, to a person, was compulsively tidy. Sam arranged his books alphabetically by author. Esther, who always washed utensils as she used them instead of leaving them in the sink until later, was a confirmed list maker. Rachel, when she lived at home, had been neat as a nurse; stored her sweaters in zippered plastic bags and labeled the coat hooks with everyone's name, a carryover, no doubt, from her boarding-school childhood. Shoshanna, trained by both parents to clean up after herself, and a neatnik by nature, couldn't fall asleep unless her curtains were drawn straight across the window and her bureau drawers shut. What was more surprising than Leah's sloth was Sam's pandering to it, his willingness to pick up after her, his uncharacteristic silence in the face of her rudeness. Fourteen years of guilt, Shoshanna decided; that was why he was coddling her. He was trying to win her forgiveness.

Sam's tolerant attitude had astonished Esther as well. Though she'd never been able to extract more than the sketchiest background details from him, she remembered the day of his showdown with Dena, the Friday when Leah stopped coming and the dour Sam began to take root. Until then, Esther had known her husband as an openhearted teddy bear of a man whose childhood seemed to explain everything about him, his temperament, his quirks, his life choices. Sam's father, Mendel Wasserman, had been a rabbi in Atlanta, venerated for his learning and beloved for his communal kindnesses, the sort of clergyman who, long before the civil rights movement, had reached out to black ministers to create joint social-justic projects and interracial dialogue; who founded a feeding program for the poor years before Johnson's War on Poverty; who established a day-care center in the basement of his synagogue before anyone heard the phrase "child care" or "single parent." Mendel took the role of Haman in the Purim spiel every year so no one else would have to play the bad guy. He dedicated the first night of Hanukkah to communal tzedakah, making sure that instead of receiving gifts and gelt, the children of his congregation donated money to good causes, did chores for the housebound, or brought presents to the needy. By example, he taught his four sons the mitzvah of giving and the definition of unconditional love (though Sam was certain he was Mendel's favorite, never having heard his father introduce him without the preamble "my wonderful son"). During services one Shabbat, after a week of torrential rains, the roof of the sanctuary collapsed onto the bimah, burying the pulpit in a crash of rubble and killing the rabbi instantly. His family watched it happen from their pew, watched him disappear under a concrete avalanche while others standing only yards away, including the bar mitzvah boy and his parents, escaped with a coating of plaster dust on their clothes. It was as if God's fist had punched a hole in the ceiling just to carry Mendel Wasserman up to heaven.

One of his sons grew up to be a doctor, two went into business, but Sam became a rabbi like his father, and seemed hell-bent on fathering the world to make up for its loss. He also became a father like his father—affectionate, gregarious, involved; a man who reads bedtime stories and builds forts out of sofa cushions. At Blue Spruce, Sam was the visiting daddy every fatherless girl wanted as her own. When he married Esther, he wrapped Rachel in his bear hug and slaked her lifelong thirst for fathering. But even after he adopted her, and after the birth of Shoshanna, it was obvious that Leah was his "zeesaleh maideleh," his most special sweet little girl. Every Sunday of the weekends she spent with them in Brooklyn, he would announce, "Okey-dokey, it's S and L Time!" and whisk her away for a cherry Coke or a carnival ride before driving her back up to school. "Most people think S and L stands for Savings and Loan," he'd explain with a twinkle. "But it really stands for Sam and Leah. And the love I've been *saving* for her all week while she's been on *loan* to Blue Spruce." Back then, Rachel wasn't jealous of S and L Time, or of Leah; there was enough of Sam to go around.

But after Leah dropped out of his life, he became a different man, a different father. Something in him shriveled, a quality Esther could never quite name except to say that it was the part she first fell in love with. "It's age," he'd snap when she asked what was wrong. "People get older, they change." Sam's transformation was a kind of emotional shrinkage, a slow fade too subtle to register on outsiders, but Esther was close enough to watch it happen, helplessly, the way Mendel's family watched him vanish beneath the roof rubble. After fourteen years, she could barely remember what he'd been like before—until she'd glimpsed in his bemused tolerance of Leah's messy ways a glimmer of his former self.

His visiting daughter, who appeared oblivious to her slovenliness, had actually been giving it considerable thought. This became clear to Shoshanna after she read the opening paragraph of "Mess as Metaphor," an essay by Leah Wasserman:

> Western culture has demonized dirt and disarray in order to pre-occupy women with domestic work. By extolling order and associating a woman's worth with clean counters and shiny floors, society coerces her into the thankless task of status quo maintenance, the endless dusting, washing, waxing, sweeping, and neatening that make up millions of women's lives. Housework is an unwinnable battle against quotidian disorder. It's time to liberate the House Wife! Too many women are married to their houses! Too many have spotless kitchens and empty lives! We have to tell them the truth: The messier your life, the richer. The existence of mess is proof that the woman who lives in that house has more important things to do. To mess is human; to ignore mess divine. All together now, repeat after me: *Fuck housework!*

For all she cared about the look of things—a room, a home, a person—Leah could as likely have written *Fuck appearances!* Her appreciation of painting and sculpture spilled over not at all to other aesthetic arenas. She loathed fashion, artifice, and personal embellishment.

"*What* are you doing?" she demanded one morning after limping into the bathroom and finding Shoshanna at the sink with a foot in the basin.

"Shaving my legs. God, Leah—I wish I wasn't so hairy."

"*Weren't.*"

"Wish I weren't."

"That's a stupid wish," said Leah. "A wasted wish." (Sam had taught her about wasted wishes.) "Don't grow a wishbone where your backbone should be, kiddo."

"I'm so *hairy*!" Shoshanna whined.

"You're not hairy, you have body hair. It's normal. Healthy. It's human. The social contract demands of us rudimentary cleanliness, not depilation. Your hair's red, mine's dark, but look at me: I never started shaving when other girls did, and now, at the ripe old age of twenty-seven, all my leg hairs have rubbed off." Leah's personal hygiene rituals were, to put it bluntly, minimal. Clean was doable, neat too much to ask. She showered every morning and washed her hair once a week, and that was *it*. Her shelf in the medicine chest boasted no razors, tweezers, hair sprays, eyelash curlers, lipsticks, makeup, skin creams, or perfumes. Only Chap Stick and Vaseline. She didn't even own a box of tampons, preferring to use the sponge.

"Couldn't be easier," she'd said, noting Shoshanna's shocked expression. "Just wash and wear, two on the heavy days."

"Yuck."

"Why yuck? You think I'd let Tampax profit from my blood? The sponge was good enough for Cleopatra; it's good enough for me."

Altering natural human attributes or excretions was "anathema" to Leah. She considered women who shaved or plucked or, worse yet, used feminine deodorant spray to be pawns of the beauty industry and captives of America's "looksist" culture. "Self-acceptance is the rock upon which we must stand before we can do anything else in life," she would proclaim, in her Feminism 101 lectures. "Or as Oscar Wilde put it, 'To love oneself is the beginning of a lifelong romance.' It may be the only love that lasts."

Her heaviest artillery was reserved for the "fashion fascists," as Shoshanna was to discover while getting dressed one day. Leah grabbed the sweater out of her hands and held it up to the window (and to ridicule). "Why turquoise?" she asked.

"Why not turquoise? It's this year's color."

"Who says?"

"*Seventeen.* The current issue."

"Does *Seventeen* know you personally? Do their editors know whether you like turquoise, or can afford another sweater, or *need* another sweater? Are they sure turquoise suits you?"

"Mom says it's very becoming." Shoshanna was feeling fidgety. She began biting her nails.

"Becoming what?" Leah stormed the closet and ran her fingers down the orderly squadron of hangers. "While we're at it, would you kindly tell me why a fourteen-year-old needs twelve blouses, six pairs of trousers, and eight skirts?" She yanked a turquoise tweed off a skirt hanger and scrunched it against the sweater. "I suppose you plan to wear these together."

"They *go* together, Leah. It's called an outfit."

"Would the fashion police arrest you if you wore a black skirt with a turquoise sweater? Would you'd be the laughingstock of the ninth grade?"

"No." Shoshanna chewed a cuticle. "But it's not as fashionable."

Leah tossed the outfit on the bed and turned on her heel, disgusted. "I leave you with Wilde's words: 'What's unfashionable is what *other* people wear.'" She was gone in a whir of black, which was just as well, or she might have noticed in Shoshanna's open drawer the turquoise knee socks.

Whatever happened, whatever anyone did or said about any subject, Leah could trot out an apropos quote, an elegant theory, or an essay she happened to have read or written on that very subject. Leah didn't just hold an opinion, she briefed it, preached it, proved it like a theorem. At first, her views scared Shoshanna, spiced as they were with unladylike obscenities, and undermining as they did the laws of feminine propriety, which the girl was just beginning to get a handle on. But after prolonged exposure to Leah, conventional thinking began to sound crazy and radicalism sounded like pure reason. Shoshanna was so intrigued by her sister's take on the world that she started asking Leah questions just to get a fuller rendition of it.

"How come you buy all your clothes from thrift shops?"

"Thoreau's injunction: 'Beware of all enterprises that require new clothes.' Beyond that, it's pretty simple: My penchant for the preowned is motivated by poverty. My fashion sense is based on what doesn't itch."

"Why do you always wear black?"

"Camouflage! Masks a multitude of sins. Doesn't distract the eye from what the ear must hear. And remember, dahling"—her voice took on a faux-haughty tone—"a monochromatic palette owes nothing to the gods of color coordination."

Shoshanna detected a residual reference to the turquoise outfit. "I never realized clothes had so much meaning."

"Everything has meaning, clothes especially. They're normative codes, class clues, signifiers that both dictate and reflect what a given society considers the proper attributes of masculinity and femininity." (Though she missed some of that, Shoshanna got the drift: it was good for clothes to be black and gender neutral.) "Had you been paying attention instead of slavishly following *Seventeen*'s dictates, you would have noticed the pernicious double standard. Women are expected to suffer for fashion; men aren't. Show me a guy who'd put up with underwire bras and three-inch heels and I'll show you a transvestite. By the time a girl is ten or twelve, she's supposed to have figured how much skin she can show without crossing the line from sexy to slutty. She's supposed to know the precise moment when today's most desirable styles become yesterday's look. Men needn't trouble their minds with such matters. Men wear uniforms—I don't mean doormen and cops, I mean men in general, and once they've sorted themselves out socio-economically, a dress code comes with the territory whether it's blue collar or white, overalls or three-piece suits. A man puts on his uniform, spends five seconds choosing his shoes or necktie, and zooms out the door without fear that his clothes might inadvertently suggest he's an easy lay or a puritanical prig."

Shoshanna's white blouse seemed suddenly fraught with symbolism. It made her feel contentious. "But we're the ones who decide what we wear, so . . ."

"Nareshkeit! Don't spout nonsense, girl. Think! Think!! Did *you* decide whether this year's trousers were to be straight or belled, waist-high or hip-huggers? Did *I* decide this was the season for fuck-me shoes that make walking hazardous and escape impossible? Did Esther declare this the year of turquoise? Did the checkout girl at the supermarket dictate how far a woman can hike up her skirt or drop her neckline and still look respectable, or when last winter's coat became passé? For God's sake, Shoshe, some people don't even own a coat, yet the fashion fascists expect a girl like you to get a different one for school, sport, rain, snow, and evening wear, yet. More coats than anyone needs in a lifetime."

"Men buy more than they need, too."

"You're being obtuse! Conspicuous consumption is practiced by both sexes—that's obvious. What I'm describing are the gender dynamics that operate *within* a consumerist culture. Take advertising. Ads directed to men promise power and virility. The subliminal message to women is: Buy our product or you'll be hopelessly homely and unlovable. Or look at the ludicrous rules we're expected to take seriously: Don't wear white before Memorial Day or after Labor Day. That's rag business propaganda to get us to buy what they call 'seasonal wardrobes.' Translation: Buy more clothes. Subtext: Honey, if you're still wearing white pumps on September 8, you're a loser and no man will want you. *Quelle* crap!"

Shoshanna didn't know the meaning of obtuse, but she hoped it didn't mean boring. What she feared most was being uninteresting to her sister. To juice up their "discourse" (Leah's word) she decided the best way to keep Leah's attention was by challenging her: "I sometimes think women dress for each other more than for men."

Leah studied her. "I sometimes think you enjoy taking men's side of every argument."

"Are you saying women aren't competitive?"

"Certainly not, but what most women compete for is male approval, because girls get points in this culture according to which boys choose us. And once we're competing with each other *for* men, we're distracted from competing *with* men for money and power."

Shoshanna raised an eyebrow. "Don't be shocked," said Leah. "Money and power make the world go round. If you can't see that, you're living in a dream."

Though her sister's idea of "discourse" could be unbearably didactic, Shoshanna kept asking questions, realizing that Leah relished what she called "teachable moments," especially the opportunity to "decode the patriarchy," and the more she answered, the more invested she became in her young protégée. "As long as we're living under the same roof, I may as well make a mensch out of you," she said after one of her tutorials. "Someone's got to raise your callow consciousness until we find you a good CR group."

"CR?"

"Consciousness-raising. It's what you and I have been doing for the last few weeks, except I've been kind of monopolizing the conversation. In a CR group each member gets equal time to talk. Usually they take up one topic per meeting and they go around the room until everyone has addressed the subject from her own perspective. It's mind-blowing how often you recognize yourself in other women's stories and how many feelings and experiences come tumbling out of other women's mouths that you thought were unique to you. Feminism begins with CR because it gets to the heart of female commonalities. It makes you feel you're not alone. It creates solidarity. Women learn more from one another than from books."

"How? I mean, exactly how?"

"Well, we usually start off with a simple question. This week it was 'Have you ever faked an orgasm?'"

(Shoshanna blushed; she couldn't help herself.)

"Nothing to be embarrassed about, kiddo. Sex is a feminist issue. Another time, the start-off question was 'If women ran the world, what would be different?' That took us into militarism, environmental destruction, public policy, the whole geshrei. A few weeks ago, motherhood was up for grabs. We asked each other, 'Would you want your mother's life?'"

"That's interesting," murmured Shoshanna. The question had never occurred to her. Her mother's life seemed so . . . so . . . *what*? She couldn't say.

Shoshanna knew she'd passed some kind of test when Leah invited her to one of Wednesday's Women's meetings. In gratitude, she dressed in black jeans and a black bowling shirt she'd found at Goodwill. Sitting there among Leah's circle of friends, with a stick of incense burning at the center "for focus" and her sister at her side, Shoshanna felt, for the first time in her life, like half of a pair. The feeling deepened as the weeks passed and she spent more time in her sister's world. To pair up with Leah meant working on *The Freethinker*, attending three or four meetings a week, traipsing to women's conferences on weekends, seeing movies with subtitles, and frequenting museums and libraries most New Yorkers never knew existed. One night, Leah even took her to a lesbian bar.

"You're too young to drink but old enough to pay attention," Leah told her, and ordered her a ginger ale. "I've heard you and your little friends laughing at lesbians. Tonight we're going to put an end to it. You're going to get to know these women and think of them every time you're tempted to ridicule a lesbian. I want you to understand their struggle. They feel safe here, but if their sexuality were known outside this bar, most of them would lose their jobs, and in some cases their friends and families. Heteros are afraid of them, so they penalize them. Congress just passed this new Civil Rights Act that protects against discrimination on the grounds of race, creed, or sex, but it leaves out sexual preference. A lesbian's only crime is loving other women or, more accurately, *not* loving men. Why should she have to hide the truth about herself before she can get work?"

"That sounds right," said Shoshanna. A tiny paper umbrella stuck out of the pineapple slice wedged on the rim of her ginger ale glass. She twirled it while Leah twirled her braid.

"I brought you here because I want you to know they aren't freaks. They're women like us and their issues are our issues. By the way, if someone comes on to you, just tell her you're Leah Wasserman's sister, you're underage, and you're straight. Unless you're not."

"Of course I'm straight."

"Don't say 'of course.' It's not the worst thing in the world to be a lesbian."

"Are you one, Leah?" Shoshanna thought this might be her sister's way of letting her know.

"Nah! Tried it once, but missed the point, as it were." (Tickled by her double entendre, she smiled.) "I come to places like this to organize women for the movement. We have to make common cause. Lesbians are the canary sent into a mine. The shit they take from the straight world is a harbinger of the shit in store for every woman if she's not a good girl."

Shoshanna nursed her drink and surveyed the scene. There were women in leather and women in lace; big, strapping women who called themselves "dykes" and petite Audrey Hepburn look-alikes; one woman was drinking beer straight from a bottle, another was smoking through a slim cigarette holder. From all corners of the room came full-throated laughter, not demure sorority-house giggles. She saw couples holding hands, necking on banquettes, and slow-dancing to Barbra Streisand's "People." When a good portion of the crowd piled onto the floor for line-dancing, a frizzy-haired, large-breasted woman who appeared to be Esther's age pulled Shoshanna off her barstool and into the line and taught her the Madison and the Hully Gully. She grooved to the music, perfecting the routines and shimmying in unison with her mentors, until Leah told her it was time to go.

"They were really nice!" said Shoshanna on the way home.

"Don't sound so surprised."

More than their adventures around the city, Shoshanna enjoyed hanging out with her sister, who seemed most like a sister when they did girlish things together at home: wrote in their journals (she'd bought a black leatherbound ledger just like Leah's). Played records (she'd packed away her Beatles albums and bought Leah's favorites—Guthrie, Seeger, Dylan, Peter, Paul and Mary, Joan Baez). Cooked up batches of My-T-Fine butterscotch pudding and ate it warm, straight from the pot. Cracked open a box of Whitman's Sampler chocolates—she found her favorite vanilla creams according to the chart inside the lid—and flaked out on the rug for one of Leah's "rap sessions," her name for the talkfests whose ground rules she'd recited to Shoshanna the week she moved in: "Nothing human is alien to us; therefore, no subject is off-limits. We can talk about anything but tell it to no one else. Everything we say is privileged. We can ask each other anything and not answer if we don't want to. But if we answer, it has to be the absolute unvarnished truth. You game?"

"Indubitably," said Shoshanna. (One of her new words.) She had questions she'd been dying to ask Leah since she'd arrived—about their father's first marriage, Leah's life with Dena, what Rachel was like as a kid. Most of all—since she'd been witnessing Sam's awkward bids for Leah's attention, Leah's evasive maneuvers, and Esther's bend-over-backward kindnesses—Shoshanna wanted to know what had happened between Leah and Sam. The rap session's ground rules gave her permission to ask, and one night, armed with two packages of black licorice, she did.

"Ahhh, Sam's first marriage!" Leah, wearing men's pajamas, sat cross-legged on the blue rug with a bed pillow behind her back and a bag of licorice open on her lap. "Dena used to call it the last battle of World War II." (Referring to one's parents by their first names struck Shoshanna as the ultimate in sophistication.) "I was four in 1941, when the U.S. entered the war. They weren't drafting men with young children, the salient point being that Sam went in as a volunteer. He was an Air Force chaplain in the European theater." (Shoshanna flashed on a sepia photograph of her father, Bible in hand, young, clean-shaven, handsome in his dress uniform.) "I think he joined up to escape my mother. The woman's a harridan. Voice of a garbage disposal. Patent-leather hair slicked back in a bun. Eyes black as pits. Stomps around the house in wooden clogs like Heidi on speed. And volatile? That's like calling

Goebbels grouchy. Even as a child I understood why he'd want to get away from Dena. What I couldn't understand was why he'd want to leave me." (Left you twice, thought Shoshanna; first for the war, then for Rachel and me. She'd look up "harridan" later if she could figure out how to spell it.)

Leah sighed, bit into a string of black licorice that matched her monochromatic palette, and pulled it through her teeth. The gummy strand made a squeegee noise as she chewed. "When the war was over, their hostility picked up where it had left off, but for some reason, they stayed together through '46, the year of living dangerously. I'll never forget the Seder when Dena got drunk and knocked over Elijah's Cup, and Manischewitz Concord grape spread like a bloodstain on a white sheet all over my grandmother's best white tablecloth. At the end of the evening, while the rest of us were singing "Had Gadya," my mother, unredemptively sloshed, was belting out 'This Little Piggy Went to Market.'"

"You're kidding." (A pig at the Seder table!)

"Hanukkah that year was pretty memorable, too. Usually, after lighting the candles, we'd run through 'Rock of Ages,' 'Mi Yimalel,' the dreidel song—you know the repertoire. But when Sam and I started singing, Dena went to the piano and pounded out a medley of Christmas carols, shouting the lyrics loud enough for the neighbors to hear. I never saw Sam so angry. He flew across the room and slammed down the keyboard lid, damn near amputating her fingers."

Shoshanna cringed. Her father violent? Unthinkable. Leah had to be talking about someone else.

"Their last fight was a doozy. Dena accused Sam of schtupping his secretary, Miss Horowitz. He accused her of sleeping with Mr. Kaplan, the president of the shul. My guess is, both were right."

Shoshanna hugged her knees. Her father unfaithful? Impossible.

Leah peeled off another string of licorice and tied it in a slipknot. "After the divorce, I lived with her for a while in Brooklyn and saw Sam on weekends. Until Dena decided to ship me off to boarding school. Said she wanted to get her shit together, a process that seemed to require Tarot cards, a macrobiotic diet, and my absence." Leah tightened the knot and bit off the loose ends.

Shoshanna loved her for saying "shit." No other adult used rough language in her presence, but Leah could be counted on to curse more than the average person coughed. Her most frequent targets, Shoshanna noticed, were associated with Judaism. Rabbis were "shit-faced poseurs" or "sexist oligarchs." Synagogues were "mother-fucking men's clubs." The Torah—"Piss-assed Patriarchy 101." Prayer books, Leah said, were "riddled with macho male metaphors—God as father, lord, shepherd, king; divinity anthropomorphized into an old white fart in a long white beard. No wonder Sam Wasserman is such an arrogant bastard. Since God is male, it follows that man is God!" Shoshanna didn't need a psychology degree to understand that her sister had conflated father and faith. If Sam could reject Leah, Leah could reject everything Sam stood for. This made some kind of sense to the girl, though she couldn't imagine anyone wanting to renounce Judaism altogether.

"I'd miss the holidays," she'd told Leah during one of their rap sessions. "How can you stand being nothing?"

"I'm not nothing. I'm a chameleon. I change with the situation."

"What's that supposed to mean?"

"Sometimes I'm a Jewish atheist."

"Isn't that an oxymoron?" (Shoshanna was thrilled to be able to use the word.)

"It's a person who knows what the God in whom she does not believe expects of her. A guy named Leibel Fein defined it."

"That's not an actual denomination, is it? Jewish atheism?"

"Not yet." Leah smiled. "It's a non-prophet organization—spelled with a 'ph.'"

Shoshanna could see she was enjoying this. "What else do you change into?"

"Sometimes I'm an Existential Jew."

"Which is?"

"A person who's Jewish because other people say she is. A guy named Jean-Paul Sartre defined it."

"What else?"

Leah tented her hands above her head and mimed a pointy hat. "Sometimes," she cackled, "I'm a Jew-witch."

Her description of life at boarding school was as discomfiting as her religious irreverence. "Blue Spruce wasn't a Dickensian hellhole, just rigid, cold, educationally inadequate, and emotionally stunting. We girls used to live for weekends. Dena missed lots of visiting days, but Sam always showed up to drive me to Brooklyn in time for Erev Shabbos." Leah was coiling her licorice strands into rings as she talked and linking them in a chain. "It used to matter to him—us eating supper together, lighting the candles and saying the blessings, having me in his synagogue, the two of us doing havdalah on Saturday night. After he remarried, he still came up and got me, only then we had Shabbos with Esther and Rachel. And little old you in your high chair." With a faraway gaze and a weak shrug, she added, "That was nice."

So far, Sam's story and Leah's meshed. What she contributed were the tones and textures, especially about Esther—the aroma of Esther's cooking, the floral fragrance that seemed to emanate from her skin, her ineffable (Shoshanna had to look it up) fuss-making warmth, the way she would scurry down the walk to greet them on Friday afternoons, cheeks dancing with dimples, apron dusted with hallah flour, arms outstretched to hug Leah even before she kissed Sam. Leah described the rush of pleasure she felt when, on top of Esther's loving welcome, Rachel would drag her to their room to talk.

"When Rachel left school to live with Sam and Esther, she was twelve and I was ten, but we always had things to say to each other—Blue Spruce gossip, since we both knew the same girls and hated their stupid behavior around the boys, but also books; we both loved to read—*Gone with the Wind, Kidnapped, Kon-Tiki, Giants in the Earth*—and naturally we cried our eyes out over *The Yearling*. We were nuts about Auden and e. e. cummings—we must have composed a hundred lowercase poems. I remember when we went by ourselves to Prospect Park with a picnic basket Esther packed with chopped-liver sandwiches and Sam's one-volume Shakespeare. We acted out *A Midsummer Night's Dream* among the trees. After you were born, of course, we did nothing but play with your ungrateful self. Actually came to blows over who could feed and diaper you. At night, we'd talk in our beds and try like hell to make you laugh, and Esther would open the door every ten minutes and yell, 'Stop the stimulation! Go shluffie now!' She was afraid you'd never fall asleep. But you always did."

Shoshanna grinned. "She still says that now."

"You were so damned cute! What happened?" Leah leaned toward Shoshanna and lowered the licorice chain over her head, like a necklace. "Anyway, all that came to a screeching halt when Dena moved me to South Boston." A scrim of sadness dropped across her face. She chewed on the end of her braid. "I didn't think anything could be worse than Blue Spruce till I saw that claustrophobic dump. Fifth-floor walk-up, two small rooms, cockroaches the size of chihuahuas. The fucking halls stank of cabbage and whiskey. Dena and I were the only tenants who didn't look like Wanted posters."

"Ugghh! How depressing!" Shoshanna reached under the bed, pulled out a box of Ring Dings, and handed one to her sister.

Leah tore open the foil, bit off half the cake, and talked with her mouth full. "When she applied to the New England Conservatory of Music, she bought this Brobdingnagian piano and had it hoisted up by an outside pulley. The thing filled the living room like a whale on legs. We slept in the other room in one bed. Can you believe your father left me sharing the sheets with a maniac!?"

Shoshanna couldn't.

"One day—I'll never forget the irony of it, I was reading *Great Expectations*—she told me I was never going to see Sam again. And I never did, not for fourteen years, until I came to New York a couple of weeks ago and knocked on your door."

Shoshanna tried to imagine fourteen years—nearly her whole life—in that Boston walk-up. "Did you ask her why the visits stopped?"

"She wasn't talking much back then. Or eating or sleeping or paying me much mind, for that matter. The Conservatory rejected her application. She started drinking big-time. Kept calling herself a concert pianist, though the last time she'd performed was in her student days at Juilliard. Still, there was always *someday*. Someday, she was going to audition for the BSO. Someday, a friend was going to book her on *The Ed Sullivan Show*. Someday, she'd do regional music festivals, rent recital space in Carnegie Hall, invite agents and critics to hear her. I would be her page turner. She'd give me private lessons. We'd play duets all over the world.

"Lovely fantasy. I actually fell for it for a while." Leah licked a smear of chocolate icing off her thumb. "She'd practice six, eight, ten hours at a time, weeks on end, all fired up. Then, without warning, she'd go into a tailspin, hit the booze, sleep all day, wake up with night terrors. Once, she tore off her nightgown and ran outside buff naked except for her clogs. Trust me, it wasn't a pretty picture." Shoshanna could only nod. "Her mood oscillations were officially diagnosed as a bipolar disorder—in other words, manic-depression." Leah said she used to imagine two polar bears pulling Dena in opposite directions until they'd ripped her to shreds. No matter how hard Leah willed a different ending, in dreams as in life she was never able to save her mother. Could barely save herself. Dena had endangered them many times. Once, she fell asleep with a lit cigarette in her hand, and by the time Leah awoke, their bed was in flames and the fire department was hacking down the door. "She blamed the electrical wiring and tried to sue the landlord." Leah sighed. "Nothing was ever her fault."

Shoshanna remembered Sam's story: Dena blamed him for everything wrong in her life, made it sound as if he'd forced the divorce on her, though Sam said she wanted it as much as he did. She made him feel guilty for remarrying. Made Leah feel guilty if she enjoyed their visits, as if by having fun she was betraying Dena. When Sam and Esther decided to move to Manhattan, to an apartment with three bedrooms, one for him and Esther, a smaller room for baby Shoshanna, and a big room with twin beds for Rachel and Leah, Dena accused him of trying to use his new baby and his fancy New York apartment to lure Leah away from her. She yanked Leah out of Blue Spruce, carted her up to Boston, and forbade Sam to see her. If he so much as wrote her a letter or tried to call, Dena swore she'd do something terrible to their daughter and it would be his fault. He didn't try. Men never got custody in those years, he'd explained to Shoshanna. He wouldn't make Leah the rope in an ugly tug-of-war. So he gave her up.

How Solomonic—abandoning his child to save her—was what Shoshanna thought when she first heard Sam's account. She never wondered how he could surrender his daughter to a madwoman or why a prominent rabbi couldn't have convinced a judge of his side of the story. And it hadn't crossed her mind to wonder about Leah, where she was, whether she was okay. But now, leaning back against one of those twin beds that was supposed to have been Leah's, Shoshanna asked, "What was it like, those years? With Dena."

Leah grinned. "Setting me on fire wasn't bad enough! You want more?" She balled up the Ring Ding wrapper and rolled it between her hands. "When I was about your age, Dena's doctor put me in charge of her antidepressants. I was supposed to hide the key to the medicine chest, dole out the pills one at a time, and make sure she didn't stockpile any for an overdose."

Shoshanna's eyes widened. Marilyn Monroe took an overdose, not someone's mother.

One oven of an evening, Leah said, she and her mother were sitting at the kitchen table in front of an electric fan. The windows were wide open, but the heat was insufferable. Leah went to the refrigerator for a cold drink and stood there considering her options—an open can of ginger ale, rancid apple juice, a bottle of cheap wine.

"Suddenly Dena grabbed me from behind and pulled my arm into a hammer lock. In seconds, she'd pushed me over to the open window and forced my upper body out and down until I was hanging halfway out of the building backward, head first, five flights up. She was leaning on my chest, pressing my spine against the windowsill. To this day, I swear it, I can feel her sweaty breasts crushing my sweaty breasts. I can smell her breath, see her black eyes—all pit, no pupil. 'Give me the key,' she screamed, 'or you're going splat on that sidewalk. I gave you life; I can kill you.'

"I said okay and gave her the motherfuckin' key, and never turned my back on her again. Didn't give a rat's ass how much dope she swallowed. If she'd wanted to cut her throat, I'd have sharpened the blade—being no stranger to self-mutilation myself . . ." Leah's voice trailed off. She aimed the crumpled Ring Ding wrapper at the wastebasket, made the shot, then brushed the crumbs from her pajamas onto the rug. "I used to stay with her because I feared her. Then I stayed because I pitied her. I mothered my mother. I was her nurse. The last ten years, I was her keeper."

Shoshanna retrieved Leah's crumbs one by one and carefully placed them on her notebook. "Why didn't you ask Daddy for help?"

"Are you *kidding*?"

"If he knew she was that crazy, he'd have rescued you."

"Bullshit! Why would he rescue me? He never tried to fight for me, never contributed a dime to my support. Dena told him, No pay, no play. That's why she wouldn't let him see me. He didn't deserve me, she said. She may have been crazy, but she was right."

"Wait a second! That's not what happened! It wasn't about money. Remember how he took you out to restaurants. And bought you all those special treats. And those beds and bureaus so you'd have your own space when you visited."

"Yeah, like you remember it."

"I heard all this from *you*, Leah, not just Daddy."

"A father shouldn't get rave reviews for one performance a week."

"But you can tell how much he cared by all the trouble he went to every week to get you. He begged Dena to let you come more often. And he only gave up when she said she'd hurt you if he didn't. He let you go because he loved you, Leah."

"Horse-cow-chickenshit! That's a flat-out lie! Don't make him out to be some kind of self-sacrificial lamb. He could have forced my mother into court and won me if he'd wanted me. By 1950, Rabbi Samuel Wasserman was a major macher. A moral exemplar. Marched with the Negroes. Met with the President. *Time* called him the nearest thing to the King of the Jews, for Chrissake. What judge wouldn't take his word over a raving lunatic's? No, he decided to pick up his marbles and move on because he couldn't take the hassle. Why be embarrassed by a loose cannon like Dena or a loose end like Leah when he had a nice new family with no complications?"

"I'm just telling you, it wasn't about money."

"Wake up, kiddo. When people say it's not about money, it's always about money. He wasn't about to blow his wad supporting yet another kid. Two daughters were more than enough. He had you and Rachel."

Shoshanna's eyes stung. Her tongue felt too big for her mouth.

Leah chucked Shoshanna under the chin. "Forget it! I'm fine. I'm a free woman." She rose from the floor and pulled the girl up beside her. "How 'bout we put on some clothes and get some air? I'll treat you to a Creamsicle."

six

SHOSHANNA COULDN'T SLEEP. In a nether place, half doze, half dream, she saw herself back on the Henry Hudson Parkway dodging cars, then floating above them, carried aloft by headlamp beams crisscrossing the night sky like Hollywood spotlights on opening night, and Leah—having dropped from a fifth-floor window—dancing toward her in a long black dress. Chagall with an urban edge.

The mind has a mind of its own, she thought, and smiled in the dark, her belly curved against Daniel's rounded back like two soup bowls. All her sleep-inducing efforts had failed. She'd named the planets, planned a week's worth of menus, reviewed her client's projects. All that remained was to launch into the ultimate soporific—her way of counting sheep—recalling her childhood apartment on West End Avenue in minute detail. First the living room: wall-to-wall rug, beige-and-rose floral on a dark blue ground. Beige sectional couches with rose-and-blue throw pillows. Philco television. Magnavox radio-phonograph. Window seat upholstered in a nubby tweed. Brass sconces. Glass doors flanked by bookshelves. Hebrew holy books mixed in with her parent's secular library, of which she could remember only Karen Horney's *Our Inner Conflicts*, because it reminded her of dinner cornflakes, and *Hiroshima* by John Hersey, because the bomb used to haunt her. Dining room: flowerpots in the south window; geraniums with furry leaves, spiky ferns, a rubber plant; mahogany table and chairs, seats covered in velvety fabric; a teardrop chandelier weeping crystal. The Chippendale curio cabinet crammed with Esther's knickknacks (Leah called them tchotchkes). Shoshanna could see each object clearly; even now—the Indonesian snuffbox; the silver-mounted ostrich egg; a blue-john obelisk; the Shabbat candlesticks that belonged to Esther's grandmother; silver hallah knives; engraved kiddush cups, one the size of a chalice; a Hanukkah menorah; two spice boxes, a silver one from pre-state Palestine and one made of olivewood from Israel. Down the long hallway with its thick Persian runner, past walls checkered with framed family pictures, to the bathroom, where she had no trouble conjuring the sea-green tiles, the matching shower curtain splashed with mermaids, the tub with its nonskid fish decals, and the man-in-the-moon night-light plugged into the socket above the sink.

Ah, the wonder of childhood spaces. The apartment she hadn't seen for three decades had returned to her fully furnished. Would that she could remember her daily schedule so effortlessly. She disengaged from Daniel's limbs and stretched her legs under the covers. Daniel, who was about as organized as a puppy, managed to memorize his calendar organically, as if the whole enterprise were some sort of natural inevitability, an extension of his thoughts. Dates that other people had to write down, he internalized, associating a day and hour with a person or event and arriving where he was meant to be without need of a note. Despite his decidedly casual relationship with time, Daniel's days unfolded smoothly, while Shoshanna's threatened to spin out of control unless programmed to the minute.

T. S. Eliot could have had her in mind when he wrote "I have measured out my life with coffee spoons." Was that why she'd lost control of her datebook—to throw a monkey wrench into her time measurements? To challenge her habit of meting out life in half-hour segments, her dependence on externally imposed order? Maybe she was unable to remember what she was supposed to do next because most of her activities were fundamentally meaningless, while her husband knew his schedule by heart because his commitments were worth remembering. Maybe the discombobulated Filofax would force her to edit her life—not just reconstruct the flyaway pages but rethink them.

On the heels of J. Alfred Prufrock, Sam Wasserman forced himself into her muddled mind and began one of his most memorable sermons.

"What do you think is the most important book in my life?" he'd asked the congregation.

"The Torah!" they'd called out. "The Bible!" "The Tanach." "The Talmud!" "Pirkei Avot!" "The Shulhan Aruch!"

"Enough already! I'll tell you." The sanctuary grew still as the rabbi pulled a small leather folder from his inside breast pocket. "The answer is, my datebook." He held it up high. "In this book I act out what I've learned from *this* book." He raised the Bible in his other hand, forming a V with his arms as if balancing his life between the two volumes. "The Torah teaches us how to spend our time on earth, but our datebooks reveal how well we've absorbed its lesson. A calendar can express our mindfulness of time—its flow, its fleetingness, the meaning of every hour, of holy days, days of work and accomplishment, days of rest. A calendar's purpose is not just to give a name and number to each temporal unit but to help us pay attention and make conscious choices about how we spend the time of our lives. Don't let passivity fill your datebook. Don't let other people fill it. Exercise whatever control a person can have over time. Fill each day with meaning and mindfulness." He'd closed his sermon with a shehechiyanu, the blessing over time.

Turning her pillow to the cool side, Shoshanna punched up a mound of goose down, burrowed in, and concentrated on her breathing. Inhale. Exhale. Empty the mind. Clear the clutter. (She imagined a huge broom sweeping away the sermon and the sea-green bathroom tiles, and everything in the Chippendale curio cabinet.) She murmured her mantra into the pillow: *"Sh'ma Yisrael / Adonai Elohaynu / Adonai Echad."* Jewish haiku. Seventeen syllables in the right order: five, seven, five. Breathe in. Out. In. Out.

Nothing worked. Transcendental meditation was no match for the rock slide of childhood memories. The clutter returned. She resumed her inventory in Rachel's old room. Pink-and-blue plaid curtains at the window, powder-blue carpeting, two beds with pink chenille spreads, and between them a night table. In her memory's video, the table was covered not with Rachel's things but Leah's, the stuff Zorro kept at her bedside when she lived in Rachel's room. Sharpened pencils in an empty peanut-butter jar, Skippy label intact. Beautiful fountain pens in satin-lined cases—a gold-toned Parker and two black Esterbrooks each with a 14-karat-gold point. A rickracked square of bubble-gum-pink cloth splotched like a Rorschach with Waterman's blue ink, Leah's pen wiper. Her blotter, which dried the written word by rolling over it, back and forth like a teeter-totter.

By 1964, everyone in America but Leah had moved on to ballpoints. Though sloppy to a fault, she was obsessed with fountain pens and the accoutrements of fastidious penmanship, and hell-bent on converting her younger sister to habits of "graphological grandeur." One night, Shoshanna was writing a letter to a friend on yellow stationery bordered with kittens when Leah, eating Cocoa Puffs straight from the box, came in without a knock and immediately looked over her shoulder.

"That's rude," said Shoshanna, glancing up.

"I'm not reading your words, I'm reviling your handwriting. It's execrable. I'm retching over those infantile circles with which you dot your *i*'s. I'm barfing over your fucking plastic pen."

"My handwriting is readable, which you've obviously discovered. So what else matters?"

"Refinement matters, you phlegmatic little philistine. Form bespeaks content. Precise penmanship signifies precision of cognition and reason. One's handwriting is a material incarnation of one's thoughts. Ball pens and bad writing are bush league, worthy of nothing but a grocery list. What's important enough to be put to paper is important enough to be written in a fine hand with a fine instrument that has the proper weight, balance, and a gold point. Ball pens are to fountain pens as the ukulele is to the violin." She drew a breath. "You'll never take yourself seriously, Shoshanna, if your script looks like pigeon droppings and your pen is a fucking Paper Mate."

Had Sam not come in at that moment to empty the trash basket, Leah would have gone on for another ten minutes. When the door closed behind him, she asked Shoshanna, "Did you ever wonder why your father is willing to take out the garbage but won't dry a dish?"

"*Our* father." Shoshanna tucked the kittenish notepaper in its matching envelope, licked the flap, then gestured toward the night table and, with Leah's blinked approval, chose one of the Esterbrooks to address her letter. "Wow! What a difference! Bye-bye, ballpoint, I've seen the light." The Paper Mate pen clattered into the empty tin wastebasket.

"As long as I'm being critical," Leah added, "I may as well raise another issue. Did you notice what your father just did?"

"Emptied the wastebasket."

"Factually, yes, but I'm talking analytically."

"Sorry?"

"You should have challenged him for being willing to empty the garbage but not to wash a dish or do anything to help your mother in the kitchen. Extrapolating from this, you should have asked yourself why, in this supposedly enlightened country of ours, so many people are still trapped in sex and race stereotypes. Why are there no male teachers in nursery schools and no female Justices on the Supreme Court? Why are black people janitors and maids but not engineers and interior decorators? Does it make sense that women are considered competent enough to rear children but not to run companies that require far fewer life-and-death decisions? Why are parking-lot attendants paid more than baby nurses? Why should a grown woman need her husband's permission to take out a loan? How come it's okay for boys your age to experiment with sex if girls have to be virgins?"

"Yeah!" said Shoshanna, warming to the subject. "How come?"

Leah disappeared into the next room and came back with a book. "Read and ye shall know."

"*The Second Sex?*"

"A.k.a. Genesis," said Leah. "Beauvoir explains how we got into such a sorry fix in the first place and why."

It took Shoshanna three days to read the 732-page book. She recited sections aloud at the supper table and regaled her mystified girl friends with her epiphanies (new word) on gender discrimination, inequality, the mythology of femininity, Woman as Other. The book's margins disappeared behind her exclamatory eruptions—"How true!" "Me, too!" "Wow!"—one chapter in particular, because it explained her fear of self-assertion, her morbid daydreams, her ardent obsessions, and named them as universal phenomena, not just hers. That passage about how every young girl becomes infatuated with a superior older woman and makes her her idol—she remembered how it had seemed to fit her and Leah to a T. What exactly was that quote? Bone weary but wide awake, Shoshanna abandoned her sleep-inducing exercises, tucked the quilt around Daniel, and tiptoed down the two flights of stairs to her office.

Shafts of moonlight cast phantasmal shadows on the floor—a tatting of bare branches, the arc of the front gate, a curlicued window grill—night lace that vanished with a switch of her lamp. (It occurred to her then that light can conceal as well as illuminate and for a moment, the thought seemed profound.) *The Second Sex* was a thicker, denser volume than she'd choose to read today, but she remembered devouring it back then, partly because it was a gift from Leah, but also because in the sixties, she'd devoured everything that had anything to do with women's liberation. The book opened by itself to Chapter 13 ("The Formative Years: The Young Girl"), her adolescence coded into its spine. Its pages were eerily familiar and the sentence she'd been looking for—underlined, asterisked, and exclamation-pointed—was impossible to miss: *In the love she gives an older woman the young girl is in love with her own future.* Scrawled beside it in the margin were the words "Yikes! This is ME!!!"

In those days, when the future stretched out ahead where it belonged, the older woman Shoshanna imagined herself becoming was Leah. She loved her mother and Rachel, of course, but she was *in* love with Leah, infatuated. At fourteen, she wanted to talk like Leah, look like her, live her life, *be* her. Compared to the gutsy young professor, Shoshanna's mother and sister seemed boringly bourgeois—ordinary women trapped in *Good Housekeeping* lives. Now Leah was the last person on earth with whom she'd trade places. Now, having witnessed how things turned out, Shoshanna knew better.

The office floor was cold. Should have worn her slippers. Should have bought a rug for the office months ago. Should, at least, have turned up the thermostat when she got out of bed. She replaced the Beauvoir and was about to return to Daniel's warmth when *The Feminine Mystique* caught her eye; it was wedged between *The Female Eunuch* and *Sexual Politics*. Movements make odd shelf fellows, she thought as she pulled the book down and settled into the club chair, frozen feet tucked under her nightgown. Even before she cracked its cover, she could hear Leah's voice echoing through time.

"Damn thing's riddled with middle-class bias! Betty Friedan makes it sound as if all a woman needs to be liberated is a fucking job. What about poor and working-class women, for Chrissake? They've got jobs, but they're not liberated by a long shot."

Wednesday's Women was debating whether to issue a press release critiquing *The Feminine Mystique*, which, to their consternation, had become a national bestseller and the putative bible of the women's movement. One WW member argued for benign neglect. "Attack Friedan and we'll only draw attention to the book. Whenever women have an honest ideological dispute, the media call it a catfight. Why give 'em red meat?"

"Because the book misrepresents the movement as the exclusive preserve of white, educated, heterosexual married women," countered Leah. "As such, it could alienate other women and hamper our organizing efforts. I say we should take an activist stance and grapple with the issues head-on before any single constituency's agenda is allowed to harden into doctrine. Why pretend that reformers and radicals are preaching the same brand of feminism? I think it's time to surface the split in the movement and fight it out." As usual, Leah's views prevailed. At her initiative, WW published a position paper called "The Invisible Labor of the Educated Stay-at-Home Woman," with the intention of stimulating public conversation about the interaction between class, race, and the homemaking role—while incidentally picking *The Feminine Mystique* to pieces. In a matter of days, the split hit the fan. WW's position paper was taken as a declaration of ideological war. It was mentioned on the wire services and in the columns. Quotes from the tract were juxtaposed against statements from Betty Friedan and her supporters. Grassroots groups took sides. Newspaper pundits fixated on the clash of personalities. Intellectuals debated the contending positions in *Dissent, Partisan Review*, and *The Nation*. In the sixties, ideas still mattered.

"The Invisible Labor of the Educated Stay-at-Home Woman" triggered Shoshanna's first serious consideration of her mother's lot. Did Esther enjoy staying home? Did she miss her life as a designer? Did she actually *like* being a rebbetzin, mother, cook, and cleaner? Only when the paper mentioned the possibility of the housewife having "burdens, talents, and dreams" did Shoshanna realize how utterly unseen her mother's life had been to her. Until then, she'd thought about Esther strictly in relation to herself. Her mother was *hers*—not a woman but her mother; not a person in her own right, but Rabbi Wasserman's wife. She had only the most inchoate sense of her mother's world. (Inchoate—"imperfectly formed or formulated.") Hooked on language because she was hooked on Leah, Shoshanna had become genuinely excited about memorizing new words and using them as often as possible, a far from simple challenge given the gems that dropped from her sister's lips.

One night, for instance, she noticed Leah's silhouette and maneuvered the two of them in front of the full-length mirror.

"Look! We have the same shape tush!" She was thrilled to identify another trait they had in common.

Leah studied the mirror. "It's the Wasserman tuchis. It's callipygian."

"Callapigeon?"

"It means 'shapely rounded buttocks.'"

"You're kidding; there's a word for shapely rounded buttocks!?"

"There's a word for everything, the exactly *right* word—what Flaubert called *le mot juste*. Callipygian is a lovely, show-offy, roll-around-the-tongue word, perfect in this context, though not terribly utilitarian. When you have to describe a complex idea or a sensitive issue, that's when you'll be really grateful to have *le mot juste* at your disposal. To name something accurately, my muffin, is to control it."

"Inchoate" certainly was *le mot juste* for Shoshanna's feelings toward her mother. Esther used to just be there, making meals in the kitchen, making nice at synagogue, doing her thing around the house. But thanks to WW's paper, Esther was transformed into a woman who might actually have needs of her own. No less eye-opening was her past, a classic immigrant's tale to which the young Shoshanna had paid little mind when she'd first heard it on the beach in Maine. Now she listened carefully to every detail until she knew her mother's story as well as she knew the ups and downs of the Swiss Family Robinson—though it was easier to imagine the adventures of a shipwrecked clan than Esther's miserable beginnings.

Wrenched as a child from a Polish shtetl, she had sailed to America in steerage, done well in elementary school, but had to drop out in eighth grade to help support her family. Six days a week, she worked on a sewing machine in a blouse factory until she married a man named Lucky, who turned out to be pathologically possessive, so jealous that he made her quit her job and beat her when he thought she was being too nice to the rag dealer, or when the knife-sharpening man gave her a discount, or whenever he felt like humiliating her, including while she was pregnant with the child who turned out to be Rachel. In the 1930s, Jewish wives lived with their mistakes, they didn't leave them. No woman wanted to be branded a failed wife or a divorcée. But the night Lucky whipped off his belt and raised it to strike Rachel for knocking over his ashtray and the tiny toddler cowered under the high-legged stove terrified, Esther decided to run away. That was when she'd scooped up the child, grabbed her grandmother's candlesticks, and taken refuge for a short time in her parents' tenement, where her four younger siblings slept in one room and there was never enough food to go around.

Listening to this part of the story rubbed a blister on Shoshanna's heart. Esther's dimples always went slack as she spoke of the bruises, the broken marriage, the shondeh of being a Jewish divorcée in 1938, the scandalous talk when she sent Rachel to boarding school. Then things began to improve. Esther got her job back. One day she noticed a design flaw in one of the blouses and proposed a change in the cutting process that saved the owner so much money he promoted her to his assistant. A few months later, she left a sketchbook of her designs on his desk, resulting in two more promotions, until she became a senior designer, known throughout the industry for her distinctive collars— shawl, draped, notched, sweetheart, scoop, V neck, squared, all exquisitely tailored and, according to the faded advertisements in a shoe box in Esther's closet, "face-flattering."

Shoshanna loved the next part of the story, when Leah arrived at Rachel's school and they became friends and hatched their famous plot. Rachel was to fake a tantrum on the phone and demand that Esther, whose regular visiting day was Saturday, start coming up on Sundays instead. (Whenever Sam couldn't pick up Leah in time for Shabbat, he'd visit on Sunday, since he wouldn't drive on Saturday.) Everyone else's parents come on Sundays, said Rachel, why couldn't Esther? (Even then, Rachel knew that her mother would do anything to be like everyone else.) Well, of course she could, said Esther, and one Sunday when Sam showed up, Esther was there, and Rachel introduced her mother to her best friend's father, and the four of them played badminton on the lawn outside the visitors' lounge. At this point, Esther always digressed to "the accident"—how the shuttlecock hit her face and started a nosebleed; how Sam raced under the net, carried her to a bench, and put her head on his lap while he stanched the flow with his handkerchief.

"Amazing how much damage a few feathers can do," he'd said softly.

"It's nothing," she'd replied, but didn't get up until it was time for the musicale.

Esther admitted having noticed that his thighs were hard-muscled and his white handkerchief was a fine linen square with hand-rolled hems. The blood on the linen reminded her of childbirth. "I got excited—being touched by a man after all those years. Then I got embarrassed. What if he knew what I was thinking?"

At the end of visiting day, Leah begged her father to take them out for pizza.

"Great idea, zeesaleh." Turning to Esther and Rachel, he executed an exaggerated bow and asked in courtly tones, "May we have the pleasure of dining with you ladies this evening at Guido's?"

The plastic laminate menu listed a dozen different toppings. "Anything vegetarian is fine by me," he said. "I keep kosher."

"What a coincidence! So does Mom!" enthused Rachel with more wow than was warranted.

"Daddy always says, 'Coincidences are God's way of remaining anonymous,'" piped up Leah. "Don't you, Pop?"

"I may have said that on occasion, bubbeleh. Speaking of coincidences, how about your names! Rachel and Leah."

"Here we go! Torah time," Leah teased.

"I don't remember my Bible that well," said Esther coquettishly.

Sam smiled. "Jacob's two wives. They were sisters."

"They hated each other," said Rachel, sliding over in the booth and resting her head on Leah's shoulder. "But we love each other."

"They didn't exactly *hate*, maideleh," said Sam. "More like envy."

Zeesaleh. Bubbeleh. Maideleh. Yiddish love names. Later, as Esther was leaving, Rachel whispered in her ear, "Can Rabbi Wasserman be my father?"

On subsequent Sundays, when their visits overlapped, Esther and Sam took walks on the grounds, with Rachel and Leah traipsing behind, or the four of them went off campus together for Carvel ice cream. Drive-in movies. Walks in the state forest. Pony rides. Miniature golf. One Sunday, Sam offered Esther a ride back to the city. The following week, they drove up together and left together. In 1947, they were married (with guess who as the maids of honor?), and Sam adopted Rachel, and Leah spent two weekends a month with them, and everyone was very, very happy.

At this point in her mother's narrative, the young Shoshanna always felt a quickening as she anticipated her own arrival and Rachel's euphoria at becoming, as she later described it, "a teenage mother without the bother of being pregnant." Still, there were things Esther never explained: why Sam had lopped Leah's branch off the family tree; how she could love a man who left his daughter in the care of a manic-depressive; how she, who'd been virtually omnipresent in Shoshanna's childhood, could have sent Rachel away to a boarding school; or why it had been so important to keep Shoshanna in the dark about all this. (Once, when Shoshanna had tried to talk to her sister about what she'd learned on the beach in Maine, Rachel had cut her off with a factoid: "Maine is the only state in the Union with a one-syllable name.") Shoshanna could easily understand Leah's anger just as she was being absorbed into a real family—with a father who loved her, a best friend who'd become her sister, an adored stepmother, and a new baby sister—Sam dropped out of her life and took everyone else with him. Like Jacob, he chose Rachel over Leah. Like their biblical counterparts, the two girls became rivals and strangers. Because of Sam.

Curled up in the club chair in her chilly office, Shoshanna remembered the day she'd pushed through the swinging door into the kitchen on West End Avenue when her mother and aunt were making matzoh balls for the Seder, in time to hear Aunt Anna say, "I'm not surprised Leah hates men. If my father had walked out on me, I'd be a women's libber, too."

Exasperated, Shoshanna had stormed, "Leah doesn't hate men! She hates male domination. You refuse to understand that we're fighting a systemic problem!" ("Systemic" was that week's word.) "It's not about one man mistreating one woman, it's about Mankind's oppression of Womankind. It's endemic" (last week's word).

Anna had thrown her mother a baleful I-told-you-so look as Esther dropped another lump of matzoh meal into the boiling chicken broth. At the table that evening, Anna said in a whisper that could pierce a wall, "Essie, maybe you shouldn't let her spend so much time with Leah. They're always in their bedrooms. Who knows what goes on behind closed doors."

Shoshanna snapped, "If you're suggesting that my sister and I are lesbians, why don't you come right out and say it, Aunt Anna?"

It had stopped the Seder cold. Leah let out a throaty "And a zeesin Pesach to all!" Rachel asked Jeremy to pour the children some grape juice. Uncle Sid mumbled something about how hard it must be for Elijah to visit every Jewish home on Seder night, kind of like Santa Claus on Christmas Eve. Cousin Warren burped. Cousin Emily kicked him under the table. Esther broke a matzoh in pieces and asked if anyone wanted a nibble, since it would be a while until dinner. Sam lifted the gnarled horseradish root from the ceremonial plate and, in a voice so flat it sounded recorded, recited the blessing over the bitter herbs. Everyone in the family was aware that Shoshanna had been inhaling feminist theory since several relatives had locked horns with her at a recent family get-together when she blasted Sigmund Freud as "the head hog of the male chauvinist pigs," knowing full well that Uncle Sid was a psychoanalyst. This time they seemed determined to leave well enough alone. Passover was no time to bicker. For the rest of the evening, however, Esther had been especially attentive to Leah, as if compensating for Anna's rudeness.

The next morning, Leah was reading in the window seat and Shoshanna was flopped on the floor making a graph, when Esther came into the living room carrying a netted sack marked IDAHO POTATOES, a peeler, a bowl of water, and a paper bag for scraps. She set herself up at the coffee table, itself completely out of the ordinary. Usually, the kitchen was the venue for food preparation; the living room was reserved for company. "What's the First Wave?" she asked as she dug out three eyes, then relieved the potato of its skin. I heard one of you say First Wave last night at the Seder. What is it?"

The poor woman is trying to understand this feminist conspiracy that's stolen her daughter, thought Leah, who normally would have jumped at the chance to deliver her standard "foremothers" lecture. But that time, she deferred to Shoshanna, both to see how much she'd learned and to give her the satisfaction of being her mother's teacher.

"The First Wave is what we call the nineteenth-century suffrage struggle, Ma; all the women who fought for the vote. Our movement is the *Second* Wave, and . . ."

"And this time it's going to be tidal," shot out Leah, "so get with the Zeitgeist, Esther."

Esther slid a peeled potato in the bowl of water. "Who were they, the First Wave?" she asked tentatively. "Did I ever learn about them?"

"Probably not," said Shoshanna, and described the women who made "herstory"—the pioneers at the Seneca Falls Women's Rights Convention. Susan B. Anthony, jailed for voting. Belva Lockwood, the first woman lawyer in America. Frances Willard, the temperance leader. The abolitionist Harriet Tubman, and the Grimké sisters. Victoria Woodhull, who ran for President.

"They were incredibly brave," said Leah, silence having proven too stressful. "And there were hundreds more like them. Sojourner Truth— an ex-slave who dared to count herself a woman like any other. Amelia Bloomer—crusader for corset liberation and comfortable clothes; also editor of *The Lily*, the first feminist magazine in the U.S., and the inspiration for my *Feminist Freethinker*. Lucy Stone, who kept her own name when she married, which is what I'd do, though it's unlikely the man's been born who would accept me as I am. I think, therefore I'm single."

"I'm sure you'll find a nice young fellow one of these days, dear."

"Who says I want to?" Leah fired back. "As you may have noticed, Esther, a woman starts out sinking into his arms but ends up with her arms in his sink."

Esther grinned. With an impish look, she retrieved a long snake of potato peel from the garbage bag and, to Shoshanna's complete astonishment, flicked it across the room. It landed on Leah's head, looking like a dirty hair ribbon. Leah flicked the peel back at Esther, who caught it and arranged the curly strip between her nose and her lips, like the mustache of a Transylvanian landlord. "I've come for zee rent," she vamped. Shoshanna had never seen her mother like this. Living under Sam's roof always seemed to demand decorum of "his" women, an expectation of refinement and restraint. Leah had changed that. Leah had made Esther saucy.

Shoshanna rubbed her icy toes between her palms and noticed in the bookcase beyond her feet the volume that had sparked her first real quarrel with her father on his own turf—*The Woman's Bible*. The flyleaf inscription, penned in blue ink with a fine hand, laid out like a poem:

> Shoshie dear,
> I offer this 19th-century critique
> Of the Scriptures
> As a counterweight
> To your father's brainwashing.
> And a gift of love.
> In sisterhood (both kinds),
>   Leah

When outrage was her daily bread, a quick skim had been enough to rile the young Shoshanna, who was already in high dudgeon thanks to Beauvoir. Sam was a convenient male target.

The confrontation happened about two months after Leah had moved into the West End Avenue apartment, and several weeks after the brouhaha at the family Seder.

"It ticks me off the way the Bible treats women," Shoshanna said to her father at the dinner table as he shpritzed a lemon wedge on his trout.

"What do you mean, kindeleh?" He cut off the fish's head and pushed it to one side of his plate.

Shoshanna turned away. At that age, she wouldn't eat anything with a face. Esther had made her spaghetti. "Why should Eve get blamed when Adam was the moral weakling?"

Sam tweezed a bone from his trout. "Anyone else you find problematic?"

"Abraham, if you really want to know. He pretends his wife is his sister and pimps her to the Pharaoh." Shoshanna saw her father flinch. "Palms her off to the harem to save his own skin and gets rewarded with a caravan of livestock and servants. And *this* guy is the founding father of the Jewish people? *Puhleese.*"

Sam began stroking his beard. "All the patriarchs are flawed, zeesaleh. But so are the matriarchs. If they were perfect, we couldn't identify with them."

"Yeah, but the matriarchs are flawed *and* powerless, which is an infuriating combination." Shoshanna heard Leah's audacity in her voice and was emboldened by it. "Sarah is passive except when she throws Hagar and Ishmael out of the tent. Rebecca's a sneak and a swindler who cheats her firstborn out of his inheritance because he's too hairy or hungry for stew or something. Rachel is jealous, mean, and conceited. And Leah is jealous, whiny, weak-eyed, and pregnant every five minutes."

"Happily, traits don't follow names," murmured Leah, as she pushed back her chair and sauntered into the living room. She set herself up on the window seat with a bag of sunflower seeds, a yellow legal pad, her Parker pen, and a copy of the Declaration of Independence, whose text she was adapting as a Declaration of Women's Liberation.

Sam followed her with his cow-brown eyes, then turned to his younger daughter. "What made you so angry, ketzeleh?"

Shoshanna raced down the hall.

Esther coughed nervously and began to clear the table.

"'*The Woman's Bible: Comments on Genesis, Exodus, Leviticus, Numbers and Deuteronomy*, by Elizabeth Cady Stanton and the Revising Committee,'" Sam read aloud when Shoshanna returned with the book and thrust it at him. His tone was just short of scornful. "I quote: 'In criticizing the peccadilloes of Sarah, Rebecca, and Rachel, we would not shadow the virtues of Deborah, Huldah, and Vashti. In criticizing the Mosaic code we would not question the wisdom of the golden rule and the Fifth Commandment.'

"Well, that's nice of them," he said sardonically, and dabbed at his beard with his napkin. Then, wagging a finger in Leah's direction, he called out, "See what you've done!"

From her utter disregard—eyes riveted on pad, teeth cracking seeds—one might have thought his outburst the hiss of a radiator or the hum of the fridge. Now it was Leah's turn to read aloud. Raising the yellow pad, she turned toward an imaginary audience across the Hudson River and declaimed, "We hold these truths to be self-evident, that all women are created equal . . ."

Shoshanna noticed the faintest crinkling at the corners of her father's mouth. Amusement? Pride? Couldn't be sure, but she'd seen him crinkle before in response to Leah's antics, as if his disapproving instincts were unable to hold the line against a deeper admiration, perhaps even delight in his older daughter's wit.

"Let's have some popcorn! Wouldn't you love some hot buttered popcorn, Sam?" Even before he nodded, the ever-mollifying Esther was backing into the kitchen, a healer retreating to the place from whence her powers come.

A few days before that, Leah, whose interest in the culinary arts usually extended no further than the ingredients on a box of Twinkies, had asked if she could watch Esther make rugalach. The process was interesting to her as a matter of "cultural anthropology," she'd said, but what she really wanted was to be close to the oven when the pastries came out. Seated on stools at the butcher-block island, Shoshanna and Leah observed as Esther demonstrated her techniques and dispensed her wifely wisdom.

"Knead the dough but don't overwork it, just like in a relationship." With a wooden rolling pin she flattened the ball of dough until it formed a large circle, then trimmed the uneven edges. "It's a woman's job to smooth the rough edges of a man's life the way I'm doing with this dough." She spread a layer of apricot jam over the whole circle, "like a woman spreads sweetness in the circle of her family," then sprinkled a mixture of sugar, chopped walnuts, and cinnamon over it and scored the dough into many small triangles. "Triangles remind us that a family needs three strong sides to be solid: parents, kids, and God to watch over them." Her fingers deftly rolled up each triangle and shaped it into a crescent. "Done! Rugalach as foolproof as *sh'lom bayit*. That's Hebrew for peace in the home. Nature gives us the ingredients, girls, but it's up to women to put them together right and make them taste like something. God makes marriages, but it's up to women to keep the peace." She brushed the little crescents with beaten egg white and slid the cookie sheet in the oven.

"Whose peace?" challenged Leah, pouring herself a glass of milk in anticipation of the first batch. "Peace for whom? Peace at what cost to which party? What you really mean is: Wife, appease your husband."

"What's wrong with that, Leah, if that's what it takes?" Esther hung her apron on a hook. "You're for the UN, right?"

"Right."

"Well, in the UN, don't they make all kinds of compromises to keep peace in the world? Why not in the family?"

"Come now, Esther, you can't equate the two." Leah appeared to be humoring her. "Treaties between nations presume give-and-take on both sides. Your formula is a one-way street."

"Sometimes you have to take a one-way street to get where you want to go."

Leah threw up her hands. "We're never going to agree on this, Esther. We're stuck in what anthropologists call a 'systemic misunderstanding.'"

"What's that?" asked Esther.

"It's when two people's basic frameworks are so fundamentally different that a misunderstanding cannot be corrected by either of them providing more information. That's our problem here. That's why we're stuck. Now, when will those ruggies be ready?"

The young Shoshanna had recalled her mother's lecture as she watched Esther back into the kitchen a few nights later promising popcorn as a peace offering.

Charming, these old brownstones, but not air-tight. A thin draft squeezed its wintry fingers through the old window frames and pulled

Shoshanna back to the present. She drew her hands inside her night-gown sleeves and tucked her feet between the side of the chair and the seat cushion. Cold feet always reminded her of her mother. At the very end, morphine dulled the pain of her cancer, but Esther could still feel her feet. "They're cold," she cried. "Warm them, *please* warm them." Shoshanna heated almond oil in a double boiler and massaged her mother's feet. She bundled them in woolen socks. Propped them between hot-water bottles, red rubber pouches like the lobes of a lung. Wrapped them in a goosedown comforter. Still, Esther groaned. The last day of her life, cold feet was her only complaint.

Before memories of her mother's death could open the floodgates altogether, Shoshanna nudged her thoughts back to her mother's life. To Esther's food, marinated in love, the fireworks of her freckles, the gentle interventions that revealed her genius for social equilibrium, a gift so delicate and intuitive that few took notice of it. With Esther Wasserman, what you *didn't* see was what you got: invisible grace. Without calling attention to herself, she ran a smooth household, calmed the first bubbles of turbulence, papered over the rough spots, and always tried to please—Sam above all. Her talent, unappreciated, offered her nothing but the secret satisfaction of knowing things had gone well or quieted down or worked out because of some perfectly timed word or gesture, a move so subtle and seamless that no one was aware anything special had taken place, only that discord had been cir-cumvented. Like a grand master of chess who forecasts every difficulty many moves ahead, the grand mistress of *sh'lom bayit* had an instinct for the rhythms of the people she loved and enabled them to behave at their best. But constantly coming to the rescue of others took its toll on the rescuer. Who brought peace to the peacemaker? And what good was invisible grace if you were dead at fifty-four? Shoshanna hugged *The Woman's Bible* to her chest.

Nothing was left in the bowl but a few blackened kernels. Leah had fin-ished reciting her revisionist Declaration of Independence to the far shores of the Hudson. Esther had loaded the dishwasher and wrapped up the leftovers and was wiping the countertop when the young Shoshanna pressed another document into her hands. Welcoming the interruption, Esther sat down and read its title: " 'The Declaration of Sentiments. Women's Rights Convention of 1848'? What's this?"

"I mentioned it the day you and Leah had your potato-peel fight. It's time you declared *your* sentiments, Mother. List your grievances. Demand your rights. And quit treating Daddy like the lord of the manse. He could be doing a lot more around the house, you know. If you write down the chores you want him to do, I'll make sure he does them." Shoshanna lowered her voice. "Or Leah will."

Esther began her list that night, but never finished it, not because she had too few demands, she had too many. Revisiting her life's choices, asking Sam to change, even changing herself was more trouble than it was worth. Much as she longed to share her daughter's revolution, she really didn't believe it possible for people to change beyond a certain age. Circumstances change; people stay the same. But maybe that was just her problem. Maybe for the next generation, things would be different.

Days later, Shoshanna remembered to ask how she was doing on her Declaration of Sentiments.

"Sorry, sweetie, I've got nothing to declare."

Now, shivering in the chill of an endless night, she wondered if that sentence had been Esther's invitation to connect with her woman-to-woman, or woman-to-teenager. If so, she'd muffed it. At the time, she'd reprimanded her mother, called her a patsy. Preoccupied with her own life—college applications, exams, boycotting the prom, political demonstrations, one thing after another—she'd been oblivious to what everyone else knew and no one would tell her. Sam, Rachel, Leah, Aunt Anna, some *adult* should have clued her in, but they'd just strung her along. "Woman troubles," they'd said, as if her mother's illness were a pesky malfunction of female plumbing. And she'd believed them, never for a moment imagining that her father and sister could lie to her again. They'd kept it from her to protect her, Sam said later, so she could get through senior year without her mother's cancer hanging over her.

What good was it to know bad news if you couldn't do anything about it? Why tell the truth if there's nothing to be gained from it? The Wasserman philosophy in a nutshell.

Because they hid the facts from her, Shoshanna never had the chance to disown her shallow self and Esther never got to rage at her unfinished child rearing or the wisdom dead-ended on her branch. Esther died with her regrets, Shoshanna lived with hers, and on nights like this, when the house was still and sleep elusive, she liked to reimagine the last months of her mother's life as they might have been had she known how little time they had left, had they not been cheated of their good-byes. She would have massaged Esther's feet every day, not just the last. Kept her company even when there was nothing to say. Listened more attentively. Asked more questions. Begged for advice— enough to last a lifetime. And Esther could have played all her strings. Passed along what life had taught her, what she wished she'd done differently or not at all, what she wanted her daughter to know, and beware of, things only a mother will tell you, and sometimes only at the end. Had Shoshanna known Esther was dying, she would have said not just "I love you," but "I love you for everything you've been, and everything you've done." She'd have thanked her for her sacrifices. Forgiven her for not being Leah or Beauvoir or Bella Abzug. Let her off the hook for the old secrets, for being ashamed of what she couldn't help, for wanting American daughters, for her conformity and her cover-ups, for always needing to blend in. She'd have asked Esther's forgiveness for neglecting her. Ignoring her. Taking her for granted. Sassing and talking back. For all the hurtful things a child says when she believes, as children do, that Mommy is unbreakable. She'd have apologized for not storing away more memories—acorns for the long winter ahead—for not seeing beyond those merry freckles. For not cherishing. Not doing enough around the house (because if Sam didn't, why should she?). For behaving as if Esther would always be there because she always *was*.

When you're young, the one event as unimaginable as your own death is your mother's. She gets sick, you assume she'll get better. You let her persuade you to "Go on along, dear, have fun." You ignore an opening line like "I have nothing to declare" and learn too late that the tiny nub in her breast had spread to her liver, and while everyone is tip-toeing around the bed fluffing the pillows and finessing the future, you sense the air being pumped out of the room and the vacuum being filled with platitudes, until finally they tell you what's really going on and it's too late to have that other conversation—about choices made and missed. At your mother's funeral, you learn more about her from other people's eulogies than you did from your mother herself, and you know it was your fault, and you spend the rest of your life remembering nothing so vividly as what was left unsaid.

Fresh tears. In flight from Leah's lamentable life, Shoshanna had run smack into the Book of Esther. Her mother's memory always made her cry, even now, nearly thirty-five years later, or maybe because it *was* nearly thirty-five years and Esther had missed so much. How surprised she'd have been to see Rachel, the über-athlete, doing needlepoint, and Shoshanna, her math-anxious daughter, running a business. How wholeheartedly she'd have approved of Daniel. How delighted to wit-ness Nelly's equestrienne elegance, Jake's irony and charm, the miracle of twin great-granddaughters. Dear, selfless Esther—cheated of all that nachas, the reward for a lifetime of invisible grace.

Regret might have ripped Shoshanna apart decades ago had she not learned from experience that the by-product of hindsight is rededica-tion. She'd kept her mother's memory alive all these years by letting it keep her up until all hours; by revisiting childhood time and space, remembering Esther's voice and smile, her recipes, her tchotchkes; by weeping over her mother's cold feet. She dried her eyes on a flannel sleeve, returned *The Woman's Bible* to its shelf, and switched off her reminiscences with the lamp. The night lace—window grille, gate, branches—tattooed itself back onto the bare office floor. Definitely need a carpet, she thought, curling her toes as she hurried up the two flights to Daniel's sweet snoring. His body heat was a blessing. She slid her frigid feet between his thighs. He stirred but let her stay. Dear man would do anything to make her happy, even in his sleep. His warmth was as generous as he was. She draped an arm across his back and, with dawn seeping in around the window shades, finally drifted off.

That next morning, she woke up with a headache. Her father's letter was on the bed table where she'd left it as a reminder to answer him, but March 8 was a week away and she still wasn't sure what to do about Leah. Why say anything to her about his visit if his name alone was enough to set off one of her tirades? Why nudge Sam if Leah wasn't going to want to see him anyway? (The last time Shoshanna had asked him to take the initiative—just to phone Leah on her sixtieth birthday—he'd been quick to remind her that Leah had ruined *his* birthday, his eightieth, and never thanked him for taking her in years ago when she had no place else to go.) Their mutual hostility had become a defining principle, the way each of them oriented him- or herself in the universe. Why bother getting them together if they were only going to bury the hatchet in each other's back? Should her effort fail, she might alienate Leah and spoil what little relationship they'd pieced together in nearly twenty years of lunches.

She found Daniel downstairs forking an English muffin.

"You just got up. Why the frown?" he asked, dropping the slices into the toaster.

"I'm wondering what to do about Daddy and Leah. I'm stumped."

"Not my call, love."

"I know, but what do you think?"

The toaster popped up, and though the muffins were still raw, he slathered butter on both slices and gave her one. "I'd say you have nothing to lose by trying, except if it doesn't work out, they'll probably blame you, and *three* pissed-off Wassermans may be more than the cosmos can stand. How would you feel if you ended up making matters worse?"

"You're saying I shouldn't mix in." She poured two cups of coffee and added milk to hers.

"No, I'm saying before you mix in, you ought to be sure they're ready to reconcile. And that your motives are pure."

"What's that supposed to mean?" Shoshanna watched him cover the butter dish and mindlessly stick it in the bread box. Without comment, she retrieved it and put it away in the refrigerator. Last week she found a carton of milk in the cabinet with the boxes of dry cereal. His absent-mindedness was driving her nuts. The man seemed incapable of doing two things at once—talking and clearing the table, thinking and timing a four-minute egg, pouring water in the coffeemaker and remembering to turn off the faucet before the sink overflowed. Now he was wandering aimlessly around the kitchen placing whatever he happened to be holding into whatever receptacle happened to be nearby. Yet the same mind that seemed irredeemably absent also seemed to be reading Shoshanna's.

"I just wonder if you're finagling this for their sake," he said gently, "or for some unresolved needs of your own."

The pocks of the English muffin held her gaze for a long moment. "Can't answer that unequivocally," she said. "But if I don't do something and one of them dies before they make up, I'll never forgive myself."

"Then I guess you have to do something."

Her head was pounding. "I probably won't decide until I'm sitting across the table from Leah. But one thing's for sure: This year I'm going to be careful not to say anything that offends her. I'm going to remember what a lousy childhood she had and how close we were for a while there when I was a kid, and how much of my intellectual education I owe to her. I'm going to be appreciative . . . tolerant . . . sensitive. And this time, goddammit, I'm going to have fun."

"My darling," said Daniel as he turned his dirty coffee cup upside down in the dish drainer, "you say that every year."

seven

THAT SUNDAY MORNING the phone rang at 9. "I know we're seeing each other tomorrow but I can't remember where; early Alzheimer's, I guess." It was Leah. She never bothered to say hello.

"You're not *that* old."

"Half-heimer's, then."

Shoshanna groaned. "We never decided where," she said. "I've been meaning to call you all week." Her W pages had not yet surfaced, so she couldn't look up her sister's number, which, thanks to the Filofax, she'd never bothered to memorize. Since Leah had appeared on TV talking about abortion rights, a barrage of death threats clogged her answering machine, and she had to unlist her phone. Leah alone of the three Wasserman daughters had kept her maiden name. Secretly, she'd have preferred to use Leo's. Besides being mellifluous, Leah *Rose* sounded like a new genus of flora, perfect for a thorny feminist; great byline, too—easy to remember, fits any column width. But taking her husband's name had been out of the question on principle. Her sisters had no such compunction.

Shoshanna Wasserman Safer used a triptych, savoring its auditory heft, the whisper of sibilant *shh*s and *esse*s, the echo of notable triple-barreled women. Edna St. Vincent Millay, Margaret Chase Smith, Margaret Bourke-White. Shoshanna had kept Wasserman not as a feminist statement but an homage to her childself, that water sprite she'd left behind on the beaches of Maine and California. She'd been resolutely earthbound since then, wings atrophied, spirit prudent, having grown a carapace appropriate to her husband's name: *Safer*.

"*Safer* means book in Hebrew," Rachel had reminded her when Daniel proposed.

Shoshanna nodded. "Mrs. Safer plays by the book. Mrs. Safer plays it safe. Suits me both ways—like Jeremy's name suits you."

"Brent? How do you see that? Brent comes from *farbrent*, Yiddish for burned."

"Exactly! If I remember correctly, your nickname used to be Hot Pants."

"*Shoshanna!!*"

"Just kidding." But she wasn't. Rachel's peppery physicality was no secret. Looking back, Shoshanna remembered, as a small child, finding a diaphragm in Rachel's drawer. At one of their lunches, Leah quipped that Rachel had "majored in sports and sex at school and was known to excel at both." Though this might suggest an avant-garde personality, virtually everything else about Rachel was Eisenhower Era. She wore penny loafers, a wardrobe from Talbot's, her husband's name. A conformist like her mother, she had happily jettisoned her real father's name when Sam signed the adoption papers, and just as blithely dropped Wasserman for Brent at the altar. Even when Leah and Shoshanna were in the vanguard of the women's movement, Rachel introduced herself as Mrs. Jeremy Brent and Leah never quite forgave her for it. Which probably explained the fight Leah had started when she was at Rachel's house for Sam's eightieth birthday party nine years ago. "You've had enough identities for three lifetimes, Mrs. Brent. You molt them like feathers."

"They're not identities, they're just names," replied Rachel. "Besides, much as I love our father, I never liked Wasserman. It's the blood test they use to detect syphilis."

"Not quite, O maven of minutiae. The syphilis test is named for August *von* Wassermann. *Two* n's." (For Leah, one-upmanship was a combat sport and information without intellect a waste of time. Unimpressed by Rachel's factoids, she never missed an opportunity to launch a zinger.) "Could be the real reason you took Jeremy's name was to mask your Jewishness. Brent sounds pretty goyish to me!"

Shoshanna was about to come to her aid when Rachel, unassisted, zinged back. "If I was looking to pass, Professor, I'd do better than Brent. And I'd be in good company with Ashley Montagu, alias Israel Ehrenberg; Al Jolson, the former Asa Yoelson; Larry Rivers, the ex–Irving Grossberg; Beverly Sills, a.k.a. Belle Silverman; and Robert King Merton, born Meyer Schkolnick, who went so far as to name himself after two colleges at Oxford. Ooops, almost forgot Man Ray, son of a Jewish vest maker, whose Dada name came not from the stingray or the man-o'-war but from letters in his original name, Emmanuel Radnitsky."

"This woman is depriving some village of an idiot," Leah snapped, though she knew she'd been bested.

"No *ad hominem* attacks, please," said Shoshanna.

"Oh, we've been working on our vocabulary again, have we?"

Shoshanna pressed her. "You're always saying you believe in freedom of choice, so why shouldn't a person be able to choose her own name?"

"A person should—assuming she's a *person* and the name's not someone else's. In choosing to call themselves Mrs. Brent and Mrs. Safer, the Misses Wasserman have declared derivative identities; they are no longer autonomous persons. Pronounce a couple man and wife—he's still a person, but she's a role. Then pity the day he leaves her or drops dead, and suddenly she has no role and she's shocked—*shocked!*—when there's nothing left of her 'Mrs.' but a monogrammed dish towel. A woman would be wiser to take a dog's name than a husband's.

"Since the dawn of creation, naming has always been a male prerogative. Men exercise their hegemony by naming things and people, continents and planets, wives and children. The giving of a name begins the process of differentiation and individuation." Rachel was chewing on her pearl necklace when the battleship *Leah* turned its guns her way. "As our resident Bible expert, Mrs. Brent, I'm sure you will corroborate that one of the first things Adam did in Eden was to give a name to all

God's creatures, not only to distinguish them from one another, but to assign each its own unique identity. That's what a name does."

"Please don't patronize me, Leah."

"Not patronizing, educating, hopeless though the task may be." The atmosphere was turning ugly, but nobody knew how to save it. "You didn't name yourself, your parents did, yet the letters R-A-C-H-E-L have come to define who you are. You wouldn't want to stop being called Rachel and suddenly be Mitzi unless maybe you were on the lam, so why would you stop being Wasserman and suddenly be Brent? Every woman should claim both the power to name *and* the right not to be *renamed*. May I quote from one of your Jewish wise guys—sorry, I meant sages: 'Have regard for your name, for it continues with you longer than a thousand great treasures of gold. A good life has its number of days, but a good name lasts forever.' Not *your* name, I guess."

"I wasn't aware that the Wisdom of Ben Sira was part of the revolutionary syllabus," replied Rachel, frankly amazed that Leah would pluck a quote from the Apocrypha.

Leah, in turn, was stunned that her sister, whose Jewish knowledge she'd assumed superficial, knew its source. "You've become totally subsumed in your husband. If one of our Blue Spruce classmates came to town and tried to find you in the phone book, she couldn't. Rachel Wasserman no longer exists. Rachel Wasserman has disappeared."

"Maybe so, but into a very good life!" With a swing of her Dutch-boy hair, Rachel wheeled toward the kitchen. "Now, if you will excuse me, I have to light eighty candles on someone's cake."

Not the best rebuttal in the world, but had they fought through the night, Leah wouldn't have given an inch. Names mattered to her. In fact, she'd agreed to a synagogue wedding—even put on a white Mexican peasant dress for the occasion—only after Leo had signed a marriage contract containing five non-negotiable demands, the first two about naming:

*She would remain Leah Wasserman—Professor Leah Wasserman—even at the dry cleaners.

*Leo, who'd always wanted four kids, would promise to stop at two. The firstborn would carry the surname Rose; the second would get Wasserman.

("Won't it be confusing for siblings to have different last names?" Leo had asked when she told him her terms. "By the time they're old enough to notice," she replied, "they'll be old enough to understand why.")

*Neither of her parents was to participate in the wedding. Not walk her down the aisle. Not stand under the huppah. Not make some bullshit toast. Dena wouldn't play the piano and Sam most definitely would not perform the ceremony. (They wouldn't have been invited at all had Leo's father not insisted, afraid that people would otherwise think the bride an orphan.)

*She would not walk seven times around the groom no matter how ancient the ritual, how beautiful, how open to modern interpretation, blah, blah, blah. No man was going to be the center of her universe, even symbolically.

*They would exchange egalitarian vows, *without* "obey."

Though Leah viewed marriage as state-sanctioned, culturally institutionalized male supremacy, Leo had convinced her that marriage to him would prove the exception. She'd let him talk her into it, having been through enough relationships and slept with enough men to know that Leo was as good as it got. She'd lived with her parents, at school, with Dena, with the Wassermans, with boyfriends, and by herself. Besides her childhood weekends with Sam and Esther, the closest she'd ever come to contentment was with Leo Rose.

When news of the wedding leaked out, her political colleagues accused her of "false consciousness." She'd forfeited the right to be a spokeswoman for the movement. She was a turncoat. A sellout. Living with a guy was one thing, but legalizing it betrayed the cause. Not the sort to take criticism lying down, Leah had fired off a press statement: "The decision about whether or not to marry, like the decision about whether or not to bear a child, must be solely the choice of a woman and her partner. Doctors, therapists, parents, clergy, tax accountants, friends, and political comrades may weigh in if asked, but have no vote.

Our right to love whom we wish is fundamentally meaningless unless we are also free to live as we wish."

Leah developed her argument more fully in a baldly self-referential article entitled "Why Wasserman Wed." "I have always prided myself on being an iconoclast among iconoclasts," she wrote. 'As such, I deplore all forms of orthodoxy, including the feminist kind. Since current doctrine deems marrying to be the ultimate transgressive act, I felt compelled to experience it, partly to demystify it, partly to transmogrify and control it."

At the time, the essay won new converts to the cause and Leah was praised for expanding the definition of women's liberation to include the freedom to choose commitment. What crap, thought Shoshanna when she came upon the essay years later in an anthology. Still, Leah's rationalizations had clearly served her needs. Having framed her decision in terms of a more-radical-than-thou feminist ideology, she never had to confront the possibility that she'd married Leo because he loved her unconditionally and treated her like a duchess, or that she'd stayed married all these years to prove she could do what Sam couldn't—be loyal, faithful, steadfast, and true. Rachel, the simplifier, had a bare-bones theory about Why Wasserman Wed: "To replace the father she'd lost."

Once Leo signed on to her five demands, Leah had gone along with the full-course Jewish wedding his family wanted (the Seven Blessings, breaking of the glass, kiddush, the whole megillah), though her impulse was to grab the fast-food version at City Hall. Leo had no problem with the naming clauses; it was Leah whose resolve was briefly shaken when a friend reminded her that her own name was actually her father's and contained the suffix *man*. For a minute she'd considered using Wasserwoman, but thankfully—Shoshanna smiled at the recollection—the echo of washerwoman squelched that one.

Her reverie was interrupted by the sound of whistling, followed by Leah's grunt. "Are you there, Shoshe? What the fuck's taking so long?"

"Sorry, sorry," she murmured into the receiver. As had been happening so often lately, a simple thought—here, the mere contemplation of a name—had vacuumed her into the past.

"Give me my marching orders, for Chrissake; Leo needs the phone." Leah started whistling again.

"Wait, I'm checking the Yellow Pages."

"Just pick a restaurant out of your frigging black book and I'll turn up."

"That's the problem—it blew off the roof."

"What did?"

"My Filofax."

"What roof?"

"The car. A couple of weeks ago, Ash Wednesday to be exact. Since then, it's been total chaos around here."

"Chaos?! Ooooh, Madame Mission Control couldn't be too pleased about that! Now you have an inkling of how the rest of us live."

"We can be mean-spirited," Shoshanna said edgily, "or we can pick a restaurant."

"Midtown, if you don't mind. After lunch, I want to stop at the Mercantile Library."

"Where's that?"

"Forty-seventh, between Fifth and Madison."

So much for Mamaleh's on the Lower East Side. "Okay, how's Café Bretagne—Forty-ninth and Madison? Twelve-thirty."

"Ooh-la-la! Crêpes. *Cidre. Magnifique!* I trust casual dress will suffice."

"As long as it's black."

"Voo den?"

Leah kept a subway map taped to the front of her medicine cabinet, the only mirror in the house and for all she cared the only one in all of Brooklyn. Usually she was more interested in figuring out how to get to Manhattan's more obscure libraries and museums than how she might look upon arrival. This morning, though, she pulled off the map and studied herself in the glass.

So much for predictability; she didn't *always* wear black. The red shawl, tossed around her neck and shoulders like an afterthought, would teach Shoshanna to make assumptions. Despite its bright, brash, Isadora Duncan insouciance, the shawl, a gift from the Schmendriks at *The Free-thinker*, came with impeccable feminist credentials, a newspaper clipping from the 1880s citing Susan B. Anthony's habit of wearing a red shawl at lectures and demonstrations because it made her stand out in a crowd.

Had Shoshanna not turned herself into a 100-proof goody-goody, she'd be wearing something socially significant as well; once upon a time, she'd gladly have stood out in a crowd. Leah had in mind a morning on West End Avenue when Shoshanna, who must have been fourteen or fifteen, appeared at the breakfast table in the uniform of a U.S. Navy ensign, complete with bell-bottom trousers and a white canvas cap. Esther had been horrified.

"Shoshie, take that off! You look ridiculous! You'll be a laughing-stock at school."

"It's not about me, Mother; it's about the politics of appropriation," Shoshanna had replied. "We have to take a symbol like a military uniform and appropriate it for the people. Shake the idolatry out of it. Remind the world that it's just a costume—cotton, wool, buttons, thread—and not a license for the U.S. to blast the Gulf of Tonkin to smithereens." She'd been a handful in those days, for which Leah took much of the credit. But those days were long gone.

Nonetheless, every year at least one of the Schmendriks reminded her of Shoshanna, the young Shoshanna who, with Leah's counsel, had grown from an unfocused ditz into a rebel with a mouth that could singe. The kid had been so remarkable in so many ways it was hard to understand how she could have degenerated into a lifestyle gumshoe for a bunch of lazy-assed Yuppies, a hired hand who spent her days tracking down British nannies and deer-proof perennials. What a waste!

Leah recalled a line from Anaïs Nin: "Life shrinks or expands in proportion to one's courage." Somewhere along the way, Shoshanna had lost hers. Someone or something had doused her fire, made her cautious and self-protective, though Shoshanna would surely have defined those same qualities as judiciousness and maturity. Moreover, she would undoubtedly point out that she was *happy*—a claim Leah could never quite make for herself, especially now that her family was such a disaster area. What mattered today was that Shoshanna had remembered that March 8 was International Woman's Day and cared enough to want to commemorate it with her sister. Leah had awakened thinking about the plight of women, who make up more than half the world's population but own only 1 percent of the world's property. At the moment, though, her immediate concern was that the radio was forecasting snow and she couldn't find her boots. Shit!

"Henry! Have you seen my galoshes?"

Silence.

"HENREEEEE!!??!!"

Heralded by slammed drawers and banged doors, her younger son emerged from the bedroom behind the kitchen in his plaid boxer shorts, hair tousled, feet bare, a Grateful Dead T-shirt skimming his flat stomach. The sight of him triggered her usual ambivalence, crosscurrents of love and letdown, admiration for his strong body, disdain for his weak ambition. Twenty-six years old and still mourning Jerry Garcia. His T-shirt wardrobe said it all; singers and sports teams, not Save the Whales. The boy had no politics.

She shoved the subway map into her backpack, then added today's *Times*, a book, and a Butterfinger bar. God forbid she should have an unrequited yen.

Rubbing sleep from his eyes, Henry shuffled across the flecked linoleum. "They're on the front stoop, Ma. They were muddy, remember?"

Double shit! After a night in the cold the boots would be frozen stiff. She opted for her black sneakers, which, conveniently, she'd left under the kitchen table with her socks stuffed inside.

Henry opened both doors of the side-by-side Hotpoint, arms outstretched—reminding Leah, unaccountably and against her will, of Sam standing at the open portals of the Holy Ark. The refrigerator contained packaged cold cuts, a bag of miniature Milky Way bars, a jar of Mother's gefilte fish, and a six-pack of cream soda—no surprises, given his mother's culinary predilections, yet he lingered there, condensation swirling around him, staring into the fridge and freezer as if deeply disappointed.

"No milk," he muttered. "Jesus Christ!"

"The only time you hear Jesus Christ in Brooklyn is when a Jew has a kvetch."

Slowly, very slowly, Henry opened the meat drawer. He threw her a sad look, though both of them knew perfectly well it would be empty. He flapped the front of the butter compartment, dug behind the jars of mustard, mayonnaise, and ketchup, peered into the vegetable crisper.

"Mmmmm." Using two fingers as a pincer, he extracted a limp, brown-tinged, barely recognizable lettuce leaf. Pause for dramatic effect. "Salad."

This was his ritual of late, and it pissed Leah off. "Close it, please," she said testily, lowering herself into a kitchen chair.

Henry rattled the tilt-out compartments. "Can't decide what to eat," he said, his silhouette backlit against the rectangle of cold white light.

Leah pulled on her socks. "Close the door, please, you're wasting energy." Wasting your life, she'd wanted to say.

He held up a plastic tray with twelve hollow craters. "How come we never have eggs in this house?" he asked laconically.

"You want 'em, lay 'em," she snapped. "Since when does your tenancy guarantee a lifetime supply of farm products? I don't remember signing on to the divine right of sons."

Even more than his indolence, she hated his arrogance. Yesterday, he'd announced, "We're out of toothpaste," as if the sun had failed to rise in the east.

"Is it too much to want some protein?" he asked. "Unprocessed wheat? Food that's green for reasons other than mold? Roughage maybe?"

"Spare me the New Age lecture, Henry. You'd have us eating the bark off the trees because it's fiber."

"Wrong, Ma. Who needs roughage when we have you?"

In the four months since he'd come home, he seemed to have reverted to adolescence. Slept until noon, brought home nameless women, ignored Leah altogether, or pelted her with putdowns. And lately his health-food mishegas had turned into this maddening daily charade before the refrigerator.

"Who the fuck gave you that disgusting sense of entitlement?" she replied, censoring everything else that needed saying.

"Must have been you, Madame Movement; you raised me. Or rather, Dad did, so I guess you're off the hook."

"To paraphrase Rebecca West, I find it interesting that a woman is called a feminist whenever she expresses sentiments that differentiate her from a doormat." She'd never been a haimishe housewife, why would she start now? Even when the boys were small, they'd pulled their own weight, following Leo's example; did their own laundry and more than their share of the housework. Truth be told, the three males had always been better than Leah at keeping decay at bay. Her idea of housecleaning was to sweep the room with a glance. Even then, she tended not to notice things like dust balls, mildew, staleness, rot. As Henry once put it, his mother was too busy changing the world to change the sheets. Leah accepted that assessment, was proud of it, in fact. High-maintenance men were the scourge of the earth and she'd be damned if that infuriating masculine combination of helplessness and dominance was going to rule the day in her house. She was nobody's maid.

"Something from each of the major food groups would be nice for a change," Henry persisted.

She thwacked one of her sneakers on the tabletop. "I said shut the fridge, Henry Blackwell Wasserman! *Enough!*"

Odd how she always invoked all three of his names when he baited her. Probably to remind him of the man he was supposed to emulate. She'd brought high aspirations to the act of naming both her sons. It was part of the pre-nup with Leo. They agreed to split the difference on Rose and Wasserman, but in return for shouldering nine months gestation plus labor and delivery, Leah would have sole control over both kids' first names. This was no newfangled idea, she'd reminded Leo. Eve named Cain, Jacob's wives named their children, and among Jews in the old country, their immediate forebears, baby-naming was often the mother's prerogative.

Leo had capitulated without a struggle and was mensch enough to do it in writing, giving her the only wedding gift she'd ever wanted—the power to name. She called it "Leo's lagniappe of love." That was before the clouds rolled in, when he was still playful and positive, his gentleness laced with whimsy, his art ablaze with sunyellows and sky-blues, the colors of Provence. Before strange questions began popping out of his mouth. "Do you ever feel like the loneliest person on earth?" he'd ask after they'd made love, or over coffee, or while she was writing. "Do you sometimes feel life is too hard to bear?"

"No, Leo, I do not. Nor do I confuse the edge of the rut with the horizon. Now snap out of it." Leo's depression had been deepening. More and more, she'd heard him disparage himself or wallow in pessimism about the future in general, his own in particular. In her worst moments, she suspected that her husband was not so much a has-been as a won't-be and maybe never-was. But back when everything was just beginning, she had believed as much in his talent as in her vision of their life together. He'd had no problem going along with the names she'd chosen for their boys, names that would add politics to their provenance and give them something to live up to—Frederick Douglass Rose, in honor of the great abolitionist, and Henry Blackwell Wasserman, for the patron saint of women's suffrage—important, inspiring names worthy of these sons of the Second Wave who were not guinea pigs for some theoretical utopia but beneficiaries of a living revolution. In the Wasserman-Rose household, fear was not feminine or anger masculine, courage had no sex, and it was all right for boys to cry. Raised on songs of protest, poems of liberation, and tales of female heroism, Frederick Douglass Rose and Henry Blackwell Wasserman learned to respect women and were well on their way to becoming New Men for a New Era. Leah had never understood what went wrong.

Her older son, Freddy, an even more flagrant travesty of *his* namesake, was currently serving five years for dealing dope from an ice cream truck. A vilde haya, that boy, a wild animal. This one, a nudnik who was always getting his life together, was still exploring his options, *finding* himself. What crap! At Henry's age, a person should be found already. He should get a job and move the hell out of his parents' house. So much for provenance. What's in a name? Bubkes.

She watched him open the cheese bin and recoil from an ashy wedge of Swiss.

"Finding yourself in there, boy?" She'd read about boomerang kids, grown children who'd been divorced or lost a job or a lease and suddenly reappeared back home, upsetting the equilibrium of their parents' marriage and wreaking havoc in the house. (Factoid according to Rachel: 12 percent of young adults in the twenty-five-to-twenty-nine age group are living at home.) Henry was a textbook case. Since moving in four months ago, he'd exhausted her patience, exacerbated his father's depression, and shaken up their household routines.

"Maybe you ought to explore your options somewhere other than in this piteously understocked kitchen," she ventured, speaking to his back. "By which I mean vacate the old homestead by April 1. How's them eggs?"

Leah watched him glare at her, then at the sneaker she'd left on the kitchen table, a Pop Art apparition alongside the sugar bowl and vitamin bottles. Everything seemed to be taunting her—her son, her shoe, her freezer.

He gestured toward the vertical tundra as ostentatiously as a magician displaying the innards of a black box. The freezer was host to a petrified lump of stewing meat, two encrusted bagels from God knows when, and an ice-cube tray shrouded in frost and bonded to its shelf. All spoke to her failings; each was a reproach. Henry gripped the ice tray with both hands and pulled back on his full weight, making much of the fact that the thing didn't budge.

Nareshkeit! He'd better stop this foolishness or else. As if he'd heard her, he released the tray and with an exaggerated lurch let his body recoil from the Hotpoint with the force of one grabbed from behind. Leah felt his movement in her body, in a sudden cell-deep shuddering that had her back in the sweltering kitchen in South Boston in front of the open Frigidaire, Dena pouncing from behind, the clomp of her wooden clogs, the sweat oozing from her patent-leather hair, her body pressing Leah's back against the sill, the upside-down view of the street five stories below, the rough brick wall, the fury in her mother's coal-black eyes. As suddenly as it came, the image passed, leaving her mind stunned by its power to slice through fifty years of scar tissue and strike bone. What triggered the flashback, she suspected, was not just the parallel image of Henry at the fridge but a parallel impulse—the urge to grab her farbissener son and throw him out the window.

She'd taken him in out of pity, the same reason Esther had let her stay at West End Avenue. Henry had been here nearly four months and (she'd never realized this before) she'd stayed four months, too, sought refuge at the Wassermans' in a moment of weakness and overstayed her welcome, unsettling the household with her slovenly habits and bold defiance. But there were differences. At twenty-seven she'd earned a Ph.D., was ambitious and self-sufficient, was teaching and writing; all she'd needed was a roof over her head until her apartment was ready. Nothing like Henry, who, seemingly launched for good after graduation, had crashed back into earth's atmosphere trailing spumes of failure, with not a shekel to his name and no prospects. She'd been a pain in the ass; Henry was an asshole. History seemed to be repeating itself in parody.

In truth, Leah allowed, her reentry was probably the more discomposing. When she boomeranged back, she'd done more than insult her father's pantry or let the cold out of his freezer. Her very presence threatened to puncture the Wasserman myth and expose the family's secrets. A cousin, they'd said, when they introduced her to their friends. A cousin from Cleveland. Leah didn't have to lie about Henry. All she had to do was accept him, and she couldn't even pull that off. While pondering the challenge, however, she'd noticed in herself an utterly unfamiliar and entirely unwelcome emotion—sympathy for her father, for what she must have put him through, and for Esther, who'd died feeling guilty, though none of it was her fault.

Not being one of those disingenuous types who always seem surprised by the impact of their actions on others, Leah knew while it was happening how much she'd wounded Esther and Sam. Having lured their precious Shoshanna out of their closed universe with its eternal verities (women's place, father's way, God's laws) and spun her into a cosmos with no rules, Leah was well aware that she'd turned her little sister into an insurrectionist, a mutineer against family and faith; not purposely, yet when it happened, the sweet taste in her mouth was Sam's just deserts.

Maybe her boomerang boy was payback for all that. Maybe life was predestined after all, ribbons of inevitability spiraling through the generations, entangling and inescapable. With each of her pregnancies, she'd vowed to be a good mother, better by far than the deranged Dena, and to raise her boys to be better men than Sam, who'd been a macher in the world but an emotional midget at home. She'd come up short on both counts. Motherhood had bored or defeated her, the minutiae driving her to distraction, the baby mess compounding her own natural tendency to disorder. And her sons had turned out as self-centered as her father, not as successful as Sam but just as solipsistic, just as smug and superior, especially toward women. Leah was resigned to Freddy the Felon being a lost cause, but with Henry, she'd held out hope, even though—apart from his seemingly effortless sexual conquests—everything he touched turned to dreck. An archaeology major, he'd signed onto a dig in the Negev but ended up on a kibbutz near the Golan Heights impregnating a seventeen-year-old Sabra whom the kibbutz governing board decided he should marry. That night, he was history. Back in New York, he'd joined an experimental theater troupe whose cast invariably outnumbered the audience, then hooked up with a traveling circus, a mangy collection of animal trainers and clowns who schlepped around the hinterlands for pennies and the right to shovel elephant dung. Massage therapy was his last gig—a complete fiasco for which Leah blamed herself, since she'd staked him to the training course. He'd managed to land a job at some chic spa, but quit after a month. Said he hated touching the flesh of strange men. Clearly, he had no such problem with strange women. A veritable May dance of chastity-challenged damsels had waltzed in and out of his room since he'd moved back. He never seemed to go anywhere with them, just bedded them behind the kitchen wall and bid them adieu in the morning.

"I can't tolerate your lubricious misogyny," she'd said the other day after one of his sleepover dates slipped out the door. "You're nothing but a sexual predator."

"Lay off the big words, Ma. If the girls have no problem with it, why should you?"

She knew why. Because his behavior had made her—conscience of the women's movement and role model to the multitudes—an enabler, a passive witness to the exploitation of young women under her own roof. "Because you're *my* son," she said, looking into his eyes without flinching. And indeed, objectively, this son of hers was wonderful to look at: Michelangelo's *David* in life tones, blessed with a halo of ringlets, high cheekbones, aquiline nose, broad chest, long, strong fingers. In someone else's family, he'd get points for all that. Being a beautiful boy would have been enough.

"Eureka!" he boomed in mock rapture. She saw his arm muscles tense beneath his skin as he hauled out the orange juice and drank it straight from the carton.

"Saved by Tropicana," Leah said. "Guess I'm not a *complete* failure." Watching him guzzle the juice, she wanted to hold him, felt a rumble of sorrow for his small rebellions and her doomed prayers. If only she could offer unconditional love to her children instead of this incessant judgmental disdain.

Leah, who lived the examined life whether or not it was worth living, saw a pattern, a family dynamic that had repeated itself in their lives, tripping them up and tying them together one generation to another. As her son's conduct was offensive to her, so hers had been to Sam. Similarly, Freddy's antisocial behavior and Henry's laconic hostility had torn the fabric of her family in much the same way as her provocations and unmitigated chutzpah had disturbed the peace of Sam's household. And though she was loath to analogize too closely, it seemed all too obvious that her sons' simmering resentments and her own sprang from the same source—the conviction that each held a low priority in a parent's heart. All three had followed a parent's example but pushed it to extremes: Leah by becoming more accomplished than her father, her sons by becoming more defiant than she. Going too far was the best revenge.

The family pattern had been out there in plain view, yet she'd missed it until now, the way she'd once failed a visual acuity test, an optical puzzle one of her Schmendriks brought to class to trick her into acknowledging the limits of her perceptiveness. It was a black-and-white drawing of a bearded man, but the student insisted it was also the figure of a naked woman. Leah stared at the picture for more than a minute before she could see the female form embedded in the man's profile. But having found it, she could never again look at the drawing without both images flickering before her eyes. Sometimes an insight can be an albatross.

Henry closed the doors of the Hotpoint, padded over to a cabinet, riffled through bags of half-eaten cookies, pretzels, and chips, and settled on a box of Fig Newtons, which he tore open with his teeth.

"Great breakfast, Mom," he said, raising the juice container as if in a toast and popping a fig bar in his mouth.

"Figs have iron," she offered as her son sauntered out the door. He turned back and smiled at her, not cruelly this time but with a look that seemed to acknowledge their mutual regrets.

Sitting there, lacing her sneakers, Leah told herself that boomerangs are made to come back and Henry had returned for a reason: To force her to think new thoughts like the one that struck her now: Though she had never abandoned her children, they were profoundly estranged from her. She'd nursed the boys, wiped their butts, seen them through puberty and holy hell—but she didn't really *know* them. And to be brutally honest, when they were dependent, raucous, and so damned time-consuming, she'd thought of bailing out more than once. Dreamed of running away to a women's commune, where she could write and think in peace. Considered giving Leo custody. Those were the afternoons when she'd called home, fabricated an excuse, and stayed late at the library in the company of Jane Austen and Emily Dickinson rather than return to *Fox in Sox* and the chaos of her children's bedtimes. But she'd never left them; she'd stuck it out. She would not be their Sam.

Now the ironies were in the fire. Her boys had left *her*. Sure, Henry was back, but only in body, and Freddy was long gone. The sons had abandoned their mother, forsaken her by refusing to be intellectuals or exemplary feminist men, by transforming themselves from good little boys into grungy male malcontents, by disappointing her, rejecting her, embracing other gods. They'd done to her as she'd done to Sam. And she to them. And Sam to her. Abandonment was yet another motif, another pattern embedded in the picture. In families, no one is merely an individual; each member is always mucking up everyone else's storyline.

She tucked her trouser cuffs into her socks and drained the last of her juice from the yahrzeit glass. (Every Holocaust Remembrance Day, she lit a memorial candle and saved the glass. Her yahrzeit glasses were her crystal set.) Leaning both hands on the table, she eased her weight onto her bum hip. It was a killer, this trip to Manhattan. To reach midtown by 12:30, she had to be out of the house by 11, leaving time for the hike to the station and the long subway ride. Yet she always did her sister's bidding for fear an objection to Shoshanna's chosen lunch locations would be interpreted as an admission of weakness, emphysema, or hip pain, and inspire one of her sister's godawful health lectures. Still, Leah wished Shoshanna would take the subway for a change and see the world from this side of the river. Brooklyn had restaurants, some damn good ones, and the old neighborhood might ring bells in her psyche. She was born here, for Chrissake.

Shoshanna's crib had been wedged at the foot of the double-decker bed in the room Leah had shared with Rachel in the apartment on Prospect Park where, for one short, shimmering time, they'd lived together as a family. Those were the only childhood memories Leah could revisit without cringing, fond associations that probably accounted for her having returned to Brooklyn as an adult and feeling at home here for the last thirty years. Ill matched though she might seem with her environment—an atheist in the Borough of Churches, an editor running an international feminist magazine from an office near the old Ebbets Field—Brooklyn was her turf. Except for cultural or academic expeditions across the river and lunches with Shoshanna, her attitude was, why leave?

Right now, escaping Henry was a good enough reason. She limped to the closet and put on the blanket cape she'd bought by mail from a Native American reservation. Aha! The cape wasn't black, either, but tan with geometric medallions in maroon and brown. It was her first new coat in years and, compared to the flea-market garments she was used to, felt like mink. She was admiring it when Henry reappeared, holding both hands behind his back like a bemused barrister. He took in the Indian cape with a grin.

"Cool coat, Mom. Betcha there's a Cherokee out there in the Great Plains saying, Hey, where's my curtains?"

"The revolution isn't over, Henry."

"Excuse me? Your cape has something to do with the war on sexism, capitalism, and racial injustice? I must have missed something."

She decided to take him seriously. "Ralph Lauren copies tribal designs and charges an arm and a leg. Do you think he's paying royalties? I choose to buy directly and contribute to the economy of indigenous peoples."

"You never give up, do you, Mom?"

"I happen to believe small gestures add up."

She was surprised when he didn't answer back, just stood there looking at her, then brought from behind his back an offering.

"Your galoshes, madam." He'd retrieved them from the front stoop. They looked calcified, the toes turned up, the leather salt-stained and chalky, but in her son's hands they were ruby slippers. Her throat tightened.

"Thank you," she said, and put them on.

eight

IT WAS MORE THAN THREE MILES from the brownstone in Greenwich Village to the Café Bretagne but Shoshanna decided to hike it. She'd promised Rachel she would add physical activity to her sit-down life, and after much discussion of the alternatives, all of which Shoshanna found odious, she'd agreed to walk a few miles a day, twice a week, moved to accept this simple regimen by the illogic of her monitoring the Evil Eye and strategizing against the one-in-a-million catastrophe, while ignoring the basic rules for health and longevity. Walking would not only keep the weight off, Rachel said, it would ratchet up her energy level. Today, Shoshanna needed all the verve she could muster to stay alert through lunch. Were she to nod off over her mushroom crêpe, she'd never hear the end of it. Leah took everything personally.

Her sleep deprivation was Daniel's fault, the result of his pre-dawn erection. "Is His Hardness trying to tell me something?" she'd murmured, dimly aware of his insistent snuggling. She'd angled her morning breath into the pillow to spare him a direct hit, but he'd sought her mouth, kissed her deeply, even rolled his tongue across her teeth, delighting her, as always, with the pleasure he took in her tastes and smells, her juices.

"You played me like a cellist," she said afterward.

"Janos Starker or Yo-Yo Ma?"

Blessed Daniel. He could always make her laugh—after sex, before, during, when she was overwhelmed, anytime at all. More than fancy love language, it was his humor, his quirky take on life, that Shoshanna found irresistible. She was his best audience. "Honey, you make me feel six feet tall," he'd say, when he *was* six feet tall. "I found the only woman in the world whose erogenous zone is her funny bone." She loved that he was sexy *and* funny, traits often incompatible in a man. In fact, Shoshanna loved everything about him—his rangy limbs and high arches, the spaniel eyes, the tousled hair, everything except his maddening mindlessness, which she'd have sworn was certifiable. On paper, they were Felix and Oscar, she compulsively organized, he the quintessential absentminded professor who wasted ten minutes every day of his life looking for his keys. Though surprised anew by each episode of forgetfulness, and freshly distressed every time he "lost" his reading glasses, he'd nonetheless proven incapable of reform. God knows, Shoshanna had tried. Countless times the lioness had entered Daniel's den and pawed through his files—alphabetizing, organizing, sorting through his desk, his mail, his journals—but no system she'd ever devised had lasted more than a week. Admitting defeat, she'd contented herself with caging her husband's chaos behind closed doors.

Now, walking up Eighth Avenue—nearly two miles into her trek—she remembered his two cellists and laughed out loud, attracting no notice at all as she approached the Port Authority Bus Terminal, where self-generated revelry was the norm. At Fortieth Street, she became aware of a crowd milling around near the taxi stand, a women's demonstration, something she hadn't seen in a long time. A lovely young black woman in hoop earrings and a headdress made of kinte cloth was pacing before a mounted display, tear sheets from a pornographic magazine. "*Hustler* hurts women!" she shouted into a megaphone that looked as if it had once belonged to a cheerleader. "Snuff out snuff porn!" The pictures showed a naked woman being shoved headfirst into a meat grinder and coming out raw hamburger; a woman's body trussed like a carcass and strapped across the hood of a car; a close-up of a man's hand holding a straight razor to a woman's nipple.

"Don't let our agony be their ecstasy! Violent pornography is not a victimless crime!" cried another, a fresh-faced Alice in Wonderland who should have been shielded from her own exhibits. Though grateful for the courage of today's feminists, Shoshanna was even more nostalgic for the movement's glory years, when such a demonstration would not have been exceptional or the crowd so small. Crossing Forty-second Street, she suppressed a fierce longing for her own past, missed being part of a group, missed the sit-downs and speak-outs, the campaigns and marches, the battle of ideas, the struggle. For a split second she yearned for the movement as if it were a lover.

Political demonstrations were major productions in those days, as elaborate in the planning as *Cats* or *Phantom of the Opera* or any of the Broadway shows whose marquees and stage doors she was passing in the theater district. She remembered the Miss America Pageant in Atlantic City where women threw bras, girdles, curlers, hair dye, false eyelashes, and high heels into a "freedom trash can" (no one ever burned a bra) and paraded a live ram along the boardwalk to the strains of "There She Is, Miss America." And the picket line in front of *The New York Times* to protest its sex-segregated classified ads (Shoshanna's sign said THE TIMES IS A SEX OFFENDER). The press conference announcing a boycott of Colgate-Palmolive for its discriminatory job policies. ("The White Knight Is a Dirty Old Man!") The abortion-rights rally in Union Square where she'd heard Bella Abzug and Gloria Steinem for the first time.

Once a week back then, Shoshanna attended meetings of Wednesday's Women, first in Rachel's—no Leah's—room in the West End Avenue apartment, and later in Leah's walk-up on Gay Street in Greenwich Village. Her "pad" eventually become the headquarters for *The Feminist Freethinker* and for Wednesday's Women, whose agenda embraced both consciousness-raising and political organizing. After Leah moved out, Shoshanna, suffering Leah-withdrawal, took the Broadway local down to Gay Street two or three times a week to lend a hand to whatever project was on the ironing board, which had never been utilized for its domestic purpose. Esther's housewarming gift (which Leah took to be a hint, the product of a Jewish mother's wishful thinking) served the group as an all-purpose work surface, sometimes laden with feminist literature, some-times with a can of tuna, its sharp lid still rakishly attached, or a box of Ritz crackers and a jar of peanut butter. Sticky plates and stained coffee cups languished in the sink from one week to the next, unnoticed until a receptacle was needed for the next combination of snacks that Leah might call "supper." Wednesday's Women, taking a cue from their leader, were oblivious to disarray. They were building a utopian world, and Shoshanna, a valued member of the work crew, was learning the tools of the trade. During months of shared activism, she felt that she and Leah had become as close as . . . as sisters. And if Leah's Hanukkah gift that year could be read symbolically, she apparently felt the same.

"My Sisterly Seal of Approval," she said as she slipped a silver ring on each of Shoshanna's fingers (including the thumb).

"Omigod, it's your trademark, Leah! I don't deserve them."

"Consider it my hecksher." Leah clicked her own ringed fingers against Shoshanna's. "If you don't deserve them now, you will before I'm done with you."

("Silver-plated brass knuckles," said Rachel when she saw them. "Watch out who you hurt with those things.")

The opportunity to prove herself arose sooner than Shoshanna expected. When the National Organization for Women was founded, Wednesday's Women saw fit to declare it an "elitist counterrevolution-ary force that would blunt the radical message of feminism." Leah decided they should make their views known to the public by picket-ing NOW's next event. The challenge was to distill WW's complex cri-tique into a message that would be comprehensible and appealing to the masses. While the group was batting around different slogans, Shoshanna was on the phone with her other sister.

"Did you see NOW's press conference on TV? Wasn't it great! Weren't those women something!" Rachel was clearly over the top about it.

"What was so great?" asked Shoshanna.

"Well, I thought they were speaking directly to me! I agreed with everything they said. Their message made me mad, but it wasn't scary."

In a flash, Shoshanna saw that the difference between the two organizations could be summed up by the reactions of her two sisters. NOW—critical of the status quo but unthreatening—spoke for Rachel. Wednesday's Women—the shake-up-the-power-structure alternative—spoke for Leah. The difference, pointillist in detail but ham-fisted in effect, suggested an image. Shoshanna grabbed one of Leah's fountain pens and dashed off a sketch of an aproned housewife (wearing pearls like Rachel's) slicing a pie in quarters while a woman dressed in black (who looked a lot like Leah) was putting a match to a stick of dynamite under the pie plate.

"NOW WANTS A BIGGER PIECE OF THE PIE," she printed in the bubble over the picture. "WE WANT A WHOLE NEW PIE!"

"Hey! Hey! Hey!" exclaimed Leah, "Genius! Pure genius!" It was her highest accolade.

Not only did WW mimeograph hundreds of copies and hand them out at the next NOW meeting, they also mailed it to their entire press list, enlarged it onto a sign, colored it in, and mounted it on the door of the Gay Street apartment.

She hit the nail on the head a second time when Wednesday's Women decided they need a stronger name, one that didn't sound like a ladies' garden club or book review circle. Leah opened the floor to suggestions.

"Womanifesto!" said one member.

"Sisters in Struggle," put forth another.

"RadicaLadies."

"Babes and Bitches."

"Lysistrata's Daughters."

"They're all excellent," said Leah. "Let's take a vote."

"Wait!" Shoshanna grabbed her bookbag, pulled out *The Collected Works of Sarah and Angelina Grimké*, and began leafing through it.

Leah tapped her fingers on the ironing board. "The Grimkés are Hall of Famers, kiddo, but what do nineteenth-century feminist-abolitionists have to do with our new name?"

Shoshanna found the passage and read aloud: " 'I ask no favors for my sex . . . All I ask of our brethren is, that they will take their feet from off our necks and permit us to stand upright on that ground which God designed us to occupy.' Sarah Grimké. 1837." She paused. "I propose we call ourselves 'Off Our Necks.'"

The reactions were instantaneous.

"Off Our Necks? What kind of name is that for an organization?"

"Nice quote, but stilted."

"I dig the historical connection, but who's going to understand it?"

Leah leapt from her lotus position, nearly knocking over the eucalyptus candle. "I *love* it! Strong, declarative, resonant, original. The phrase has yichus, it links us with the First Wave. Explaining it, we'll educate people." She turned to Shoshanna. "Can you give us an image to go with it?"

A supine woman, fist in the air, shaking a man's boot off her neck. The cartoon said it all. The vote was close, but Off Our Necks won in a runoff and Shoshanna's drawing became the group's logo. She copied her sketch onto a huge poster, the sign they would rally under at the upcoming antiwar demonstration in Central Park, the big enchilada. Now she'd earned the rings.

The first Sunday in November dawned gray and blustery. But by nine in the morning, the Sheep Meadow in the park had been transformed into an urban beach party with colorful bedspreads and grungy blankets laid out edge to edge like a giant patchwork quilt. Women nursed their babies in the open. Hippies played guitar or rolled joints. Bottles of wine were emptied before noon. New arrivals looked for helium balloons tied to belt loops and baby strollers to locate their families, schools, unions, fraternities, and "affinity groups." Though the demonstration was called as a protest against the Vietnam War, a variety of cause-related organizations took the opportunity to trumpet their messages to the huge crowd. Off Our Necks commandeered a patch of scrubby turf at the southwest corner of the meadow and set up a folding table loaded with feminist literature, each pile secured by a rock. A sack of apples, a giant Hershey bar, and a couple of six-packs of beer were stashed under the table, sustenance for a long afternoon. Leah's portable radio was reporting two hundred thousand people in the park. To Shoshanna, it looked like a million.

"Down with sexism! Equality now!" the women of Off Our Necks bellowed between blasts of the PA system. "Women should make policy, not coffee!" they chanted as they hawked their pamphlets and solicited signatures on a petition asking the New York State Legislature to legalize abortion. Their table attracted the already committed and the merely curious, women eager to join the group on the spot, and men who stopped to bait and debate. Leah, the rapid-response expert, was the group's first line of defense against the hecklers.

To the man who shouted, "You're all a bunch of lesbians!" Leah yelled back, "What are you? Our alternative?"

When someone called out, "Crackpots!" she answered. "One step ahead, I'm a genius; two steps ahead, I'm a crackpot. Let's hear it for the cracked pots!"

A woman who identified herself as a member of the Jewish Defense League asked Leah her religion.

"Born-again feminist."

The woman frowned. "Where does it get you, this female separatism? You should be working for our people."

"When women get together, it's separatism and bad, but when Jews get together, it's Zionism and good? You ought to rethink that one, sister. Women are your people, too. May I remind you that only 2.5 percent of Americans are Jews but more than half of American Jews are women. So why aren't you working for *us*?"

If Leah was the battleship, Shoshanna was the Statue of Liberty. All afternoon she held up her drawing of a woman throwing off the boot, while chanting a paraphrase of Sarah Grimké's line: "We ask no favors for our sex / Just take men's feet from off our necks." She lifted the heavy placard until the blood drained from her arms, then lowered it, shook her arms until her circulation returned, then started the process all over again—up-down, up-down, hour after hour. By 4 p.m., her arms were dead weights. The harangues from the stage had become white noise:

U.S. imperialism, capitalist warmongering, military-industrial complex, blah, blah, blah. The wind knifed through her windbreaker and two layers of sweaters. She was tired and cranky. The day had lost its luster.

"I have to leave," she said, handing the poster to Leah.

"How so?"

What should she say? Tired arms? She'd sound like a spoiled princess. Homework? Too self-centered. Mom wants me home by dark? A lie, and infantilizing besides. Thinking fast, Shoshanna assumed a worldly wise tone and replied, "I'm sick of carrying water for the male antiwar movement. Have you heard any of their speakers talk about women? When they come out for our demonstrations, I'll be back for theirs."

Leah steepled her eyebrows and glared. "Nothing wrong with being a know-it-all unless that's *all* you know. Fuck the speakers, Shoshanna. *We* know why we're here. Militarism abroad, machismo at home. Violence begets violence. Only a cretin could miss the connection." She turned away as if the sight of this pathetic quitter was making her sick.

Shoshanna kicked at an empty Marlboro box and rubbed her aching arms. "Okay, give it back," she said, reaching for the poster.

"Forget it. Take these." Leah slammed a stack of yellow flyers against the girl's chest.

"And . . . ?"

"And hand them out, cretin."

The headline on the flyer said: "DON'T BUY BOMBS WHEN YOU BUY BREAD! Boycott Wonder Bread, Profile Bread, Hostess Cupcakes, Twinkies, Morton's Frozen Foods. These products are made by Continental Baking Company, a wholly owned subsidiary of IT&T."

So that was why Leah had stopped eating Twinkies.

"What if someone asks me what IT&T is doing wrong?" Dumb question. Knew it the second it left her mouth.

"Maybe you *should* go home. At least until your IQ rises above room temperature." Leah grabbed a flyer and read aloud from the small print, didactically, like a teacher explaining why rain falls: " 'IT&T manufactures components for the electronic battlefield in Southeast Asia. IT&T makes the equipment that guides the bombers to their targets. IT&T's

sensors cannot tell the difference between women, children, and soldiers. Say No to IT&T. Boycott Wonder Bread, Profile . . .'"

"All right, already." Shoshanna snatched the flyers and plunged into the crowd, waving one yellow sheet in front of her and praying someone would take it. Someone did, an elderly woman who read a few lines, then tucked the paper into her purse as if it mattered, as if she would study it later. Encouraged by her interest, Shoshanna yelled, "Read what IT&T is doing in Southeast Asia. Boycott Wonder bread, Twinkies, Hostess cupcakes." A bearded man with a headband took one, then a woman wearing bell-bottoms with miniature American flags sewn on each knee, a WASP-y guy in a Sherlock Holmes cap, and a parade of long-hairs who yelled "Groovy!" or "Right on!" whenever she said the word "cupcakes." On the PA system someone was lambasting Lyndon Johnson. The air smelled of marijuana and burning draft cards. When the last sheet was gone, she wended her way back to the corner of the Sheep Meadow and, drawing closer, heard a new chant:

OFF OUR NECKS! OFF OUR NECKS!

OFF OUR NECKS OR NO MORE SEX!

With Shoshanna's poster as their backdrop, the group formerly known as Wednesday's Women had arranged themselves chorus line–style, arms linked, legs kicking in unison to the rhythm of the chant. A phalanx of reporters was pitching questions at Leah while TV crews and still photographers jostled for position. Leah, spotting Shoshanna, called, "Author! Author!" as she shepherded the girl toward the press.

"They *love* your drawing, kiddo," she whispered into Shoshanna's hair. "It's going to put us on the map." Kiddo again. No more cretin. To the reporters she announced, "This is my sister, Shoshanna Miriam Wasserman. It's her drawing and her slogan."

As the cameras closed in, Shoshanna had only one thought: Leah knew her middle name.

Their chorus line made the eleven o'clock news on all three networks. A shot of the poster went out on the wires and appeared on the front page of the *Daily News* with the headline RADICAL ROCKETTES KICK A – –. Off Our Necks got a sidebar of its own in *Time* magazine with a picture of the Wasserman sisters and a historical note on the Grimké sisters. In a matter of days, "Off Our Necks or No More Sex" had become the chant of choice at women's events all over the country, and Shoshanna's illustration—which had materialized overnight on buttons, posters, T-shirts, and tote bags—had begun to rival the female biological sign with a clenched fist in the middle as the symbol of women's liberation. Even Rachel was impressed. Shoshanna's poster was for sale at her mall.

"It pisses me off that someone's making money on all this and you're not," groused Leah, sounding like a running dog of capitalism.

Shoshanna smiled. "It's okay. Neither are the Grimké sisters."

She turned east on Forty-ninth Street in the direction of the café, still reliving the Days of Rage when Leah became her closest comrade and Rachel almost a stranger, a fact that had been embarrassingly palpable when the family gathered for Sunday dinner at Rachel and Jeremy's house and several of them got into an argument about whether biology or environment exerted the stronger influence on human development. Shoshanna, a high school senior at the time, came down on the side of biology. "It explains why Leah and I are so alike," she said ingenuously. "It doesn't matter that we weren't raised together. We both have Dad's genes and we both inherited his intellect." Years later, Shoshanna recognized not only the cruelty of her words but how foolish she'd been to abandon her solid suburban sister in favor of the fiery, flashy one. But that Sunday night, the young Shoshanna was oblivious when Rachel quietly excused herself from the table, then came back red-eyed. And for a long time she was unaware of Leah's campaign to alienate her from their other sister.

When Shoshanna returned from one of her increasingly rare sleepovers on Long Island, for instance, Leah asked, "Have fun?"

"Uh-huh."

"What'd you do there?"

"Played with the kids. Babysat when Rachel drove to the train to pick up Jeremy."

"Woody station wagon?"

"Yeah! How'd you know?"

"What else happened in paradise?"

"We had a barbecue in the back yard."

"A barbecue!" said Leah. "Is that when the woman buys the groceries, washes the lettuce, chops the tomatoes, dices the onions, marinates the meat, and cleans up afterward, and the man throws the steaks on the grill?"

"I guess so."

"Then what?

"He had to go to a meeting. I helped Rachel bathe the kids. Read them stories. Then we watched *Gunsmoke*."

Shoshanna was well into her twenties before she heard Rachel's side of it. "You were so disdainful of my life. I thought I'd lost you for good."

She was almost at the restaurant. Passing the gilded Prometheus at Rockefeller Center, Shoshanna couldn't help recalling the night she and Leah scaled the statue and unfurled Off Our Necks' banner: WOMEN OF THE WORLD UNITE! YOU HAVE NOTHING TO LOSE BUT YOUR CHAINS! If Prometheus reminded her of Leah, the ice rink would forever be associated with Rachel, who, when Shoshanna was four and dressed in a bunting that made her look like a knee-high snowball, taught her to skate here, starting her off on double runners strapped to her shoes. It seemed to take forever before she graduated to single blades and a satin skating costume, though Rachel swore Shoshanna was suited up in sequins and acquitting herself quite respectably by the time she was five. Dear, patient Rachel. How bewildered she must have been— this natural athlete whose supple body always did her bidding—at having to demonstrate every movement dozens of times before her clumsy little pupil could even approximate it. But she'd stuck with the enterprise, devoted nearly every winter weekend to it that first year, drilling, coaxing, praising, correcting, until Shoshanna's figure eights made Sonja Henie's look like sevens.

Shoshanna checked her watch: 12:10. This walking business was easier than she'd anticipated. Twenty minutes to spare and the café was only blocks away. Plenty of time to hang out and watch the skaters. She wasn't sure which were more diverting, the weak-ankled novices hanging on to the rail and each other or the graceful pros performing complicated routines at the center the oval. She zeroed in on the show-offs, the backward racer, the twirling demon, the girl with the muff. Even now, she could measure up to the best of them. Except, maybe, for the one in red. Technically dazzling, weightless as a butterfly, the woman couldn't be missed even if she weren't wearing that close-fitting Valentine-red jacket with the black fur collar and cuffs, and that tiny black circle skirt whose red lining flashed like a tongue with each turn. Her hair was honey-blond, shoulder-length, crowned with a black headband. She was so breathtakingly lovely, her skating so fluid and buoyant, that it was a while before Shoshanna noticed her partner.

Jeremy! Rachel's Jeremy, looking even more distinguished than usual in a white cable-knit turtleneck and slender black pants, his hair silvery and thick, like a cap of soft icicles. The red queen was far younger than he (late thirties, maybe forty) but nearly as tall, with legs as long as winter. They were waltzing to "Garden in the Rain," his arm around her waist, hers stretched across his chest, hands clasped in front and behind though neither needed help staying balanced. Rounding the bend as one body, their legs moved like currents in a stream, swirling sideways and whooshing forward, ankle over ankle, blade over blade, skimming the blue ice.

Their eyes never left each other's face until, coasting down the length of the oval, they kissed and smiled and kissed again, then separated only long enough for him to twirl her like a vase on a potter's wheel and swivel her back into his arms without nicking an edge.

High above the rink on the observation deck, it was Shoshanna who hung on to the rail, wobbly-ankled, as the song ended and the skating couple skidded to a stop, blades gleaming, an ice storm grinding in their wake. They kissed again, longer this time, commanding the center of the rink with the authority of the bride and groom at the top of a wedding cake. Around them, the other skaters awaited the next piece of music fidgety in their idleness, practicing their turns, tightening their laces, or wiping the frost from their runners, while the woman in red planted one blade tip in the ice like a ballet toe shoe and stood with her head erect, her body poised in a kind of alert serenity, a heron in a flock of jittery ducks. When the PA system poured forth Frank Sinatra singing "I've Got You Under My Skin," she flew back into Jeremy's arms.

Watching them made Shoshanna feel like a voyeur in a boudoir closet, yet she could not turn away. Her outrage seemed an ugly thing beside their erotic pantomime. Her muscles felt the athleticism of their grand jetés, the liquidity of their glides and turns, the serifs at the close of each carved figure as they coasted and curled around each other, sinewy whorls of red, black, and white, their hair blown back like wings, his silver, her gold.

Who was this woman? Secretary? Colleague? Maybe a client, since he seemed to be far more attentive to her than he'd ever been to his wife or anyone else in the family. Jeremy was the sort of man whose mind wanders when he isn't talking. She'd known that about him since she was six.

When he came to the apartment to pick up Rachel for their first date, he'd asked Shoshanna the questions everyone asks little girls: "How's school?" "Where'd you get that pretty dress?" "What's the name of your doll?" But unlike her big sister's other boyfriends, who'd listened as if everything she said was astoundingly clever, Jeremy paid no attention to her answers. She'd thought it strange at the time because his ears were kind of big so he should have been able to hear things better than anyone. She'd also hated his calling her "sis"—suspected he couldn't remember her name—but decided to forgive him when he gave her a set of Kidsmetics, with *real* lipstick and perfume, the same night he gave Rachel a ring. And because she got to be flower girl at their wedding.

As she grew older, she noticed that Jeremy didn't pay much attention to adults, either, unless they were interested in what interested him, which was mostly his cases—personal injury, products liability, medical malpractice. At family gatherings Rachel, well aware of her husband's social deficiencies and eager to keep him from dropping out of the conversation altogether, would make reference to a matter he was working on, and someone else, usually Daniel, picking up Rachel's signal, would ask him about the case. Invariably, then, Jeremy would perk up like a watered plant, become quite animated, and talk about his client—the victim of a defective toy or a bungling surgeon who amputated the wrong leg—and amplify the facts so the questioner understood what was at stake. When you reacted sympathetically to the wrong that had been done, or engaged the details of his argument, Jeremy listened—lasered in on you with those sky-blue eyes, tilted his handsome head and cocked his Clark Gable ears, and made you feel like the most important person in the room, someone who might very well have a new perspective on the case that would alter his tactics or help him convince a jury that his client could be made whole only by being awarded several million dollars.

Shoshanna couldn't fathom what her sister saw in him until the night his lasers were turned her way. It happened in the ballroom of the Pierre Hotel, where the Brents were hosting a dinner dance following their son Gideon's bar mitzvah. ("Nouveau riche excess," proclaimed Leah, who hadn't been invited, but Shoshanna, then a college student, found the celebration quite "glam.") After he made the motzi over the hallah, Gideon returned to the kids' table while Jeremy and Rachel had the first dance. Then, following family tradition, Jeremy took each of the female relatives onto the dance floor in order of seniority. When it was her turn, Shoshanna, knowing his taciturn indifference, prepared herself for an awkward and interminable fox trot. To her amazement, her brother-in-law, who looked even handsomer in his tuxedo, not only danced like Fred Astaire but started a conversation.

"You'd be interested in the case I'm working on now, Shoshanna."

"Really? Why?" Glancing up, she noticed that his bow tie wasn't one of those pre-set winged numbers held in place by a hook but was a satin sash that had been tied by hand. And unlike the Old Spice crowd, he smelled from lemon and pipe tobacco.

"Because you're a women's libber and it's a rape case."

That he knew she was a feminist—that anything she did had registered on his consciousness, much less been given a label—and understood that rape was her issue was incredible to her. She looked up again, bow tie, Pepsodent teeth, flared nostrils, to the arctic eyes that had always seemed hard as blue marbles, and in them found a hot orange flame.

"I didn't realize your practice included criminal defense cases," she said, wanting him to know she knew the difference between his usual caseload and a rape case. But obviously she didn't know enough.

"Hold on! I'm not defending the rapist, I'm representing the victim. It's a civil action. We're suing the housing project where my client lives. But I think women's lib ought to be following this case like any other high-profile rape trial. Most of the tenants are poor women and kids, and the security in these projects is a joke. The guy got into my client's apartment like a steak knife cuts through cream cheese. She never had a chance."

Shoshanna nearly tripped over Jeremy's feet. "Oh God! Did he kill her?" She unlocked from his laser gaze and concentrated on her footwork. His shoes were black patent leather with a grosgrain bow where the laces should be.

"Not quite. Held a gun to her head, tied her to the bedposts, pillowcase over her face, raped her for a couple of hours, put out his cigarettes on her breasts, but left her alive. She'll never be the same, though, and it wouldn't have happened if the city gave a damn. All they had to do was put a guard at the entrance and a chain lock on every door. But they don't give a damn about the safety of poor people. They don't care if a poor woman gets raped. People who live in the projects, they're garbage."

Shoshanna flashed on the time Jeremy and Rachel were driving her back to the city after an overnight visit, and as they crossed the Triborough

Bridge, Rachel, pointing out a grim complex of brick buildings in upper Manhattan, had said, "The one on the end's where Jeremy grew up."

"Look, Shoshie! There's the Empire State Building!" Jeremy had burst out, as if she hadn't been looking at the thing practically every day of her life. Obviously he was trying to distract her, and obviously Rachel tuned into his discomfort, because suddenly she was spouting factoids like an automated tour bus.

"The Empire State Building was completed in 1931. Weighs 365,000 tons. Used ten million bricks. Vertical to within five-eighths of an inch. Over six thousand windows. In 1933, some guy jumped from the eighty-sixth floor but was stopped by a ledge on the eighty-fourth and suffered only broken bones. Two years later, a woman the papers called a 'moody Manhattanite' pulled it off successfully and set a record for distance— 1,029 feet. After that, they fenced in the Observation Deck."

Though Shoshanna had allowed herself to be diverted, she'd never forgotten that her brother-in-law, who dressed impeccably and wouldn't drive anything but a Mercedes, had grown up in a housing project and was ashamed of it.

When the fox trot ended, he kept her hand in his. She was embarrassed that her palm was sweaty. "I hope you win this one, Jeremy; I mean, how can you lose?"

The band started playing "Cherry Pink and Apple Blossom White." Showing no inclination to trade her for his next partner, he'd adjusted to the new beat and, exerting firm pressure on the small of her back, led her across the floor in a rumba.

"Oh, I could lose, all right," he said. "Any lawyer can lose an open-and-shut case if the jury doesn't buy his argument. Suppose you were sitting on my jury, Shoshie. What was your reaction to the facts as I described them?"

She paused, not sure she could rumba and answer simultaneously. "Actually, I thought about how the people in our apartment house expect our landlord to keep the place running right. Once, my parents and some other tenants got together and asked him to fire a night elevator man who didn't respond when we buzzed him because half the time he was asleep in the basement. Our friends on the ground floor made the super put bars on their windows after a robbery happened in the neighborhood and they didn't feel safe. I guess someone who lives in a housing project—especially a woman living alone—ought to get the same service from *her* landlord."

"Good analogy. My argument's a variation on it. Plus I've got precedent, the case of a famous actress who was raped in her hotel room and won a multimillion-dollar judgment against the hotel chain because of its lax security. If a corporation can be held responsible for a guest's safety, I say the city ought to be held responsible for a tenant's."

"Why not sue the rapist?" Shoshanna asked.

"He doesn't have a pot to piss in. That's why you go after the deep pockets. The city'll probably say my client let the guy in, and no landlord can control what happens after a woman opens her door to a visitor. I'm going to have to prove he was a stranger, an intruder who wouldn't have made it past the lobby if the city had a goddamn brain in its bureaucratic head and put a few bucks into basic security measures. Someone's to blame for the fact that this brute got into my client's apartment. It didn't happen by accident, it happened because of gross, unconscionable negligence, right?"

"Right!" Shoshanna said, with the fervor of a convert.

"Shouldn't the negligent party be held responsible for the assault and violation of this poor woman?"

"Yes, absolutely."

"Isn't her bodily integrity as sacrosanct as yours? Isn't her safety and well-being as important as that of the women on West End Avenue? And wasn't her pain and suffering as horrific as the famous actress's?"

"Of course it was! Of course!"

"So, if the rapist is indigent, who should pay the price?"

He concentrated his blue lasers on Shoshanna's face. Though his feet moved in perfect time to the Latin beat, she sensed him listening for her reply as if nothing else mattered, not the rumba or the next girl he was supposed to dance with; not the champagne toast he should have been making to his bar mitzvah boy or the beef gravy coagulating on his plate. All he cared about was what Shoshanna Wasserman thought.

"The city, definitely!" she said and, at nineteen, understood for the first time how a woman could be thrilled to the marrow of her bones by a man like Jeremy.

Shoshanna watched her brother-in-law's hands slip under his partner's short black skirt and cup her buttocks, not compromising for an instant his own grace as he dipped her down and let her hair sweep the ice. Jeremy was an even better skater than dancer, and why not? Rachel had been *his* teacher, too. She's given him so much, the bastard. Five kids, a gorgeous home, a beautiful life. Served up haute cuisine whenever he deigned to eat at home. Entertained whomever he invited, sometimes on an hour's notice, always with style and hospitality. She'd put the icing on his career. Also planned wonderful vacations in the hope of luring him away from his work. (Most years, he claimed he was too busy to travel, said he'd seen enough hotel rooms on business and he'd sooner stay home and relax, which, in fact, he almost never did.) He told her to hook up with Shoshanna and Daniel. Or with the kids. Simon and Roy often asked her to join them, Tamara and Seth seemed to enjoy her company, and she had an open invitation to visit Zelda in Seattle and Dalia in London. But Rachel never wanted to go anywhere without him. Never criticized his antisocial ways and binge absences, covered for him at the kids' ball games and school plays, carried the load without resentment, held the family together after Gideon died. And *this* was her reward.

Jeremy's current treachery aside, Shoshanna had always marveled at her sister's loyalty despite evidence of such neglect and disregard as might drive another woman to divorce. "You never really know what's going on in someone else's marriage," Daniel reminded her whenever (once or twice a year it seemed) she'd been moved to inform Rachel of how badly her husband was treating her. The one time Shoshanna couldn't contain herself, Rachel jumped to Jeremy's defense. "It's because of what happened to Gideon. He gets overinvolved in his cases 'cause he's thinking about the brakes that failed on Gideon's car and it goads him to fight companies who make gas tanks that explode, or dump PCBs in rivers, or sell pajamas that burst into flame while a kid stands five feet from a stove. That's why he works so hard."

Only because of their conversation on the dance floor could Shoshanna understand how Jeremy's representation of the injured and impaired, the healthy who'd been made sick, the innocent who'd been misled, the pure who'd been polluted and despoiled, might inspire his long-suffering wife to excuse everything else, and by reminding herself of his impoverished beginnings take a kinder view of his materialism. "He never had fine things when he was young," Rachel would say when he bragged about a rare wine he'd bought at auction or insisted that people stroke the baby-soft leather on his briefcase. "He can't believe he can actually afford such good stuff. It's still a miracle to him." No matter what he did or said or failed to say, no matter how rude or arrogant he was, Rachel found a reason for it.

The secret ingredient, Shoshanna concluded, must be sex. Rachel's trim athleticism, blunt haircut, and forthright gaze were misleading. Behind that no-nonsense exterior lived a passionate woman who, if Leah could be believed, had always been "an erotic prodigy." And to judge by the incandescent expression on Rachel's face whenever the subject of sex came up, Jeremy must have satisfied those appetites. Until her change of life, Rachel said they made love three or four times a week, virtually every night he slept at home, and being statistically inclined, she rated him "in the top 1 percent." With his wife beaming all that unconditional love at him, how dare he cheat on her? And in the middle of Rockefeller Plaza yet, where someone they knew was bound to see him and carry the tale back home. Didn't he care? Or was he literally skating on thin ice, hoping to get caught?

Shoshanna wished she'd never turned east on Forty-ninth Street. Had she made her right on Thirty-fourth or Forty-second she wouldn't have caught him in the act. Had she been running late and not had time to watch the skaters. Had she taken the subway or a cab. Had she suggested another restaurant for lunch. Had Jeremy picked another day for his ice capades, or gone to Sky Rink or Wollman, or waited until after work to do his thing. If only. In the futility of hindsight lies proof that one can never control *everything*. It's the choices we make without thinking, the coincidences, the accidental confluence of person, place, and time, that chart destiny's detours. Only after the fact can we see how many minor decisions, how many small moves and tiny turns led us to the point of crisis.

The route that landed her at Rockefeller Plaza at 12:10 p.m. had dropped her in the middle of Can This Marriage Be Saved? with every hackneyed stereotype intact: The devoted stay-home wife. The dashing philandering husband. The beautiful young home wrecker. To rise above chiché the story needed a poet to give it grandeur and a therapist to provide motivation: Does the rich lawyer love the woman in red, or is she a mere flirtation, perhaps one of many? Does the red butterfly want the silver-haired lawyer for a husband or just a skating partner? Most urgently, does the sister tell the wife what she's seen? Does stumbling upon a criminal act automatically require a witness to testify? Or does the moral obligation to tell the truth shrink in direct proportion to the truth's capacity to wound? And are there different rules for family than for everyone else?

Shoshanna searched for answers in the face of the Titan Prometheus, who stole fire from the gods, gave it to humanity, and was tortured by Zeus for his effort. If truth were analogous to fire, what guidance could be gleaned from the myth? Fire warms and illuminates, but it also incinerates. The same can be said of truth, of information, of knowledge. Yet we would rather possess fire than live in darkness, preferring to decide for ourselves how to harness the flames. What punishment lay in store for her if she played her sister's Prometheus? Would Rachel ever forgive her for being the carrier of this truth? Shoshanna had forgiven her cousin Emily for her gin rummy revelation because, however hostile its intent, it armed her with facts she could parlay into self-protection.

Mightn't Rachel do the same with these facts? But what *were* these facts? Shoshanna shoved her gloved hands in her pockets as her eyes sought the elegant couple on the rink. Skating, though sensuous, wasn't sex. Before she could say a word to her sister, she would have to find out what actually was going on, which meant she'd have to tail Jeremy and gather more evidence. She could put her staff to work on it or hire a private investigator, which was doable—she had the contacts—but that would throw the matter into high gear before she was sure exposing Jeremy was the right move.

On the other hand, if she passed along what she'd seen without checking further, it would merely shift the burden of discovery onto Rachel, who would enlist Shoshanna's help anyway, thereby sending her back to square one. Even more probable, her straight-arrow sister would skip the surveillance phase and ask Jeremy point-blank if he'd been unfaithful. God only knew how he'd respond, but whatever he said was sure to break her sister's heart. He might admit he was in love with someone else and clear out without a struggle, as if he'd been waiting for an excuse to go. Or say he needs time to let the new relationship develop and tell Rachel to take it or leave it, propelled in his dispassion by some belated sense of midlife entitlement. Or hit her with a list of wifely infractions and inadequacies, including menopause, to suggest she'd driven him away. Or he could admit the affair, say all the right things, beg her forgiveness, promise never again to stray—and promptly resume his extracurricular activities, less reckless next time, but basically undeterred. Shoshanna had no doubt there would be a next time, having seen nothing furtive about his demeanor in Rockefeller Plaza, no sidelong glances at the spectators, nothing to suggest that he wasn't a seasoned veteran of illicit dalliances and entirely at ease in his double life. She knew enough about Rachel's marriage—or rather Rachel's perceptions of it—to anticipate how his betrayal would shatter her universe. Were she to find out about his philandering, she'd feel like a fool for having mouthed off about her ideal sex life. She'd be crushed and humiliated. Just knowing that he'd skated romantically with another woman could be as devastating to Rachel as if she'd caught them in bed together. Skating was Rachel's province and she, more than most, knew the high temperature of intimacy on ice.

Mulling all this, Shoshanna realized with no small degree of astonishment that she who usually wanted nothing more than to control everyone's fate now held Rachel's future in her hands. She felt overwhelmed by the burden. It was in her power either to destroy her sister's innocence or to blot this scene from her memory and let sleeping dogs dream. Her conscience froze at the thought of withholding the truth, but the idea of telling Rachel was almost paralyzing. Ultimately, Rachel might find a way to excuse Jeremy—judging by past behaviors, she was fiercely motivated to protect her marriage—but what parallel motivation would lead her to forgive Shoshanna for having witnessed his transgression? As with all embarrassing confidences, that was the core problem. Divulge what you know and the aggrieved person will not be able to face you without wondering if you're thinking about it. Even if she's ready to move on, knowing that the incident lives in your mind will not allow her to be free of it. The very sight of you will be a permanent reminder of what she most wants to forget. Shoshanna refused to play such a pain-triggering role in her sister's life. Though all her options were fraught with unintended consequences, Don't Ask, Don't Tell seemed the one with the least chaos-producing potential. Her silence would spare them both.

Yet how could she do to Rachel what she'd resented Rachel for doing to her? Ever since Sam picked up the sharp stick and drew his circles in the sand, Shoshanna believed that deception was more damaging than the worst of all possible truths. As the casualty of her family's well-intentioned cover-up, she used to be absolutely sure that the right to know trumped the impulse to protect. Why was she equivocating now? Worse yet, how was she going to get through the next two hours? It would be a relief to bring her dilemma to the lunch table and hear Leah's views, which no doubt would be incisive and helpful. But given that she'd been withholding key information about Sam, how in good conscience could she discuss the merits of candor with Leah? What's more, to elicit Leah's advice, Shoshanna would have to convey what she'd just seen, which would require her to compromise Rachel's privacy, and she wasn't willing to do that, especially in front of the "Bad Sister," who would surely savor Rachel's comeuppance.

At 12:25, she tore her eyes from the rink and resumed her walk to the restaurant, turning back only long enough to catch a glimpse of Jeremy twirling his butterfly in a pirouette, her short black skirt spinning like a gyroscope around her thighs.

nine

FOR LEAH WASSERMAN, March 8 was a disaster from start to finish. The lunch with Shoshanna never happened, and after downing half a bottle of Smirnoff for dinner, she basically lost the following day altogether, having slept until three in the afternoon. But today, she was determined to get her life back on track.

Wednesday, March 10. Today she would visit Freddy come hell or hip troubles—endure two subways to Columbus Circle, an interminable bus ride with other inmates' relatives who, like Leah, would make the trip upstate only to gaze at their beloved through a thick pane of Plexiglas, talk to him through a telephone receiver, then reboard the bus and go home. She usually visited him every six weeks, with or without Leo, but this time four months had passed since her last trip, four months of writer's block, academic inertia, and physical lassitude occasioned no doubt by the irksome presence of her other son, the boomerang boy, and exacerbated by her husband's deepening funk. This morning, Leo had felt a cold coming on and wasn't about to venture out in the howling wind. Henry, who'd yet to visit his brother even once, said he had other plans. So Leah was traveling solo.

Though the walk to the subway was hard on her hip, a taxi was out of the question. Most of her teaching salary went to support *The Free-*

thinker, and Leo had been landing fewer and fewer portrait commissions; boomers wanted a prestige artist to immortalize their children, not some obscure Brooklyn painter, however talented. Whether due to the dried-up commissions or the advent of a new muse, Leo was now doing abstracts. A gallery owner in SoHo, a woman given to body-piercing and thigh-high boots with stiletto heels, seemed excited about his new work. If she found him an audience he might never again have to fawn over another VIP tot, one of those pink-cheeked children in brass-buttoned blazers or velvet jumpers whose parents propped them in front of some marble fireplace with a Welsh terrier curled up at their feet, as if they were heirs to the British throne. That her boys never had fancy clothes or pedigreed pets was not the issue. What bothered Leah was Leo's never having painted them. She knew oil and tempera were expensive; watercolor would have suited her fine. Pastels. Charcoal. Colored pencils. Fucking Crayolas.

"Quit nagging," he'd say.

"Nagging's just another word for the repetition of unpalatable truths."

"I'll get to it."

"Yeah, like the cobbler gets to his kids' shoes."

Finally, she'd stopped asking. The paintings weren't the problem, anyway. What was poisoning their lives were his impenetrable stupors and sudden attacks of worthlessness, his ambivalence toward the boys, his way of distancing himself from them without ever neglecting them.

It all began with his frigging sperm count. Low. Very low. Too low to ensure conception anytime soon, the doctor said after they'd been trying to get pregnant for more than a year. Fertility treatments being unknown at the time, the doctor had recommended a sperm bank, but using Carl as the donor had been Leo's idea; he hoped his brother's semen would produce a child with Rose traits, maybe even one that resembled him. An inspired solution, thought Leah. Leo was desperate to have a family, and Carl, a compulsive bachelor with zero paternal instincts, was in good health, with a demonstrable though misapplied intelligence and a discernible likeness to his younger sibling. These factors made his sperm more desirable than the hyperactive tadpoles donated by horny college boys (or the hubris-heavy semen of septuagenarian Nobel Prize winners too impressed with themselves to imagine there might be a correlation between birth defects and superannuated sperm). Most important, Carl had agreed to ejaculate with no strings and to keep his role a secret for as long as he lived.

Damned thing took, first shot out of the box, as it were. Between gales of laughter, Leo had inseminated Leah with a turkey baster on their kitchen table. But before undertaking the "procedure," they'd spent hours discussing its ramifications and implications, during which Leah, assuming her academic persona, conveyed her views (also available in print wherever feminist treatises were sold) as methodically as if she were lecturing a grad-school seminar. "Understand that the value assigned to biological paternity is socially constructed," she told Leo. "The purity of the male line is of consuming interest to patriarchal cultures intent on perpetuating male wealth and power. But to a child, all that matters is, Was I wanted? Am I loved? Will I be cared for? A seed is not a father, Leo; a father is a man who rears a child." She acknowledged the shame associated with artificial insemination, dispelled it by tracing its roots to three misguided notions: (1) the stigma of male inadequacy (Real Men Make Babies), (2) the implied connotation of cuckoldry ("You put another man's come in *your* woman's womb?"), and (3) the negativity associated with masturbation (which, despite its universality, is commonly ridiculed as an act of desperation, or religiously condemned for detaching sex from procreation).

Leo, tired of his wife's intellectualizing, finally said, "All right, already," and promised never to give another thought to his sluggish sperm or his brother's thirty-second contribution of speed swimmers. That's what he said, but his gut reneged. Over the years, Leah watched a sense of masculine failure block his abandonment to fatherhood. Not that he didn't look after the boys—better than she did, in fact—and not that he wasn't affectionate with them, or happy to take responsibility for them even if it meant leaving a painting unfinished on the easel. In all those ways he'd acted the parent to them. But he never made them *his*. Missing, always missing, was that shock of surrender that transforms a man into a dad, the heart-stopping lurch that makes a pair of indifferent eyes go soft or sparkly at the sight of his own child. Leah felt sad for him, a crabbed compassion. Pity.

When the boys were in elementary school, his obsession with virility and paternity acquired additional layers. He started hocking her about whether Freddy and Henry suspected the truth, and he began questioning his right to exercise authority over them. Convinced that rationality could master monomania, Leah called upon every pedagogical trick she knew—suasion, syllogism, case histories—to bully him out of it. After reading about a South Dakota woman who underwent in vitro fertilization with her son-in-law's sperm and gave birth to her infertile daughter's baby, Leah teased out the analogy.

"The story's all over the papers, Leo. Some are playing it as the personification of maternal sacrifice. Others as a respectable form of incest. No one is suggesting that because the daughter is infertile she's an inauthentic mother or a failure as a woman. So I wish you'd stop insisting you've flunked manhood."

Leo pulled at his ponytail. (Was his hair substituting for the cock he'd found so deficient?) "It's different for a man," he muttered.

"Sorry, mister, I give out those grades and I say you pass."

"You wouldn't tell me the truth, anyway."

"Come *on*! When have I ever protected you from the truth? The point is, this couple in South Dakota wanted kids. So did we. They found a rational solution to a physiological dilemma. So did we. Families do all sorts of things to help one another get what they need.

"This is different," he insisted, but couldn't say why.

"You're being a jerk, Leo, but I'm going to pretend your feelings have merit and give you three new ways to reframe them." She took him by the shoulders and wouldn't let go until he looked into her eyes. "Number one: You, Freddy, and Henry are each one step removed from Carl—you horizontally, the boys vertically—which puts the three of you on a par with one another. That's the biological truth: you're *blood*! Number two: Your parents would have been the boys' grandparents whether their father had been Carl or you, but the Rose line is enjoying generational continuity because of *you*, not Carl. Without you, there would be no Freddy and Henry and no next generation. You're the Rose who shot two arrows into the future. That's the genealogical truth. Number three: You're always saying I'm as close to you as your own flesh and blood. Well, if you really mean it, then my literal flesh and blood, the children of my body, must be as close to you as I. That's the emotional truth. Now, will you please shut up?"

He gave her a half-smile but shook his head. "It's not enough."

Nothing ever was enough.

"I feel like I'm dead," he said one morning. "And you're already in a levirate marriage."

"Excuse me?"

"Levirate marriage. You know, when a man dies childless and his brother is expected to marry his widow and procreate with her. It's a biblical commandment. Orthodox Jews still observe it."

"I don't give a shit if Orthodox Jews observe Lent. All I know is that you've been a terrific father and your boys adore you."

"I've been rearing my brother's sons."

"A few spurts in a turkey baster doth not a father make."

"It makes a man."

That's what fucked everything up, she thought, on her way to the subway. Wussy sperm. The goddamned male obsession with the three Ps—potency, paternity, patrilineage. Even when there's no kingdom to pass on, they have to leave their mark.

She stopped in front of a bodega, rounded her back to the wind, and lit a Gauloise. Catching sight of herself in the shop window—galoshes, Indian cape, Susan B. Anthony shawl, purple sunglasses—even Leah had to admit she looked eccentric. Wouldn't she have relished the expression on her sister's face had she shown up at the Café Bretagne in this outfit on Monday?! But March 8 had been a bust. Waited nearly a year for lunch with Shoshanna, looked forward to it with more excitement than she was willing to acknowledge, but never made it across the East River. In fact, she'd gotten no farther than the subway platform. To put it bluntly, Monday was fucking surreal. Everything had turned weird, herself included, and lunch had gone belly up. Now she was on her way to the subway again, missing Freddy, excited about seeing him, and this time she was going to make it to her destination. Four months between visits was too long.

A strong headwind made the walk more arduous than usual, but her hip was behaving and the cape was warm. She took care to hoist her hem above the slush as she descended the subway steps. The smell of fuel, sweat, and urine—*L'eau d'MTA*—wafted toward her, a dank, fetid breeze. Except for a woman carrying a cat in a traveling case with a mesh opening on the side and a man in a black wool cap eating an apple, the station was deserted. As she waited for her train, Leah took note of the clots of dead chewing gum on the cement, the light grid made by the sunlight spilling through the sidewalk grating above, the windsong in the tunnel. She pulled her *Times* out of the backpack but couldn't concentrate. New Yorkers are a strange breed, she thought: not comfortable in empty public spaces, need a mob around us before we can claim our zone of privacy. Her ubiquitous Butterfinger bar called to her, but she resisted—later, on the bus, she'd want it even more. She was still teaching herself the rewards of delayed gratification.

As the subway roared into the station, the man in the black cap threw his apple on the tracks. Leah wanted to give him a piece of her mind: "Use the receptacle, you slob! This isn't a compost heap. What would the transit system look like if every creep dumped his refuse on the tracks? Who raised you, anyway? Feral wolves?" But she said nothing, just boarded the train, sat down, and read her paper. She'd been thoroughly chastened by Monday's encounter.

Monday was International Women's Day, and Leah, wearing a huge WOMEN HOLD UP HALF OF THE WORLD button on her lapel, had been waiting on that same platform for the train that would take her to

Shoshanna. A grotesquely disheveled man was leaning against a pillar a short distance away. No one else was near him, doubtless because of his odor, pungent even at ten feet. His face was stubbled, one shoe lacked a heel, the other its laces, and the gray coat he held closed with his hands in its pockets was caked with muck and grime. Lost soul, she thought. Homeless, probably. It took a lot to threaten Leah but not much to arouse her sense of injustice. Though his stench seared her lungs and his looks were beyond unsavory, it wasn't her sensibilities that were offended, it was her belief in human decency. How, in the richest city in the world, could a person be so neglected, so alone and overlooked as to fall into such a primitive state? She decided to hold her breath, give him a five-dollar bill, and explain about the soup kitchen in the church down the block. They'd direct him to a neighborhood agency that would help him clean up and find shelter and work.

As she was about to speak, he suddenly flared open his coat flaps, unzipped his fly, and directed a stream of steaming urine against the nearest pillar, like a dog relieving itself at a fire hydrant. Probably couldn't help himself, Leah reasoned quickly. Homeless people, by definition, had no bathrooms. Nevertheless, urination was unacceptable public behavior. "You mustn't do that," she said, quietly but firmly, reaching for his putrid sleeve. "Come, we'll find you a toilet."

Before she could back away, he wheeled around, still holding his penis, and aimed his urine at her, tracing an erratic trail on her Indian cape, like a garden hose gone wild. She watched in disbelief as the liquid soaked into the wool. It smelled like sewage.

"No! Don't!"

"Suck my cock, bitch!" he sneered, shaking the last noxious drop from its tip.

Leah's empathy evaporated on the spot. Concern for the homeless, ruminations on social policy, all her do-good impulses simply vanished, and the man became, not a mentally disturbed vagrant, but a despoiling, woman-hating monster, cousin to the Cossacks who had raped and ravaged her ancestors, and to every marauding male who'd ever pissed on the vanquished. But she didn't say a word, and she didn't move.

When faced with the enemy, she'd just stood there, holding the soiled cape away from her body, and stared at the stain. The subway chugged into the station. Its doors opened and closed. When she looked up, the man was inside, sitting smugly at a window, his demonic face sneering at her through the glass until the train disappeared into the tunnel.

What a hypocrite she was! What a fulminating, fainthearted, fucking fake! Always picking fights with the power structure. Always spouting the socialist line. Counseling others to buck the system. But when confronted by a real-life contradiction—some poor guy who was a casualty of the system and also happened to be a misogynistic, foulmouthed public pisser—she'd clammed up. Maybe it had been understandable for her initial burst of social worker compassion to dissipate once the man turned his dick on her (though she had to wonder if a belief system that collapsed so easily under fire had been very well rooted in the first place). What she couldn't explain was why, once she'd changed her view of him, she hadn't kicked him in the balls or called a cop and filed a complaint. She'd been preaching activism and self-defense for the last thirty years, for Chrissake; why had she let him get away? The answer was alarmingly plain: in the crunch, when it really counted, she was a weakling, a girly-girl, a quitter. Sending mental apologies to the women who might, due to her inaction, be victimized by this man in the future, Leah staggered through the exit gate and upstairs to the street.

No way was she going to meet Shoshanna stinking of piss and self-loathing. Besides, a mushroom crêpe seemed unappealing right now. She would go home, rid herself of this loathsome garment, phone her sister, and make another date. A taxi skidded to a stop the instant she raised her arm. Settled in the back seat, she tried not to glance at its galloping meter. Or the stain whose acrid stench, despite her open window, was strong enough, distinctive enough, to carry her back . . .

"It's been three weeks!" yelled the heavyset matron, thin lips protruding from her double chins like a beak. Leah had wet her bed every night since Dena dropped her in the driveway of the Blue Spruce Boarding School and took off in the same van that brought them. Now a dorm's worth of scared little girls looked on as the fat matron with the thin lips stripped the sheets off Leah's cot and another matron, a sallow woman with a mole on her nose, pulled off Leah's soiled nightgown and slapped her with it. "Twelve years old and still fouls her nest!"

"Dummies," shouted Leah. "It's involuntary! It happens in my sleep. It's a reaction formation." She always seemed to understand herself better than the adults around her, yet they were the ones with the power. The two matrons dragged her to the communal bathroom and wrestled her into a claw-footed porcelain bathtub. "Leave me the fuck alone, you stupid farts!!" The one with the mole gagged her with the urine-soaked nightgown. The wet flannel tasted of yeast, smelled metallic. She tried to kick her way out of the tub, but Double Chins held her down while Mole Nose shackled one of her ankles to the faucet.

She spent the night in the cold tub, naked, with neither blanket nor pillow, and no tears. From their narrow cots beyond the bathroom wall her schoolmates whispered comfort, but Leah made a joke of her ordeal, called it "*The Tale of a Tub*—with apologies to Jonathan Swift." The next day, the matrons let her return to her bed. "We're finished with you," they said; but she hadn't finished with them. If they thought she'd peed on purpose, well, now she would oblige them. After lights-out, she crept to the water fountain, swallowed thirty mouthfuls, and, when her bladder felt ready to burst, voided lavishly into her mattress.

"We've washed the last of your smelly sheets!" said Double Chins. "You can drown in your stinking urine for all we care." Back in the tub, manacled, injustice fueling her outrage as it would for the rest of her life, Leah jerked and strained against the chain while bellowing every curse she knew as alliteratively as she could. "Bullies! Bitches! Brutes! Barbarians!" Though unable to break free, she succeeded in heaving the upper part of her body out of the tub and throwing her hip out of joint in the process. Her subsequent howls, caroming off the bathroom tiles, attracted the security guard, who threw a bath towel over her nakedness and released her. "Cruel and excessive punishment," he wrote. The doctor's report said, "Dislocated hip." (She'd read it upside down on his desk.) Nice guy, she recalled, though he'd left her with the limp.

The headmaster fired both matrons and ordered up a child psychiatrist, a kindly woman with rimless spectacles, who pronounced adolescent bed-wetting a normal regressive reaction to the trauma of family dislocation. My diagnosis exactly, thought Leah. The new matrons spread a rubber mat under Leah's bedsheet to protect the mattress and changed her linens without complaint until, in time, she began waking up dry. But she'd never forgotten that smell or how it felt to be ashamed, alone, and absolutely powerless.

Though costly, it had been a quick trip home in the taxi on Monday and therefore worth it. As soon as she'd set foot in the house she'd thrown the stinking cape in a plastic bag and dropped it on the front stoop for the cleaners to pick up. In the bedroom she'd found Leo flaked out on their bed, glass in hand, a bottle of vodka on the side table only a quarter full. Since he'd been aware of her lunch date with Shoshanna, she waited for him to ask why she was back so soon. He'd barely looked up.

"What's the matter?" She dreaded the answer. It was always something.

"My brother." He poured himself a gezuhnte double. "Heart attack."

"Heart attack?"

"He's dead, Leah."

"I'm sorry." She meant she was sorry for Leo, not his brother. It was so typical of Carl to get off this parting shot, to drop dead exactly when she needed to be the only crisis on the block. Instead of coming home to wallow in her post-traumatic stress, instead of claiming what little succor Leo might offer, she would have to minister to him.

"You're not supposed to drink alcohol, Leo. You know what it says on your medication."

He took another swig. "It's a shame we weren't closer, Carl and me, but . . ."

"Carl and I," she corrected.

". . . but it's sad he's gone." Leo's eyes puddled.

"Not *that* sad. The man never missed a chance to put you down, so let's deep-six the tears."

"It's not about me, Leah, and it's certainly not about you," Leo insisted, and guzzled more vodka to prove it.

Chastened, Leah paused. "How did you hear?"

"It was his lawyer that told me."

"*Who*. It was his lawyer *who* told you."

"Stop with the grammar, Leah; the poor man's dead."

"Oh, *give* me a break! Carl wasn't poor in any sense of the word. *We're* poor. He was a rich prick." She was sitting on the edge of the bed, pulling off her galoshes.

"He *was* poor. Because he died alone. Sounds like the only one he had at the end was his lawyer—this Driscoll—the guy *who* called." It would have been spunky if Leo had said this to taunt her; it would have shown some spine. Instead, she knew, he was trying to please, which perversely made her meaner.

"Carl had whomever he wanted, and face it, pal, it wasn't you. So don't suddenly make like mishpochah. The two of you were about as close as a fox and a chicken."

"Stop being cruel, Leah."

"If you stop bullshitting yourself. The man was a solipsistic sybarite. Filthy with lucre. Never even gave us a wedding gift."

"Since when are you so materialistic?"

"Since Carl was. He splurged on his women, but the fist closed tight when it came to his family. Need I remind you that he never got our boys a birthday present? Never bought one of your paintings. Prided himself on his fucking art collection—eclectic, bold, yada yada yada, Goya, Grosz, Picasso, Pop Art, Popsicle sticks—but wouldn't shell out a measly five hundred bucks for an original Leo Rose." Now she was really being cruel.

"My stuff wasn't up his alley, you know that. Besides, I couldn't take money from my own brother."

"So you gave him a freebie—that gorgeous Nantucket landscape. And what'd he do? Sold it! If he didn't like the damn thing, why the fuck didn't he return it? It galls me to this day that Carl was making money off your work when you weren't!" She kicked her galoshes under the bed.

"I'm not thinking about art or money right now." Leo sighed, sounding weepy. "He was my last living relative."

"Horseshit, honey. You're mourning the brother you *wish* you'd had, not the one you did."

She hated herself for turning on Leo, something she did reflexively whenever he became masochistic. He was a decent man, *too* decent. Not stubborn or bull-headed like most Leos, her Leo was always excusing bad behavior (hers included), always giving the other person the benefit of the doubt. And what did it get him? Bubkes. And what did it get her? A sweet, solicitous husband who brought out the worst in her, more for what he exposed of her ideological fault lines than for any of his actual shortcomings. Leo was everything she'd always insisted a man be permitted to be—sensitive, emotional, nurturant, compromising, noncompetitive, math-anxious, hardware-challenged, willing to ask for directions. The problem wasn't that he was weak, it was that his strengths were so quiet and unassuming—gentleness, consistency, commitment to the people he loved. His long suit: unshakable devotion. So devoted had Leo been to his parents that the only time he'd ever put his foot down in all these years was when he'd insisted on a traditional Jewish wedding so his mother could kvell at a ceremony he knew she'd never get from Carl. So devoted to his boys was he that he treated them like sons, though he felt they weren't his. So devoted to Leah that he knew her better than anyone else—and loved her anyway.

Sadly, the qualities she'd treasured in Leo that made him *un*like other men had, over time, metamorphosed into irritating inadequacies that made her wish he were *more* like other men. Someone who didn't take to his bed with spells of world pain. Someone who could hold his liquor, fix the plumbing, talk back to assholes like his brother, and solve her problems for a change instead of always depending on her to solve his. Someone who would grab her and rip her clothes off. She resented him for making her miss the stereotypical male traits he lacked. She blamed him for confounding her belief in the dysfunctionality of traditional masculinity, a credo that informed her work but crumbled in her marriage, and for arousing in her, after all these years, the wish to be taken care of.

Leo threw a baleful glance at the vodka bottle, but seemed to think better of it. He slumped back on the pillows, his silver hair spreading around his head like a halo in a medieval painting. The owner of his new gallery, who'd recently pierced the center of her tongue with a small emerald, had insisted he grow his hair shoulder-length, a dashing affectation he'd have been incapable of assuming on his own. Artists need a marketable image, said Madame Stiletto, implying that Leo had none. She'd sent him a picture of Leon Wieseltier and recommended he emulate the Byronic look, which he'd done to great effect until last August, when, after a few 90-degree days, he'd announced he was off to the barber's.

Leah had practically barred the door. "We've saved a fucking fortune on your haircuts; why start up again?" She'd convinced him to tough out the heat wave, but her real reason wasn't budgetary. She thought his long hair sexy—the Samson effect, maybe. Anything to make him seem stronger.

"It's killing me," he'd protested the next night, lifting the mop off his neck.

That was when she'd pulled the rubber band from her braid and gathered his hair in it. Eureka! Even sexier. Senior hippie. Gray Panther in a ponytail. Striking, she'd thought, and wondered how he'd look in an earring.

But on Monday, lying there half-soused in his halo, he was anything but Samsonesque. "The lawyer says we're in Carl's will, you and me and the boys," he said wanly.

"You and *I*" sprang to her lips, but all she said was "I should hope so."

"We have to go to the law firm next week to hear it read aloud."

"When exactly?"

"March 15."

" 'Beware the ides of March.' " (Leo looked lost.) "The soothsayer's warning. *Julius Caesar*." She uncapped her Parker pen and went to the calendar hanging in the bathroom on a towel hook. "What time?"

"Seven. They're sending a car for us. Carl left instructions."

"What do you mean, instructions?"

"We're not supposed to eat beforehand; they're giving us supper."

She stepped out of her black slacks and pulled the black sweater over her head. Her underwear exuded vapors of sweat and subway. She decided not to tell Leo what had happened. It would make him feel worse, which would make her feel worse, which would defeat the whole idea. "Where's the funeral?" she asked.

"No funeral. He's been cremated."

"Judaism forbids cremation."

"Carl wasn't much of a Jew."

"When'd he die exactly?"

"Two weeks ago, Thursday." Leo turned his head to the wall.

So much for fraternal intimacy. His only brother, gone a fortnight, and he'd just found out about it. She didn't rub it in. "I've had a mother of a morning, pal. Excuse me while I grab a glass and help you demolish that vodka." She peeled off her bra and panties, left them in a heap, wrapped herself in the apricot chenille robe she'd owned since college, and padded to the kitchen. Were it possible to wrap herself in the simplicity of student life, she'd have kept that on a hanger in her closet as well. There was a clean yahrzeit glass in the dish drainer. She was about to bring it to the bedroom when she remembered Shoshanna and put in a call to the Café Bretagne. The maître d' recalled Ms. Safer very well indeed. She'd waited almost an hour, then left.

"My Time Is Your Time," announced a brisk British voice. "Fiona speaking."

"Shoshanna there?"

"She's out to lunch, madam," said the voice. "Message?"

(Tell her I stood her up because of some pisher. Tell her I was the victim of a drive-by shooting. Tell her I pissed away the morning.)

"Just tell her Leah called."

She filled her glass and started a bath. Tubs were not her normal milieu. Wasn't it patently absurd to spend a half hour in a hot sitz bath, when, after two minutes, one was in effect stewing in self-pollution. Besides, bathtubs reminded her of boarding school and she was disinclined to arouse the memories encrypted in the warp of her hip. But after her encounter with the subway creep, she would do whatever it took to feel clean; multiple purgations, if it came to that. She would soak in the tub until every ounce of humiliation was leeched out.

She shpritzed a stream of shampoo at the running water (instant bubble bath at half the price) and watched a carpet of bubbles spread across the surface. The phone! If it woke Leo, she'd be on bedside duty for the rest of the day. She shut off the tap and ran to stop its ringing.

"Where were you?" For weeks, Shoshanna had been priming herself for their lunch, practicing her lines, rehashing Sam's letter but when Leah failed to show up, she'd been both disappointed and grateful for the last-minute reprieve that spared her having to discuss either their father's visit or Jeremy's indiscretion. Leah's default had solved both dilemmas by postponing them. Still, Shoshanna was curious. "You stood me up. What happened?"

Shit-free. Leah liked that. She carried the portable phone into the bathroom and closed the door. The mirror, stripped of its subway map, had misted with condensation. Suds licked the rim of the tub. She sat on the toilet lid wondering if she should tell her sister the truth. Apart from being owed an explanation, Shoshanna might actually be the one person Leah could confide in. Others in her life—the kids at the magazine, her retinue of Schmendriks, the purists of progressivism and women's studies—would think less of her, not because a man had urinated on her, but because of what she hadn't done in response. They would fault her either for letting him get away without slugging him, or for surrendering her social conscience as soon as a living, breathing member of the underclass impinged on her comfort and safety. But Shoshanna, activist manqué herself, would understand, and with Leo being blotto and her misery starting to fester, Leah felt she had to tell *someone*. Only in the telling could she begin to distance herself from the ordeal, cherry-picking the tolerable details and repressing the rest as one does when recounting a hard birth or narrow escape. The objective, she'd learned from *The Tale of a Tub*, was to fashion a narrative that would lend itself to repetition and anesthetize the teller until what began in humiliation could become manageable as myth.

They talked for the better part of an hour. Leah couldn't have done it face-to-face. Even on the phone, she fidgeted with everything in sight—her brush and comb, Leo's razor, toothpaste, floss—as she revisited the subway platform, the foul act, its odor, her mute, contemptible inertness. Leah's narrative was uncharacteristically spare, few adjectives, no alliteration, no zingers. When her tears came, so strange, so unlike her, she let them. Yet she kept apologizing for her "aphasia." Never felt so inarticulate, she said; never been so incoherent. "I can't seem to capture what it was like. The whole thing sounds trivial now—a shot of piss. Big deal. It never even touched my skin. So why am I so upset?"

"Anyone would be upset. Especially you."

"What's that supposed to mean?" Leah asked, provisionally tense.

Shoshanna, never having known her sister to be vulnerable, chose her words with care. "It means you're not someone who's used to feeling diminished. And you're not someone who typically answers bad behavior with silence. But this guy shut you up. He didn't just drench your cape, he drowned your voice. It was probably the first time in your life when you didn't talk back."

Leah sighed into the phone. Cushioned in flattery, her passivity seemed less devastating. She heard Shoshanna saying, "You start from a higher perch than most people, that's why the fall hurts so badly. Being ordinary is a shock to your system." This made sense to her.

At the end of the conversation, Shoshanna asked if they should schedule another lunch date, then, thankful for having been entrusted with Leah's confidence—or perhaps feeling sorry for her—said, "Never mind lunch. Why don't you and Leo come for Passover? March 31. Henry, too, if he's free. We're doing the first Seder at our place."

The invitation was proffered casually, as if they'd been trading home visits all these years, but Leah reacted to it with a noticeable leap of the heart. The idea excited, then immediately panicked her. She hadn't been to a Seder in nearly thirty-five years. Seders reminded her of the father she'd spent the better part of her life trying to forget, a goal she'd come close to achieving partly because Sam had emigrated to Israel, but mostly because she'd distanced herself from all things Jewish. To avoid being reminded of him, a child abandoned by a dentist might eschew annual checkups and suffer the consequences of bad teeth. But the daughter of a deadbeat rabbi had only to steer clear of synagogues, simchas, and Jewish holidays, which Leah had done quite successfully through the years. She was surprised, therefore, that her response to Shoshanna's invitation was temptation, not outright rejection. Another reaction, no less startling, was tenderness; how touched she was that Shoshanna remembered Henry had been living at home, that Shoshanna carried this detail around in her head.

"The Seder?" Leah combed her shaggy bath mat with her toes. She hoped her voice hadn't sounded shaky. "You've just spared yourself a trip to Brooklyn. I was going to insist we do our next lunch on my turf."

"Impossible. I get the bends when I cross the river."

"I'll grant you a special dispensation for Passover, but the subject of future venues is not closed."

"We'll talk about it at the Seder. See you on the thirty-first," said Shoshanna.

By the time they hung up, Leah's bath had cooled. She opened the drain for a minute or two, refilled the tub from the hot faucet, and added a few more squirts of shampoo. Lowering herself into the tub, she closed her eyes, and—braid undone, hair afloat on the foam— awaited purgation.

The last time she'd taken a bath with a purpose was the night before her wedding. Though Leah found the practice of mikvah offensive and had written a twenty-page paper explaining why, she'd agreed to visit the ritual bath because she believed in honoring women's history. She went because Leo asked her, and Leo asked her because his mother had asked him to, and his mother wanted her to go because *she* went to mikvah in Brooklyn and *her* mother had gone to mikvah back in Poland. Leah went only after she had recast the mikvah as a rite of passage that would connect her to generations of women who didn't have the option of refusing, because in those insular little shtetls where everyone knew everyone else's business, a bride either went to mikvah or she didn't have a sex life.

Before he dropped Leah off at the nondescript building in the armpit of Borough Park, Leo extracted from her a promise of good behavior, which she'd actually kept. She did as the mikvah lady instructed—removed all her clothes, entered a tiled space the size of a suburban bathroom, and descended into the lime-green waters of the ritual immersion pool that, by Jewish law, had to be exactly four feet deep, seven feet square, and filled with at least two hundred gallons of water. No bubbles. The mikvah lady told her to squat and plunge three times, to say the blessing, and not to let any part of her body touch the walls of the tub or it would invalidate the whole thing. Fully submerged, feeling ridiculous, she peered up at the lights overhead and realized with a kind of water-logged wonder that this immersion could serve quite well as a symbol of her willingness to plunge into marriage despite a dozen reasons not to. At that moment, unyoked from her father's Judaism, the mikvah became *hers*, and years later, when feminists appropriated and reinterpreted the mikvah for ceremonies of healing and renewal, Leah knew she'd been Sacagawea to their Lewis and Clark, the first pioneer to find modern meaning in an ancient space.

One of the Schmendriks had defended mikvah on the grounds that rituals of purity and impurity impose order on a chaotic world. Leah remained unconvinced. The notion that an involuntary hormonal cycle made a woman ritually impure struck her as inane, anathema, and—assuming female hormones were divinely created along with Eve herself—theologically flawed. She refused to accept that sacrificial blood, animal blood, was holy, while menstrual blood was profane.

That an observant Jewish man couldn't shake hands with a woman in case it was one of her "unclean" days. That a husband couldn't touch his wife for two weeks of every month. In her 1970 essay "Pulling the Plug: The Ritual Bath and the Hatred of Women," Leah pointed out that almost every Torah law concerning impurity had become obsolete after the destruction of the Temple except for the halachah regarding menstruating women.

Why? [she asked in the article]. Short answer: Men were in charge. Long answer: Fearing women's mysterious power to give birth to life, and needing to assert their own power and supremacy, men arrogated unto themselves the bloody sacrificial rites and proclaimed women's monthly blood unclean. But wait, guys! The Torah tells us women were created in the image of God, so God, too, must have menstrual cycles (though surely not PMS). Does that mean God, too, is unclean for two weeks of every month? The Torah also tells us that every Jew belongs to "a kingdom of priests and a holy nation."

"Oh," say the rabbis. "He didn't mean *you,* hon."

"Why not us?"

"Because you're unclean," the rabbis reply, unfazed by their circularity. "You can't be holy if you're untouchable."

"Actually, it's vice versa. We can't be untouchable because we're holy."

Leah's invented dialogue ended with her throwing down the gauntlet:

You can't have it both ways. Either humans are created in God's image or only half of us are. Either Jews are a holy nation or only half holy, a chosen people, or only half chosen. Are you guys suggesting that God was only half right? Sounds like heresy to me.

Obviously, the mikvah had made her mad. Yet she remembered her premarital dunk as rather pleasant, even with a rabbi barking instructions from behind the door and the mikvah lady handing her little cotton bedikah cloths "to see if you're clean or not" and checking under her fingernails for an errant speck of schmutz. Having detached the ritual from *taharat hamishpacha*, "the laws of family purity," Leah's one and only mikvah visit remained, in retrospect, an homage to her foremothers and a symbol of her plunge into matrimonial waters. Nothing more.

The Borough Park mikvah was an upscale spa compared to the pitted tub in which she'd soaked herself on March 8 not for reasons of women's history, tradition, or revisionist symbolism, but to decontaminate from the pisser even if it took all night, which it very nearly did. She'd refilled the tub twice more before she toweled off and went to bed in her apricot chenille robe.

That was Monday, this was Wednesday and she still felt out of sorts, as if she'd been lugging around Sandburg's "bucket of ashes," her past. Hindsight being stubbornly nonlinear, she'd been revisiting events in size order, the salient before the recent—last week, fifty years ago, subway, school, bathtub, mikvah—a life without a time line, one memory careening into the next with no propulsion but related pain.

A trip to the penitentiary might not be the best antidote to attacks of temporal dislocation and spiritual melancholia, yet being with Freddy always seemed to cheer her up. Her older son accepted suffering as natural, even when he himself was its cause, and took the consequences of his acts with mordant humor. His worldview was vaguely Buddhist, its distinguishing trait a remarkable gift for equanimity, an optimism gene, was what she'd called it. After each setback, he would recover from reality's blows by way of mental discipline and moral rededication. But when the next temptation came his way, with its promise of a fast buck or an easy make, off he'd go sporting his all-knowing smile and briny charm, trouble nipping at his toes.

She'd been Freddy's first sucker, Leah reminded herself as the bus rolled up the thruway. Even as a child, he could make the preposterous plausible. Though his powers had been displayed often enough to have cured her of her gullibility, and though she saw herself as a cynic with a Ph.D. in shit-detection, she'd kept buying his line. At ten, he talked her into letting him go swimming off Coney Island in March to study the relationship between air and water temperature and he'd nearly died of hypothermia. At sixteen, he finagled her into hosting an open house for the high school football team without mentioning that its opponents had also been invited and, given the two teams' virulent emnity, broken lamps were a foregone conclusion. Then there was the time she caught him stealing from her wallet when, by the end of their heart-to-heart, she actually believed he was taking the money to buy her a birthday present.

His last gambit was a doozy. He'd quit his research job at the chemical lab and announced he was going to drive an ice cream truck. "Don't be a schmuck!" said Leah. "You've got a great future there."

"I know, Mom, but . . ." That's when he'd spun his gossamer tale. He'd be selling his wares in the inner city, where other companies feared to tread. He'd make sure underprivileged kids got the same quality ice cream as kids in the 'burbs. He'd bring Good Humor to the grass roots. Leah remembered berating herself for her bourgeois instincts, for worrying about his financial security while her son, taking a leaf from his mother's book, had chosen to dedicate his labor to the have-nots. When it turned out that the appetite he yearned to satisfy was a drug habit, not a sweet tooth, no one was more shocked than Leah.

Kids and ice cream, what could be more pure? It was the perfect front. An ice cream van could park anywhere (great for market reach) and serve people of all ages well into the night without arousing suspicion. At the window of an ice cream truck, money changed hands in the open. A paper napkin was proffered with the product, so it was easy to slip a glassine envelope between its folds, wrap the napkin around a chocolate chip cone, and accept payment in the form of a five-dollar bill that happened to have a couple of C-notes in it. *Voilà!* A transaction as innocent as the cherry on a hot fudge sundae.

The same creativity applied to a legitimate enterprise would have made Frederick Douglass Rose an entrepreneur. He'd invested in a friendly white refrigerated truck and bought enough ice cream to keep the kids coming. Stocked a full menu of dexies, acid, ecstasy, coke, crack, smack, pot, goofballs, angels, tranquilizers, inhalants, and diet pills, and stored the pharmaceuticals behind the legitimate stock. Stuff that could take the chill he'd stashed in a gallon-size ice cream vat under the parfaits, the rest behind the pyramids of sugar cones. Then he'd jingled his bells and raked in the cash. Until one night a plainclothes detective had a hankering for a coconut pop and happened to be waiting in line behind a customer whose napkin slipped. Freddy was in handcuffs before the glassine envelope hit the ground. Mandatory sentence for possession and sale of narcotics in New York State: five years to life. Two down, three to go if he was lucky. And dozens more bus trips, if her hip didn't give out.

The guard detail at the gate had been changed since her last visit, and since no one recognized her, they observed the security rigmarole to the letter. Picture ID. Sign-in (Leah's name, Freddy's number). Coat on hook. Knapsack in locker. Empty pockets. Shoes off; back on. Metal detector. Pat-down. Pass into a wire cage whose entry gate slammed shut before its egress gate slid open onto another reception area from which an escort led her through a quarter-mile of hallways to the visitor's room. Finally seated at a table behind a Plexiglas partition, Leah waited for her son.

It was just as well Leo hadn't come; these visits usually left him wallowing in regrets. He'd been a lousy role model. He'd failed Freddy twenty different ways. He should have picked up the signals. Leo had always been, as current parlance had it, "in touch with his feelings" while Leah used to think of herself as the stoic. Not anymore. Now she was just another hand-wringer hounded by her errors—the Edsel of mothers. Were she to count the ways she'd failed Freddy, there'd be no stopping at twenty, and if Leo was a lousy role model, what was she? From which parent did Freddy learn to manipulate people? From whom did he get his golden tongue? Who was the calculating strategist and who was guileless? Who was ego-driven and who was selfless?

No, this boy was *her* acorn.

The metal door opened and the guard came toward her without Freddy.

"What's wrong? Is he okay?"

"Oh, he's fine. But he won't come down. Says you haven't been here in four months so he doesn't want to see you now."

"What?"

"He won't leave his cell."

The guard was young. Leah noted a patch of whiskers on his neck where he'd missed shaving and, at the corners of his mouth, grains of powdered sugar, probably from a wolfed-down doughnut.

"Can't you make him?" she asked. It struck her that the guard probably had a father who'd taught him how to shave and a mother who'd raised him to wipe his mouth. But they couldn't make him.

"I dunno. Never had one like this. Usually they're champing at the bit to come down." He looked at Leah kindly. "You want me to make him?"

"No." Leah twirled her braid. "That won't be necessary." She stood up. The guard unlocked the door and let her out.

ten

SHOSHANNA ORDERED A DRY MARTINI and considered her options. It wasn't like her to take a midday breather on a barstool, but two days after witnessing Jeremy's ice capades, she was leaving the French Tourist Office (where she'd been researching the wine festivals of Alsace for a Francophile-oenophile) when she realized that his office was a block away, and the idea of confronting him became so compelling that she ducked into a cocktail lounge to mull it over. Now, gripping her martini glass by its stem, she fished out the olive and wondered if the assembly line workers whose only job it was to stuff in the pimiento were women. A bad case of female pity threatened, extremes of male misbehavior having overloaded her circuits with the confluence of Leah's subway pervert and Rachel's cheating spouse. Men are priapic pricks, she thought. (It was one of Leah's more memorable alliterations from the old days, though when Shoshanna had looked it up, priapic seemed redundant.) The alcohol cleared her sinuses.

Assuming Jeremy was in his office—rather than out skating—what then? How does one accuse a brother-in-law of adultery? "Gotcha! Confess and repent!" He'd laugh in her face. Since their ancient conversation on the dance floor, to which she'd doubtless assigned disproportionate weight, he'd taken no notice of her beyond polite condescension. Once

the children and grandchildren began monopolizing everyone's attention, family gatherings were hectic enough to mask their banal interactions and allow them—like millions of accidental relations—to navigate
a lifetime of Seders and Sunday dinners on a ship of platitudes. (Nothing wrong with that, thought Shoshanna. Except for her and Rachel, ties
of birth or marriage hadn't made great confidants of anyone else in the
family, either. People routinely tell a stranger on a plane things they'd
never divulge to most of their relatives.) The memory of a well-nursed
grievance—when Gideon died and she'd tried to communicate her grief
to Jeremy in an honest, unhackneyed way and he'd blown her off—
made it all the more difficult for her to imagine herself standing at his
desk to demand he do right by Rachel.

Since she'd never before ventured into his sphere, Jeremy would give
her his undivided attention out of curiosity if not good manners. But
why would he take her seriously, or care one whit what she thought, or
decide to shape up simply for having been found out? From what she
knew of Jeremy, she could expect a vehement counterattack conducted
with all the adversarial zeal for which he'd become famous. "Calling
Jeremy adversarial is like calling Saddam Hussein testy," Leah once
commented after she'd caught him in action on Court TV. Were
Shoshanna more like her tough-tongued sister, she might go head-to-
head with him, but being herself, she would fold like a fan, and if her
office visit accomplished nothing more than to remind her of what a
gnat she was in his eyes, why waste the effort?

Confrontation was out. She drained the last of her martini and contemplated the original dilemma: Should she or shouldn't she? Tell
Rachel or keep mum? She paid her check. Daniel's last class would let
out in ten minutes; she'd cab down to ask him.

He was leaning back in his chair, chewing on a pencil. "Don't you think
there's something morally wrong with you having more information
about your sister's husband than she does?"

For someone who prided himself on clear thinking, Daniel's faculty office was a paper-strewn, book-burdened mess. "I suppose so." She could see where he was heading.

"Then don't you think you owe her that information?"

She hated when people—namely her husband—insisted on delivering a statement in the form of a question, as if their rising inflection could mask how opinionated they really were. Usually, it was women who did this—intelligent, strong-minded women who affected tentative tones while saying things like "This is probably crazy, but I think American foreign policy would benefit from a closer analysis of Third World economic forecasts, don't you?"—women who were afraid to sound too sure of themselves for fear their conviction would be read as conceit. Shoshanna had done exactly that in the presence of men who she knew expected deference. Daniel, however, tended to affect his quizzical tone in the presence of nonacademics, probably to temper his professorial authority and make the untutored feel comfortable. Irresolution, however disarming in a man, annoyed her anyway. Questions that insinuated their own answers registered on her as patronizing, and dredged up the inferiority complex she'd been wrestling with since she had given up larger aspirations for the illusion of control that came with running a service business. There was a price to pay for playing it safe.

She answered him talmudically, with questions of her own: "Don't *you* think it's morally wrong to carry tales? And don't you think it's nasty to tell someone you love a lot something you know is going to devastate them and unravel their life—the life they've been happy with until now? And if so, wouldn't you agree that kindness might outrank candor and the more humane thing would be to say nothing?"

"Kind but patronizing," said Daniel, unaware that the pot was describing the kettle. "Rachel's a grown-up, Shoshe. She'll cope. She'll survive." He gathered up some papers and stuffed them into his battered briefcase.

"It doesn't have to come to that. If I keep quiet, things can just go on as they are." She bit off the last shred of a jagged thumbnail and started gnawing its cuticle.

"I think you're playing God, don't you?"

Again, that infuriating question mark. "No, Daniel, I think I'm playing sister."

"Okay, then, turn the tables. Would you want Rachel to know something about me that you didn't know?"

"You're not Jeremy!"

"You're not answering." He locked his file cabinet, tossed his keys on his desk, led her to the door, and turned off the lights.

"Don't be disingenuous, Daniel. You know I can't tolerate secrets. I don't want anybody deciding how much I can know about anything." She buttoned her coat and flashed on her parents.

"I rest my case," he said, and took her hand as they walked across Washington Square Park, leaving her other hand, and its fingernails, openly accessible. A pinky made its way to her mouth.

"Don't be dismissive," she replied testily. "There are consequences to consider, not just principles."

"*Not* telling has consequences, too. For the rest of your life, your relationship with Rachel will be distorted by this enormous secret, by what you know and she doesn't. You'll hear double entendres she misses. You'll be even more hostile to Jeremy than you are already, and overprotective of Rachel whether you realize it or not. It's the proverbial pachyderm, this secret. There's no business as usual with an elephant in the house."

"There is if I discipline myself. I'm good at denial. I can forget what I saw."

"Even a control freak has her limits." He tousled her hair.

She dropped his hand and pulled on her gloves to keep her fingers out of reach. Esther had painted some foul-tasting liquid on her nails that cured Shoshanna's habit when she was nine or ten. But under stress, she reverted, then hated herself for destroying what had taken so long to grow. Now she thought about how long it takes to grow a marriage. "I can't tell her, Daniel. I'm a coward." They turned into their street.

"Think of it as a mitzvah," he said gently.

She shot him a look.

"Seriously. Revelation can be the beginning of redemption. And if I may say so, your sister could use a new life." As they climbed the brownstone stoop, he began digging in his coat pocket for his keys. Shoshanna suddenly remembered where they were—on his desk, three feet from the file cabinet he'd so carefully locked. She extracted her own set from her purse and opened the door while he was still searching.

"I doubt she'd agree with you. Don't forget she's the child of a broken marriage. She lived through our mother's divorce. She wants to spend the rest of her days as Mrs. Brent. You've heard her say that."

"Never happen. It's only a matter of time before Mr. Brent takes a powder. He's been cheating on her for decades."

"Come on!!" Though the same thought had already occurred to Shoshanna, she was shocked to hear it spoken. "How do you know?"

"He once asked me, man-to-man, as it were, if I wanted a little hanky-panky on the side—not realizing, of course, that my hanky already provides all the panky a body can handle." Daniel fell on the couch and pulled Shoshanna down beside him. "Let me put it this way, love: it's a wonder he finds time to practice law."

"Rachel would die if she knew."

"Last I checked, murder by truth was not a homicidal category. Besides, she's a survivor. Never mind her childhood; think of what she's lived through as a mother. Gideon's death. Simon's coming out—at sixteen, yet. And those daughters put her through a few wringers."

Shoshanna jabbed him in the ribs. "Rachel's girls are terrific."

"Sure they are. One moves to London, becomes a Lubavitcher, and has six kids . . ."

"Dalia's not Lubavitcher, she's Orthodox."

". . . Tamara's a stand-up comedian, eight months pregnant, lives with the baby's father but won't marry him . . ."

"She's always been way-out," Shoshanna agreed. "Kind of like Leah."

"The third's a dot-com hotshot who hasn't seen her family in two years."

"It's hard when you own your own business. Zelda never leaves Seattle. Anyway, none of those things is unusual anymore."

He grinned. "The point is, Rachel won't die when she hears. Now let's wrap this up. You've asked for my vote—I say tell her."

Shoshanna could have predicted Daniel's response. He hated duplicity for the same reason she did, having been kept in the dark for so many years about *his* past. On their first date, they'd discovered they had this in common—a family secret revealed long ago that proved large enough to change their lives. But Daniel's was worse. He'd been brought up to believe he was a Christian—German-American Lutheran, to be exact. When he was eighteen, against his father's wishes, his mother decided to tell him the truth and let him sort things out for himself. She did it the night before he left for Columbia, after he'd packed the last of his clothes and his trunk was standing by the door of the Book Barn, where his mother and father made a modest living selling used books, the barn where Daniel, an only child, had read his way out of rural New Hampshire long before he'd actually left. After closing time that hot night in early September, she'd sat him down on the old sofa with the faded cabbage-rose upholstery and pulled over the rocker with the flattened-out seat cushion, and there in the glow of the alabaster lamp with the tassel at the end of its pull cord, amid books as musty as dry leaves, books that had kept him company his whole life like an unending stream of well-worn babysitters, his mother had rocked and rocked until she rocked out her secret.

"Your dad and I are Jewish." (Daniel could hear the crickets' wings rubbing together; he could feel the blood in his veins.) I mean we've lived a Christian life, but we aren't really. He and I were both born Jewish and we never actually converted, just sort of fell into the church when we first moved up here and the neighbors invited us to Sunday service and we went, just to be friendly, and the hymns were lovely and the people were so nice that we went back the next week and everyone just assumed we were Christians like they were—Safer could be any kind of name—and it would have been awkward to correct them."

By the time Daniel was born, his mother was singing in the choir and his father was running the church book bazaar, and when their boy got old enough, it seemed only natural to send him to Bible class along with his playmates. Sometimes, she said, they felt guilty, what with the rest of their families having perished in the Holocaust, but neither of them believed being Jewish had been worth dying for, so how could it be worth living for? Once his parents were safe in America, all they'd wanted was to stay alive, just blend in and stay alive, his mother said, and since they were orphans, with no embarrassing relatives likely to show up with sheytls or shtraymels on their heads, his parents felt secure in their new identities and gave themselves to the small town's embrace, and their friends became their family, and anyway, it was easier to pass for Protestant than to practice Judaism in a place where a synagogue was as rare as a jar of schmaltz.

His mother had smoothed the creases in her faded cotton skirt and stopped rocking. "So that's it. From now on, you can choose your own path," she said, as if offering him alternative hiking trails.

The alabaster lamp seemed unbearably bright. Daniel reached for its tassel and pulled. In the darkness, his mother resumed her rocking and Daniel remembered the time when he might have figured all this out for himself but didn't, the day he'd asked his father why, since there was so little call for them, he kept so many books on the Holocaust. "I bid on someone's library, I get everything in it," his father had answered tersely. Few of those volumes, however, were casual acquisitions. His parents had been piecing together their pasts from the diaries of others, documentary histories, parallel lives. As he listened to his mother, something else had become clear: The Book Barn was his parents' fortress, its stacks (those tall, tireless companions of his inquisitive youth) provided protection from exposure. The profession of antiquarian bookseller accommodated a Yiddish accent well by allowing his parents to appear cultured and literary rather than frightened and Jewish.

Eventually, Daniel would hear of other World War II refugees who hid their Judaism from their children, but when he had first learned his family's story, he'd thought they were the only underground Jews and he was the only kid who came home from college carrying a secret that could get him in trouble in the small town where taunts of "kike" and "Jew boy" erupted in the movie house when Tony Curtis appeared on the screen. Choosing the path less traveled, he'd become Jewish with a vengeance—majored in Judaic Studies at Columbia, joined the Hillel group on campus, taken graduate degrees at the Jewish Theological Seminary, married a rabbi's daughter beneath the huppah at Congregation Rodeph Tzedek—with his faux-Lutheran parents weeping on the bimah—and under the tutelage of his new father-in-law, celebrated his bar mitzvah the same year as his wedding. Twenty-five years later, Daniel Safer, the son of New England conversos, was one of America's leading Jewish ethicists.

So his vote was predictable. Still, Shoshanna needed to hear his reasoning. "If it's such a slam-dunk for you, how come I'm having so much trouble with this?"

"Maybe you enjoy having information Rachel doesn't. It evens the score from when you were a kid and she knew things about you that you didn't. If knowledge is power, then hoarding knowledge might be a power trip, right?" He noted Shoshanna's discomfort. "Look, we can swing on the horns of this dilemma till the cows come home—to milk a metaphor— but it's really not a tough call."

Daniel could be very clever. And *very* annoying. She pulled back and faced him. "If you've been aware of Jeremy's philandering all this time, why didn't *you* tell her?"

"Because what I heard was guy talk. What you've seen is real. Big difference." He kissed Shoshanna's hair.

All this draying around was making her crazy. She was quiet for a long while. "Okay, I'll do it. But in my own way, when I'm ready."

Shoshanna might have reached the same conclusion on her own, after many more martinis and contorted rationalizations, but working it through with Daniel, however irritating the process, shortened the agony. This was one of the perks of her marriage—having a second conscience, a live-in Jiminy Cricket who had your best interests at heart, wanted you to do the right thing, and wouldn't let you be a schmuck. Shoshanna provided a similar service for Daniel. For example, when he once mentioned he was taking Jake helicopter-skiing and she said, "You're doing WHAT!?" in a voice that by itself canceled the trip. Later he'd confessed that he wanted to turn Jake down but was afraid to appear overcautious in his son's eyes. Blaming Shoshanna made it easy. "Mom doesn't want us to go," he'd said. "She'd be too worried." Eventually Jake went helicopter-skiing on his own and Shoshanna blamed Daniel for making the sport sound reasonable in the first place. She would probably blame Daniel for whatever happened between her and Rachel. That's what spouses were for. But at the moment, thankful for his third degree, she kissed him deeply and felt the mound in his lap register an immediate barometric change, 30 degrees and rising. She unbuckled his belt.

"That's twice this week," he said afterward.

"Twice what?"

"That you've hit on me. Seduced your husband."

She zipped up his khakis. "I'm just a regular Circe."

"Seriously," he said. "Twenty-five years ago, if someone had told me I'd be turned on by a fifty-year-old and get a blow job in my living room in the middle of the afternoon, I'd have tried to sell him a bridge." (Fifty sounded surreal. Spooked, she thought of her hot flashes and Rachel's sandpaper innards and wondered if post-menopausal drought runs in families.) "Wish I could hang around for thirds, but the Scrolls beckon."

Daniel disappeared into his chaotic study. That the Dead Sea Scrolls were as captivating to him as the modern novel was to Shoshanna seemed incredible, until she realized that interpersonal problems—sex, adultery, sibling rivalry, deceit—hadn't changed much in three thousand years, and the questions she was grappling with right now, relating to her father, sisters, and brother-in-law, weren't all that different from those her ancestors had pondered in the desert.

She put on lipstick and went down to her office, where a flinty sun gleamed on the hardwood floor. "Buy rug," she scribbled on a pad, remembering her cold feet. Absent the Filofax, she didn't know where to put the note. Thankfully, her intrepid assistants were almost finished sorting through the ruins of her Dead Road Scrolls, organizing the tattered pages and piling the loose items in categories. If her private chaos took up any more staff time, she'd have to change the company name to My Time Is *Mine*.

"Remind me about this, would you, Fiona?" She gave the rug memo to a tall, big-boned woman wearing a Black Watch plaid jumper, black tights, and cloddy, sensible shoes. At the coffee machine, Shoshanna bypassed her usual decaf and opted for the hi-test. "Either of you come across today's page? I have no idea where I'm supposed to be tonight."

"Your memory improvement course?" joked Fiona, whose Oxford accent and British efficiency more than made up for her sarcasm.

Shoshanna hissed.

"Don't tease her today," said Elliott. "She's feeling fragile."

"If you hearken back to my intake interview," Fiona continued, "you'll recall instructing me to lay off your appointments; you said you'd handle them in your Filofax and I was to restrict myself to tracking the company projects, which I have done. Ta-da!" She flipped open her electronic organizer, punched a few buttons, and read, "By May 15 we're to locate two thousand square feet of sunlit rental space—East Side preferably—for the Manhattan branch of a Chicago ad agency. Linda Tarrero gave us till April 1 to inventory all the appliances in her new apartment and order the necessary service manuals, since the sellers left none behind and she has no idea how anything works. The Sackowitz bat mitzvah is March 20; we're doing the party." (Shoshanna had forgotten about Fiona's master calendar, bless her Anglo-Saxon soul.) "But what really makes me twitch in my knickers is this California job; it's turning into a major megiller and it's due St. Patrick's Day."

Yiddish wasn't Fiona's strong suit. "Refresh me on that?" Shoshanna poured herself a second cup of coffee. Her mind was a complete blank.

"You ran into a man who runs the California Visitors Bureau, old college chum, if I remember rightly. After you told him what you do for a living, he sent us crates of tourism brochures—best places for fishing, spelunking, summer theater, stuff like that. We're to fact-check every leaflet, make sure what they say exists still exists and its particulars are current—prices, phone numbers, e-mail addresses—and post it all on one mega-list for their Web site."

"Sounds straightforward enough; what's the problem?"

Elliott, an elfin man in his thirties who might have passed for a grown-up had his eyeglass frames not been tomato red, replied, "The problem is, a number of the brochures were printed two or more years ago—the Ice Age when it comes to the Internet. Now every pickle factory and petting zoo has a Web site and E-mail address that has to be added. I've spent two days on this one file alone and I'm still not done." He handed Shoshanna a fat folder marked *Greater San Diego*. "Here, have a look."

"E-mail, Web site, perfect segue, thank you, Elliott," said Fiona, pronouncing his name Ell-yutt. "Makes my point that paper is passé." She waved a few Filofax pages in Shoshanna's direction. "Time to join the electronic age!"

"I'm thinking about it," Shoshanna muttered.

"Here's a proposition. Buy yourself a Palm Pilot and I'll input on my own time even though it's not in my job description."

"I *said* I'd give it some thought, Fiona. Now, let's have the bad news. How many pages are missing?"

If you owned an electronic organizer, *nothing* would be missing. The little gizmo's foolproof. It reads your handwriting, you push a button, it downloads everything into the computer. So all your data is backed up in seconds and you can put the whole file on a floppy, just to be safer. Get it, *Safer*."

"Not funny."

"The latest Palm is so small you can pop it in a pocket," Elliott added.

"You two sound like a commercial. Even if I had a . . . a gizmo, a lot of what I need is not . . . not . . . inputtable?" She hadn't even mastered the lingo, much less the technology.

"What you *need* is highly debatable," replied Fiona. "Does an American citizen *need* to carry her passport from Greenwich Village to

Riverdale? Does one *need* to staple theater tickets for next September into one's calendar?"

"That reminds me," said Elliott, "tomorrow night you're seeing *Death of a Salesman* with Rachel. I found these." Like a proud archaeologist, he held up a smudged page, Thursday, March 11, with two crumpled mezzanine tickets attached.

"Let's hear it for the Luddites!" Shoshanna beamed. "My system works!" She marched back to her office and shut the door. Since Daniel had seen *Salesman* twice, she'd invited Rachel, but now it seemed like the wrong play, the absolutely wrong play for them to see together. That scene where the son barges into his father's hotel room and catches him with his mistress—Shoshanna couldn't bear to watch it with Rachel. That must have been what Daniel meant when he said everything would be distorted by the secret.

Had she not been so fatutzed (Leah's word), she'd have realized Torrey Pines would be in the Greater San Diego folder and she'd have passed it back to Elliott like a hot coal. But now that the file was in her hands, she couldn't resist flipping through it, and when she found the brochure, of course she picked it up.

Torrey Pines State Reserve is a wilderness island in an urban sea. With its panoramic views of the Pacific from Del Mar to La Jolla, it is one of the crown jewels of the California coast, a spectacular five-mile stretch of jagged bluffs and red-rock buttes with sandstone hiking trails that overlook the crashing surf.

The brochure showed a stand of Torrey pines with twisted trunks and gnarled branches. And that long view of Yucca Point, its cliffs slicing straight into the water like the walls of a medieval moat. And Razor Point Trail, where she and Stefanie had glimpsed a jackrabbit in a wind cave.

Senior year, spring break, their last blast before graduation. In June, they would go their separate ways, Stefanie to St. Thomas, where a job awaited her as a scuba-diving instructor in her uncle's business, Shoshanna to New York to live with her widowed father and work with Leah on *The Feminist Freethinker* until she could figure out what to do next. She wasn't looking forward to spending so much time with Leah, who'd been less enthusiastic about Shoshanna since the "kiddo" had developed strong ideas of her own. In fact, Shoshanna hadn't been particularly close to either of her sisters once she'd gone off to Oberlin and discovered a soul sister in her roommate. Stefanie was the person who'd pulled her through freshman year after Esther died. (Rachel was too distraught to be of any comfort, and Leah wasn't the comforting kind.) If not for Steffie, she wouldn't have shown up for a single class or turned in a page of homework, and she'd never have stopped drinking. "Quit or get out," her roommate had announced after one of her more revolting binges. Shoshanna had chosen sobriety rather than lose her best friend. It wasn't even a close call.

They'd come a long way since Freshman Orientation, when Stefanie, brown eyes flashing, took one look at Shoshanna and announced she preferred to room with an African-American. The college had insisted she make the effort for a month, and though Shoshanna was a pretty sad sack—still mourning her dead mother and openly romancing a fifth of Dewar's—Stefanie gave it a go and eventually declared the white girl tolerable. "A kike and a nigger-lady—paydirt for the KKK," she said, bopping around the room like a yahoo. They'd been living together ever since.

Race and religion weren't their only differences. Stefanie was an über-jock like Rachel, while Shoshanna, functioning as Leah's branch office, was the campus revolutionary. Shoshie carried the weight of the world on her shoulders. Steffie epitomized *joie de vivre*. Shoshanna, having absorbed her mother's timidity, was physically timid, while Stefanie was a world-class daredevil.

"You're too serious, Shishkebab!" she thundered one day as she pushed a long-toothed comb through her Afro, then left it standing straight up, like a crown. "There's more to life than meetings." A firm believer in self-improvement, her own and everyone else's, she spent four years cultivating Shoshanna's "underdeveloped strengths" until the girl she called Shishkebab became what Stefanie said she could be—as daring physically as she was politically, an adventurer whose escapades would have given Esther shpilkes had she lived to see them.

For their final spring vacation, they'd planned a serendipitous journey down the California coast in which each of them would plan the agenda on alternating days. It had worked beautifully so far. Sunday, Stefanie had chosen ballooning. Monday, Shoshanna had arranged for them to spend the day helping out at a San Diego women's center. (Stefanie had pitched in wholeheartedly, though she considered the women's movement a rip-off of the Black Power movement and insisted on calling feminists "libbers.") Tuesday, Steffie picked kayaking, and Shoshanna, close to fearless by then, was a wholehearted accomplice. Wednesday, Shoshanna, counterintuitively, programmed them into a day spa for massages and pedicures.

Thursday, Stefanie's choice was Torrey Pines. They were going tide pooling, she said. Shoshanna hadn't a clue what tide pooling was, but she scrambled along behind her roommate on a goat trail between vertiginous cliffs that plunged hundreds of feet from the wind-sculpted bluffs to the canyon floor. At the base of the bluffs signposts warned UNSTABLE CLIFFS: STAY BACK!

"*Now* they tell us." Shoshanna laughed.

In the shadow of a half-dozen hang gliders who looked like flying reptiles, the two girls made their way to the beach through a narrow passage scooped from the cliffs by seventy million years of geological time. Along the rugged shoreline, marine terraces had been exposed by the receding tide, with shallow pools filling the interstices between rock and coral, creating hundreds of self-contained aquariums, each teeming with marine life. Stefanie explained that tide pooling meant leaping from rock to rock and peering into every puddle. It was her idea to add the challenge of a competition: whoever saw a species first and identified it won a point.

"Two-spotted octopus!" Stefanie shouted as she knelt at the edge of a ribbed basin and pointed to a multiarmed creature with a beak like a parrot's. She called it a "rare sighting," though Shoshanna had been just as impressed by the sea cucumbers and hermit crabs, urchins and anemones, and the shells Stefanie identified embedded in the striated shale. Hours passed in the dazzling sunlight as Steffie racked up fifteen points to Shoshanna's zero.

"You're a regular Jacques Cousteau, Steff! Is there anything you can't do, for God's sake?"

"In Barbados, if I couldn't name nine out of ten living things in the ocean, my uncle wouldn't be giving me a job."

So intent were they on their sightings that they never noticed the tide coming in. It happened fast, the shallow pools disappearing into a blue-green blackness, the sea rising, closing over everything, until suddenly there were no rocks to leap to, no more shale jutting out of the water, and no one left in sight, only Stefanie, much farther out, chest deep now in the Pacific, waving and shouting, "Go ashore! Hurry!" just as Shoshanna lost her footing and fell in. The tide inundated the beach, the sea swirled and deepened, the waves gathered force and pounded the base of the cliffs. Her sneakers were waterlogged and her shorts billowing, making it impossible for Shoshanna to stay erect and move ahead at the same time, so she gave up trying, kicked off the sneakers, and tried swimming to shore. With every stroke, the current pulled her laterally. The undertow ground her down. Her bare legs scraped and slammed against rocks she couldn't see, geological protrusions that earlier had cradled those placid little tide pools and now stabbed through the ocean floor like the spikes in the road you're not supposed to enter at a car park. Instead of advancing toward the cliffs, she was dragged sideways. Still, her arms churned. She kicked and plowed through the heaving chop, losing all track of time until, overcome by fatigue, she let her feet drop and, miraculously, met a hard surface underfoot. Rock or sand, the ledge was firm enough to support her slow, hard push toward the cliff wall, where, out of a crevice, a root, like a gnarled hand, offered help. She grabbed it and hung on fast as the swells surged and eddied around her waist. Her eyes combed the surface of the sea, expecting to see Stefanie treading water or heading to shore with her strong, sleek crawl. But there was no nappy head bobbing in the waves, no brown arms slicing through the water. Neither did the cliff line, going off in both directions, yield the sight of her roommate clinging to a sister root or waving from a similar perch.

The current must have separated us, thought Shoshanna. Steffie's probably around a bend by now or in a cove. Trouble was, Shoshanna could see down the shoreline in both directions and there were no inlets or coves, just the soaring cliffs, a wall of bluffs that hid no secret refuge. The only signs of life were a glide of gulls and a red-throated loon diving and swooping above the spray; the only sounds, birdsong and the echo of her own screams. Her throat ached. She must have been shouting Steffie's name for a very long time. She must have been in the water for a very long time too; the root had chafed a red band between her thumb and forefinger and her skin was as puckered as that of a child who's been dillydallying in the bath. Hope spent, she clung to the root until the waters began their retreat and a stripe of sand exposed itself along the canyon wall, a path wide enough for her to mince and claw her way to the point of egress, all the while praying that Stefanie would be waiting there, exhilarated by nature's furies and eager to hear what activity Shoshanna had planned for them for Friday. But the goat trail was deserted. In the sky, where storm clouds should have been raging to match the wrathful surf, an improbable orange sun hung like a huge helium balloon. The day dared to remain beautiful.

Stefanie's body washed ashore in the morning. Head struck a rock, the Coast Guard said. Probably unconscious before she drowned.

Beaches were her downfall, her traumas, bi-coastal. In Maine, she'd lost faith in her parents; in California, her faith in her future. A sodden fatalism descended upon Shoshanna after Torrey Pines. Life seemed entirely beyond human control. Everything she'd learned in school, everything her family taught her, everything she'd been promised by Leah and the women's movement had turned out to be a hoax. Nobody had warned her about the derailments—that mothers die young and friends get sucked into the sea. Nobody told her that two young women reveling in life's wonders would be catnip to the stalker, that wearing one's happiness in public was like wearing diamonds to the docks. Stefanie said they'd be red meat for the Klan, not carrion for the Eye. Nobody told her that everything she'd been taught to value in herself was ultimately of no use—top grades, high ideals, feminist convictions, Irish-setter hair—none of it counted for squat when the chaos came. In a few hours on that California beach, she was pitched from a past that delivered rational rewards for effort to a warped present, one charged with a terrifying sense of her precarious purchase on the world, one that mocked the narrative of youthful omnipotence and replaced it with a craving for order and peace.

Shoshanna did not attend her college graduation. She spent a week in Barbados with Stefanie's family, then moved to New York and took a secretarial job in an import-export company, hoping to anesthetize her brain. She didn't officially leave the women's movement, there being no place to tender one's resignation, but did bow out of its leadership, which was fine with everyone but Leah; in movements there's never enough honor or power to go around anyway, and one less face in the camera lens, one less spouter of the creed, left more room for the others. Though still a believer, she'd lost her taste for battle, felt impotent, inconsequential, too weak to inspire others to be strong, too meek to matter. She wrote checks to support pro-choice advocacy and kept up her subscription to *The Freethinker*, but she had no desire to reconnect with Off Our Necks or any other organization. Group politics paled now beside the enormous significance of one life, one irreplaceable person. That was how she'd come to see the world.

Leah browbeat her for a while—not understanding, because Shoshanna couldn't explain it and didn't try—until finally, she'd washed her hands of the apostate, resigned to having lost her investment in her most promising protégée. But every so often, at one of their lunches, she'd let loose a tirade about her little sister's surrender to the status quo.

"Your purview has shrunk! Your vision has narrowed. You're wasting your talents, kiddo."

"What you call shrunken, I call focused," Shoshanna had replied. "What you see as narrowed, I see as deepened."

"You're a yellow-bellied, hen-hearted deserter. Finking out. Leaving it to others to get the job done. Who's going to advance the agenda if women like you abandon us?"

"I haven't abandoned anybody. I'm doing it differently, that's all. You're trying to change the world in big ways. I'm trying to help one person at a time."

"Oh, right! Like slavery could have been eradicated one plantation at a time?"

"I don't do slavery, nuclear proliferation, world hunger, or war crimes. I do what I can do."

"Which means finding the perfect vermeil berry spoons for Mrs. Pritchett's table?"

"Sometimes—if it makes Mrs. Pritchett happy and frees her to do more important things. Other times it means finding a safe house for a battered woman, or a support group for an incest survivor. I'm not a movement person, Leah. I'm a gun for hire."

Though her answers sounded polished and confident, Shoshanna was still trying to understand her own trajectory and the reasons why so many onetime activists had dropped out of the movement. What put a damper on the spirit and energy that fueled that early fervor? How did the banner-waving troublemakers of the sixties and seventies morph into well-behaved feminists who, at the end of the twentieth century, almost dared not speak the movement's name?

By now Shoshanna could lecture on the subject, if anyone cared. For one thing, the founders of the Second Wave were, like her, entering their fifties, sixties, and seventies, and were somewhat the worse for the wear and tear. Age takes its toll and the years can grind a rebel down (though you'd never know it from Leah). Some foot soldiers drifted away because circumstances changed, for good and for ill. For good, because so many battles were won. For ill, because the conservatives whipped up a backlash and demonized feminists as man-hating, anti-family lesbians. Under attack, younger women disavowed the feminist label, afraid it would mark them as unlovable, career-crazy "feminazis" whom no man would want as the mother of his children. Fear of the f-word was not just a semantic problem, it was the by-product of a right-wing strategy to destroy what a movement needs most—solidarity. The opposition took the movement's vocabulary away—appropriating words like "pro-life" and "pro-family" for policies that were anti-woman and anti-child. They ridiculed movement leaders, their looks, clothes, and language. Some critics called the women's movement radical and dangerous; others said it was obsolete and unnecessary. After the media proclaimed the "post-feminist era," anyone who was still talking about inequality or date rape or sex stereotypes was accused of being "politically correct." A friend of Shoshanna's who worked with welfare mothers was attacked as a "victim" feminist." Other activists were called "strident" and made to feel like relics from another era.

Not every woman could stand up to such castigation and ridicule. Some ran scared and retreated altogether. Some affiliated with more moderate organizations, doing the same work but with less fanfare. Some stuck with the struggle but discovered the press was no longer interested. When one newspaper failed to cover the thirtieth anniversary of *Roe v. Wade*, Leah fired off a scathing Letter to the Editor that Shoshanna treasured for its clarity:

> Thousands of Americans celebrated the anniversary of the Supreme Court's abortion rights decision yesterday, but you'd never know it from the news blackout in your paper. No matter how many thousands show up at one of our demonstrations, you find a way to say we're irrelevant, either by reporting a much smaller turnout, ridiculing us by your choice of photographs, or not covering our events at all. Without media coverage, it's hard for a movement to make its work known or attract adherents. How can a woman join a movement she can't find? How can a movement grow if its older leaders are pronounced has-beens, its young leaders ignored, its name made a pejorative, its precepts systematically distorted, and its most triumphant victories cited

as proof that it isn't needed anymore? You keep saying feminism
is dead when the truth is, you keep trying to kill it.

"The good news is, they published the letter," said Shoshanna at
lunch that year. "The bad news is, the pundits are spinning the story
like mad."

"Fuck the pundits," said Leah. "They've announced our demise
every year since we were born. Check the microfilm. Check Nexis. Same
headlines in 1973—'R.I.P. Women's Lib' 'Hello, Post-Feminist Era.'
What crap! We're here to stay."

Leah certainly was. But other women had fallen by the wayside, and
Shoshanna, whom Leah counted among the deserters, thought she
understood why. Some left because they were burned out and wanted
their personal lives back. Some considered the job finished because
they'd won their litigation or legislation and weren't hurting anymore.
Some got fed up with the sound and fury of political combat, or got
tired of speaking in the plural. Some had worked for years on one issue
and were ready to move on. Some were disheartened by defeat, scarred
by infighting, frustrated by foot-dragging and backsliding. Some were
intimidated by the backlash. And some pulled back from the front lines
because they needed to make money, or missed their families, or were
just plain tired. They didn't become converts to the Moral Majority,
and they didn't repudiate feminist goals or give up hope. They left
because they wanted to reconnect with other human beings around
something other than political struggle.

Shoshanna left because her best friend drowned.

"I need my file, sweetums," crooned Elliott, red-rimmed glasses in the
lead as he poked his head through her office door. "Gotta finish the rest
of those San Diego calls."

She looked up vacantly. The ghost image of her roommate's caramel
face grew dim around the edges, like a movie fade-out. Shoshanna put
the Torrey Pines brochure back in the folder and handed it to him.

"Oh, you forgot this," he added, holding out tomorrow's smudged calendar page with the two tickets attached.

She took the page and reached for her staple remover. "How'd you like to see *Death of a Salesman*, Elliott?" His eyes widened as she gave him the tickets. "Offer the second one to Fiona. If she can't make it, take your roommate."

When the door closed behind him, Shoshanna picked up the phone. "Hi, Rachel. Sorry this is so last minute, but I have to cancel the theater tomorrow night," she told her sister's answering machine. "I'm totally swamped. Rain check soon, I promise."

eleven

TONIGHT THEY WERE GOING INTO THE CITY to hear Carl's last will and testament. His last wink and testicle, Leah called it. His last whoop and tetany. His last leer and lunacy. The schmuck had to "set things straight," or so he said in the side letter that Desmond Driscoll, Esq.— right from Central Casting in a three-piece pinstriped suit—read aloud the evening of March 15. Later, she would fault herself for missing the mischief in that phrase, for wasting time being pissed at the ostentation of the evening rather than anticipating the havoc to come. By the time she'd tuned in to Carl's Grand Guignol, it was too late.

Driscoll had already carried out the first part of his client's instructions. He'd sent a white stretch limousine to pick them up and ferry them to Manhattan, a vulgar amenity that Leah had vigorously protested, relenting only after Leo accused her of putting her ideology above his brother's last request. She'd slouched in the back seat and, with anthropological detachment, studied the vehicle's excesses while Henry helped himself to papaya juice from the well-stocked bar and activated a small TV that rose from the floor like a periscope. To her horror, Leo found a cigar in the humidor and lit up.

Upon arriving in the conference room of a Lexington Avenue law office with a drop-dead view of the Chrysler Building, they discovered that the promised meal was to be a four-course feast catered by Le Cirque. That alone should have tipped her off to the circus to come, but she'd been too busy deploring Carl's extravagance and hadn't thought to suspect the basic absurdity of his dead hand reaching beyond the grave to ply them with food and drink. Snowy napery blanketed the long conference table. A multiarmed compote laden with fruit, petits fours, and hand-dipped chocolates stood on a marble sideboard flanked by urns filled with calla lilies so smooth they might have been coated in cream. Across the room, a chef in a starched white jacket and toque guarded a rolling cart topped by a silver dome polished glossy as a mirror. Along one side of the conference table were three place settings, silver gleaming, crystal twinkling, candles kindled despite the overhead lights.

Leah took the middle chair—which she knew was intended for Leo—determined to rebel every way she could. Facing them, like a grand inquisitor, sat Driscoll with no setting at his place, just a glass, a pitcher of water, and a small stack of documents. His thin-lipped grimace and dour demeanor suggested his felt his current task beneath him.

Two waiters in black tie brought a tray of drinks. One poured champagne for Leo while the other filled Henry's crystal flute with apple cider at his request. Leah, hunched like an angry troll, ordered water. "Not Evian. Not Perrier. Not San Pellegrino. New York *tap*." She resented having to schlep into the city for a dinner she didn't want, summoned by a brother-in-law she despised, to hear the text of a will she knew would disappoint no matter how low her expectations. But the extravaganza was Carl Gustav Rose's last chance to rub their noses in the life they'd missed, the life Leo had repudiated when he chose art over business and Leah over "all the normal girls in the world." Carl always made it clear that he thought her a raving radical, which to Leah was a badge of honor.

"I bet your CommiFem wife would like me better if I spelled my Carl with a K," he'd once sneered to Leo, though nothing could make Leah like Carl better. He'd built a fortune in real estate and lived in a world far removed from theirs, yet he insisted on taking his artsy brother and dowdy sister-in-law out to dinner several times a year, just to lord it over the peons. It was as if he couldn't enjoy his conspicuous consumption, his house on the North Fork, the Park Avenue duplex, his supermodels and supper clubs, without exercising his bragging rights and showing off to them. A few weeks before he died, Carl had driven them out to Teterboro Airport to visit his new plane.

"Today a peacock, tomorrow a feather duster," she said of her brother-in-law's ostentation. "The man is insufferable, Leo. Knows the price of everything but the value of nothing. Why do you think he keeps flaunting stuff you and I don't give a fuck about? He's making a big tzimmes to convince *himself* he's happy? Only someone who's pathologically insecure needs three houses, four cars, six girlfriends, and a dozen jars of mustard in his pantry. What's he afraid of—running out?" Leah saw her husband's brother as a hopeless reprobate, the wormy fruit of patriarchy, capitalism's turd. She loathed him. The feeling was mutual. To Carl, Leah embodied the uppity bitch in combat boots who dared to challenge the natural order of the universe.

"You ladies will deserve equality when you can piss standing up," he said once, abandoning all pretense of family amity. When Leah gave as good as she got, the insult Olympics were under way, their rancor intensifying with each round.

"When your IQ reaches 50, Carl, you should sell."

"When your boobs hit the floor, you should consider a bra."

"If a man speaks in a forest and there's no woman there to hear him, is he still dead wrong?"

"If they made penicillin out of mold, why can't they make something useful out of you?"

"When you open your mouth, Carl, it's only to change feet."

"Never trust anyone who bleeds six days a month and doesn't die."

"May you fall into the outhouse just as a regiment of Ukrainians finishes a prune stew." (Yiddish curses were Leah's specialty.) After a while, she realized he was enjoying the duel too much, so she changed tack and hit him with her full frost. Though Leah had begun speaking in sentences when she was sixteen months old and hadn't stopped since, she kept quiet no matter what his provocation, diverting herself by making mental lists of Shakespeare's plays, the chemical elements, the major constellations. Finally, he'd quit trying. Carl hated to be ignored.

Had it been up to Leah, they would have stopped seeing him altogether after the insemination, but Leo the Gentle-hearted was determined to maintain fraternal contact, especially after their parents died. It was his way of honoring their memory. Afraid the raging bull might gore her husband or perforate the family secret, Leah continued to accompany Leo, ready to play the matador's cape. The likelihood of Carl exposing them was remote. He'd shown zero interest in the boys from the start, which was a relief to both Leo and Leah, though for different reasons. She, a die-hard proponent of nurture over nature, judged Carl's disregard of Freddy and Henry as proof that the parental "instinct" is a cultural invention. Leo was relieved that his brother wanted minimum contact with the boys, since he was having enough trouble feeling like their real father as it was. Now that Carl was packed in an urn, their secret was safe.

Leah asked the lawyer the circumstances of Carl's death. Driscoll stammered that his client had been in the company of a woman known as the Moscow Masseuse. He had not, as Leo had feared, been alone.

"Died in the saddle." She chuckled. "John Garfield, Nelson Rockefeller. And now Carl Rose." She rearranged her four forks, two spoons, and three knives to match the Deco sunburst on the spire of the Chrysler Building as Driscoll began reading the side letter, which described precisely what Carl wanted to have happen during this command performance—the canapes, his wine and food choices, the after-dinner liqueurs to accompany the reading of the will.

Their first course was smoked Norwegian salmon with capers, lemon, and onions, after which a flourishing sweep of the silver dome revealed a majestic crown roast, which was carved table-side and served with Potatoes Dauphinoise (Carl's affinity for Louis XIV) and baby asparagus. Leah got the message: "See how great this is?" Carl was saying. "You guys never knew how to live." Still, she savored every dish, and though her sweet tooth was normally satisfied by an Oreo, she found herself eagerly anticipating the Belgian chocolates from the compote on the sideboard. Instead, dessert was a mountain of thin pancakes layered with hot apple slices, over which the chef tipped a copper saucepan, struck a match, and poured a fiery stream of cognac. "Gâteau de Crêpe à la Normande!" he announced in Frenchified tones. If the service got any fancier, they'd have to bring the after-dinner liqueurs in a Rolls.

She was licking her spoon when Driscoll checked the clock and donned his glasses. "As executor of Carl Rose's estate, I have called you, his heirs, to this office according to my client's wishes, and with the permission of the Surrogate's Court, I shall now read his testamentary document." From that point on, the lawyer kept his eyes riveted to the text. Later, after the mayhem, Leah would wonder if he knew what he was about to unleash and couldn't bear to witness it.

Carl left his real estate holdings and his stock portfolio to the United Jewish Appeal, a wildly eccentric bequest given that he'd shown no prior interest in the Jewish community or the State of Israel. "The officers of the UJA shall make every attempt to enhance the profitability of my properties," Driscoll read, "thus ensuring that Jews everywhere may have a lifelong supply of prescription drugs and polyester yarmulkes." Leah burst out laughing. The bastard had a sense of humor. According to his will, Carl was leaving this fortune to the UJA because it was his father's favorite charity. The subtext would soon become obvious. He had left almost nothing to his mother's favorite charity—Leo.

At ten, Leo had learned from a maiden aunt that when he was six months old, his mother had become seriously ill and the boys had to be separated. Three-year-old Carl, robust and indestructible, was allowed to stay with his mother, while Leo, a premature baby, skinny, sickly, and difficult to care for, was sent to live with the aunt. That arrangement lasted for more than two years, until his mother was fully recovered and strong enough to provide the attention Leo needed. His only conscious memory of that period was the chocolate cake that greeted him the day his aunt brought him home. His mother, consumed by guilt, could not do enough for Leo, while Carl, whom she perceived as having been unfairly privileged, was shunted aside as if he'd already received enough attention to last a lifetime. At twelve, Leo was struck by polio, a mild case that left him temporarily enfeebled but not crippled. Aware by then of where he'd spent his first two years, he was terrified of being sent away again, though to Carl's everlasting resentment, their mother responded to Leo's illness by drawing him even closer.

Leah was convinced that, in his psyche, her husband remained the sent-away child. She took an academician's interest in the difference between his reaction to his *fear* of his abandonment and her reaction to having had two parents who in fact or feeling, abandoned her for real. Whereas she had reinvented herself as a tough broad with the grit to go it alone, Leo became a good Jewish boy who'd do anything to avoid being cut off from those he called family. What else could explain his being so fucking nice? Guilty for having displaced Carl as their mother's favorite, he'd turned himself into his brother's punching bag, but no matter how nice he was, Carl could never forgive him for putting an end to the idyllic years when he, Carl, was the prince. He'd been punishing Leo ever since. Why would he stop now? thought Leah, as Driscoll read the rest of his bequests.

Leo got an Andy Warhol he'd once ridiculed, but none of the paintings he'd coveted. The rest of Carl's art collection—Miró, Kandinsky, Shahn, Marsh, the Halsmann photographs, the Giacometti sculpture— went to the Museum of Modern Art. The Metropolitan got his eighteenth-century furniture. Leah couldn't care less about that; it was what he'd done with his books that left her speechless. The first editions, maybe two hundred of them, and the leatherbound sets of Maupassant and Dickens went to the library at the University of Miami, Carl's alma mater. Leah, his English professor sister-in-law, was the beneficiary of works by a few select, perniciously chosen authors whose names Driscoll mispronounced as he read through the list: "the Marquis de Sade and Sigmund Freud, August Strindberg, Lionel Tiger, Phyllis Schlafly, George Gilder, Midge Decter, Norman Podhoretz, Paul Weyrich, Camille Paglia, Richard Viguerie."

She asked for a glass of red wine. Carl wasn't stupid, but she hadn't imagined he could know her nemeses, each name a slap in a feminist's face.

The lawyer continued in his brain-dead voice: "My final bequest requires a preamble. Though I promised to protect my brother's secret, I said I would do so for as long as I lived. That pledge has been fulfilled. But now that I am dead, I want the truth put on the record for posterity so that Henry and Frederick can benefit from it. Given advances in DNA testing and gene research, they probably would have stumbled on the truth eventually. I prefer that they get it from me, their father."

A fist down Driscoll's throat, a chair through the plate-glass window, set fire to the document, feign a heart attack—nothing she could think of would stop Carl's bullet from leaving its chamber. Henry leaned forward trying to understand what the lawyer had said. Leo went limp as a rag. His groan was the sound of a dying animal.

"It would be disingenuous to claim that because women's lib says so, the sperm is incidental. From *Oedipus Rex* to *Star Wars*, the identity of a man's father has always mattered to him. The boys deserve to know their genetic heritage should they ever wish to procreate. Furthermore, as their father, I feel it only right that I should provide for them."

He left them five million each. Payable over five years. Looking up for the first time, Desmond Driscoll sent a book of bank checks skittering across the table toward Henry. "With the surrogate's permission, I have already transferred the first million to an account in your name. Frederick's inheritance will not be available to him until he is released from prison." The lawyer returned to the document. "Since it is clear that neither of my sons possesses the financial acumen to manage wealth responsibly, I also bequeath to them five years of paid investment advice to increase the possibility that, rather than dissipate their fortunes, they might prosper further. I do not mean for them to abstain from sybaritic pleasures. On the contrary, I want to enable them to pursue a lifestyle far more gratifying than the one in which they were raised. I do not claim to love my sons, but I wish them well."

Henry stared at the checkbook. Leo appeared comatose. Across the way, in the Chrysler Building, a suite of offices went dark as the cleaning crew finished its work and doused the lights. Leah remembered a line from Lenny Bruce: "Comedy is tragedy plus time." Maybe for the ancient Greeks. But what had happened on the ides of March in the year 1999 would never be funny to her, not in ten years or fifty. Had she thought it through in the limo instead of focusing on all that diversionary luxury, she'd have known that Carl would deliver his death blow posthumously, when he could do it without having to face them. She'd have sensed what was coming and told Henry the truth herself, understanding as only she could that Carl would reveal their secret, not just to destroy his little brother once and for all, but to settle the score with *her*.

At first, the deal had been quite straightforward. Leo wanted Rose family DNA to increase the chance of the baby's physical resemblance. Carl agreed to provide enough sperm for two inseminations because he fancied the idea of witnessing what his genes could produce without having to take responsibility for the product. (Wasn't that every bachelor's dream?) But once they'd begun to formalize the arrangements, he'd got it into his head to impregnate Leah "the old-fashioned way." Unless she slept with him, he said, the deal was off. Clearly he wasn't turned on by her—to say the least, she wasn't his type. He wanted to humble her, to make her come crawling to his bed.

"When turtles sprout wings! When the White House turns purple! When the fucking Pope is a woman!" she'd roared the day he called with his ultimatum. She'd slammed down the phone.

The chutzpah of his demand amazed her less than his change of heart a week or so later when he'd called back and, without embellishment, announced that he would go ahead with the original plan. The next day, he'd jerked off to an XX-rated movie and delivered himself of two turkey basters' worth of active swimmers, a soupçon of which Leo had deposited into Leah's vagina to produce Freddy. Two years later, after a spell in the freezer at the local sperm bank, another squirt was shpritzed upstream to spawn Henry, and what was left, Leo poured down the drain. Knowing nothing of Carl's ultimatum, Leo always felt his brother had done him a mitzvah. At the time, Leah, who couldn't figure out why a man as combative as Carl had given up so easily, chalked it up to the male animal's compelling urge to reproduce himself. But tonight she understood what had been obvious to Carl twenty-eight years ago. The mere possibility of his going public with the secret would be torture enough for Leo. As for Leah, he didn't have to sleep with her to humble her. So long as he controlled the secret, he had the power. He had only to decide when to use it.

The neon zigzags on the Chrysler Building calmed her with their symmetry and made her wonder if people became architects because they fear anarchy. Anyone looking in from across the way would not have known what to make of the three figures sitting on one side of the long conference table, motionless. They could have been a George Segal tableau. Leo, his face a flat tire, slumped in his chair. Henry had begun hyperventilating, arguably a sane response for an instant millionaire who'd just learned that his uncle is his father. Leah, for the second time in her life, the second time in a week, was at a loss for words. Pissed on again by another creep.

"Stay as long as you like," said Driscoll, who'd gathered his papers and was backing out of the room. "The car will wait."

She had no idea how long they'd sat there before they finally dragged themselves to the elevator and into the limousine. Speeding over the Brooklyn Bridge, she recalled sitting in that same back seat a few hours ago with nothing on her mind but automotive excess. She hadn't known how happy her miserable life had been.

At home, Henry went straight to his room.

"Henry?" Leo said in a whisper.

"He's gone to bed."

"He hates me."

"It's okay, Leo."

They climbed the stairs together.

Leo undressed slowly and lay down in his underwear. "I'm not real."

"Of course, you're real. Don't be ridiculous."

He was staring at the ceiling fixture. "Not his real father. Nothing real." Carl had seen through him—knew he'd been a weakling as a child, an impotent husband, a false father, a failed artist. But the boys hadn't known what an imposter he was.

"Stop it, Leo. For Chrissake, if you aren't real, who's been giving me such a pain in the ass lately?"

Not a flicker. There'd be no reasoning him out of this one. Her words were useless against the silent weeping and the agony in his eyes. She spread both blankets over him, held his ponytailed head against her chest, and, when he didn't stop shivering, covered his body with her own and cried with him.

The next morning, there was a note propped against the sugar bowl:

This time I'm gone for good. You can throw out the stuff I left in my room. Don't try to find me. I never want to see you again.

What happened last night explains things that didn't make sense before. Now I understand why Freddy and me ["Freddy and I" she corrected reflexively, despising herself for it] *are so fucked up. But I don't understand how you could have made it with Carl. And I don't get why Dad . .* [he'd crossed out "Dad" and written] *Leo stuck around, unless he never knew you were boffing his brother. If he didn't know, I feel sorry for him. If he did know, then I owe him something for all the years he took care of me even though I wasn't his. Either way, he's having a rough time now, so give him this and tell him thanks.*

Henry

Attached was one of his new checks. Pay to the order of "Mr. Leo Rose," he'd scrawled in his loopy, childish script: "One Hundred Thousand Dollars." She noted the signature: "Henry Blackwell Wasserman." Through welling tears, she read the letter twice more. While it aroused the searing pain of a rejected mother, a woman falsely accused, what struck her most was his last line. This son she'd given up on, this wastrel she'd thought selfish and amoral, had, in the crucible of his distress, felt sympathy for the broken man he no longer considered his father, felt it keenly enough to sign away 10 percent of the first year of a fortune that had been his for less than a day. She hadn't thought him capable of such an act. For the first time ever, her love for her son was tinged with respect, and though he'd maligned her terribly, making her the heavy of the tale, she wondered if she might have raised a mensch after all.

Carl's will told the truth but not the whole truth, yet lacking information to the contrary, Henry had to be excused for assuming himself the product of an affair between his mother and his uncle. The will never said Leah had rejected Carl at the risk of remaining childless. It didn't explain that Henry was conceived, not in his uncle's bed, but on the kitchen table in a Greenwich Village apartment. It didn't describe how they held a mirror between her legs and pored over the self-insemination diagrams they'd found through the Reproductive Rights Underground, the same folks who published "Ten Ways to Induce Your Own Abortion." It didn't recount Leo's search for the perfect turkey baster, or the rituals he devised to make the baby his, the incantations and force of will that transformed Carl's sperm into a generic fertilizing agent so disembodied from its source that it may as well have been mail-ordered from a seed catalogue.

She read Henry's note again. If it was a tactical mistake hiding his provenance all these years, not fleshing out the rest of the story last night when they'd had the chance was just plain dumb. Instead of sitting there in wounded silence, they could have comforted their son, described his immaculate conception and all the love that went into it, conjured the laughter in that kitchen. Once they got home, she could have made a pot of tea and insisted the three of them stay up and talk. Could have bullied Leo out of his funk rather than let him crawl under the covers as if he were the only shock victim in the house. He had nothing to be ashamed of, for Chrissake, he was the good guy in the saga, a father in all the ways that counted. But neither of them had said a word. So no wonder Henry had figured his father for a cuckold, his mother for a whore. Still, that wasn't why he'd left. He left because he'd been lied to. No one likes to be lied to. Lying is why bad things keep happening to smart people. The longer a secret is buried, the more ballistic it is when exposed, its fallout more damaging than the facts one meant to conceal. Oedipus, upon learning that Polybus is not his father, asks, "How could he love me so, if I was not his?" Twenty-five hundred years later, Henry was asking the same question. From Greek drama to Jewish farce, same story.

He'd have survived the shock had they told him the truth themselves. But shock compounded by deceit and humiliation can be too much to bear. Leah remembered, at one of their lunches, asking Shoshanna how she'd felt when she first learned about her secret sister.

"Like a fool. Like I'd been duped by the people I trusted most in the world. Like a dummy for not having figured it out." Judging by her adult obsessions, Shoshanna had yet to recover from her parents' secret. In her way, Leah, too, remained similarly obsessed, wanting to know whatever Sam had been hiding for fifty years that would explain his leaving her. It drove her wild to think her parents might die before she could learn the truth, yet there was little likelihood of her hearing it from either of them. Dena Dearest, now in her eighties, had been committed to a mental hospital since what she quaintly termed "the incident," when she'd put on her clogs and run through the New England Conservatory with a can of kerosene, setting their Steinways on fire. (A jury found her not guilty of arson by reason of insanity, the same grounds on which Leah eventually found her not guilty of pyrotechnic mothering.) Sam was still lucid, at least according to Shoshanna, but just as unreachable, and not just because he lived thousands of miles away; because he was Sam.

She folded Henry's letter and shoved it in the silverware drawer. The check she carried to the bedroom. Leo was still asleep, though it was nearly noon. Surely Henry's generosity would take the edge off last night.

They didn't have to cash the check; once they sold the Warhol, they'd be in good shape. The important thing was that Henry had written it.

"You're not going to believe this!" she trilled as she tugged at Leo's blanket. His head was a gray blob against the marshmallow pillows. "Wake up!"

His lashes fluttered.

She held the check in front of his face. His eyes were an empty room. She found a pair of reading glasses, set the nosepiece in place, half-circled the stems behind his ears.

"Henry left you a present. Look!"

He turned his face to the wall.

"I know you're upset, Leo; I know you're sad. But think about what this means. He's telling you you've been a good dad and he's grateful. It's his thank-you." She couldn't stop babbling. Having lived through so many of these episodes, she knew by now what to expect. If she couldn't snap him out of it, his paintings would grow dark or he'd stop going up to his studio altogether. Food would sit on his plate untouched, conversation would grind to a grunt. Usually, medication brought him back, but sometimes the plunge was unstoppable until, for no apparent reason, it would stop. Waiting it out, she would remark upon what an inexact science psychology was, not a science at all, really, just a bunch of contradictory speculations and obfuscating terms. Nothing like her discipline. Any two professors in any English department in the country could identify a sonnet or a simile, even if they disagreed on what makes a poem great or whether postmodernism was a crock. But psychology was the sum of a hundred years of theory, and its practitioners spoke in jargon and often disagreed about the basics—diagnosis, prognosis, treatment. Leo's psychiatrists said he was suffering from "clinical depression," a category too amorphous to be meaningful to Leah. The only expert who'd made sense explained Leo's condition through metaphor, comparing his type of depressed personality not to a tree that snaps in a storm but to a reed that bends low, then swings back when the wind dies down.

three daughters

Sitting on the edge of their bed watching her husband sleep, she loathed herself for being so impatient with him, so unappreciative and unfeeling. She made herself recall the things she'd once found so remarkable about him, especially for a man. His bone-deep decency. The intense way he listened. The empathy that showed in his eyes. The luminosity of his early paintings. His benevolence to the boys. (Even after becoming paternity-obsessed, he'd remained attentive and caring, more so by far than she.) And other astonishments: his lack of arrogance, the way he would offer to negotiate their disputes even after he'd won, his fierce hatred of hypocrisy. What Leah had loved most about him, she realized, were the many ways he'd loved her. His solicitude. His admiration for her intellect. His respect for her passions. His pride in her work—not romantic to every woman perhaps, but to her more seductive than sex.

She shook Leo by the shoulders. "You have to wake up! It's after twelve." He turned toward her. Gray whiskers stubbled his cheeks.

His eyelids dropped like shutters. "I can't, Leah. I'm sorry."

After March 15, every day was like that. He'd have slept sixteen hours at a crack had she let him. Instead, she badgered him with books, played CDs, held animated one-way conversations in which she talked to him as if he were actually listening. She told him urban legends she'd found on the Internet, propped an art book on his lap as if it were breakfast in bed, brushed his long hair, and sang "Darling, you are growing old / Silver hairs among the gold." Her talent to amuse surprised even her, but the audience of one remained unmoved. Little remained of her husband—the man on whom her independence had depended, the man who'd been her net as she trapezed through life— but his sorrow.

"I'm tired," he said.

She remembered Samuel Beckett's "Every word is a stain upon silence" and gave up trying.

twelve

THE CARDWELL NIGHTMARE. Rachel had dreamt it again last night. (Factoid: "Dreamt" is the only word in the English language ending in *mt*.) Other people had recurring nightmares—dreams of falling, forgetting their lines, being chased, taking an exam they hadn't studied for— anxieties anyone could relate to. Rachel's nightmare lacked that universality. It wasn't something you could laugh about the next day or confide to a friend, unless the friend happened to be a lesbian pedophile.

Frequent reruns had taught her what brought it on, and while there were other incitements, the most potent catalysts were symbols associated with St. Patrick's Day. This time it was a needlepoint pillow ordered by one Bridget O'Malley as a surprise for her fiancé. The design had a green clover in the center—Bridget insisted a proper shamrock was a three-leaf clover, not four—and above it the words "You can always tell an Irishman, but you can't tell him much." Though Rachel had been working on it full-tilt, by March 17, the saint's big day, the pillow still was unfinished. It was the first delivery date she'd ever missed. Since last week, when Shoshanna canceled their theater date because *her* business was overextended and Rachel had made the mistake of volunteering to help out on the California project, she'd fallen behind on everything. Fact-checking those tourism brochures should have been a slam dunk, but she'd run into bed-and-breakfasts that no longer served breakfast, a rafting outfit without liability insurance, endless misspellings. The job was taking forever.

Rachel promised to hand-deliver the pillow within forty-eight hours, but Bridget said if it couldn't be a St. Patty's Day present, forget it. So now it was front and center in Rachel's showroom awaiting a customer whose affection for a Donohue or O'Reilly might recommend its purchase. Not only did the sight of it remind her of stress and overwork, it had probably triggered the dream: Miss Cardwell was wearing a three-leaf-clover brooch the day Rachel's real-life nightmare began.

Blue Spruce knew how to do St. Patrick's Day, she'd give them that. Over the school's bronze sign they'd draped a canvas that changed the word "blue" to "green." The kitchen turned out corned beef and cabbage, Irish soda bread, and green Kool-Aid. After dinner, a squadron of visiting bagpipers filled the assembly hall with competing plaids and deafening wheezes. One of the gym teachers taught the girls a jig, which Rachel learned quicker than anyone and performed with the light-footed finesse that distinguished all her physical efforts—field hockey, modern dance, ice skating, skiing, whatever she put her mind and muscles to. Rachel lived in her body in a different way than most girls; there was nothing tentative in her movements, no anticipatory fear of strain or injury, no squealing when her feet touched the boggy bottom of the lake. She could swim longer, throw farther, and run faster than any other girl at school. Her body always seemed to deliver what she needed—a burst of energy for the sprint, a deeper breath for the dive, euphoria between her thighs.

It was hard for her to understand how something that felt so good could possibly be wrong, yet the student handbook listed her secret pleasure among the six infractions that warranted expulsion: stealing, lying, cheating, fighting, smoking, and "self-abuse." When she'd first learned to read, she'd had to ask an older girl what that meant. *"Masturbation,"* said the student in a whisper. Then Rachel had to ask what *that* meant, which was how she found out at the age of six that her favorite physical activity was strictly prohibited (though that hadn't stopped her). The girls in the nearby cots knew it was just a matter of time before Miss Cardwell caught her rubbing and humping under the covers, which was exactly what happened during bed check on St. Patrick's night, two years before Sam rescued her.

"Trollop!! What are you *doing*?!" Miss Cardwell pushed the sleeves of her green sweater above her bony elbows as if to administer a blow. Instead, she ordered Rachel to follow her to her room, a garret off the first-floor stairwell that served as the dorm proctor's quarters. Shivering in her nightgown and bare feet, Rachel was prepared for the worst—a thrashing, humiliation, expulsion. Instead, Miss Cardwell closed the door behind them and, with the turn of her key, became another person, a reverse Frankenstein monster whose knife-edged features turned soft and blurry as she lilted, "There's nothing to be afraid of, dear, we're just going to put on a play together, a fantasy . . ."

When she wasn't being dorm proctor, Miss Cardwell was the drama coach in charge of school productions. But a play in the middle of the night? In the teacher's bedroom?

Miss Cardwell opened the drawer of her night table and lit two votive candles. "I'll be the Queen and you'll be my lady-in-waiting. That means you have to do whatever I tell you." She turned off the lights, then slowly, with a regal stateliness, removed her plaid skirt, the green sweater with the shamrock pin, the brown brogues and woolen stockings, and finally, to Rachel's astonishment, the sensible white cotton underwear. "Come here," she said.

Rachel inched toward the teacher and stood there in her nightgown, afraid. Never having seen a naked middle-aged woman, not even an unclothed Esther, she was repulsed by the teacher's crepey breasts, the pumpkin hips, the matted triangle of hair at the base of her belly.

Miss Cardwell stroked the girl's cheek. "Curtsy to Her Majesty," she said.

Rachel curtsied. Every Blue Spruce girl knew how.

The woman stretched out on her bed, raised her arms over her head, and opened her veined thighs. "Now come up here and do as you're told," she said in a voice that had grown burrs.

However repugnant the Queen's orders, the ten-year-old performed as commanded, never imagining she had the choice to do otherwise. From the day she'd entered the nursery division, Rachel had been trained to respect authority, especially Blue Spruce authority, and tonight that authority was a dorm proctor whose desires required cold cream, a hairbrush, a candle, Rachel's fingers, Rachel's tongue. When Her Majesty was sated, the lady-in-waiting, fighting nausea, expected to be summarily dismissed.

But to Rachel's confusion, Miss Cardwell, the lilt resettling in her throat, indicated that their play wasn't over. "Act II. A reversal of roles," she said, smoothing the bed linens. "Now you're an Egyptian princess and I am your slave." She gently removed Rachel's nightgown and panties. "And I must make you happy." She placed a pillow under the girl's head and another under her buttocks, and slowly, deftly, with lotions and feathers and consummate finesse, brought forth a bliss more thunderous than any Rachel had ever produced for herself.

The teacher was all business after that. "Now, this must remain our little secret, young lady. Say anything to anyone—that includes the new girl you've been hanging out with, that troublemaker in the bathtub—and I'll have you thrown out of school. Remember, there were witnesses. Five girls saw you playing with yourself. Expulsion will be automatic, understand?" Rachel, who'd been searching for her panties, looked up and nodded. "If your classmates ask how I punished you, tell them I made you write 'I shall not abuse myself' one hundred times." With that, Miss Cardwell put on her flannel pajamas and terrycloth robe and escorted Rachel through the darkened corridors back to her dormitory.

All the girls were asleep, their breathing soft as the rustle of a taffeta skirt. She crawled under the covers and tried to grab hold of the sensations that careened with the tree shadows on the moonlit ceiling, sensations that would have to remain *her* secret—the throbbing, the lingering warmth, the puzzling contradictions. It was a gruesome ordeal, ministering to Miss Cardwell, whose body, vile in itself, had been all the more loathsome for its incongruous juxtaposition with her own. What she'd been forced to do had left her feeling dirty and used. But there were other feelings, too, an inkling of the sublime, and she who knew her body so well was bewildered by it now. She felt rapture and repulsion, both. Satisfactions of the flesh and pangs of conscience. The rage of the overpowered child and the greedy ardor of the woman she would become.

During her remaining two years at boarding school, Rachel would periodically recall her mortification and feel overwhelmed by shame. She thought about telling on Miss Cardwell, who would flatly deny it and accuse her of inventing this bizarre story to cover for having been caught misbehaving under the sheets; expulsion would follow as sure as breakfast followed reveille. Then she thought about Esther, how proud she was of her little Blue Spruce lady, how hard she'd worked to pay the school's fees, how devastated she would be were her daughter to be kicked out for self-abuse. Clearly, the truth was not an option. So Rachel kept Miss Cardwell's secret. And her own.

That really happened when Rachel was ten. What never happened, *except* in her dream, was Act III, in which Esther—dressed in her Persian-lamb coat and the pillbox hat with the netted veil—makes a surprise visit to the dorm proctor's room. In a white-hot instant, Esther sees her daughter naked with Miss Cardwell on all fours, licking her like a mangy old cat, a denouement that, by itself, qualified the dream as a nightmare. So palpable was her mother's shock, so sharply etched Rachel's horror at having been discovered, that the dream always woke her up.

If not Bridget O'Malley's pillow, it would have been a "Kiss Me, I'm Irish" button that brought it on, or the shamrocks in the shopping mall, anything with a clover like the one on Miss Cardwell's cardigan. In a good year, March came and went without the dream. When Irish eyes stopped smiling and the local pubs yanked the cardboard leprechauns from their windows, Rachel would breathe a sigh of relief and pray she'd seen the last of it, only to have it blindside her in August or October. Nightmares have their own calendars. Sometimes years would pass unhaunted and she'd let herself believe it was gone for good, but then it would return as it had tonight—only this one had awakened her with a shudder and an altogether different finale. Unimpeded by the arrival of the censoring mother, this dream climaxed in Rachel's loins. Not one for introspection, she didn't bother to wonder why, after all these years, her unconscious had changed a hellish nightmare into a wet dream. Instead, she lay on her damp sheets, alone in the king-sized bed, regretting that her husband was in Miami and had missed the greening of her lust, its comeback from the menopausal weeds.

Friday morning, bursting with energy, she ignored the cold gray drizzle and went out for a run. Keeping in shape was Rachel's way of keeping her life under control. As long as she could do an eight-minute mile, thirty push-ups, and swim the same number of laps as last year, she felt fine. After her shower, she drove her Lexus into town to the bakery whose owners knew how to make a decent hallah, which was more than she could say of the local supermarket. Because of the time crunch with the pillow, she'd had no time to bake her own, but the shop's braided loaves were almost as good—dense, eggy, and studded with either poppy or sesame seeds. She bought one of each to take tonight to her daughter Tamara's. Since Jeremy was away for the weekend and they knew she hated to spend the Sabbath alone, Tamara and Seth had invited her for Shabbat dinner, and Rachel had insisted on contributing at least the bread to make it easier on her daughter, who was eight months pregnant. She would drive herself and the hallahs over before sundown, have dinner with them, walk to synagogue, and let Seth walk her home. Sunday night, when Jeremy got back from Miami, he'd ferry her over in the Mercedes to pick up her car.

The light on the answering machine was flashing when she returned from town. Shoshanna's message sounded strangely perfunctory; she was driving out to Long Island right now, by herself, on a Friday, for no apparent reason. Her voice was odd, too—breathy and rushed, with that stilted quality heard in movie scenes where the kidnap victim is forced to make a phone call with a gun to her head. Rachel replayed the tape to be sure she'd got it right.

"Hi, it's me. I'm coming out to talk. ETA one o'clock. Hope your needlepointers aren't around. We need time alone. Don't make lunch. I'm bringing sandwiches. If you're not home when I get there, I'll wait in the car." Click. Beep.

It made no sense. Just yesterday, they'd had a long chat on the phone and everything seemed perfectly normal. Shoshanna said a lost Filofax page had made her miss a friend's retirement party, but she didn't sound that upset about it. Rachel told Shoshanna about Bridget's pillow. Shoshanna said she'd gained five pounds and asked if it might be menopause-related. "From now on, honey, everything's menopause-related," Rachel had replied, and recommended a low carb diet. Nothing unusual there. Jeremy had left that morning for a Bar Association conference in Miami and Rachel told Shoshanna that watching him pack his bathing trunks had made her want to go along; she was sick of swimming laps at the health club. He'd said the trunks were wishful thinking—he'd be in back-to-back seminars and probably never see the ocean. He'd encouraged her to come anyway, as long as she didn't mind spending most of her time on her own. The idea of socializing with a bunch of lawyers' wives wasn't in the least bit tempting, so she'd said no, but now that the weather had turned raw, she wondered if she should have gone anyway, packed a few novels and just lolled on the beach for three days.

That was when Shoshanna said she had to hang up; a client was on the other line. All in all, a perfectly ordinary conversation. Rachel couldn't imagine what might have happened between then and now that upset her sister enough to launch her on this journey. A business problem, maybe; but why would she need Rachel's advice? Unless it was more specific—something Rachel had done, a blunder on the California project, that fact-checking job she'd helped out on (and hated).

If that was it, Shoshanna could have reamed her out on the phone; it didn't take a special trip to Long Island.

Must be some sort of health problem. Bad news. Something terrible with Daniel. One of her kids. Shoshanna herself. That had to be it. Her sister was sick. They'd often worried together about breast cancer and wondered which of them was going to meet Esther's fate. Shoshanna had probably found a lump in her breast—not something she'd want to talk about on the phone. That's why she was driving all the way out here on a Friday. To tell Rachel she had cancer.

Rachel gave her needlepointers the rest of the day off, set the table, and waited for her sister's Volvo to pull into the driveway.

Anyone glancing into Shoshanna's car would assume she was singing along with the radio, but she was actually rehearsing. There's no right way to tell your sister her husband's been cheating on her. It was going to be a terrible blow however she phrased it, maybe bad enough to give her sister a stroke. She wanted Daniel to drive out with her, but he refused.

"She shouldn't have to face anyone but you until she's had time to absorb the shock and gather her resources," he said. "Her dignity's at stake here, not just her marriage."

"I'm scared, Daniel. What if she has a stroke? I mean literally." Shoshanna was chewing her nails.

"You'll call 911, which is all I'd do anyway."

"How should I tell her? What should I say?"

"Can't help you with that, love. That's the hard part."

For a control freak Shoshanna was feeling awfully weak-kneed. She'd considered unloading the task on one of Rachel's grown children, assuming a mother is less likely to fall apart in front of her offspring. The problem was, the offspring might fall apart first: the philanderer, after all, was their father. She'd thought about writing to Rachel, a carefully worded letter sent by overnight FedEx so it would arrive before Shabbat and Rachel could open the envelope, but thought better of the idea when she imagined her sister reading it all alone in that big house with two gas ovens in her designer kitchen, razor blades in all five bathrooms, and a garage she could lock herself into with the motor running.

After yesterday's conversation, Shoshanna felt she could procrastinate no longer. Back-to-back seminars, my foot! Unable to listen to another word about Jeremy's Miami "conference," she'd hung up the phone and decided to drive out to Rachel's the next day and get the thing over with. This morning, after failing to recruit Daniel to the cause, she'd put on a pair of chinos and a denim shirt, filled a thermos with coffee, stopped at the health food store for two vegetarian wraps and a couple of apples, and headed to the Midtown Tunnel with a heavy heart.

On this bleak March day, Rachel came to the door like a ray of light, wearing a lemon-yellow cashmere sweater set, her omnipresent double-stranded pearls, tan gabardine slacks, and brown toggle loafers. Her cropped pewter bangs stopped just above her brow, straight as a hedge and sleek as a tassel. Gym-thin as always, her pelvic bones protruding like parentheses at either side of her flat stomach, she looked like a cover girl for *Modern Maturity*. Shoshanna could only hope to age as well, but whether genes from their common mother or from Rachel's biological father were to thank for her youthfulness was not subject to speculation. Esther hadn't lived long enough to *get* old, and Rachel's father was a complete unknown. As for Sam's side, Shoshanna wasn't keen on inheriting his post-fifty transformations, or Leah's either, for that matter. Both looked older than their years. Shoshanna was disappointed in herself for indulging such ageist preoccupations, but turning fifty seemed to have that effect.

Like herself, Rachel's living room radiated a warm, welcoming energy. Wood fire blazing, lamps aglow (multiplied by her mirror collection), Vivaldi on the CD player, red amaryllis on the piano, orchid plant on the coffee table, pink roses spilling from a pitcher on the mantel. As amiable a scene as Shoshanna could have hoped to encounter, and unbearably sad.

They hugged each other hard. Shoshanna because she knew what was coming; Rachel because she thought she did.

"Silly Shoshie, bringing food when you know my fridge is bursting!" Rachel said as she transferred the wraps to her Bernadaud plates and poured the contents of the thermos into a silver carafe.

"I don't want you fussing in the kitchen. I want us to be able to talk."

Rachel nodded knowingly. "Shall we eat at the table or bring our plates over to the fire?"

"That'd be nice." Shoshanna wasn't thinking about ambiance, only how to begin.

They carried their place settings into the living room, went back for the cups and carafe, and settled in the wing chairs facing the hearth.

"What's up?" asked Rachel, her usual straight-to-the-point self.

Shoshanna reached for a wrap. "Let's eat first; I'm starved." She was stalling. "You'll love this combination—goat cheese, spinach, and roasted beets, believe it or not, with a raspberry vinagrette." As if there were nothing strange about her having driven forty miles for lunch, Shoshanna talked about mundane things. "Nelly's thinking about applying to Ethical Culture for the twins."

"Your alma mater—wouldn't that be great!" enthused Rachel, waiting for the breast-cancer bulletin.

"Tell it to my daughter! She won't let me write a recommendation. Says it's too pushy."

"Tell her the pushy hinge gets the oil."

"You mean squeaky."

"Did I tell you about Simon and Roy's commitment ceremony?" asked Rachel.

"You did, and I think it's wonderful."

"It'd be even better if they could get legally married."

"Simon and Roy are great together, Rache."

"My son has good taste in men."

When they finished eating, Rachel carried the empty plates to the kitchen and returned with the apples in a Wedgwood bowl. Shoshanna focused on the beauty of the crimson fruit against the blue porcelain. How in the world was she going to begin?

"Coffee?" Rachel filled Shoshanna's cup and handed it to her.

"I have some upsetting news," said Shoshanna, squeezing her cup handle.

Rachel poured coffee for herself and sat down with the saucer on her lap. She looked at Shoshanna with sympathetic eyes, waiting.

"It's about Jeremy."

"Jeremy?" Jeremy had cancer?

"There's no right way to say this. I saw him with someone else."

Rachel slumped against the back of the wing chair as if she'd been shoved. Her coffee sloshed into her saucer and splashed on the lemon-yellow sweater. Shoshanna kept talking, afraid if she stopped she'd never start again. "It was just a coincidence. I was passing through Rockefeller Center that day and happened to look down at the rink . . ."

She told it as fast as she could, in the most neutral words she could find—said she'd seen them together, didn't say they'd been intertwined like a vine; said they were kissing, but left out his hands reaching under the little black skirt; said the woman was young, not that she was beautiful and skated like an angel. "The whole thing was probably just a flirtation, probably nothing serious at all."

Rachel stared at the fire until she seemed to have figured something out, or thought of something she'd forgotten. Her face was so naked, Shoshanna was almost ashamed to be looking at it. Then, without a word, she sprang out of the wing chair, grabbed an apple from the blue bowl, and pitched it like a fastball against one of her mirrors, an antique in an arched frame which dropped straight down to the floor without breaking. Shoshanna, shaken, started toward the wall to rehang it, but before she could take a step, Rachel hurled the other apple at a huge rococo mirror that must have weighed a hundred pounds and shattered in a hailstorm silvery splinters. She threw a cup across the room next, spraying coffee over the needlepoint rug that had taken her five years to finish, then a saucer, followed by the beautiful Wedgwood bowl. Everything was moving too fast. Shoshanna started toward her, intending to stop the blitzkrieg, but Rachel, wild-eyed, kept her sister at a distance as she seized the silver carafe, coiled her pitching arm, and, turning toward her clock collection, flung the pot at an ultramodern timepiece whose minute and hour hands appeared to be floating in space. On impact, they sailed through the air like arrows while the crystal clock face crashed to the floor, blanketing the rug with jagged shards. Rachel raised the orchid plant over her head like a trophy and hurled it at the eighteenth-century grandfather clock, whose long glass door cracked with a sickening crunch, setting the pendulum clanging. Pandemonium. Shoshanna grabbed her wrists, hung on tight, yelled in her face, and only then did the tempest cease and Rachel fall limp and wasted into arms that had never held her older sister before, never had reason to comfort her.

Rachel pulled out of her embrace. "I have to know if he's having an affair."

"How do you propose to find out?"

"Search the house. There must be clues. Will you help me look?"

"Let's sweep up first." Shoshanna was afraid of what they might find.

"No time for that."

"Come on, Rache; broken glass is dangerous."

"No! I want to get started and be done before sundown. Damned if I'll violate Shabbat for that snake."

Shoshanna knew Rachel had taken a deeper interest in Judaism lately, but her religiosity seemed to have ratcheted up several notches, with more frequent references to "the sages," more mention of prayer.

"Okay, we'll leave the mess for now. Where do you want me to start?"

"His desk; you're better at that kind of research. I'll go through his closets and drawers." Rachel picked her way around the broken glass and ran upstairs.

Jeremy's study adjoined the living room and had French windows overlooking gardens that were gray but groomed in preparation for a spring that seemed very far off. His desk was the size of a billiard table, surfaced in Moroccan leather. Shoshanna sat in his swivel chair and tugged at the lower-right-hand drawer, the deepest drawer, meant for storing files. It was locked. Shoshanna had reorganized enough desks in enough homes and offices to know that people tended to hide the key to the file drawer somewhere in the desk itself. Painstakingly, she searched the rest of the drawers, every slot and compartment, looked under stationery boxes, manila envelopes, map cases, packets of diskettes, legal pads, paper supplies. About to give up, she suddenly remembered a client who'd nailed a metal plate to the underside of his desktop and to it, stuck a small magnetized key case. She tipped the desk lamp, shone it in the knee niche, then looked under the desktop and there it was, attached to a small metal plate: a similar magnetic container in which lay the key to the locked bottom drawer. Inside, Jeremy's files were lined up like a drill team and neatly labeled: *Health Insurance Claims. Life Insurance. Taxes. Deductibles.* Couldn't have organized it better herself. The folder marked *January 1999* held a sheaf of bills—gas, electric, telephone, car repairs, Amex, MasterCard, Visa—but it was impossible for Shoshanna to distinguish the guilty charges from the innocent. She shouted for Rachel to come downstairs.

"Do you ever pay the bills?" she asked.

"No, that's his department."

"But you'd know if something's suspicious, wouldn't you?"

"Maybe."

"Here's the January Visa bill. How's it look?" Rachel studied each item: meals at businessmen's restaurants near his office; a subscription to *American Lawyer*; charges at the Metropolitan Club; the monthly invoice for his parking garage; hotel bills from Minneapolis, Detroit, Pittsburgh, Wheeling, West Virginia, cities where she thought he had pending cases. Everything seemed legit.

"He travels a lot," said Shoshanna.

"The average American takes about five business trips per year and averages three overnights each. Jeremy takes four or five trips a month, but he's usually away only one night at a time. Except now, he's in Miami through Sunday."

"Yeah, you told me." Shoshanna noticed, handwritten at the top of the Visa bill, the notation: *Submitted, 2/1/99.* "Looks like he uses the Visa card for his expense account."

"That makes sense. We have American Express for personal and household expenses. Same number, but he's the primary; I'm the secondary."

The word bounced between them like a ball.

They went through the January Amex statement together—hardware, haircuts, Rachel's clothes (Shoshanna was dazzled by the size of her sister's Bergdorf's bill; she'd forgotten that her brother-in-law was a rich man), appliance repair, gardener, car service, restaurant meals that Rachel recognized, the pair of shoes ($350!) she'd encouraged Jeremy to buy for himself when they were in town together a few weeks back. All aboveboard.

They returned the Visa and Amex bills to the file folder and with distraught fascination pored over Jeremy's MasterCard statement. Here were the trysts and treats, the splurges, the man's secret life writ large in dollars and cents—charges from upscale restaurants, jewelers, airlines, hotels in places Rachel had never been. Boutique bills that made her Bergdorf's spree look like bargain day at J. C. Penney.

"How'd he manage to go to St. Bart's in January without you knowing it?"

Rachel's cheeks reddened. "Must have been the time he went to California for a deposition . . . *said* it was California. Said it was a deposition. It was the middle of the week, why would I . . ." Her voice cracked like a mirror.

"First-class tickets to St. Bart's, two nights at a snazzy resort, $1,500 worth of jewelry, nightclub, golf club, beach club . . ."

"He came home with a tan. Even before I said anything about it, he commented on his tan. Told me those nutty Hollywood types insisted on *taking* their meetings around their swimming pools. The phrase was ridiculous but the outdoor meetings sounded reasonable. I never thought twice about it." She wiped her eyes on the yellow cashmere sleeve, leaving a swath of mascara that reminded Shoshanna of Ash Wednesday and the widower on the snow-pocked lawn. (She'd bet he'd been faithful to his wife.)

Rachel now had a map of her husband's infidelity. From the Caribbean to Columbus Avenue, extravagances galore—$200 at a florist, a staggering bill from the Four Seasons, hefty charges from Restaurant Daniel, Bernardin, Chanterelle, Jean-Georges—only the best. Most crushing of all was a modest little entry—January 14, Rockefeller Center Skating Rink. March 8 hadn't been his first time.

"Why don't you lie down now, Rachey." Shoshanna couldn't believe she'd invented a diminutive for her sister at this late date. "I'll call Tamara and tell her you're not feeling well. I'll fix us a nice dinner."

"But I bought hallahs for them. For Shabbat."

"They'll make do, they'll use rye bread, don't worry. Come to bed. You'll take a nap. You'll feel better." She was sounding like an old Jewish mama. Like Esther.

Leaning heavily on her sister, Rachel let herself be helped upstairs. Shoshanna, who'd seen the master bedroom countless times before, was stunned yet again by its size (twice that of her living room) and the luxury of the adjoining suite with its exercise gym, sauna, steam room, and vast His and Hers dressing alcoves. The sleeping area was decorated in creamy tones of beige and peach, with thick beige carpeting and peach moiré draperies rippling from ceiling to floor, and a king-sized bed topped with a puffy down comforter and strewn with a dozen beige and peach throw pillows. Shoshanna tried to guide her sister toward the bed, but Rachel headed straight for Jeremy's dressing room, said she hadn't finished going through his things. She'd started and she wanted to finish.

"Why? You have the bills. What more do you need to know?"

"Everything," said Rachel. "I need to know everything." She yanked open a drawer and began flinging her husband's undershirts and boxer shorts on the floor. A second drawer, full of workout clothes and tennis whites, met the same fate. The next held nothing but socks, each rolled into a ball, tight as a fist. The instant it occurred to Shoshanna that they'd make good projectiles. Rachel picked one up and heaved it at Jeremy's photograph on her dressing table, knocking it flat.

"Hey, enough with the pitching practice, Rachel, *please*. I'm the one who's going to be cleaning up once you begin your day of rest."

"It's your Sabbath, too. We'll make Jeremy clean up." Rachel churned her hands around in the sock drawer. Both women heard something scrape against the wood. Rachel felt for it. A small box.

Shoshanna thought of how the sight of Tiffany's distinctive aquamarine box triggers a thrill even before a person opens it. When a menopausal woman finds a box of condoms in her husband's sock drawer, the reaction is less than thrilling. Condoms. Ramses condoms. One dozen. Lubricated.

"Know who Ramses was?" asked Rachel in her flat, factoid tone.

Was the question rhetorical? Should Shoshanna respond? For the first time, she felt as nervous with *this* sister as she usually did with Leah. "An Egyptian pharaoh?" she ventured.

"Not just any pharaoh. The one who fathered more than a hundred and sixty children. Hardly a man you'd expect to name a condom for." She dropped the box as if it were electrified.

Shoshanna charged across the room and held her sister again, feeling lumpish and maternal. "Hang on," she mewed, as if she could stop the sobs racking the tiny, twiggy frame. She hunted down two tabs of Tylenol PM and got Rachel to swallow the pills and lie down. "You rest, I'll start dinner," she said, stroking her sister's hair. "Don't worry, I'm not leaving you alone; I'm sleeping over, assuming there's a spare bed in this shack."

Rachel blinked her gratitude. Her legs were stiff and her hands, clasped across her chest, gave her the look of a dead body arranged for viewing. Shoshanna kissed her sister's forehead, then went downstairs to call Daniel and tell him she wouldn't be home until tomorrow.

In Rachel's well-stocked refrigerator she found celery and carrots to spruce up canned chicken broth. Greens for salad. Flounder filets, which she defrosted in the microwave and sautéed. Leftover potato dumplings. Based on the look of the table at lunch (how long ago that seemed), she set two places at one end. She fetched a bottle of merlot from the wine rack. Laid the two hallahs side by side on a wooden bread board and covered them with linen napkins. Carried the brass candlesticks from the sideboard to the dining table. Everything looked properly transformed for the Sabbath except that, after rummaging through every cupboard, she could find no candles. Maddening how there was always one flaw, the zit on the perfectionist's cheek.

A door in the pantry opened into the garage, where she found a large plastic bin labeled RECYCLABLES. She lugged it to the living room and set it on sheets of newspaper to keep the carpet clean. Retrieving her lined leather gloves from her coat pocket, she disposed of the largest glass shards by hand, then swept up the slivers and vacuumed whatever tiny sequins still glittered on the rug. The empty mirror frames and battered clock cases she stacked behind the couch, not sure what could be salvaged. It fascinated her, the different ways people handled disorder. Rachel, usually so self-contained, had committed Kristallnacht, wreaking havoc outside to match the chaos she was feeling inside. When Shoshanna was upset, she did the opposite, straightened up the outer world to soothe the inner mayhem. That's what she was doing now, coping, devising a system to restore order, just as she had on the Henry Hudson Parkway. Her pattern was obvious: Angry, she cleaned closets. Frustrated, she filed. Scared, she labeled shelves. Until the Filofax debacle, she'd never met a mess that couldn't be put right. And now, with the table set and the glass cleaned up, she felt the old magic at work again, the *appearance* of order having restored the equilibrium she'd lost this afternoon in the wake of her sister's rage. Still, it troubled her to realize she was the initiator of the explosion, the one who brought a concealed grenade into her sister's home along with the goat-cheese wrap, and her reactions to Rachel's meltdown were anything but admirable. Not just paralyzed amid the airborne cups and carafes, but worse than that, she'd been exhilarated to watch her sister fly out of control.

three daughters

. . .

When Shoshanna returned to the bedroom, Rachel was in the exact same position, stretched out like a corpse. Rivulets ran from the outer corners of her eyes into her hair. Her voice startled Shoshanna:

> "See, he hatches evil, conceives mischief,
> and gives birth to fraud.
> He has dug a pit and deepened it,
> and will fall into the trap he made.
> His mischief will recoil upon his own head;
> his lawlessness will come down upon his skull."

She unclasped Rachel's hands and held them in her own. They were cold. Like feet. "Who's the poet?"

"David. Seventh Psalm."

"You haven't slept at all."

"I've been thinking."

"What?"

"Jeremy—he had a lot of women before I married him. I mean a *lot* of women. I never told you, but a week before the wedding, I almost called it off. He begged me not to. Swore he was done playing around. Said he didn't need it anymore 'cause he had me. I believed him."

Shoshanna breathed on Rachel's icy hands, warm air, the breath of life. "Shouldn't you get some sleep before dinner?"

"Time, please?"

"Twenty past five."

Rachel jumped to a sitting position and wiped her eyes. "Gotta bentch."

"Bench?"

"Bless, in Yiddish. Light the Shabbat candles. At 5:48 exactly. Eighteen minutes before sunset."

Shoshanna smiled. "I thought you said *bench*, like chair. Believe me, I know what *bentch* means. Mom and I used to do it every Friday

243

night." (She could see her mother in a white scarf, like a picture in a locket, kindling the flames, murmuring the blessing, sealing it with a kiss on the girl's forehead.) "Dinner's ready when you are," Shoshanna said, missing her mother. She wondered how Esther would have comforted Rachel, what magical meal she would have produced for her devastated daughter. "But where the hell do you keep your candles?"

"I'll show you." Rachel skimmed off the coffee-stained sweater and replaced it with a white silk blouse, the tan slacks with a slim black skirt.

"You don't have to change, Rache. It's just us," said Shoshanna.

"Us and God," said Rachel. "The Talmud says, 'Thy Sabbath garments should not be like thy weekday garments.' I always dress up to greet the Sabbath Queen." She ran a comb through her hair and slipped her stockinged feet into a pair of heels. "We both know my clothes won't fit you, but this might perk up your outfit." She took off her double-stranded pearls, slipped them over Shoshanna's wild red hair, and arranged them around the collar of the denim work shirt. "Chic," she said.

Downstairs, she opened a lower cabinet that Shoshanna had somehow missed. Its top shelf held a box of white tapers, seven silver kiddush cups, a large platter with a picture of a hallah painted on it, and seven silver candlesticks. "My Friday-night shelf," said Rachel. "Stuff to welcome the Sabbath." Shoshanna flashed on Esther's curio cabinet and the pair of candlesticks that had belonged to her grandmother. Esther used to compare those candlesticks to the timbrels the Hebrew women carried with them out of Egypt. Though they left in haste, the women remembered to take their timbrels so that wherever they ended up, they could sing God's praise. Esther's mother had carried *her* mother's candlesticks to the New World from the shtetl, and Esther had rescued them when she left Lucky, and Shoshanna had inherited them from Esther and kept them now in a place of honor on her dining table in a shtetl called Greenwich Village. There were Shabbat candlesticks in every Jewish home, often because Jewish women had rescued them, carried them through thick and thin so that, wherever life tossed them, they could bentch licht on Friday night and say thank you to God. Shoshanna remembered Rachel quoting a line from G. K. Chesterton: "The sad thing about those who are not believers is they don't know whom to thank."

"The bottom one is my Saturday-night shelf," Rachel was saying. "Stuff to bring Shabbat to a close and welcome the new week." She pointed to a couple of spice boxes and a thick, braided candle made up of several wicks. (It reminded Shoshanna of Leah's hair.) "The havdalah candle puts out a huge torchlike light. Ismar Schorsch, of the Jewish Theological Seminary, says it has a bounding, restless flame because it anticipates the hectic state of our lives as we resume a new week. Hectic isn't the word for what's going to happen in this house next week."

Shoshanna was amused by Rachel's show-and-tell. Minutes before, the woman was a corpse, but now, composed and serene, she was educating her less observant sister, creating her island in time, preparing her home for God's day. And surveying the table with a critical eye.

"You won't be insulted if I change to my Friday-night stuff, will you, Shoshe?"

"Be my guest; it's your house." Shoshanna watched as her sister returned the bottle of merlot and substituted a crystal decanter of kosher sacramental wine, moved the two hallahs from the wooden bread board to her special hallah platter and replaced the plain glass goblets with embossed kiddush cups. When she returned the brass candle holders to the sideboard and brought out six silver candlesticks, Shoshanna pointed to the one she'd left behind in the cabinet, thinking she'd overlooked it.

"I'm never lighting that one again. It's Jeremy's."

"Don't say that. You might feel different later." (After Gideon died, Rachel had continued lighting his candle. She'd retired his kiddush cup, but not his candlestick, because, she said, his memory still lit up their lives.)

"There won't be any *later*. I don't want his candle on my table and I don't want him in this house. I want him gone."

"Take it easy, now. When he gets back Sunday, you'll see what he has to say. Talk it over. Maybe work it out. People get past this sort of thing all the time."

"I'm not people."

It was just like Rachel to pare things down. "You're also not in the best condition to be making final decisions, Rachey. This is a difficult situation." Rachey again. She was infantilizing her sister.

"No, it couldn't be simpler. He's been cheating on me for years. I just didn't want to see it." There were other occasions to suspect him, hundreds of them: hushed phone conversations in his study, sudden departures, explanations that made no sense. Have to go to the gym, he'd say, though he'd installed that state-of-the-art exercise room upstairs. Have to meet a client who's only free on Saturday night. Huge workload. Gotta spend Sunday/President's Day/Veterans Day/Columbus Day at the office. Gotta write a brief. Gotta leave right after dinner/theater/the kids' ball game. Times he stormed out of the house after an argument, came back hours later, told her he'd been at a bar. But there was no liquor on his breath; he smelled of other things. With all this, she was surprised by how distraught she felt. Why was it so hard to hear evidence of his betrayal? Why was she suffering now? She'd known the kind of man he was from the start. He hadn't really misrepresented himself. He lied about where he went, but he hadn't faked who he was. She was the fake. She'd been cheating herself. She'd always understood who Jeremy needed her to be and she'd become that woman—for him, but also for her, because she wanted the same things he did. She understood what he needed in the way of image and accoutrements before he could stand tall in his world and his own eyes, and she'd accepted it. Her perfidy, her willingness to trade authenticity for security had led to this. The original betrayal was the pact she'd made with herself.

Shoshanna, sensing her sister's torment, had no interest in speaking up for her brother-in-law, largely because she'd never been fond of him, but also because she knew that some messes can't be cleaned up. If Daniel ever cheated on her, she wouldn't take him back either. (God, what a thought!) She hugged Rachel. "Are you going to be all right?"

"I'll be fine; don't worry. The Talmud says, from the moment we bentch until the third star appears in the sky on Saturday night, God gives us a *neshama yeterah*, an extra soul. Two souls ought to get me through this."

"But tomorrow night? When you're back down to one?"

"I will go from strength to strength."

At exactly 5:48, Rachel draped a white scarf over her head and lit her six candles. *"Baruch atah adonai, elohaynu melech ha'olam, asher kid-shanu b'mitzvotav vitzivanu, l'hadlich ner shel Shabbat."* Her graceful hands drew three sweeping circles over the flames, scooping the light toward her and ending with the fingers of both hands resting lightly on her closed eyelids. Shoshanna knew this was the moment when the woman of the house traditionally thanks God for her blessings and prays for whatever she needs. Though not the biggest believer in the world, Shoshanna shut her eyes, thanked God for Daniel, her children and grandchildren, and beseeched the Almighty to grant her sister's wish.

thirteen

LIVING WITH LOONIES seemed to be her fate. After the debacle in the lawyer's office and Leo's swan dive, Leah, who'd never believed in God as puppeteer, couldn't help wondering if the reason she'd been charged as a child with the care of a meshuggener mother was to prepare her to watch over a clinically depressed husband. At the very least, it made her grateful for the temperance of his affliction. Where Dena had sputtered like hot fat, Leo was Crisco at room temperature, a benign lump of a man who slept too much, talked too little, dragged around the house in his pajamas, and refused to go up to the attic. Even a cheerleading visit from the stiletto-heeled gallery owner, who'd buttressed her various body piercings with a snake tattoo on her arm, failed to goad him back to his easel.

The loyalty forged in the crucible of her mother's madness would have predicted that Leah dutifully minister to her husband for as long as they both shall live. Yet only days after the reading of the will, when the antidepressants weren't working and his psychiatrist suggested a quiet place in the country where he might be treated with an experimental drug regimen and monitored on a daily basis, Leah, who prided herself on sixty years of resisting authority, went along with it. Not because she had faith in shrinks or medication, only for fear that on her watch, her husband might kill himself.

They took a train to a station just above Poughkeepsie, where a man carrying a WELCOME LEO ROSE sign picked them up in a pristine white van and drove them to a Georgian-style mansion that reminded Leah of the main house at Blue Spruce. There were hills in the distance and trees all around and manicured lawns where, instead of frolicsome girls from three to sixteen, people of all ages walked slowly in the thin sunlight. For all its apparent tranquillity, the place, like most institutions, intimated that its surface was not its truth and the people in charge were hidden from view. After Leah filled out some forms, a smiling woman in a navy suit showed them to Leo's room, a decent-sized oblong with a small bathroom at one end and a window overlooking the hills. Leah unpacked his suitcase, barely filling a small chest of drawers. To her dismay, when she was finished, the smiling woman told her she had to leave.

"Get better," Leah said to Leo. She hadn't meant it to sound like an order.

"Don't worry," he replied, in the depths of their hug. "I'll be back soon."

Small towns slid by her window as the train whistled through the Hudson Valley, past old wooden station houses, boarded-up warehouses, scruffy kids at play in the weeds alongside the tracks. Leo's sanitarium called itself a rest home. Maybe that was all he needed. Rest. A respite from her, Henry, and Carl's taunting legacy, from the badgering gallery owner in her Nazi boots and whatever canvas was moldering on the easel in the attic. He'd had too many reverses lately, too many tough breaks. Under a comparable onslaught, Leah would have lost her mind a little, too, and it probably would have taken fewer setbacks to do it. She'd always thought of Leo as the weaker of the two of them, but now, tallying how much he'd tolerated before he cracked—and how little he'd leaned on her while it was happening—the premise seemed false. As the train burrowed into a tunnel, Leah dove deeper into her thoughts.

The question was not just, how long would it take him to heal? The question was, how long could she function without him?

In the gray flannel of a cold March evening, she opened the door to her empty house, poured a fist's worth of Scotch into a yahrzeit glass, and dialed the Safers' number.

"I'll be coming by myself tomorrow night. Hope it doesn't fuck up your table." Surely her hyperorganized sister had an anal-compulsive seating plan for the Seder.

"What happened to Leo and Henry?"

"We've had a convergence of crises hereabouts. I can sit at the children's table if it's easier."

"Stop with the table. Tell me what happened."

Leah tried to answer briefly, but her dam wouldn't hold. Everything poured out, a trickle, then a torrent. Even as soap opera, it was overwrought. Victimhood was not her style; she hated unburdening herself to her sister at all, much less right on the heels of the subway saga. Yet here she was again, pride in tatters, cataloguing a new litany of catastrophes: Carl's will. Henry leaving. Leo . . .

"Oh, Leah—how awful for you! Can I do anything?"

"Nah, onward and upward. Enough with my nugatory hametz."

"Your *what*?"

"Hametz. Metaphor for the unwanted shit in life, the crap you want to get rid of."

"I *know* what hametz is," said Shoshanna. "Daniel and I have been on hametz patrol for a week. My holier-than-thou sister wouldn't come to our Seder unless we promised to clean the house by the book."

"Saint Rachel," snorted Leah.

Ignoring her, Shoshanna described how she and Daniel had scrubbed the range, boiled the silverware, scoured the cabinets, and locked up the regular china, replacing it with Esther's Pesahdikeh set—the blue glass, maybe Leah remembered it from West End Avenue. (She did.) They'd disposed of everything forbidden—bread, cake, cereal, anything made of wheat, barley, oats, or rye, down to the very last kernel. The unopened packages Daniel had dropped off at a homeless shelter, the open ones went into the trash. "Tonight after sundown, we have to go around the house with a feather to search out the last bits of leaven. Then we're going to burn the crumbs out in the garden. We promised."

"Are you saying you've moved leaven and earth for Rachel?"

She could still be punny; that was a good sign. "I'm saying I know what 'hametz' is. What's 'nugatory'?" asked Shoshanna.

"Trifling. Worthless."

As a teenager Shoshanna had kept a journal filled with words she'd learned from her sister. She hadn't added to her vocabulary in years, but "nugatory" she would have to remember, if only to put a label on the minutiae cluttering her life. The Filofax fiasco had motivated her to clean up her calendar; Passover had motivated her to clean up her house. If only she could hold on to the scoured-cabinet feeling she had at this moment standing in her spotless kitchen. If only Leah could get rid of *her* hametz, the puffed-up ego, the yeasty personality that always got a rise out of others. Leah could use a fresh start, too.

"Maybe all this was meant to be," Shoshanna said into the phone. "This avalanche of crises. It could be your signal to turn over a new leaf."

"Spare me the mixed platitudes."

Shoshanna backed off. "Anyway, you won't be the only single. Rachel's coming alone, too. She and Jeremy have split."

Leah let out a low whistle. "What's the story? Married in '56, was it, or '57, and it takes them till now to discover they're incompatible?"

Shoshanna hesitated, not wanting to reduce Rachel's life to phone gossip. If regular sisters keep secrets from one another, surely she was entitled to hold things back from a half sister, especially one who'd distanced herself from the family. Hadn't Leah forfeited the right to intimate information? Yet Shoshanna had invited her to the Seder—a calculated risk at best—so she owed it to everyone else to prepare the ground. If Leah was capable of empathy, she might be moved to hold her tongue and leave Rachel alone. But first she'd have to know the truth.

"Jeremy had another woman." Essentials only, no flower pots, no mirrors, no condoms.

"Jeeezus!"

"Rachel found out about it while he was away. The night he got home, she threw him out. Called a lawyer the next morning. That was ten days ago, so she's still pretty churned up."

Silence at the other end.

"Leah?"

"A fifty says she takes him back. She's helpless without him."

"You're going to lose fifty bucks. She's been firm from the start. Really adamant."

"Firm? Adamant? Are we talking here about Mrs. Jeremy Brent?"

"She says it's over."

"Amazing."

"When you think about it, the amazing thing is that all three of us stayed this long with the men we married in our twenties. What is it now, half of all marriages end in divorce?"

"Please," moaned Leah. "One statistician per family is enough."

Shoshanna wanted out of this conversation. "Can you come at six? We'd like to start early, before the twins get cranky."

"I'll be there at 5:55." Downing the Scotch, Leah switched on a light and went looking for a Chinese takeout menu. She called in her order: steamed dim sim, pork fried rice, shrimp in lobster sauce, the perfect Erev Passover meal, 100 percent traif. She would feast on the taboo, foods banned from the Jewish mouth: pig, for not chewing its cud; crustaceans, for want of fin and scales. The dietary laws were well-known to her—which animals were ritually unclean and which acceptable—but she'd defied them for years, a disobedient child in revolt against a dismissive father. She poured herself a double and wondered how she was going to get through the night.

The Scotch tasted even better in the living room, where the evening light was somewhere between gloom and darkness. She flicked on the radio, not caring what was on. Glenn Gould, Bach, the *Goldberg Variations*. Leo had the dial locked onto WQXR. She felt her way to the beat-up Barcalounger. Leo called it his Papa Chair. She called it the Shtarka-Barca. He used to come down from the attic around five, still in his paint-spattered clothes, fall into his chair, and listen to classical music without moving. The man was capable of utter stillness, but when his legs stayed up too long on the footrest, they'd go numb. Grinning, he'd demonstrate their rubbery uselessness and stamp and shake them back to life. (Which always reminded Leah of Shoshanna shaking the blood back in her arms that day in Central Park.) "Let's hear it for blood," he'd say. "Everyone's always focusing on the muscles—pumping them up, showing them off. Without blood, muscles are useless." She knew, in his quiet way, he was talking about his art.

Each of the Wasserman daughters had used marriage to recover from her childhood. Rachel, reared by a school, found a wealthy husband who underwrote the home of her dreams. Shoshanna, deceived as a child, married an ethicist who would never lie to her. Leah chose a man who was the antidote to her parents, sedate and soothing where Dena was a bipolar hysteric; sensitive and open where Sam was the quintessential shut-down male. All Leah ever wanted from Leo was a share of his quiet calm. She'd gotten more of it than she'd bargained for, however, and when the stillness turned to stupefaction and his spirit went numb, neither of them could stamp the blood back into it.

Teaching graduate students about Chekhov and the poignancy of longing, she'd been struck by that bit of dialogue in *The Three Sisters* where Irina says of the husband she'd once thought so brilliant, "He is the kindest of men, but he is not the cleverest." That's Leo in a nutshell, she'd thought, then had to acknowledge that *she* was also Irina, and the problem wasn't her husband's changed personality but her altered perception of him. People don't always rust from the inside out; corrosion can begin in the eyes of the beholder. If the beholder was someone like Leah, with an irresistible impulse to critique everything—books, character, motivation, syntax, husbands—and if the process happened to yield doubt and disillusion, well, such were the hazards of the analytical life.

In a Scotch-lubricated insight, she saw the men in her family as archetypal male juveniles: Sam, the neighborhood bully. Leo, the sullen baby. Freddy, the quintessential bad boy. Henry, Peter Pan. Jeremy, the arrogant Jewish prince. Only Daniel remained unlabeled. Of what was he emblematic? The egghead? The mensch? Were Shoshanna calling the shots, she'd dub him the angel. But if the academic grapevine could be trusted, Daniel wasn't quite so perfect. Leah heard that a book he'd published early in his career not only had been researched by a graduate student but had largely been written by her, yet he'd refused to share authorship, acknowledging her contribution in the book in the most reserved terms. She was a doctoral candidate, but he made her sound like a research assistant, barely a step up from a typist. Supposedly, this transpired during the period when his father was dying and Daniel was commuting to the barn in New Hampshire every week to be at the old man's bedside. If that was so, Daniel had probably found himself in a time bind, maybe stood to lose his book contract, and chose to meet his deadline by appropriating more of the student's product than was considered ethically acceptable—an unwise move for any scholar but fatally damaging for the author of a book on Jewish ethics. Rumor had it he was so afraid the student would expose him that he'd threatened to sabotage her subsequent work and bad-mouth her thesis if she didn't keep silent about her role. She may well have complied, since the rumor died quickly, and some years later, when she published *her* first book, Daniel gave it a rave review in the most prestigious journal in their field, a clear conflict of interest. Since he taught at NYU and Leah taught at Brooklyn College, and never the twain did meet, she had no way of confirming the story. But in her experience, rumors rarely traveled that far from their source unless the story had some truth to it. If it didn't, Daniel had been cruelly maligned; if it did, Shoshanna's angel had singed wings.

Wasserman women were harder to categorize than the men, though one thing could be said about all three: they hadn't become their mothers. Unlike Esther, Shoshanna had chosen a man who treated her as an equal. Rachel had ultimately repudiated *sh'lom bayit*, the willingness to sacrifice herself for peace in the home. And thus far at least, Leah had not succumbed to Dena's madness.

three daughters

The doorbell shrieked. "Super Szechuan!" called a young voice with a Chinese accent.

Damn! She hadn't wanted the food so fast, knowing she'd devour it as soon as it arrived and then the night would stretch out ahead of her with too many hours and nothing to fill them. She never watched TV, had no hobbies, and wasn't the type to distract herself from her misery by washing floors or mending socks. Reading was out of the question; she'd already had trouble absorbing the menu.

"Just a minute!" Rocking forward, she nearly tumbled out of the Shtarka-Barca. While she knew the rule was 10 percent tip for a delivery, 15 in a restaurant, Leah believed in rewarding the working class, so she gave the kid 20 percent for pedaling through the carbon monoxide on this raw wreck of an evening with a half-dozen plastic bags swinging like a cow's udder from his handlebars. Overtipping might not advance the socialist revolution, but it let her sleep at night.

The plastic bag looked forlorn on her kitchen table. She wished for the self-discipline to postpone opening it, but found herself yanking at wire handles and tearing open cardboard flaps to find her first course, dim sim. "Heart's delight" in Cantonese. Leah's passion for vegetarian dumplings had begun when she was Sam's heart's delight. On visiting days, or during S and L Time, he would take her out for Chinese food, and since he kept kosher, he would order only vegetarian dishes. Now, stabbing a dumpling with a chopstick, she had an inebriated thought: she'd been stabbed herself so many times in the last few weeks, she ought to be perforated. Instead, she was attacking her food like a ravenous teenager and schlurping green tea straight from its paper cup. Shoshanna, she suspected, would have poured the beverage into a mug and transferred the dim sim to a proper plate. Tomorrow night, there would be more than enough silver and china to make up for this grungy picnic. What there wouldn't be enough of was men. When the dumplings began morphing into testicles, she decided to let up on the booze. The source of her hallucination was obvious: two husbands, several sons, and a father would be present at the Seder table only in the palpability of their absence. Yet counting Jeremy and Leo among the missing wasn't quite the news flash it seemed, since both of them had been phantoms for some time now, and both wives had been basically on their own, Rachel unilaterally shoring up the structure of her marriage, Leah the spirit of hers. Now, however, the women were clearly alone, one-person households; the Wasserman sisters, manless now as they'd once been fatherless; together again in a hard place.

A shrimp escaped her chopsticks. She rescued the slippery bundle with her fingers and popped it into her mouth. Voraciously, with a carnal hunger and the manners of a ferret, she wolfed down the rest of the shrimp, then wedged a corner of the paper carton in her mouth, schlurped the lobster sauce, and, also without benefit of utensils, attacked the fried rice. She remembered what Nehru had once said while shoveling pilaf into his mouth with his aristocratic fingers: "Eating rice with a fork and knife would be like making love through a translator." In Western culture, where etiquette demanded a translator, solitude's reward was the freedom to eat with your hands.

Leah hadn't meant to suggest—even to herself—that because both were without husbands, her situation and Rachel's were comparable. They most certainly were not, and as the difference between kosher and traif mattered to Rachel, drawing critical distinctions mattered to Leah, whose intellectual mandate, as she saw it, was to distinguish between elegant reasoning and idiocy, the Platonic and the Aristotelian, subjective and objective truth. One major difference between herself and her sister was sex. Rachel valued sex more than she did; therefore Jeremy's sexual betrayal wounded her pride and self-esteem, while no comparable humiliation attended the wife of a depressed husband. Another difference was dependency. Manlessness had to be more jarring to Rachel because her primary persona had been Wife Of, whereas Leah had always been a person in her own right, with her own work. She was accustomed to moving in a world of women, writing about, teaching, studying, and advocating for women. Men had always been on her periphery—or had they? In the stillness of her scruffy kitchen, with night wrapping itself around the windows like a cloak, she realized with some wonderment that beneath the ovular curves of her feminist enterprises, she'd always had the harmonizing balance of an angular, edgy maleness, the thrum of her husband's step on the stair, her sons' robust vivacity, the rumble of male voices behind the walls. All this time—little noticed, little cherished—her men had been taking care of her. Henry did errands and schlepped her clothes to the cleaners. Freddy, until his troubles, fixed her computer and made her laugh. Leo did everything. Bailed her out when she was arrested for chaining herself to the South African consulate. Painted signs for her demonstrations. Marched with her against welfare cuts. Designed covers for *The Feminist Freethinker*, a square for the AIDS quilt, flyers for her conferences. She'd taken them for granted, all three.

The steaming Chinese tea brought to mind the uncountable cups Leo had quietly delivered to her desk—tea, hot cocoa, hazelnut coffee, espresso. She remembered how he'd come up behind her, massaged her neck and shoulders when she was writing. His quotidian kindnesses, whether doing their bills or her laundry, or replenishing her office supplies before they could run out. His shepherding the boys out to the park or the movies so that, unburdened by nugatory hametz, she could think large thoughts. His tolerance for her volatility and self-centeredness. Always, she was foreground, Leo background, attending to the ordinary, clearing the pebbles from her path.

One by one, the men had disappeared. It was almost too schematic, as if each of them personified a pathological response to the masculine role. But *her* men were supposed to be different, vaccinated by feminist humanism and immune to male dis-ease. So why had they succumbed? What was the bottom line here? The system always triumphs? Don't mess with a patriarchal God? Never underestimate the power of a man to disappoint a woman? Did the fault lie with their weakness or her worldview? Could she herself be the problem? For once, cognition and logic seemed floppy tools, unequal to the task. All she knew right now was how she *felt*. Unsure. Unsafe. Abandoned. Alone. For the first time since Dena had dropped her off at school and driven away in a yellow van, Leah Wasserman was afraid.

fourteen

IF ONLY TONIGHT WERE AS PERFECT as Shoshanna's Seder table. Tall tapers stood guard over her best Judaica—the kiddush goblet from her bat mitzvah pressed into service as Elijah's Cup; the white satin matzoh envelope encrusted with gold embroidery; the porcelain Seder plate that she and Daniel had hand-carried home from Israel after their honeymoon, miraculously without mishap. Best of all, her mother's Pesahdikeh dinnerware, disks of blue glass, dotted the damask cloth like cobalt Frisbees on a snowy field. To Shoshanna, the sentimental was sacred.

"Elegant," said Daniel, admiring her handiwork. "Splendacious. Grand!" He'd done his part, too, adding leaves to the table, lugging up extra chairs, unearthing the Haggadahs and distributing one to each setting.

"We're twelve tonight," Shoshanna announced when everyone was seated. "Like the tribes of Israel."

"Or Christ's disciples."

"Leah!"

"Sorry. The twelve minor prophets." Leah poured wine for herself, for Shoshanna's daughter Nelly and son-in-law, Ezra, and grape juice for their three-year-olds, Ruby and Pearl. Can you believe those names? she thought, but held her tongue. Cartier and Tiffany would have been worse.

Rachel, glancing around the table in those first few minutes, could see only the people who weren't there. The missing husband who, when confronted with the box of condoms and his MasterCard bill, had done as she'd requested and moved out, but only after a stream of protestations. He was pathetic, but she'd listened; it was the first time she'd ever seen him desperate. Despite appearances to the contrary, he said, he really loved her. Hadn't he proved that with his generosity? Hadn't he supported the start-up of her needlepoint business and paid for all those Jewish courses she was always taking? Hadn't he admired her handiwork and given her complete freedom decorating the house, and trusted her to make all the decisions about the children? He told her how important she was to him, and how much in his life depended on her, and how badly he needed her. That part, she knew, was true. His house of cards had rested on her queen.

She'd met his words with a hardened heart. Maybe the marriage had ended years earlier and there was nothing left to feel bereft of, or maybe, without realizing it, she'd been anticipating such a showdown and Jeremy's pleadings. She was surprised, though, by her lack of ambivalence, which is not to say she didn't mourn the collapse of her own house of cards, or feel the need to pray almost nonstop since the day of the broken mirrors. But the help she was seeking had less to do with the end of her marriage than with the beginning of her new life. She was going to need God's providence to make a future.

Gideon was also among the missing, gone twenty years, yet still a part of Rachel's mental roll call. And the daughters who'd moved away—Zelda, the Yuppie, too busy to tear herself from her computer business in Seattle (her father's daughter!); and Dalia, the über-mom who lived in London with a Hasidic husband and six kids of her own, and who'd declined to fly her family across the ocean for a Seder that could never be kosher enough for them. Probably just as well they hadn't come. Rachel hated the sight of Dalia in a wig and thought her son-in-law's fur-trimmed hat and long frock coat not only religiously unwarranted but anachronistically absurd. Half her time would have been spent arguing with them, since Rachel—observant, egalitarian, pious, and reverent—would not have tolerated her daughter or son-in-law dismissing her as an inauthentic Jew.

Dalia had been sucked into Orthodoxy by a vacuum cleaner known as Lubavitcher outreach the summer before her junior year, when she'd lived in Israel in a boardinghouse full of new immigrants from the Soviet Union who kept to themselves and spoke only Russian. Lonely and homesick, she had wandered over to the Western Wall to stick a prayer in the cracks, a wish that the summer would end. There, in the women's section of what used to be called the Wailing Wall, a Hasidic woman who spoke Brooklyn English befriended her and invited her to Meah Shearim for Shabbat dinner. In no time at all, the woman's family offered her a room, took her into their life, and, in Rachel's opinion, brainwashed her.

"Orthodox Judaism really speaks to me, Ma," Dalia had told her mother on the phone from Jerusalem that August.

"Arranged marriages speak to you!?" The geshrei was involuntary. To Rachel's mind, the Hasidim had kidnapped her daughter. "What exactly speaks to you, Dalia? Not being touched? Cockamamie outfits from eighteenth-century Poland? Having eight children before you're thirty? *What?*"

"I didn't call to fight, Ma." Dalia was patient, but steadfast. "The Fifth Commandment says we should honor our father and mother. I called to tell you I'm getting married." Which she did. At twenty. Dropped out of college, moved with her new husband to London (where he'd been assigned to spread the gospel of Hasidism), and now, at thirty-three, was already halfway to *Cheaper by the Dozen*. Rachel had to travel three thousand miles every time she wanted to see her grandchildren. Sitting at the Seder table amid the hubbub, she realized that her once-picture-perfect family was intact now only in home movies that no one ever watched, and she was a fallen matriarch and a betrayed wife. Still, she was *there*. She had driven herself into the city without pausing to jump off the Triborough Bridge. She'd managed not just to stay alive but to function, keep up her fitness regimen, and dress neatly. What she hadn't done was meet her needlepoint deadlines or put fresh flowers in the vases. That degree of perfection belonged to her former life. Her goals were different now: Getting through each day. Being true to herself. Planning for the future. She was counting on the Seder's rituals of rebirth to help her heal.

At least hers wasn't the only sundered clan. Her sisters were also missing family members. All three had their incompleteness in common; Leah, in fact, had no one, which made Rachel all the more grateful for her remnant family, the presence of whom had pulled her out of her doldrums: Simon, her only surviving son, in his late thirties now, and his long-time lover, Roy, who sat thigh to thigh, joking like an old married couple, their intimacy more blithe and natural, she realized sadly, than anything she'd ever known with Jeremy. And her youngest daughter, Tamara, who seemed improbably cheerful despite an uncomfortable pregnancy and no marriage license.

"You guys have Mom's permission to have a baby?" teased Simon, a gibe at his sister's stubborn refusal to tie the knot with Seth, her perennial live-in. Rachel called him her son-out-law. Seth was a marathon runner and struggling jazz musician whose day job, carpentry, paid the bills, but just barely. He'd spent a couple of months building the yarn cabinets in Rachel's needlepoint studio, and during the many hours they'd whiled away talking as they both worked, or taking a jog together at the end of the day, she'd grown to love him. He was no Gideon, but he felt surprisingly sonlike.

"You guys have the Pope's permission to hold hands?" countered Tamara, who made a sometime living as a stand-up comedienne. She's a kinder, gentler version of Leah, thought Rachel, studying the thirty-year-old from whom bartenders still demanded ID. Rachel watched Seth lean over and kiss Tamara's almost full-term belly, something else Jeremy had never done, not once in Rachel's five pregnancies. She watched Tamara tousle Seth's curly hair and Simon squeeze Roy's knee, and she wondered how, with her forced mirth and faked marriage, she could have spawned such happy children.

"I wish Jake was here." Shoshanna sighed. (Clearly, the ghost of missing persons had moved down the table.) Her son was at U.C. Boulder, stuck there for midterms. He'd arranged to attend a community Seder with some other Jewish students, and though Shoshanna was pleased he'd be observing Passover, she worried when he went off campus since Colorado had had more than its fair share of tragedies—a Denver talk-show host shot by a white supremacist, the murder of six-year-old beauty queen JonBenét Ramsey, the Kennedy who skied into a tree and died—weird happenings that bore the stamp of the Evil Eye on a Rocky Mountain high.

"*Were,*" said Leah. "You wish Jake *were* here." She'd met Shoshanna's son only once, nine years ago at Sam's eightieth, but remembered him as a tall, gangly kid with his mother's auburn hair and his grand-mother's Milky Way of freckles. He'd written a limerick for his grandpa: "There once was a rabbi named Sam / Who refused to eat pork or ham" was all Leah could recall right now, but she had a feeling she was going to miss Jake tonight, too.

Shoshanna missed her father. She remembered how he loved to run the Seder, explaining each ceremony in the Haggadah to within an inch of its life, and how beneficently he'd preside over his growing tribe. Since he'd been living in Israel for twelve years, the family took his absence for granted, at least that's what Shoshanna assumed, since no one had mentioned him, she quite purposely. No way could she men-tion him without discussing his forthcoming visit, and she wasn't will-ing to take a chance on Leah's reaction to the news. Why fess up now and risk ruining the evening?

"Then again," continued Shoshanna, "thirteen's unlucky at a dinner table."

"The devil's already done a job on this family," said Rachel. "Leah and me—we've had enough lousy luck to last till Tisha B'Av."

Leah controlled herself, didn't scream *I, you numskull, Leah and I!*, only shifted in her seat and added, "Don't forget Shoshe. Since her datebook blew off the car, her future's been bollixed up, too."

Bollixed, not fucked—that was progress. Though monitoring Leah's motormouth and trigger temper was less stress-producing in her own dining room than in a public restaurant, Shoshanna was so invested in the evening's success that she'd already leveled her pinky nail, the one she usually gnawed first, thinking it the least noticeable. She studied her sisters—Leah, all slouchy and serious in a black sweater dusted with cigarette ash; Rachel, with her ramrod posture and lemony silk blouse— and felt a fierce desire to keep the two of them not only in her *life* but in each other's. It could happen, if everything went well tonight, if Leah didn't get out of line. Damn it! Was she ever going to let go? Her addiction to Keeping Things Under Control had become almost uncontrollable. She remembered, at one of their earliest lunches, Leah calling her a control freak.

At the time, Shoshanna had neglected to point out Leah's need to control *her*. Tonight, however, she was pondering her sister's *self*-control. Her uncharacteristic willingness to let Rachel's grammatical gaffe pass without reprimand after correcting Shoshanna's might be evidence of her empathy for Rachel, which was just what Shoshanna had hoped to elicit on the phone last night. Or it could be a side effect of Leah's own malaise. Either way, she hadn't made a scene and Shoshanna began to believe Rachel might actually escape tonight unscathed. Everything was chugging along better than she could have imagined. People were being solicitous of one another. Conversation was humming. She let go of her ragged pinky nail and folded her hands in her lap.

"How's the Filofax Reconstruction Project coming along?" Leah asked her. "Pages still missing?"

"Twenty-seven from the calendar alone. I've been standing people up for six weeks and there's no end in sight." Shoshanna's voice trailed off.

"Oy!" said Leah, realizing guiltily that her sister had remembered their lunch date, then got stood up herself. "Chekhov is on point here. In *The Three Sisters*, Kuligin says, 'The most important thing in every life is its framework . . . what loses its framework comes to an end.'" She finished the sentence with a faraway look and began twirling her braid. She was thinking of Leo, her own collapsed framework, the decisions that lay ahead. She had no idea where he kept the mortgage or the tax folders or anything else. If he was going to be gone for a long time and Henry wasn't coming back, she probably ought to sell the house.

Modest as it was, five rooms were more than one person needed. There was so much to think about.

Rachel watched Leah's face crumple. "I guess all three of us have lost our frameworks in one way or another . . ." Maybe, when you've made a mess of things, she thought, you have to break everything apart, frame and all, and reconfigure it before you can start anew.

"Let's get started," interrupted Daniel, who'd sensed a downward slide. He approached his sister-in-law's chair and put his hands on her shoulders. "I'd like you to run the Seder, Rachel, if you don't mind. I've been doing it long enough." (He'd been their leader since Sam moved to Israel. Everyone had agreed he was the rabbi's natural replacement—and no one else wanted the job.) Shoshanna's eyes watered pridefully. Her husband was ceding the role not just to buttress Rachel's self-esteem but to tilt the spotlight away from himself. He understood that his very presence underlined the other two husbands' absences, and he knew the contrast would be minimized if he wasn't at the head of the table. Putting Rachel in charge of the Seder was a mitzvah.

"Great idea!" exclaimed Tamara. "Go, Ma!"

Rachel blushed. "Oh, I can't, Daniel. But thank you."

" 'Course you can," he insisted. "I wouldn't be surprised if you could recite the entire Haggadah by heart."

"Easy for her; she's suffered all ten plagues." Tamara was only half joking.

"Please, Rachel. Take my seat," Daniel said, pulling slightly at her chair. "You're the only one who can embellish the story the way your father used to. What did he call those digressions of his?"

"Educational eruptions," Rachel replied with a soft smile.

"Interminable interruptions was more like it," said Leah.

Shoshanna added, "Dad's Seders always took forever."

" 'Our father oppressed us with education.' " Leah was quoting yet another line from *The Three Sisters*. Though loath to credit Sam with anything positive, anything that might vitiate her hostility, she couldn't help remembering how deftly he used to unpack the Haggadah's boring passages, layer by layer, until they became vibrant with fresh meaning. His Seders were as engaging as the best graduate seminars she'd ever taken. Or given. But unless someone held a blowtorch to her eyeballs, she would never admit that, or the fact that it was her father who'd inspired her to become a teacher.

"*Do* it, Mom!" Simon was urging.

"We want Rachel!" Nelly and Ezra chanted.

The twins chimed in, "We want Way-chel!"

Rachel smoothed her lemon silk lapels and tugged at her pearls. She closed her eyes, continuing the struggle beneath the tender skin of her eyelids, wondering if she was up to it. She'd been a student of Judaism for years, but not a confident, articulate intellectual like certain people at this table. She remembered once contradicting her father on some obscure biblical reference and feeling almost apologetic when she turned out to be right. Delighted by her expertise, he'd pushed her to go deeper, but she'd demurred. He used to accuse her of underplaying her brains because athletics came so easily to her. He used to tell her she was smart.

Now, without Sam's encouragement (unless he'd taken up residence in her subconscious), she was pushing herself to go deeper. It was no more complicated to lead a Seder than to follow a needlepoint pattern, she told herself. If she could do that, she could do this. Ten years in her father's house, twenty-odd years of adult education, countless courses on Exodus, and a whole semester on the Haggadah as Literature, had taught her how. And she'd never missed a family Seder, two a year every year of her life, a hundred and twenty-eight in all. For the last decade, though none of her relatives knew it, she'd also been attending a third Seder, a feminist ceremony led by women who dared to read women into the ritual, to conjure their Jewish foremothers, to speak of the Four Daughters and ask the Four Questions as women might have written them: Why on this night do women serve and men recline? Why do our brothers lust after shiksas? Why can't our daughters say kaddish for their parents? Why are so many women in the Torah nameless? She'd gone at the urging of a friend who'd read about the feminist Seder in

The Jewish Week (told Jeremy she was going to the city to visit a friend, afraid of his mockery), but she'd returned by herself every year after that, and now *that* Seder, the transgressive one, felt the most traditional, because it counted women *in*. She'd come to realize how impossible it is to feel viscerally connected to a tradition that counts one out. Over time, as she'd watched different women run the Seder, she'd found herself thinking, I can do that, and this year, without Jeremy here to roll his eyes and diminish her, maybe she would. If Dulcie of Worms could lead a prayer community eight hundred years ago, and Ray Frank could deliver the High Holy Day sermon to a congregation of a thousand Jews in Spokane in 1890, and Regina Jonas could stand in the pulpit at the Berlin synagogue in 1935, Rachel Brent could run one little Seder in her sister's dining room in 1999.

"I guess I can give it a try," she said finally, fingering her pearls. "But I'll need everyone's help." It struck Shoshanna that all three sisters were fidgeters, she with the fingernails, Rachel with her pearls, and Leah with the braid, which she was twirling now in barely controlled fury.

What audacity! Leah wanted to shout. *Who the hell do you think you are, Rachel Brent? Leading a Seder isn't like running a fakrimpteh Sisterhood meeting!* She was the last one to care about guarding Sam Wasserman's turf, but the idea that Rachel would even consider stepping into his kittel was utterly ludicrous. Leah's first impulse was to laugh out loud and offer to run the Seder herself, which, despite the remoteness of her last exposure, she was sure she could pull off. Yet, just as she had stopped herself from reacting to the twins' jewel names and Rachel's grammatical blunder, she held herself in check now, realizing how bizarre it was that she—who'd sworn off Judaism, scorned religious holidays, and chowed down cheese Danish while her sisters' mouths were dry with matzohs—cared about the Seder at all.

Why was this night different from all other nights? Because tonight Leah wanted her family to like her. This most extraordinary desire seemed to be driving her toward good behavior, though she wasn't sure what good behavior was after a lifetime of letting it all hang out. What was different about tonight was not her sudden concern for the integrity of the ritual but her hunger for acceptance and her self-restraint. At this very moment, in her mind's ear, a voice was reaming her out: Who are you to object? You're the newcomer here, a guest in your own family, the stranger at the Seder table, not to mention a defector from the faith. You lack what lawyers call "standing." If everyone else is willing to let this . . . this . . . *housewife* run the show, why don't you shut the fuck up?

"This was Sam's kittel; he gave it to me when I took over the Seder," Daniel was saying as he guided Rachel's arms into the sleeves of a long white robe. "A Jew—albeit a *male* Jew—is supposed to do three things in this schmatta: get married, lead Seders, and be buried. I wore a tuxedo to my wedding, but the kittel has seen me through many Seders and I expect it will be my shroud. Until then, it's my pleasure to pass it on to Sam's eldest."

Rachel wrapped herself in the robe and tied its sash around her waist. As she assumed Daniel's seat at the head of the table, everyone beamed except Leah, who kept puzzling over the intensity of her negativity. A woman in a kittel symbolized everything she'd been fighting for the last forty years—a woman's right to be a judge, cop, priest, senator, or Seder leader. So what was wrong with this picture? *This* woman was! The first female to run the Seder in a family like theirs ought to be a sage not a fact fetishist, an imposing presence, not a ninety-nine-pound needle-pointer. What should have been an exhilarating breakthrough was spoiled by this suburban schmeggegy. She looked ridiculous in the kittel, like a child in dress-up clothes. *We don't need you,* Leah wanted to holler. *We can read the Haggadah to ourselves and be out by 8.* But again, the ire died in her throat, squelched not by rachmoness for Rachel (tonight wasn't *that* different from all other nights) but by self-interest. If she made trouble, Shoshanna might ask her to leave, and she desperately wanted to stay, couldn't bear the idea of going home to Leo's empty Shtarka-Barca, her sad little study, their empty bed. Enough losses. Too much space had been yawning around her lately, and she wasn't about to alienate the only people left who might fill it.

She swallowed her antagonism the way she'd once made herself gulp down an oyster and silently toasted her sister's chutzpah with

Manischewitz Concord grape, the nectar of memory. One sip evoked Passovers past. Maxwell House Haggadahs. Barricini's chocolate-covered matzohs. Bowls of unshelled walnuts and pecans, and everyone clamoring for the family's only nutcracker. Seders before the divorce, when Leah got to ask the Four Questions and drink from Sam's cup, the enormous silver goblet that depicted the crossing of the Red Sea. Seders after the divorce, when Grandpa Moishe, an old man with matzoh crumbs caught in his beard, gave her a box of Barton's Passover candy to bring back to school and Dena confiscated it for herself. Leah's happiest Seder, the last one she'd ever attended, when Rachel sat on one side of her and Shoshanna, in her high chair, on the other.

"Please open your Haggadahs to page 1." Rachel began reading the text aloud. "'We cried out and God heard our cries and saw our affliction, our misery and our oppression. And God took us out of Egypt with a strong hand and an outstretched arm, with awesome power, with signs and with wonders.'" She looked up from the page and continued, haltingly, in her own words: "Those lines from Deuteronomy summarize the story we are about to tell. Not just *tell* but *live*. We Jews are commanded to experience our ancestors' enslavement every year no matter where we are or what our circumstances. To feel as if we are slaves, as if the Egyptian bondage were actually happening to *us*. Because we once were strangers in a strange land, we are expected to identify with the oppressed of our own time, to feel an affinity for the stranger, meaning the downtrodden, the outcast, those who are poor or sick, belittled or different. Through three millennia, Jews have experienced the miracle of memory. We know that ritualizing the past can make it even more vivid than the present. And so tonight, we once again grind the gears of Jewish history, and as we recall how God liberated us from Mitzrayim, we rededicate ourselves to the liberation of all who are suffering in heart, mind, or body in today's world."

"A-men! You could have given that speech at a gay-rights rally!" exclaimed Roy, who was turning out to be this year's karmic relief. "The message is so . . . *now!*"

"The Bible was way ahead of us," said Rachel, grateful for his enthusiasm.

"I guess there's nothing new under the sun," replied Simon.

"Ecclesiastes!" declaimed Leah.

"Duh—who doesn't know that?" said Tamara.

Embarrassed to have blurted the obvious, Leah snapped, "Nothing wrong with being a know-it-all except when that's all you know."

Central Park. The antiwar rally. Leah remembered that moment at the end of the day when she'd slammed Shoshanna with the same line. But Tamara wasn't offended; she was smiling. Leah relaxed. Blessed are those who can laugh at themselves, for they shall never cease to be amused.

"Our task is to imitate God," Rachel was saying. "As God helped us throw off our oppressors, we must do the same for ourselves and each other." Her small shoulders broadened at the thought of having freed herself from her personal oppressor. She asked her sisters to rise and join her in lighting the holiday candles.

Leah thought it incredibly strange to be taking instruction from Rachel, stranger still to see this conventional little woman flex her muscles in a role for which she seemed so miscast, strangest of all to feel a lump in her throat when the three sisters stood and said the blessing, ending in perfect unison: *"l'hadlich ner shel yom tov."* Rachel couldn't help thinking about last year's Seder, when she and Shoshanna had their husbands at their sides and Leah wasn't there at all. What a difference a year makes. "Amen," they said, and sat down, not looking at one another, as if in eye contact they might be forced to acknowledge *how* different.

"Seder means order," said Rachel. "Following a set sequence helps us remember everything we have to do this evening. The Haggadah is our guide."

Leah, who never had much use for set sequences, who usually disdained the call for order as an excuse for fascism or a crutch for the indecisive, allowed herself to acknowledge the pleasures of the predictable and the comfort to be found in regularity and structure. It wasn't as if she'd been living in total chaos. Leo had brought order to her world simply by being so reliable. She recalled Flaubert's "Be regular and orderly in your life so that you may be violent and original in your work." Orderliness had been the cornerstone of Leo's creativity, and while it hadn't spawned violence in his work, it had freed Leah to be original in hers. His regularity had made possible her life of the mind. From now on, she would have to create her own structure or get it somewhere else.

"I'm sure you're all acquainted with the symbolism of the items on the Seder plate, but tradition requires me to point them out anyway and review what they mean." Rachel held up the matzoh. "Matzoh is called the Bread of Affliction for obvious reasons, but it's also called the Bread of Freedom, because it was the first sustenance the Israelites provided for themselves. It symbolizes self-sufficiency and survival. It was made on the run, so it's not puffed up with air. It's here to remind us to get rid of our own hot air, our hametz, our puffed-up self-importance."

Shoshanna checked to be sure Leah was listening.

"Karpas, the parsley, signifies springtime and rebirth. It stands for our capacity to grow and change, to make a fresh start, which is the essence of the Exodus story. Maror, the bitter herbs, represent the bitter experience of slavery, and all the other bitterness we store in our hearts—hatred, resentment, jealousy, envy." (She had in mind her feelings for Leah.) She went on to explain the shank bone, the roasted egg, and the haroset. "This delicious mixture of apples, wine, and nuts symbolizes the mortar used by the slaves to build Pharaoh's pyramids." (She flashed on Ramses.) "Why do we designate something sweet to recall the hard labor of pyramid-building? Because the Hebrews previously were expected to build *without* mortar, which was a heck of a lot harder."

Heck?! Leah hadn't heard "heck" since *Ted Mack's Amateur Hour*. She chose that moment to let loose a zinger. "Ex*cuse* me, Mother Rachel. Doesn't it strike you as rather delusional, maybe even voodooistic—assigning all this iconic significance to food?"

Shoshanna tensed, but Rachel seemed to welcome Leah's challenge. "Ever heard the famous story about Niels Bohr?"

"Not sure I have." Leah assumed she was leading up to a factoid.

"One of Bohr's students was shocked to see a horseshoe hanging outside the office door of the great physicist. 'Surely of all people you, Professor, cannot believe in such nonsense,' said the student.

" 'Of course not,' Bohr replied, 'but I understand it works even for those who don't believe in it.' "

Leah grinned despite herself. "Touché."

Rachel had everything under control. Her forehead, so deeply lined earlier in the evening, had ironed itself out. She pointed to the silver goblet at the center of the table. "Elijah's Cup. Later, our youngest will open the front door to welcome the prophet, who symbolizes the eternal hopes of the Jewish people. If Elijah actually arrived on earth, it would signal that redemption is at hand, for he's the precursor of the Messiah. Surreptitiously, adults often shake the table to stir the wine and fool the kids into thinking he's taking a drink. Everyone wants to believe the Messiah's on his way."

"Or *hers!*" said Leah.

"Or hers," repeated Rachel, raking her fingers through her bangs, a gesture Leah remembered from their schooldays. "The other large goblet, the ceramic one, is Miriam's Cup. I bought it at my synagogue gift shop, that's how common it is for Moses' sister to be added to the Seder table. Miriam's Cup is filled with spring water to symbolize the Nile. Water also reminds us of the basic things that sustain human life. Without water, no wine. Without Miriam, no Moses, no Elijah, no Messiah. But I'm sure you've noticed which of the above gets the headlines. The other unusual addition to our Seder table is the orange on the Seder plate. I asked Shoshanna to put it there to remind us of the woman who wanted to read from the Torah on Shabbat. Instead of welcoming this serious young scholar, her rabbi refused her request, saying, 'A woman belongs on the bimah the way an orange belongs on the Seder plate.' "

Neat bit of consciousness-raising, thought Leah. Very nice.

Rachel broke the middle matzoh in two, wrapped the larger piece in a cloth napkin, and slipped the package behind a couch cushion. "I'm hiding the afikomen," she said coyly. "Let's hope someone finds it."

Since Ruby and Pearl were only three, it fell to their mother, Nelly, at twenty-six the next youngest at the table, to recite the Four Questions.

"Those are ancient questions," Rachel said when Nelly finished. "Now it might be interesting to ask the questions we've been pondering in our own lives. Anyone have a question? Anything at all?"

"Me," burst out Shoshanna. Watching her twin granddaughters, she'd been struck anew by the thought that when Rachel was their age, she was already living at boarding school. "If you really mean *anything* . . ." Why was she hesitating? She was among family; she ought to be able to ask this question: "How could Mom send you away so young? I just don't get it."

"Because she was a single mother with a full-time job," Rachel answered without hesitation. "I guess she couldn't handle it all." (Too easy, thought Shoshanna.) "I think she honestly believed Blue Spruce would turn me into a real American. Though it might have had something to do with Coco Chanel, too. Chanel had a boarding-school childhood, and she was Mom's idol. Mom probably thought she was doing me a favor."

Could Rachel be as resilient as all that? Where was her anger? "I made the best of it" was all she would say whenever Shoshanna asked about her years at school. And last week Rachel gave the same answer about why she'd stayed so long in her marriage. "I made the best of it." Shoshanna was beginning to think her sister could teach her a thing or two about wresting order from chaos.

"You want my question?" said Tamara. "Why can't this baby be born already?" She rubbed her belly as if summoning a genie.

"Why am I always late grading papers?" asked Daniel.

"Ditto." Leah.

"Why am I so dependent on my Filofax?" Shoshanna asked. "Strike that; too egocentric. I meant, why can't there be an end to hunger, violence, and nuclear proliferation?"

Simon leaned forward. "If we're getting serious—why are my friends still dying of AIDS?"

"The Hebrew word for Egypt, mitzrayim, means the narrow place," Rachel said, taking her son's hand. "Most of us still have mitzrayim in our lives, places where we suffer, get stuck, or feel powerless. Others of us have left Egypt but are still wandering in the desert; we've been released from slavery but not from the mentality of the slave. For those who are b'derech, on the path, in transition between bondage and freedom, the Promised Land can seem very far away." Her last words faltered. She let go of Simon's hand, flicked at her bangs, and, fighting tears, fell silent.

Suddenly the table itself seemed like a narrow place. Instead of Elijah, the stalker had entered the room, trailing vapors of danger. Shoshanna glanced at Daniel, hoping he might say something to shift the mood, but he was reading ahead in his Haggadah. He hadn't noticed the demon party crasher and its ghostly attendants—Leo hovering over Leah, Jeremy goading Rachel into blaming herself, and beyond them, the specters of worldly despair. Shoshanna felt her perfect evening slipping away. Rachel was still not ready to trust her voice. The younger generation was baffled but too respectful to question the swelling silence, so it fell to the third generation to break the sound barrier, Pearl and Ruby having burst into tears for no apparent reason, unless collective angst is something children pick up on. While Nelly and Ezra comforted the twins, Leah did the unthinkable—tapped out a Gauloise and leaned forward to get a light from one of the tapers.

"*Ohhhh* no, you don't!" bellowed Shoshanna. "Not in the house!"

"That candle has been blessed, Leah; it's not a Bic," said Rachel. "Besides, we don't smoke at the Seder table."

Leah shrugged and squeezed the cigarette back in the pack. "Chill out, girls. I can live without it."

"Well, you sure as hell won't live *with* it," said Tamara under her breath.

It took Roy to put the evening back on track. "I used to be a chain-smoker, myself. Quit cold turkey. You could try my system, Leah; whenever I got the yen, I ate a carrot; hundreds of carrots, maybe thousands. Skin turned orange, but haven't had a puff since."

That broke the tension. Roy had led them through the narrow place.

"Let's move on," said Rachel, composed now. "We'll read the Ten Plagues together, top of page 10."

They named each plague, dipping a finger in their wine and tapping the droplet on their plates. "Blood. Frogs. Vermin. Beasts . . ." Shoshanna used her pinky; the alcohol stung where she'd bitten her nail down to the quick. Rachel flinched at number ten, death of the first-born son, but this time recovered fast. "Does anyone have a modern plague to add to this list?"

"I do," said Tamara. "Labor pains."

"Being overdrawn at the bank," put in Seth. Was he worried about supporting the new baby? Rachel resolved to write them a check in the morning—without asking Jeremy.

The others called out their plagues. Insomnia. Global warming. Homophobia. Envy. Gossip. Channel-surfing.

"Academic jealousy," said Daniel. (Leah looked at him. So the story was true.)

Shoshanna added, "Fear."

"That's ten," said Rachel. "You can keep going. With plagues, the list is never closed."

Mental illness, thought Leah, but didn't say it, only rubbed her droplets together on the blue glass plate.

After the singing of "Dayenu" and more readings, and after the second cup of wine and the ritual hand-washing and the eating of the matzoh and the bitter herbs, Daniel, sensing his sister-in-law's distress, put her to work. "Grab that pitcher, would you, Leah. I need you to fill everyone's ramekin with salt water." He disappeared into the kitchen and came back with a bowl of hard-boiled eggs. Applause greeted his return.

"Thank God—*food*!"

"Since when do hard-boiled eggs qualify as *food*?"

"Eggies," said Pearl.

"Why don't boiled eggs taste this good the rest of the year?"

"Because we don't dip them in salt water the rest of the year."

"No, because we don't *deserve* them."

Leah dipped her egg, symbol of life's continuity, into her salt water, the tears of her people. She hadn't been to a Wasserman Seder in thirty-five years, but the banter was exactly the same, a symbol of their continuity as Jews and as Wassermans. She was beginning to feel at home. "Which came first, the chicken or the egg?" she asked the group.

"We give up," said Shoshanna.

"The rooster. Then he lit a cigarette, turned over, and went to sleep."

It was Leah's dream menu—gefilte fish, chopped liver with schmaltz, matzoh-ball soup, brisket, boiled chicken, tzimmes, potato latkes. Honest kosher carbs. As the meal progressed, she noticed that everyone, not just the women, pitched in with the serving and clearing. She tried to be helpful as well, though, deep in conversation, she was loath to leave the table. Sometime during dinner she realized to her amazement that she was having a very good time.

Rachel walked over to the couch and looked behind the cushion. "Oh my God!" she said, miming melodramatic shock for the benefit of the twins. "The afikomen! It's gone! We can't finish our Seder without it. Where can it be?"

Ruby and Pearl giggled as their mommy, the youngest, held up the wrapped matzoh and demanded a ransom. "Always be generous to your children," Nelly teased Rachel. "We're the ones who will choose your nursing home."

(Not my children, thought Leah. She would have to choose her own, probably join Leo up at the Georgian mansion. That way, at least, she'd have one less institution to visit.)

Rachel, having been a last-minute recruit, was unprepared to ransom the afikomen, but Daniel had laid in a stock of silver dollars. He gave a coin to his daughter, Nelly, and to Ruby, who promptly tried to put it in her mouth, and to Pearl, who dropped hers in her bowl of salt water. Then he passed out coins to everyone else. "Tonight you're all the youngest." He winked at Shoshanna. Relax, he was saying; the evening's almost over and everything's going great.

"I know you're all salivating for the macaroons, but the afikomen is the best dessert of all." Rachel held the two halves of matzoh together. "Now that the special matzoh has been made whole, our brokenness is repaired and we're permitted to finish the Seder." Her broken marriage flitted across her mind like a housefly, but she swatted it aside. "So, thank you, Nelly."

" 'Twas nothing."

"No, it was very important. If you hadn't returned it, we'd be stalled here for the rest of the night." Rachel broke the ransomed matzoh into bite-size pieces and passed them around on a plate. "That's how much power the Haggadah gives the children. A child starts us off with the Four Questions and ends our journey by giving us the afikomen. Lovely, don't you think?"

"Next year, I'm ceding my power to my girls," said Nelly, smoothing Ruby's copper hair. Shoshanna's genes had gone straight to her grand-daughters' heads.

Tamara protested. "Wait a minute. Next year *our* kid will be the youngest. Maybe it'll be a prodigy. Maybe it'll come out of the uterus asking questions."

"It?" repeated Roy. "I thought everyone knew their baby's sex in advance."

"We don't want to know," said Seth, lacing his fingers into Tamara's. "We're having this baby the old-fashioned way."

"If it's a boy," asked Leah, "will he have a bris?"

Tamara looked shocked. "Of course he'll have a bris."

"What do you mean, *of course*?" Leah's fighting tone.

Here we go, thought Shoshanna. "Macaroons?" she asked brightly.

"I can give you a dozen reasons why a parent would reject circumcision. Beside the obvious barbarity of it, there's the avoidance of pain, the possibility of a botched procedure—it happens, you know—and, contrary to popular belief, the uncircumcised penis is not unhygienic. The findings are clear on that." When the macaroons reached her, she deliberated between plain and chocolate.

"Have one of each, they're both great," said Shoshanna. "We made them from scratch."

"The recipe will cost you one Susan B. Anthony dollar," said

Daniel, giving an assist to his wife's bid to change the subject. But Leah would not be diverted.

"Then there's the issue of male supremacy. The whole purpose of the bris is to ceremonialize the covenant between God and the Jewish male. And *only* the male. Some say women can be covenanted symbolically through a kind of circumcision of the heart. Others think we should tattoo girls with some generally agreed-upon sign, to mark them physically the way we do boys."

"How 'bout we tattoo a penis on the baby girl's tummy and when she gets pregnant it grows." (Tamara, of course.)

"I'm sure they were thinking of a Star of David, dear," said her mother. "Or a Lion of Judah."

Leah knew she was dominating, but felt this was a lecture everyone needed to hear. "Nowadays, there are rituals and naming ceremonies for girls, an attempt to correct the inequality. But dipping a daughter in a mini-mikvah or planting a tree in her name will never measure up to the primal power of a blood sacrifice. The bris is a coronation, for Chrissake. Hail to the son, the boychik is king!"

"Christ again," muttered Rachel.

Leah barreled on. "Since we're asking questions, here are four more for you: What are the larger implications when a society celebrates the birth of one gender with so much more fanfare and import than the other? Shouldn't all children be equally welcomed into the Jewish people? How are girls supposed to feel about their inherent worth if we make a fuss only over boys? Isn't every baby a miracle of Jewish survival?"

Those who'd never heard Leah on a tear didn't know what to make of her. Nelly and Ezra, being the parents of girls, couldn't help nodding in response to each question. Simon and Roy busied themselves arranging their macaroon crumbs into lines and circles on the tablecloth. Tamara retreated from the conversation and Seth looked confused. Thank God, Sam wasn't here, thought Shoshanna. He'd be livid. She wasn't sure what should happen next. Her antennae picked up oscillations of impending chaos, but she saw how calm Daniel was and decided to take her cue from him. She didn't have to be responsible for *everything*. There were ten other people at the table; let them handle Leah.

The normally reticent Rachel, perhaps emboldened by the kittel, spoke first: "It's a divine commandment, Leah. Genesis 17—'Every male among you shall be circumcised.' That's pretty non-negotiable."

"If you're a fundamentalist, maybe. But we're rational people. We make choices all the time. I'm sure even you don't obey every commandment."

Rachel flashed on the half-month of sexual denial she'd never observed, the mikvah she'd never visited. She put one strand of pearls in her mouth and sucked on it.

"What about historical continuity?" asked Daniel. "Doesn't it count for something that the bris is a 3,500-year-old ritual? Abraham circumcised himself when he was ninety-nine; he also circumcised his son, Isaac. Some commentaries say Moses was circumcised by his wife. Some say the ancient Hebrews circumcised themselves in Egypt; it wasn't just the lamb's blood that spared them from the tenth plague but their own. I'd say any ceremony dating back that far deserves respect."

"Thanks for the history lesson, Professor Safer, though I rather doubt you'd make the same claim for animal sacrifice. And you needn't remind me that Jews circumcised their sons in secret in times and places when, for want of a foreskin, a man could be killed. No one respects that history more than I. But this is another time and place, and today the ceremony is a sexist anachronism."

"It's not that simple, Leah," insisted Daniel.

"You're right, it's not. It's about Jewish women's fundamental status as Jews. Rachel said we're commanded to empathize with the stranger. Well, I'm asking you to empathize with the strangers in Judaism—our girls and women. The discrepancy between male and female birth ceremonies insults us. The utter *maleness* of the bris excludes us. It's a fraternity initiation. Skull and Bones, Cock and Foreskin. Testosterone Central."

"You sound so hostile," said Tamara. "Like you really hate men."

"Don't be silly, some of my best friends are men." She forced a chuckle.

"Actually, there's nothing in Jewish law that requires those roles to be filled by males," corrected Daniel. "The bris is so important that even a woman, a minor, and a slave may perform it." He smiled sheepishly. "I realize that doesn't put women in the best of company, but you get the point."

Rachel, repressing her mikvah guilt, said, "As a feminist, Leah, you ought to know that women now serve as sandeks. Some have even trained as mohels."

"I can hear the Orthos now: *Don't trust your son's pecker to a feminist!*"

"It's not a joke," Rachel persisted. "You should be proud. We have your movement to thank for those advances."

Before Leah could answer, Shoshanna turned to her and asked, "Were your boys circumcised?"

She flushed and reached for another macaroon. "Yes, but not at a bris. By a doctor in the hospital."

"Why did you agree to it at all if you feel so strongly?"

"My husband wanted his sons' penises to look like his. That's the only reason I went along."

"It seems to me that's a pretty good reason," said Shoshanna gently. "When you really think about it, what Leo was saying was, he wanted his boys in his tribe. He didn't want to break the chain. Remember Philip Roth's wonderful quote about this? It was in a recent *New Yorker*. Wait, I don't want to mangle it. I'll get the magazine from my office."

Nelly rolled her eyes. "Mother and her infernal clippings." She beckoned to Ezra. "Let's take the girls upstairs. It's late." Shoshanna had made the beds in Nelly's old room so the twins could sleep there while the Seder ran its course. Leah used the break to go outside for her deferred smoke, but was back at the table with a fresh dusting of ashes on her chest by the time Shoshanna returned with the magazine, an issue from the previous December.

"Here. It's from this amazing letter Philip Roth wrote years ago to Mary McCarthy:

'I think you fail to see how serious this circumcision business is to Jews. I am still hypnotized by uncircumcised men when I see them at my swimming pool locker room. The damn thing never goes unregistered . . . I asked several of my equally secular Jewish male friends if they could have an uncircumcised son, and they all said no, sometimes without having to think about it and sometimes after the nice long pause that any rationalist would take before opting for the irrational.'"

"What can you expect from Philip Roth?" said Leah. "The man writes with his prick."

Everyone laughed. Leah noticed the ashes on the front of her black shirt, tried to brush them off, and, when they smudged like chalk, rubbed them in instead. That used to be her strategy. If you can't brush it off, rub it in. This time, she brushed it off and laughed along with them.

Shoshanna, pleased to have bested her snappish sister with a literary source, couldn't help but puff up a bit, hametz or not. And Daniel, who might have been reading her mind, made her feel even bigger when he sang out, "Let's hear it for my wife! I'll bet no one else at this table could have located a story in a four-month-old magazine in three minutes and twenty seconds."

Rachel tried to recall a time in nearly four decades of marriage when Jeremy had praised her in public. "Forget about *The New Yorker*," she said, "*this* is our text, page 26." She tapped her Haggadah and began singing "Adir Hu."

The melody cued the words into Leah's throat. As surprised as she was to be singing along, she was even more astounded to realize that she'd lost an argument and been willing to let it go. Shoshanna had caught her in a logical inconsistency—compromising her principles for the sake of her husband's feelings. But she'd done it because Leo had given up synagogue, Seders, Hanukkah, Yom Kippur; everything, for her. She'd thought she owed him the circumcision after cutting him off, so to speak, from his Jewish roots. Pity he wasn't here tonight to share her return to her family Seder. At least she *had* a family. He had psychiatrists and that woman in the flight-attendant outfit who'd shooed Leah away. In his last letter, Leo had written:

We're going to have a Seder here. A sign went up on the bulletin board this morning saying one of the patients would run it, this guy who used to be a rabbi. It makes me happy to think you'll be attending a Seder too this year, especially with your sisters. It was nice of Shoshanna to invite you. I always liked her. The few times I met her, she seemed kind.

She was kind, thought Leah. Watching Shoshanna replenish the macaroons, Leah felt enormous gratitude to her. For sitting through Leah's lunchtime perorations all these years. For listening to her accumulated mishegas without being smug or sanctimonious. And now, for inviting her to the Seder and letting her sermonize on circumcision without dispatching her back to Brooklyn. Leah ate her macaroon in one bite. It was hard to admit this, but she also felt gratitude to her other sister, for coming through tonight without shaming her sex, for her nuanced commentaries, for allowing humor at the Seder table. Rachel might not be the sharpest knife in the drawer, but she gave good ritual. More than a pretender to the throne or a substitute teacher, she'd proven herself the real thing, a woman at ease in a kittel.

Rachel, it so happens, was summing up her evening as well. She'd come alone and would leave alone, yet in the last few hours her feelings about her single state had changed dramatically. Like the prophet Miriam, she'd performed well, with no husband crouching in the bullrushes barking orders. (Though, in one sense, he had been; his betrayal was so flagrant that he might as well have been ordering her to leave him.) Now, reclining on her Passover pillows and feeling quite pleased with herself, she realized that tonight had been a proving ground, a test of not only her competence but her self-sufficiency and self-confidence. She'd be in great shape, if only she didn't have to drive home to an empty house. A house sounds and feels different once someone who has always lived there is gone. There was barely a trace left of Jeremy—some tools, his rowing machine, the furnishings in his study—and he'd been away so often over the years that she was accustomed to being alone. But now the emptiness felt different. If only she didn't have to leave.

Rachel caught Leah looking at her. Despite the purple-tinted glasses, she could see that Leah's expression, for the first time in decades, bespoke no contempt.

Simon got up to go. "Great Seder, Mom! Loved it!"

"It's the Jewish people's favorite ritual." Rachel was back in factoid mode. "Eighty-seven percent of American Jews attend at least one Seder, which is pretty impressive when you realize that only 28 percent light Friday-night candles and barely a quarter engage in Jewish study."

Leah marveled at the things her sister knew.

fifteen

"HI, MOM."

It was Jake from Boulder. When Shoshanna was growing up, long distance was for heart attacks. Nowadays kids called cross-country to check the time.

He said he was worried. Was everything okay at home? It was so unlike her to ignore one of her children's or grandchildren's birthdays, events she'd marked every year with fuss and fanfare, much as her birthdays had been celebrated by Esther. Every May 3, since he'd gone away to college, Shoshanna sent Jake a singing telegram, a humongous tin of homemade cookies, and a UPS box full of birthday presents. This year, May 3 had come and gone unnoticed.

Shoshanna, appalled at herself, promised to FedEx a batch that afternoon.

"We've got cookies in Boulder, Mom. I just wanted to be sure nothing was wrong."

Nothing wrong, she assured him, though clearly something was. Those pages blowing around somewhere on the Henry Hudson Parkway were no excuse; she should have remembered her son's twenty-first birthday. Dismissing her apologies, Jake, who was studying for his Psychology 101 final, volunteered that, as much as he appreciated her treats, he didn't need them, and her life might be a lot simpler if she didn't go overboard celebrating everyone's birthday, anniversary, promotion, or lost baby tooth. He wondered why she felt the need to lavish such attention on others. Maybe she was overcompensating. Maybe she felt fate had dealt her too much good stuff and she had to keep putting out and making others happy so it would be okay for her to have what she had.

"Psych 101," she laughed, but he had her nailed. She'd inherited her mother's kaynahoras—the crazy fears about having too much, the obligation to be grateful for the good stuff but not to get smug or showy lest she attract people's envy, which would attract the Evil Eye, which would strike her with some horrible affliction to cut her down to size. Esther's kaynahoras were supposed to keep Shoshanna humble but instead had left her with a mammoth case of Jewish guilt and the sense that whatever blessings came her way would eventually have to be paid for. To preempt the Eye, she had to be extra kind and generous and thoughtful; that was the price for being so lucky.

She hung up the phone and burst into tears. Forgetting Jake's birthday was her worst lapse yet. It had vanished from her brain because its page had disappeared. Other missing pages—Fiona called them MPs—had kept her from a dentist appointment (the mercenary billed her anyway) and a block association meeting (she never got to vote on whether ginkgoes or maples should replace their damaged street trees). Because of an MP, she and Daniel had missed a dinner party whose hosts called afterward to find out what had happened and were quick to forgive once they'd heard. The mere *idea* of losing their datebooks was chilling, they said. Then again, it might be a relief to skip half the things one signs up for in life. The message was clear: she'd become too busy, but also too passive. She had to change her ways. It wasn't enough to be happily married and sexually fulfilled if she was going to be losing her mind.

Turning fifty wasn't incidental either. One result of the Filofax fiasco was that she'd conveniently blanked out her own birthday; June 14 remained among the MPs. No matter. It was coming up fast, with or without its page, her self-imposed deadline for a radical retooling. She was going to separate the meaningful from the mundane and simplify her life—that would be her present to herself, that plus a Palm Pilot. Leaving the computer store, she recalled Leah's axiom: "When men get depressed, they invade another country; when women get depressed, they go shopping." Shopping was better.

She brandished the electronic organizer under the noses of her assistants. "Look what I bought."

"Praise God, she's done it!" bellowed Elliott, who removed his red-framed glasses with a flourish.

Fiona dropped what she was doing and immediately unwrapped the organizer and began to copy appointments and phone numbers from the leftover Filofax, and enter project deadlines from her own Palm, which, as she put it, "had saved Shoshanna's arse, clientwise."

The brownstone's back garden was lush and verdant in the morning sun. Stalks of jaunty bluebells dotted the postage-stamp lawn. Pink and red tulips nodded along the brick borders of a weedy flagstone path. Outbursts of azaleas and lilac brightened the split-rail fence dividing Shoshanna's property from her neighbors'. As she meditated on her precious patch of earth and its tireless springtime rebirths, she worried that it might be too late for her to learn new things, like how to operate an electronic organizer, or teach herself to remember dates. She opened the glass-paned door and followed the path to a fountain of weathered stone topped by a curly-haired Cupid. With the flip of a faucet at its base, she set the first waters of the season spouting from the cherub's tiny penis to the scallop shell below. What about her own fountain? she wondered. Was it running dry? Would her garden stop blooming? Was she losing it? Thinking in clichés embarrassed her, yet such questions were arriving daily now, shadowed by a new threat, a fear not of rising tides or malfunctioning fire extinguishers but of the havoc in her own head. It had never occurred to her that the stalker might be after her mind.

She decided to test herself this minute. Back at her desk, she grabbed a yellow legal pad, made a list of friends and relatives in one column, then tried to recall their birth dates in the other. The exercise made her sweat. She couldn't remember Leah's birthday, much less those of Leo, two of Rachel's kids, or half her friends. Once, she'd known them all.

"I forgot Jake's birthday," she told her assistants, carrying the pad to the outer office.

Elliott said, "No, Shoshanna, you do *not* have a brain tumor."

"But I *do* have a problem." She dropped the list on Fiona's desk.

"Mmm, lots of blanks there," murmured Fiona, then noticed an entry beside her own name. "Hey, thanks for remembering."

"Who could forget? That's the date you never come to work."

"Me mum always said birthdays deserve a person's undivided attention."

"Maybe when you're twenty-eight they do."

"Aha!—only six weeks till the big five-oh."

"Thank you, Fiona," Shoshanna said caustically. "Without your timely bulletin, it might have slipped my mind."

"Well, you'll never forget another birthday from this day forward and forevermore. Guaranteed! I'm transferring your birthday notations from the grungy Filofax sheets. Rachel's going to help fill in what she can and I'll check with Daniel to see whose he remembers. Eventually, everyone's birthday or anniversary will pop up on this little screen on each person's special day."

"Thanks," said Shoshanna, but she'd be damned if she'd need an electronic brain to remind her of her children's birthdays. She certainly needed no help remembering her own. Rachel had been reminding her about it on a daily basis. She wanted to make Shoshanna a party and Shoshanna was resisting, having been to too many fiftieths—black balloon balls where everyone got sloshed, told incontinence jokes, and made vacuous toasts about the prime of life when they were really thinking, God! How depressing! Shoshanna was already depressed enough, couldn't get a handle on why she loved her life yet was preoccupied by death. Perfect health, terrific husband, great kids, nice little business, looked good for her age, yet none of it seemed to outweigh the angst. In Washington Square Park the other day, she'd seen a T-shirt that summed up her feelings: "Aging ain't for sissies." Fifty was nothing to celebrate and no one could convince her otherwise, though Rachel still called twice a day insisting on a party.

"You've gotta have one. It's the halfway point."

"More like three-quarters."

"Not if you're like Dad. He's nine-tenths and still going strong. Besides, fifty's just a number."

"A gloomy number."

"You're obsessing over it, Shoshie. Tell me you're not."

"I am."

"Okay then, the cure for obsession is celebration. Look, I'm definitely giving you some kind of party, so you may as well tell me what you want."

Shoshanna wasn't sure why her sister was pushing so hard, but it occurred to her that party planning might be good therapy for Rachel. "All right," she sighed into the phone. "A small one, no more than ten."

"Ten?"

"Ten women, including me."

"You only want women? Wait a minute—are you saying that to make your suddenly single sisters feel comfortable?"

"No, to make *myself* feel comfortable. You asked what I want. That's it."

"How come?" The notion of a social evening without men struck Rachel as peculiar, though, undoubtedly, Jeremy had gone out many evenings with just the boys. When he zoomed out of the garage, maybe he wasn't always en route to a woman but to a bunch of guys who were similarly afflicted with testosterone poisoning. Maybe they told each other how impossible their wives were, or paid some lap dancer in a thong and pasties to rev their motors. Rachel had always found all-male groups grossly primitive, their enthusiasms vulgar.

"Because when there are no men around, women are more honest," replied Shoshanna, who'd discovered the phenomenon in Off Our

Necks years ago (when Leah pointed it out). "I don't want to hear any crap about aging gracefully or how young I look. I want help."

"Can we do the party on your actual birthday, or is Daniel taking you out?"

"He's reserved me for Saturday night. Monday's fine." Again, she sighed into the receiver. "But you'll have to take care of everything and just tell me where to show up."

"This isn't torture, Shoshie."

"What I meant to say was, thank you, Rache, I know I'll love it."

The invitation list was easy. Besides Rachel and Shoshanna, there was Shoshanna's daughter, Nelly, Rachel's daughter Tamara, Leah, who'd become a real presence in their lives, and the tall Brit Shoshanna always raved about who worked in her office. That made six. Rachel called the Brit for advice about the last four slots.

"Shoshanna's four closest friends? Easy," said Fiona, and named them. "Ask me a hard one."

"Any restaurant suggestions? I'm from Long Island."

"Are we talking London? Florence? Rio? . . ."

"New York, Fiona."

"If you're into four stars, it's Jean-Georges."

Rachel remembered the name from Jeremy's secret MasterCard bill. "What about a half star, someplace casual where ten women can sit around for three or four hours and schmooze?"

Fiona named an Italian restaurant in the Village with a small private room. "It's bellissimo! Big round table. Seats ten, maybe even twelve."

"Ten is all she wants. Would you mind making a reservation for us, June 14, 7 p.m. Oh, and, Fiona . . ."

"Yes, ma'am."

"You're invited."

"Jolly good. I'll make sure to be done with the Palm by then so I can give it to her fully packed and programmed, along with my present. She'll be glad to have things back under control!"

Shoshanna's birthday fell on Flag Day, a distinction that would have failed to impress her childhood classmates had it not been for Esther's parties. Short of fireworks, Esther Wasserman celebrated her daughter's birthday the way the rest of the country celebrated the Fourth of July. She dressed her Yankee Doodle girl in a homemade tricolor costume, decorated the birthday cake with miniature flags and the table with a Statue of Liberty centerpiece, stacked the phonograph with patriotic tunes by George M. Cohan and John Philip Sousa. Esther considered it an act of God for her daughter to have been born on the day honoring the Stars and Stripes, and with an immigrant's awe for the quintessentially American, made much of the coincidence. In fact, Esther made much of every birthday and holiday, American or Jewish, utilizing her designer talents to decorate the apartment more lavishly than Lord & Taylor's windows at Christmas. Not content to carve pumpkins into jack-o'-lanterns on Halloween, she set up a ghoul scene in the window seat with a backlit skeleton that could be seen from Riverside Drive. For Purim, she made edible Queen Esthers (stuffed celery with a cherry tomato head and parsley skirt) and homemade groggers (gravel in empty oatmeal cylinders). She threw Hanukkah parties with themes drawn from the story of the Maccabees. "Illumination" one year; "Miracles" the next. Her Rosh Hashanah dinner table had a centerpiece made of real ram's horns and everyone in the family was invited to practice blowing the shofar. Shoshanna had inherited her mother's fuss-making proclivities. A three-ringed surprise for Jake was one of her productions, also parties with a horsey theme for Nelly, and ethnic birthday dinners—a Hawaiian luau, Texas barbecue, Mongolian hot pot—with a book of little-known facts about each culture for Rachel, who'd decided this was payback time. This year, Rachel was going to revive the Flag Day theme for her baby sister and take it over the top.

She designed the invitation herself, an American flag with a photo of Shoshanna where the stars should be and the text printed on the stripes:

Dress code: Red, white, and blue
Gifts: Whatever will make Shoshanna feel good about turning 50
Toasts: Inspiring advice (she wants help)

She ran them off on a color copier, sent each in a bright red envelope with a flag stamp, and had all her RSVPs in hand by June 1. Everyone was coming and no one knew what to wear. "Tell my generation to think Tommy Hilfiger," said Tamara. "Yours—Abbie Hoffman."

Shoshanna's present would be a flag pillow with fifty *S*'s instead of stars on a field of blue, and in the red-and-white stripes the names of famous women who had achieved prominence or done their best work *after* fifty. Sometimes, thought Rachel after completing her research, a few well-chosen factoids are more effective than a book of inspiration. She gave her needlepointers until June 5 to finish the pillow. That way, if it was late, it would still be on time.

The restaurant manager was as excited as a kid when Rachel described the party's theme. It was he who'd proposed a color-coordinated menu. "Mother Nature doesn't really do blue," he apologized, "except for blueberries. But we'll go heavy on the reds and whites—white cheeses, red peppers, shrimp with cocktail sauce, pasta and tomato sauce—and we'll put them on blue plates. How's that?"

"Great," said Rachel. "But no shrimp." (Bad enough the food wasn't kosher.)

"We'll set the table with a white cloth and red-and-blue napkins," the restaurant manager said. "I'll ask the Village Democratic Club to loan me some of that bunting they drape around speaker's platforms. Maybe scare up a couple of Uncle Sam and Miss Liberty hats for the wait staff. How about sparklers? They're not exactly legal, but I could get some if you want."

Men can be kind, she thought fleetingly. "Can you decorate the cake like a flag?"

"Piece of cake," he answered. "Hey, if your sister has a sense of humor, we could write Old Glory on it, or You're a Grand Old Gal. Something like that."

"*Nothing* like that, please!" Rachel threw him a look that could have nailed a man to the wall. "Just write HAPPY BIRTHDAY, SHOSHANNA."

Male kindness, she noted, has its limits.

three daughters

. . .

Leah could hardly believe it was May 9. The afternoon was as dark as slate. Rain pelted the attic roof and poured down the skylight in slithery sheets that reminded her of a long-ago car wash, an automated, assembly-line operation with huge scrub brushes that soaped up the body and blasted the windows with torrents of rinse water while she and Sam sat in the front seat of his old Chevy, cozy and dry inside their bubble. The attic was dry, but not cozy.

Though the weather made it feel like Groundhog Day, today was Mother's Day, a date that had never before registered on Leah except as something to criticize. She'd always insisted her family ignore such celebrations—birthdays, Mother's and Father's Days, Thanksgiving, July Fourth, even Labor Day, which had been perverted from a paean to the American worker to an end-of-summer clearance sale. May Day and International Women's Day were the only dates that meant anything to Leah, though 90 percent of the population either didn't know what they commemorated or thought you were a Communist if you did. In articles and speeches, in more venues than she could recall, Leah would regularly denounce the commercialization of national holidays and life-cycle events. She deplored the mass-marketing of Mother's Day, the Hallmarking of sentiment and the advertising hype that bullied millions into department stores to buy bedroom slippers and toaster ovens nobody needed, or drove them into restaurants on "Mom's day off"—one day, mind you, one.

Not much had changed since the Second Wave. Motherhood was still being exploited for politics and profit. The difference this year was in Leah herself. An hour ago, she'd fled a local coffee shop before ordering her sandwich, saddened by the tables full of other people's families, the messily wrapped presents set before smiling moms, the hugs and kisses passed around. She wondered how her sons were doing and whether they might be thinking of her. Not likely. She'd mothered them poorly, that was incontrovertible, but she used to think they'd forgiven her for it. Now, alone in the attic with the driving rain, she was having trouble forgiving herself. Without Leo around, she couldn't seem to remember what was so lovable about her, what it was exactly that had made up for her maternal failures. Without Leo she'd been wandering through the empty rooms feeling sorry for herself. After more than a quarter century, she had mixed feelings about the house, an attachment born of familiarity and old-shoe comfort melded with a deep sense of rue based on all the tsuris that transpired here, more troubles than a one-family dwelling should hold. A marriage had withered under its roof. Its floors had cradled her husband's fall from promising young artist to brush-for-hire; his slide from marriage partner to millstone. Its walls had witnessed her transformation from star scholar to aging has-been, from feminist trailblazer to a name in the magazine retrospectives. Its doors had shut on two young men who'd had all the right equipment for life's journey, yet quickly lost their way. The foundation had crumbled along with its inhabitants, their frustrations leeching into its concrete, their bitterness cracking its plaster and corroding its pipes. In every room, the air had the consistency of wet cement. She'd gone up to the attic to escape Mother's Day and find Leo.

A hodgepodge of storage took up almost half the space, his studio the rest. Under the rain-smeared skylight, his battered easel stood like the skeleton of a small A-frame hut, beside it, a table of supplies. Tubes of paint, squashed and speckled, were lined up in a plastic tray. A jumbo-size Sacramento tomato juice can held his brushes, a bouquet of hairy flowers. Though she hadn't been up here in months, it didn't surprise her to find Leo's work space so orderly (he was always as tidy as she was lax), but she hadn't imagined it would be so peaceful, that the rain would be so lulling or Leo's paint-spattered chair so poignant. She turned on his radio. As if playing Leo into the room, a Vivaldi flute concerto wound itself around her, an aural embrace.

At one end of the attic, leaning on its kickstand, was the tandem bike they'd bought at a yard sale. With a little reconditioning, he'd said, it would take them riding in Prospect Park, but like the portrait of the boys he was always promising to paint, he'd never gotten around to it.

Stacks of books circled the bicycle like an audience in the round. Even at a distance, she recognized his old art books, her outdated textbooks, piles of notebooks, blue books, scholarly journals, the family album she'd begun when the boys were small. Keeping the album current had overwhelmed her—she was no Shoshanna—and before long she'd abandoned it and commandeered a Macy's shopping bag, the one on the floor over there, as the repository of the photographs they'd accumulated over the years. She couldn't remember when she'd last looked though them.

The steamer trunk under the dormer window groaned as she opened it; so did Leah when she saw her sons' baby clothes. (Who was she saving them for—grandchildren?) Under the layette was Leo's tuxedo from the wedding, her cap and gown with its doctoral stripes which she'd refused to wear during the anti-Establishment era, sheets and pillowcases she'd been reluctant to dump though they were coarse and yellowed. She stopped at the pink quilt, the one Sam had brought up to Blue Spruce when she'd complained that the school's blankets were too itchy. Pink was never her color—especially this shade, which was more like poached salmon than strawberries and cream—but the quilt, witness its torn stitching, had seen more than its share of use. Lightly, as if trolling the waters of a stream, she let her fingers brush its silky surface. Rayon, most likely; Sam would have thought silk too extravagant. She leaned down and burrowed her nose in the scents of her past: pine from school picnics in the woods. The musk of Dena, who'd sometimes cocooned in the quilt at the end of a boozy night. Incense from the Gay Street apartment where Wednesday's Women used to spread it on the floor like a beach blanket. She lifted the quilt out of the trunk and draped it around her. Dust drifted like a train in her wake as she hobbled toward the skylight, woozy with nostalgia and grateful now for the laziness that accounted for the quilt's never having been cleaned. She contemplated each stain and its source. Brown smudge? The Hershey bar Rachel had brought back for her after visiting day and secreted in its folds, where it had melted when Leah, unknowing, set the quilt on the dorm radiator to warm it before bedtime.

Coffee stains? Her college years. The white smear had come, literally, from the young man she'd loved when she was still technically a virgin—or from the Wite-Out she used to correct the typing errors on her thesis. The dime-sized brown spot was Shoshanna's menstrual blood, which had seeped through her sister's jeans during a women's group meeting. The blue ink recalled the night she'd fallen asleep in the window seat on West End Avenue, pen in hand. Her tearstains, it seems, had vanished.

The trunk disgorged the last of its contents—Leo's old flannel shirts, a chipped platter, table linens that had never been used. Junk, someone once said, is what you throw away two weeks before you need it. But she couldn't imagine a circumstance when she would need the embroidered banquet cloth and twelve matching napkins that Leo's mother had given them before she'd realized her daughter-in-law wasn't the entertaining type. A small chamois pouch lay wedged in a corner at the bottom of the trunk, its drawstring a snarled bow, its suedy surface pilled with lint. Decades had passed since she'd last seen it, but she recognized the little bag at once, knew what it contained and how it would make her feel to open it. She let it rest there for a long moment, stared at it, then looked away, as deep-sea divers might when they happened upon a treasure chest they were too awed to open. Finally, she leaned down and scooped it up. The string took some untangling until she could untie it and upend its contents into her hand. Esther Wasserman's watch. Gently, she closed her fingers over the delicate timepiece as if it were a wounded bird, then held it up to the skylight's glare. Its face was more miniaturized than she'd remembered, its marcasite facets more glittery, and she'd forgotten the band altogether, a thin silken cord, dark blue with a silver clasp. What she did remember in crisp detail was the day Esther had given it to her.

She was ten. Rachel was twelve. They were in the bride's dressing room after the ceremony. Esther was wearing her wedding gown (her second), a white satin dress that looked like a slip. The tulle veil, thrown back on her head, made a diaphanous hood for her copper hair.

"Presents!" she called, beaming, a pouch in each hand. "To celebrate our becoming a real family, the four of us." She directed the girls to sit on a chintz loveseat. "I felt terrible when I couldn't afford to buy you something new. Then I thought, if I gave each of you a piece of myself it might be even better. Tell me if I'm right."

Rachel opened her pouch first while her mother narrated: "They're very precious, these pearls. Cultured. Your grandma gave them to me for my eighteenth birthday." The pearls were double-stranded, each bead glowing from within, like a firefly. Attempting eloquence, Esther said something about how Rachel's happiness would double like the two strands now that she had a real father, and how she hoped Rachel would grow up to be as cultured as the pearls.

When Leah opened her pouch, Esther could barely contain her excitement. "It's the most expensive thing I ever bought myself." She circled the watch around Leah's wrist and fastened the catch with her polished fingernails. "Took me two years to save up for it and I only wore it for special occasions, but you can wear it every day. To remind you of your new family and the happiness we're all feeling today. I know it will last forever." Leah remembered Esther's tight embrace and her scent—a blend of baby powder, vanilla, and Joy perfume. In fifty years, no flower had ever measured up to it.

The watch might as well have been a Fabergé egg, so wondrous did it seem to the young Leah. But from that day to this, she'd never worn it. Blue Spruce permitted no jewelry, and the first time Dena saw the piece and heard where it had come from, she threatened to smash it. So Leah kept it hidden, always in a different place, and surprised herself whenever she happened upon it, buried deep in the toe of a shoe or a scrubbed-out Vaseline jar. After she moved to New York, the watch stayed in the box with her fountain pen collection—the full extent of her "valuables"—and whenever she cleaned the pen nibs, she would wind the watch and tell herself that it was too lovely to wear. And she would remember that Esther had been wrong about forever.

There was a logic to recalling her stepmother on Mother's Day. Esther was the only maternal presence she'd ever known; briefly, but long enough to reveal what she'd missed. Fifty-two years later, Leah dropped the chamois pouch in her pants pocket, closed the trunk, and wondered if it might make sense for the watch to get some use. Not that she needed another watch—her Timex served just fine—but she needed to revive the *idea* of the watch, the feeling of being loved and treasured, of deserving something that precious.

In Leo's work area a dozen new canvases, white as bedsheets, stood in a large vertical rack beside his easel, awaiting the portrait commissions that would never come. Stacked loosely off to the side were his used canvases—Leo liked to buy old paintings in junk shops and country auctions, picked them up cheap either for their frames or because a picture was nondescript and he could whitewash it and paint over it— several of them tilted against one another at odd angles, as if arranged that way while the paint was still wet. Good, she thought, he'd actually made use of them. With a slight shove, she got that group of canvases settled one behind the other and tilted them back against the wall, the better to look at them.

The first was a serene, undulating abstract, reminiscent of a trance state or a moonscape and unlike any work of Leo's she'd seen before. Its background, a fluid wash the color of sea foam, was tracked through with subtle, grainy lines in blue and gold, gossamer strands that seemed to weave in and out of the canvas itself like afterthoughts of sun and sky, or thoughts themselves. She found the painting remarkably beautiful. Calming. She tipped it forward against her thighs to reveal a second canvas as dark as the first was pale—a brooding composition of jagged lines and broken squares rendered in the colors of dried blood and brackish water. Anguish. Blight. Despair. Each daub of paint seemed to have been raked across the plane of the picture as if its creator were a gardener at war with the soil. In these two works, Leah saw her husband's extremes rendered as precisely as if he were there in the attic acting them out. She admired his technique, how he captured feeling in form, embodied a mood, mixed colors that seemed to whisper or shout, and made images that, whether they tread lightly on the eye or abraded it, wouldn't let it go. She used to think he'd have been more successful had he been more aggressive—promoted himself, hired the right agent, shown at a better gallery. But these marvelous abstracts made her wonder if the fault was hers for having kept Leo from his work. Would he have been more productive had she not been such a high-maintenance mate with such commanding priorities? And though this was the classic *wife's* question, would her husband have realized more of his gifts had he not had primary responsibility for the children?

The next canvas made her blink and start, the way cartoon characters do when shocked. A refined, richly detailed, museum-quality portrait—two golden children set against lush crimson draperies, light glinting in their hair, creamy flesh tones, luminous eyes fringed with long lashes, soft smiles on their pillowy lips. She'd have taken it for a Sargent or a Gainsborough if not for its subject. Her sons. Her *sons*.

Leo had placed them in a gracious formal room with an Oriental carpet and book-lined walls. Freddy, who appeared to be around eight in the painting, stood erect, a slim leather-bound volume in one hand, the other resting on the shoulder of his younger brother, who was shown seated with a leg folded under him on a deeply fringed hassock. Both boys seemed to be looking straight into the eyes of the viewer. They were wearing velvet clothes they'd never owned, Little Lord Fauntleroy suits, one forest green, the other royal blue, and both had on white knee socks and shiny black shoes. Napping at their feet was a dog they'd never owned either, a cocker spaniel.

She drank in the painting as if parched, as if she'd never seen her children before. All those years when she was badgering Leo to paint them, she'd imagined something literal, like one of those snapshots that had ended up in the shopping bag, the boys in sneakers and baseball caps. But this was a nineteenth-century tableau, an upper-class fantasy; no, not a fantasy, a vision of the boys as Leo had always viewed them— from a respectful distance, his beloved Others. He had taken ultramodern children from a postmodern marriage and placed them in another world and another place, set them in a time when the mere survival of a baby was a miracle in itself. Studying the composition, she saw in it not only his perception of Freddy and Henry as miracle children but the lesson he'd learned and she'd missed. That children are valuable only insofar as adults assign value to them. And by dressing their kids in velvet outfits and placing them in elegant settings, his Park Avenue clients (bourgeois boobs, philistines, whatever she might call them) were telling the world that they prized their offspring, maybe for the wrong reasons, some undoubtedly only as props and possessions, but nonetheless, that they appreciated them in their current incarnations, valued them as *children*.

Leah had skipped that phase. When her boys were young, they seemed to her nettlesome creatures, tolerable only as precursors of their grown-up selves. She recalled with embarrassment the time she'd shoved a couple of dollars in Freddy's jacket pocket and sent him to the stationery store for a typewriter ribbon. He was six years old. When he didn't return, she told Leo what she'd done and they'd gone out and combed the neighborhood. They'd found him sitting on the steps of an abandoned building, crying. "I got lost," he'd said between sobs, and she saw that he'd wet his pants.

Leo looked at his wife with eyes as hard as steel. "Don't *ever* do that again, Leah. You don't understand children. You don't *see* them."

He'd always known that about her. She suspected that was why, despite her nagging, he'd never done the boys' portraits. He wasn't willing to immortalize them the way she perceived them—as inadequate and ordinary—and, had he painted a picture that looked like this one, he knew she'd have ridiculed it as faux-baronial, affected, absurd. So he'd painted it in secret, waited perhaps until he was teetering at the brink of despair to represent Freddy and Henry as *he* perceived them— idealized and beautiful and better than himself.

Gently, she raised the painting to the easel, then dropped into her husband's chair and lost herself in her children's eyes.

The rain had stopped. A Haydn sonata was playing on the radio, a piano solo, music stripped to its bare essentials, as Leah had been since Leo left. She returned to the old canvases, looked again at the two abstracts, then tipped them forward to expose the next painting and this time heard a cry, her own. The composition was casual but sublimely painterly, the brushstrokes fine, the colors clear and true, the subject as magnificent as a man could be without being thought pretty. Henry stood off center on the canvas, looking as he did now—or did in March, when she'd last seen him. He was wearing a plain white T-shirt and jeans with no belt, his face tanned and smooth, his hair curling over his ears. He was leaning against a long refectory table, fingers resting lightly on its surface, eyes staring out of the painting with the same bemused expression he'd worn the morning he'd brought her frozen boots into the kitchen as a peace offering. Leo had painted him with bare feet, the tendons almost sculpted, one ankle crossed over the other, as if to actualize his father's desire for him to be in no hurry to leave. At one end of the table a platter overflowed with blushing pears and plump persimmons, cherries doubled on their stems, bunches of grapes, a pomegranate cut open and pregnant with seeds. Abundance. The other end of the table held a vase of long-stemmed roses, each bloom so perfectly rendered that she could make out its thorns. But none of Henry's thorns were visible, his stubborn perversity, his irresponsibility, his carelessness. In the painting, he was all sweetness and sexual magnetism.

She imagined the pleasure it must have given Leo to control these images, glorifying his little boys and giving grown-up Henry the WASP-y insouciance of the young Robert Redford in *The Way We Were* (a movie she'd seen, she liked to believe, only for its political content). On canvas—the only place in his life obedient to his will—Leo had created the perfection that forever eluded him. That deeply human urge to reimagine the world through the transactions of art was not so different, Leah realized, from her efforts to change the world through revolution (or, for that matter, to change literature through criticism), or Shoshanna's need to subdue random terrors by controlling every aspect of her environment, or Rachel's attempt to invent a storybook life. The son Leah had found wanting, Leo had found wonderful. With his version of Henry on the easel before her, she understood how having been shamed in front of this beautiful boy could have been the brush-stroke that broke the artist's heart.

She expected to find among the old canvases a romanticized painting of Freddy—sailing, perhaps, or playing polo (neither of which he'd ever done)—and, in all honesty, a portrait of herself. Trying to put the best gloss on her absence, she speculated that Leo had never felt the need to glorify her in art because he'd found her perfect in life, but she knew that was bullshit. The rest of the old canvases, though white-washed, were bare. Freddy's story, she guessed, had been too painful to sanitize in art, his fall from grace too tragic to contemplate even for as long as it would take to transform the truth into a redemptive ideal. The blankness of the canvas told its own story. Freddy's crime had left an empty nothingness where once Leo had kept his dreams for his son and the images that went with them. Or maybe the blank canvas *was* Freddy's portrait, filled from edge to edge with the white powder that he sold from the back of an ice cream van until it whited out everything else in his life.

A blinding haze blanketed the skylight and drenched the attic in glare, a migraine waiting to happen. She wished she'd brought her purple glasses upstairs with her. Sam would have called that a waste of a wish. On her tenth birthday he'd given her a private sermon on the subject of wasted wishes. They were having dinner in a restaurant, and he'd arranged for a cupcake with eleven candles, one for good luck, to be delivered to their table at the end of the meal. Before she could make a wish and blow, he'd put a hand over her mouth. "Wait, kindeleh. Wishes are like prayers, and birthday wishes are the most special prayers of all, so you don't want to waste them. Close your eyes and think hard. Make sure you ask for something that deserves God's attention. Not a new dress or a good grade, but something you couldn't possibly get or accomplish for yourself, something that would make you very happy if only it would come true." Leah closed her eyes. There was only one thing she wanted—for Sam to marry Esther. By her next birthday, her wish had come true.

Returning to the easel, she gazed at her little Fauntleroys and, lacking candles, lit a cigarette. What she wished for was a different childhood for herself and her children. She wished it hadn't taken a journey to the rim of madness before Leo could paint his sons. She wished Henry and Freddy could see themselves as Leo saw them and could make him understand that sperm were just a mess of tadpoles compared to a father's love.

sixteen

EARLY EVENING on Shoshanna's birthday brought June weather squared and cubed, with a pink-purple dusk and a light breeze. The party guests, obviously having taken Rachel's patriotic dress code to heart, arrived at the restaurant in their Flag Day outfits—blue blazers, white pants, and red tops; blue slacks with white shirts and red suspenders; red trousers with blue belts, and tricolor scarfs. Tamara, having landed a stars-and-stripes tank dress on Canal Street, teased her mother for being too tame. Rachel was wearing a crisp candy-cane blouse with a tailored navy suit. When Shoshanna showed up in a plain white shift, everyone scolded her for breaking rank until she reached into her bag, whipped out a Wonder Woman cape, child-sized, and tied it around her neck. "My mother made this for my last birthday party." The diminutive cape perched on her shoulders like star-spangled wings. "I was twelve."

"Doesn't impress me," sneered Fiona. "No magic bracelets."

"They're invisible; only virgins can see them."

"Oh, right."

When they lined up for a snapshot, the group's combined effect made everyone laugh.

"We look like the chorus line from *Stars and Stripes Forever*," said Nelly.

Tamara: "Or the Honor Guard for the DAR."

When Leah hadn't made an appearance by eight o'clock, Rachel grew antsy. "She wouldn't want us to wait for her, Shoshie. Let's get started."

Shoshanna stared at the door. "Something must be wrong."

"A million things can happen to hold a person up," said Rachel. "I'm sure she's fine."

Shoshanna thought of the creep on the subway platform. "An optimist is nothing but an ill-informed pessimist," she replied. The line was Leah's.

Having planned the party, Rachel felt entitled to direct it. (Since the Seder, the idea of running things was no longer daunting to her.) She seated everyone at the round table, placed herself at her sister's right, and was about to put Nelly on her sister's left when Shoshanna asked that the seat be saved for Leah. A tiny flicker of rejection crossed Nelly's face. Shoshanna would have to explain later why she wanted to monitor Leah at close range. Not to control her this time, but to protect her. Vulnerability was new to Leah.

The empty chair was making Shoshanna nervous. She wanted her sister to be safe, wished this party wasn't happening, was trying to enjoy her birthday, but felt reluctant to celebrate an age that didn't fit, that was too big for her, just as the Wonder Woman cape was too small. Yet again, her fear of happiness put her in a double bind: to have the evening go badly would depress her further; to have it go well might trigger the Evil Eye. Did there have to be a booby trap in every prize? Would she ever let herself feel pleasure without first putting her head through the wringer? The night of the Seder she'd been worrying about Rachel's wounds, Leah's volatility, and keeping sparks from erupting between them. Now she was struggling with her inner conflicts, the weirdness she felt about being fifty, the alarming realization that her losses would escalate from now on, and more and more would be taken away from her—health, energy, memory, looks, the people she loved most. At the same time, in that zigzag way of hers, she was aware of her present blessings and determined to enjoy them.

A tinny sound broke through her thoughts: the restaurant manager beating a drumroll on a pie pan. Rachel was on her feet. "Welcome, everyone! As you know, we're here to celebrate Shoshanna Wasserman Safer" (applause, cheers) "and the flag of the United States of America" (guffaws, a few hummed bars of the national anthem). "The food and the wait staff are part of our theme." Rachel gestured toward a waiter in a top hat right off the UNCLE SAM WANTS YOU! poster and a waitress wearing a spiked Statue of Liberty crown made of Styrofoam. Shoshanna's eyes stayed glued to the floor.

Just then, Leah came bustling in, hair askew, her barrette having slid halfway down her braid. A long red scratch had welted on one cheek, the other bore a charcoal-gray smudge. Despite the requested color scheme, Leah was wearing black, a loose peasant blouse and a long skirt that almost hid her black high-top sneakers—her "I can-look-like-a-matron-if-I-want-to" look. The outfit, which she'd deemed appropriate for both the demonstration against police brutality from which she'd just come and the birthday party, was noticeably disheveled. One sleeve was torn at its shoulder seam, and the skirt had the dipping-down look of a hem that had been stepped on while its wearer was in motion. Watching her approach the empty chair, Shoshanna realized that she'd never seen Leah in a skirt. Rachel, witnessing the same journey, wondered if Leah had noticed *which* chair they'd left free for her, or if she even cared. Always alert to where she stood (or sat) in the scheme of things, Rachel would have registered its significant location next to the birthday girl, but Leah noticed the empty chair only because she was dying to sit down. Her shoulder throbbed, her hip was acting up, and her neck ached like a son-of-a-bitch. Had she not felt beholden to Shoshanna for her recent kindnesses, she'd have gone home to bed.

"Sorry, kiddo! I got arrested. Don't want you to think I *always* get in trouble en route to meeting you, but the cops wouldn't let me leave the station house no matter what curses I inflicted on their mothers."

"Not to carp, but you could have phoned," deadpanned Fiona.

Leah shot her a heavy-lidded look. "How foolish of me to use my one call to reach my lawyer."

No one said a word about Leah's face, though her sisters each squelched an impulse to dip a napkin in water and mop the smudge. Nine red-white-and-blue outfits had turned toward the new arrival. "Arrested!?" "Are you hurt?" "What happened?"

Bedraggled as she was, when Leah barged into the room straight from the barricades, Shoshanna felt something come in with her, something vital and alive that also shimmered around Nelly whenever she bounded through the door in her dusty riding clothes, flushed and thrilled after breaking a horse or jumping fences. Shoshanna remembered feeling the way Leah looked, but long ago. Now she was a well-behaved woman in a neat white dress, navel-gazing her flaws and obsessing about a stupid birthday while the ageless Leah, a workhorse with the brash of a war hero, was still firing away at the flaws of the whole society.

The story of Leah's arrest, which she recounted with relish, lasted through the appetizer (roasted red peppers and white mozzarella on blue platters), the tricolor salad, and the main course (halibut in white sauce, grilled tomato, blue Peruvian potatoes). In the telling, her report became a morality play full of dramatic tension and salty characters. Demonstrators marching. Picket signs waving. Lines of police in riot gear trying to look impassive. Then trouble: A man shouts, "The NYPD are racist pigs." A beefy cop thuds his nightstick on the man's back. Leah jumps the beefy cop, locks her hands behind his neck, and pulls him down with her full weight. He grabs one of Leah's arms and twists it behind her back until her shoulder is nearly unhinged. She screams: "Clay-brained maggot! Shit-eating dickhead! Fat-ass mother-fucker!"

"Leah!" interrupted Rachel. "We can do without the direct quotes!"

Leah told the party guests about the skin-scraping handcuffs. The ride in the paddy wagon. The scarred and scruffy desks in the station house. Getting fingerprinted. 'I stand before you, a woman felled by the city's constables for the third time in as many decades, a woman who came this close to being a cop killer." She positioned her thumb and forefinger an inch apart; then, frowning as if displeased with the measurement's accuracy, shrunk it further.

What she left out of her report was how the ordeal had made her feel: like a geriatric weakling. Worn-out, time-scarred, moss-backed, and moth-eaten, her joints fossilized, her reflexes rusty. Had she known she was going to live this long and stay this rebellious, she might have taken better care of herself. Eaten smarter and smoked less. Anticipated how hard it would be, trapped in a superannuated container and ruined by her own bad habits, to stay the course.

Another pinging sound. Rachel suddenly remembered she was the host and was clinking her glass with a spoon. "We all know Shoshanna is taking this birthday kind of hard . . ."

"Talk straight, Ma. She's freaked," interrupted Tamara.

"Okay, she's freaked. She can't believe that *she* of all people could possibly be fifty. Fifty is surreal, she told me. It's our parents' age. She's traumatized. She wants advice and we're gonna give it to her. Each of you has been asked to pretend you're a wise woman and tell her how you coped with turning fifty or, if you're not there yet, how you think you're going to handle it when it happens. Nothing morbid, please. And keep it under two minutes. I've got a stopwatch. I'll go first, then we'll work our way around the table." She threw a candy-striped arm over her sister's shoulders (a vaguely patronizing move that set Leah's teeth on edge but pleased Shoshanna immensely. After all these weeks with her arms around Rachel, she welcomed the switch). "My advice is, Get into your body, Shoshe. Two-thirds of Americans say they'd gladly live to a hundred if they weren't afraid of becoming helpless and frail. I know you. You're hyperactive from the neck up, but from the neck down you're half dead, except, I suppose, for sex. I promise you'd feel a lot better about being fifty if you got stronger physically. No matter how down I've been, I always knew I could run six miles or swim laps or keep up with all those toned young women in step class, and knowing it made me feel better. And remember, this is *sixty-four* speaking, not *fifty!*" The whispers reassured Rachel that she didn't look her age.

"Finally," Rachel rasped a little, "I wanted to say a shehechiyanu, the blessing we Jews offer to express our gratitude for the gift of time. The shehechiyanu is our way of thanking God for letting us live long enough to reach this joyous occasion." She recited the b'racha, then retrieved her arm and checked her watch. "A minute fifty-four seconds. Let's see if the rest of you can be as disciplined."

Quintessential Rachel, thought Shoshanna, who hugged her sister with enthusiasm but discounted her advice. Not only couldn't she imagine herself an athlete, but she viewed her body as a magnet for her fears—the bones she might break, the skin she might lacerate, the lungs that might fill with water. Maybe she could change, but she doubted it.

The notion that step class was the key to a contented old age struck Leah as absurd; nonetheless, having broken enough laws for one day, she'd decided to follow the rules and keep quiet. Since Rachel had started the roundelay to her right, Leah would be the last to speak, which was fine with her. She had time to formulate two minutes' worth of freeze-dried philosophy, but what could she possibly say? "Here's to a woman who squandered her talent!" "Here's to a really accomplished Stepinfetchit!" She speared a chunk of broiled tomato, a Peruvian potato, and a slab of halibut onto her fork tines and fit the multi-layered assemblage into her mouth. She still couldn't understand how Shoshanna ended up an errand girl for a bunch of spoiled jerks when her younger self would have been out there on the barricades leading the charge against police brutality. What's more, she couldn't under-stand how Shoshanna could sit still for this ridiculous party.

The premise of a flag theme had made sense when Shoshanna's mother put on her 1950s extravaganzas, but that was because Esther was a wide-eyed greenhorn who'd nursed a lifelong love affair with the United States and felt genuinely grateful to this country for giving a fresh start to a penniless immigrant like herself. Since passing through Ellis Island, she'd reinvented her life not once but three or four times before settling into the role of the rebbetzin of West End Avenue. To Esther, the flag had symbolized everything hopeful and new. But Rachel was no Esther. And Shoshanna—former standard-bearer for Off Our Necks, a "Clean for Gene" hippie for whom Bobby Kennedy was too conservative, a flag burner, in fact—had to be thinking this patriotic parody was a joke.

As a matter of fact, Shoshanna was thinking no such thing. Over time, red, white, and blue had become the colors of her childhood, her mother's colors, not her country's, and the symbols she'd rebelled against in her youth had recast themselves in their original incarnations, as Esther's Americana, party decorations, nostalgia not politics. She was happy to wrap herself in the flag.

"Your turn, Nelly," said Rachel. "Help your mother out here."

"I don't have any advice for you, Mom, because to me you're already perfect—even if you can't do pushups and don't know a gallop from a trot. And if you think you're feeling weird about turning fifty, imagine how disconcerting it is to have a mother who looks like my sister and has the energy of my daughters." Nelly had the knack of saying exactly what a person needed to hear. She raised her glass. "To the best mom in the world. I love you."

Shoshanna reached in front of Rachel and squeezed Nelly's hand. "Love you, best daughter!"

"Do you want to skip your turn for now?" Rachel asked her own daughter, who was nursing two-month-old Max.

"I'm not Gerald Ford, Mother, I can breast-feed and talk at the same time." Tamara draped a baby blanket across her chest until all that showed of Max was a pair of tiny feet, ladyfingers sticking out from a tea cloth. "I have only one piece of advice, Aunt Shoshanna: Lighten up. You worry too much, even though you seem to have nothing to worry *about*. Maybe you make stuff up, I don't know. All I know is, you could relax more. I brought you this quote from Gilda Radner's book. Remember her?" (Tamara, a comic herself, got most of her axioms from comedians.)

"Vividly," she replied. When Radner had died from ovarian cancer ten years earlier, Shoshanna had memorized her symptoms.

Tamara cleared her throat. "Gilda wrote: 'Life is about not knowing, having to change, taking the moment and making the best of it without knowing what's going to happen next. I may never be able to control the fear and the panic, but I have learned to control how I live each day.' Take her advice. Live each day as it comes. Go with the flow, like Seth and me. And happy birthday!"

Seth and *I*, dammit, thought Leah. You and your mother are *both* grammatical Gidgets.

Shoshanna puckered an air kiss in Tamara's direction. If a child raised by someone as buttoned-down as Rachel could become an expert on relaxation, there was hope for Nelly to escape Shoshanna's worst traits and to not pass them on to Ruby and Pearl. That was another strange thing about being fifty—suddenly she was aware of her legacy.

"Tamara can be cavalier about time, 'cause she's young," put in Dede, Shoshanna's friend, who was fifty-seven.

"Not *so* young; pushing thirty," said Tamara.

Shoshanna looked around the table. Three women were in their twenties, two over sixty, the rest in between.

"When you're thirty," said Dede, "you can afford to blow off the future, but some of us don't have that much wind left. If we don't second-guess the future, we'll find ourselves out on a pretty long limb."

The mushy metaphors were getting to Leah.

Rachel reset her stopwatch. "No side conversations, please. Okay, Fiona's next."

Shoshanna's assistant stood up, hooked her thumbs in her red suspenders, and, in the voice of the pre-Higgins Eliza, said to her boss, "I've been watching you struggle with the MPs and the Palm Pilot, and it made me think of me mum. Mum always says, 'Well, I can't be young again, but I *can* be new.' Keeps rejuvenating herself, she does. Learned to play chess at sixty. Left my dad after twenty-eight years of marriage, then started raising Airedales. Not that I'm recommending *either*. But Mum says every time a person adds something new to her life, she can let go of something she doesn't need anymore. You've added the Palm and let go of the Filofax. Don't stop there."

"Thank you, Fiona." An English accent, even a cockney one, had a way of making anything sound smart.

"I've always loved Airedales," mused Helen, who'd given birth for the first time after turning forty and now had a three-month-old. "But maybe raising a child at my age qualifies as enough newness for a while."

"I agree with Fiona's mama," offered Ernestine. "I'm fifty-one and I just started taking Japanese. Can't possibly live long enough to speak it well, but I'll be fluent in the tatami room."

"Fiona only used fifty-eight seconds," said Rachel. "Shows how much can be said in a short time when it's well put."

Leah squirmed in her seat. If the party's purpose was to make Shoshanna less uptight about time, someone ought to tell Rachel that this two-minute shtick of hers was having exactly the opposite effect— it was making everyone hugely time-conscious. (Though that someone wasn't going to be Leah.)

Ernestine raised her hand. "Hold it, girlfriends. I'm having trouble relating to this so-called problem from the getgo. For black folks, it's not a catastrophe to get older, it's a triumph. That blessing Rachel gave us before—to me, that says it all. Be grateful God let you live long enough to *be* old. Not that fifty's old, honey. Didn't mean that. But some of us don't even make it that far." (Stefanie hadn't. The caramel face appeared to Shoshanna complete with laugh lines and wrinkles. She'd have turned fifty March 4.) "And when we make it, our men don't," Ernestine concluded. "So, to hell with the calendar."

Right then, Shoshanna felt that it might not be so terrible to grow old if this was the company she could keep along the way.

"Shoshie, I just have one word of advice for you . . ."

"Not your turn, Dede," scolded Rachel. "Helen, you're next."

The white stain on the shoulder of Helen's navy blouse had to be a motherhood mark—spit-up or Desitin—the badge of the over-whelmed and underslept. Had Shoshanna given birth to her kids start-ing at age forty, Nelly would be only ten now, Jake not even in kindergarten. The thought so unnerved her that being fifty with grown children suddenly seemed an enviable state.

"If you value time—and who doesn't—don't wear a watch," said Helen. "Maybe not every day, but once or twice a week." (That sounded gimmicky and superficial, neither of which Helen was; there had to be more to it.) "I decided to give up wearing one when I read an essay of Montaigne's. He recommended it as a way of savoring time. Without a watch, I have to stay alert to the subtleties, tune in to the baby's needs. Instead of putting her down for a nap because it's noon, or nursing her because a clock says it's been three hours since her last feeding, I have to read her signals. When I'm out in the world without a wristwatch, I notice the sky, where the sun hits the buildings, the lengths of the shadows. I figure out what time it is from clues. Are the stores open yet? Is the lunch crowd out on the sidewalks? Have the kids been dismissed from school? Is the commuter rush over? I notice all sorts of things that used to pass me by. If you're watchless, you can't be mindless. It forces you to pay attention. And you'll find time slows down and stretches out when you're paying attention."

Shoshanna nodded thoughtfully. "I'll give it a try and let you know what happens."

"Okay, Dede. Now you can go," said Rachel.

Dede planted both elbows on the table. "I have one word for you, Shoshe—*travel.*"

"Thank God," said Tamara. "For a minute there I thought it was gonna be plastics."

Dede's counsel could have been item nine in any magazine article on "Ten Ways to Turn 50." However prosaic, it touched a nerve in Shoshanna. She and Daniel had flexible work lives and lots of vacation time—so why did they travel so rarely? Because of her fears. (Even when they went away for a weekend, she always left everything shipshape in case she died on the trip.) It wasn't a fear of flying that haunted her, but of the off-the-itinerary stuff that happens when travelers are in an unfamiliar place and don't know the local quirks and can't possibly be prepared for every contingency. Like high tide.

Shoshanna paraphrased Janis Joplin in her head: "Freedom's just another word for nothing left to fear." If she could recapture her pre-anxious, pre–Torrey Pines state of mind, it would be like recapturing her youth.

Leah had tuned out Dede's travel advocacy and the advice of Ginny, the last of the four friends, who was talking about the importance of keeping romance alive in a long-term marriage. Coals to Newcastle, thought Leah. Without even trying, Shoshanna would go home tonight to a peony in her toothbrush glass. When Ginny was allowed to exceed her time limit, Leah wondered if it was because she, the Bad Sister, was next and Rachel was worried she'd say something to ruin the party. True, she'd made a scene at Sam's eightieth, but that was because it was Sam's. For Shoshanna, who'd done so right by her lately, Leah was behaving.

When her turn came, she removed her purple glasses and cleaned them with the overhang of the tablecloth. For a moment, it looked as if she might demur altogether, but then she opened up with "According to Oscar Wilde, 'Nothing ages like happiness.' He'd never have written that had he met you, Shoshanna. Happiness has kept you young. Your looks, that is. But your spirit has aged before its time. The wild child, the brave babe you once were, what the fuck happened to her?" Rachel felt everyone's pulse stop. Leah fished for her braid and, holding its fringe like a paintbrush, traced swirls on her grimy cheek. "Age is a high price to pay for maturity, but you're old enough now to have discovered that the greatest mishegas in the human repertoire is the compulsion to conform. For Pete's sake, turning fifty isn't a signal to start the day with stewed prunes. It doesn't mean you have to acquire a taste for melba toast, mash your carrots, learn to play canasta, cut your hair, switch to harlequin glasses, or quit wearing jeans. Conformists give nothing new to the world, nothing audacious or life-changing. You may think there's safety in order and convention, but the truth is, they're deadening. Someone once said, 'Without freedom, order is oppression. Without order, freedom is chaos.' It's the paradox political philosophers call 'ordered liberty.' But your life, if I may say so, suffers from too much order and not enough liberty. At fifty, a woman has earned the right to be herself. *Be* it. Be Shoshanna." She stopped twirling. "As T. S. Eliot reminds us, 'Only those who risk going too far can possibly find out how far one can go.'"

The clink of dishes and cutlery sounded like a musical interlude as Miss Liberty and Uncle Sam cleared the table.

"That was only a minute and twenty seconds," said Rachel. If anyone was going to disregard the time limit, she thought, it would be Leah. Regretting her own rules, wanting more, needing the pep talk for herself, she urged, "Go on."

"My dear Rachel," replied Leah, as she languidly chose a wafer with red-white-and-blue sprinkles from the platter of cookies that had just materialized on the table. "Though I'm famously prone to prolixity, even I know when less is enough." She raised her glass. "To Wonder Woman at fifty."

"Hear! Hear!"

When Shoshanna leaned over and planted a kiss on her wooly head, Leah sputtered, "Hey, I forgot the disclaimer. If the advice doesn't fit, I don't give refunds."

Reflecting on her battle-scarred, brutally honest sister, Shoshanna began to wonder if she'd worked so hard to keep Leah in her life because Leah still believed in Shoshanna's wild child. Year after year, in uncomfortable proximity at one restaurant table or another, her feisty, argumentative sister had been reminding Shoshanna what the wildness was and what it was for. Their lunches were her annual tune-ups and Leah her access to the unfettered, the last utopian, the only brave babe left standing. At sixty-two, Leah was the model of how to live one's life after fifty, her belief in a perfectible future the very definition of youth. Shoshanna had refused to let go of this prickly woman because Leah exuded the oxygen of hope.

Covering for how intensely she'd been moved, Shoshanna asked, "Do you take exchanges?"

A pinprick of the old jealousy pierced Rachel's navy-blue aplomb. "Fetch the presents, Nelly," she called out. "Time to give your mama something tangible."

"Open mine first!" Nelly said, holding out a manila envelope.

Shoshanna released the clasp and removed an official-looking document: "The Statue of Liberty–Ellis Island Foundation proudly presents this Official Certificate of Registration in THE AMERICAN IMMIGRATION WALL OF HONOR to officially certify that Esther Frank Wasserman came to the United States from Kiev, Russia, joining the courageous men and women who . . ." Shoshanna couldn't read on.

Nelly jumped in, "I contributed to this foundation so Grandma Esther could be listed on the wall that wraps around the whole island." She turned to Shoshanna: "It's not exactly a present about *you*, but since your birthday is Flag Day, I thought I'd give you family and American history all rolled up in one."

"It's wonderful!" Blinking back tears, Shoshanna passed the document along for others to see.

"Signed by Lee Iacocca," Tamara noted when the paper reached her. "Does it come with a sunroof?"

After the wall of honor, other gifts might have seemed anticlimactic had not each in its way been as personal. Fiona, with a nod to Shoshanna's memory slippage, gave her a T-shirt that said, *Over the hill? What hill? I don't remember any hill.* Tamara had put together a tape of the records Shoshanna remembered from her childhood parties—Sousa marches, "Yankee Doodle Dandy," "America the Beautiful." Shoshanna's four friends had chipped in on a Ralph Lauren sweater, navy blue with a flag knitted into the front.

"Hey, I happen to know how much this sweater costs. Even split four ways, it's too expensive," Shoshanna protested.

"We think you're worth it," replied Ginny.

"They plan to borrow it," said Leah. "All four of them."

Shoshanna relaxed in the grip of an epic completeness. "Thanks for talking me into this crazy party," she whispered to Rachel, who countered with "Open mine!"

The needlepoint pillow brought cries of admiration as Rachel identified the names on the stripes: "Louise Bourgeois, sculptor; Margot Fonteyn, ballet dancer; Bella Abzug, congresswoman; Sarah Vaughan; Tillie Olsen; they all had great successes after they were fifty."

"Hey, there's Mom's name!" shouted Nelly. "Shoshanna Wasserman Safer."

"That's how sure I am that your mother's best years are still ahead of her." Rachel smiled. "As soon as she gets over her panic attack."

Leah was surprised to find herself touched by this overenthusiastic little celebration, but then again, why not? It was a female rite of passage, with many elements of feminist ritual. An all-woman guest list. Caring but honest advice. No subject off limits. Equal time for all. Morale-boosting gifts. Role models in needlepoint. Leah tried to think of nine women in her life who would do this for her but couldn't come up with one.

Shoshanna grabbed Rachel's face and kissed her. "God, what patience! Those little S's must have taken you weeks!"

That her assistants had done the actual needlepointing wasn't something Rachel chose to confess at the moment. Not that she wanted to take credit for other people's work, it was just that she wasn't ready to tell her sisters or anyone else that she wasn't a needlepointer anymore. That phase of her life was over.

Shoshanna reached for the last gift. It wasn't wrapped, that's how she knew it was Leah's. Rachel watched closely as the lid came off the small brown box, and when she saw the chamois pouch, she felt the oddest tickle at the back of her throat, a feeling she associated not with illness but with gravity, a moment of consequence. As she loosened the drawstring, Shoshanna thought it might be one of those trick presents—container inside container until the last eensy-weensy bag disgorged a kidney bean. But when she turned the pouch on her palm, a tiny watch fell out, its marcasite twinkling like stars. She tried to reconcile this elegant piece of jewelry with its source. Why would Leah, of all people, give her a watch, and why such a vintage beauty, so obviously beyond her means? Was it a metaphor about time's value, an accidental rebuttal to Montaigne's watchless days?

"It's beautiful! Look, everybody!!" She held it up for inspection. Immediately Rachel snatched the watch, another bewilderment. Was she afraid Leah's present had outshone hers?

"Sorry. I just wanted to have a closer look," said Rachel, blushing. For her, the watch was no metaphor but the purest incarnation of memory, a relic of her past as seen through the wrong end of a telescope. She looked at it closely, then returned it to Shoshanna, who held it on her wrist while Leah circled the blue silk cord and fastened the catch, exactly as Shoshanna's mother had done fifty-two years ago for Leah. It looked lovely on Shoshanna's tanned skin, but Rachel conjured it against Esther's softer, whiter flesh, a wrist splashed with freckles. "Let me wind it for you," she said, and rotated the stem back and forth. Raising the face to her ear, she marveled, "It still works."

"Still?" Shoshanna was lost.

Rachel and Leah caught each other's eye across the thatch of Shoshanna's coppery hair and remembered the last time they'd been in a room with the same treasure.

"It was your mother's," said Leah, in the tone of a viola d'amore.

"My *mother's*?" Shoshanna's eyes flew from one sister to the other.

"I'm told it's a bourgeois tradition for the bride to give presents to the women in her wedding party. Rachel and I were your mother's only attendants. She couldn't afford to buy us something new, so she gave me her watch and Rachel her pearls." Protectively, Rachel clutched her necklace, the double-stranded pearls she always wore, the ones she'd put around Shoshanna's neck to dress up her denim shirt in honor of the Sabbath Queen. Rachel had never told Shoshanna the pearls were Esther's, and Leah had never mentioned the watch. Rachel wondered if this family would ever be cured of its secrets.

"You've had it all these years," whispered Shoshanna. It was not a question.

The question was Rachel's. "Why would you give it up? Don't you wear it?"

"Jewelry's not my thing." Leah touched her earlobes for emphasis, then held up her hands and laughed. "Except rings."

"You can't imagine how much it means to me to have this, Leah. *Thank* you!" Shoshanna pressed the watch to her lips.

"I'm just the conduit, kiddo. Think of it as Esther's present." The waiter in the Uncle Sam hat and vest poured coffee all around. Leah took another cookie and helped herself to a piece of birthday cake with HAPP written on it. She thought of Fiona's mum. A person can let go of something she doesn't need if she adds something new to her life.

Remembering her mother's excitement as she gave them their gifts, then seeing the watch pass to Shoshanna, a daughter who wasn't even born when it first changed hands—the whole thing was too much for Rachel. After a polite interval, she escaped to the ladies' room. She shut herself in a stall and, without disturbing her neat navy skirt, plunked herself down on the toilet seat, balled up a wad of toilet paper, pressed her cheek to the cold metal divider, and wept. Her emotionality upset her at first; its persistence after more than three months eroded her faith in the healing powers of time until she realized she wasn't crying for herself or her situation: her tears were for Leah. She just wished she could feel things without also feeling that she couldn't handle the feelings.

Someone pushed open the outer door. Flushing the toilet, Rachel used the interlude of whooshing water to regain her composure. When she emerged from the stall, Leah was at the mirror scrubbing her cheeks with a wet paper towel.

"Someone should have told me New York's Finest left their filth on my face."

"Never noticed it," lied Rachel, checking to see if her eyes were red. (They were.) "It was really amazing of you to give her the watch. It was the *most* marvelous present for her, especially this year."

Leah shrugged. "Seemed a good time to me, too." She splashed water on her face, then tore off a fresh towel and wiped.

"Do you have anything else of my mother's?"

"Nope. Unless you count her voice in my head."

Leah was out the door before Rachel could ask what she meant.

The blueberry birthday cake was a great hit, judging by how little was left of it, just a wedge with "HDAY '99" in red writing on white icing. Miss Liberty was offering to wrap it for Shoshanna to take home when Daniel stuck his head in the door.

"Thought you'd need help running your presents home in a cab," he said after they'd kissed and clinched.

"Not yet, Daniel. Wait. I haven't finished saying good-bye to every-body."

Rachel, privy to his plan, helped it along. "Actually, we should all get going. The manager needs the room for a late party." When Daniel winked his gratitude, Rachel discovered in herself a horror of dying without ever having known the devotion of a man who would go to such lengths to please her. It wasn't the fear of death or of never remarrying or never having another sexual partner, but of her own *formlessness*, the lack of a shaped self sufficient to inspire another person's passion.

The party group piled outside where a white lacquered hansom cab awaited, its every protuberance festooned with red-white-and-blue streamers, its bonnet pleated and folded away so the cab was open to the summer night. Cone-shaped vases of white gladioli were strapped to the vertical posts. The benches facing each other at the center of the cab bore tufted blue cushions. The driver sat on a high perch, wearing a pair of blue jeans, a red cowboy shirt, and a white top hat and tails. Perhaps in recognition of Shoshanna's birthday—or maybe it was always there—a tiny American flag rose from the bridle of a fine white horse.

"Your carriage, my love," Daniel said, opening the half-door. She watched her husband sweep into a low bow, then rise to his full height like a coachman, his hair cowlicking his forehead, his teeth white as Chiclets under the broad band of lamplight.

The women beamed on him, oohing and cooing like doves. Shoshanna, damp-eyed, was overwhelmed, but also mystified. Her husband was a romantic, yes, but not the Prince Charming type. His courtliness always had a sophisticated flair: Cole Porter, not Old King Cole. The horse-drawn carriage—a fairy-tale cliché—was clearly his attempt to jar her out of her birthday malaise, to make her feel like an old-fashioned princess, not a princess who'd grown old.

She took his face in her hands and pressed their foreheads together like palms.

"I couldn't let the actual day pass without some husbandly flourish," he said, the bow having left his shirt askew. "But we'll have to take in washing to pay for it. Seems these hackers only travel between the Plaza and the Bethesda Fountain. To get this guy to go below Fifty-ninth Street, I had to promise him our first-born grandson."

Gingerly, Daniel hoisted Shoshanna into the carriage, loaded her gifts on the facing seat, and settled in with his arm around her, careful not to dislodge the Wonder Woman cape. Having already sung "Happy Birthday," the women sent them off with a spirited rendition of "For She's a Jolly Good Fellow." Rachel took great pleasure in the tableau, then thought to check Leah's reaction and was pleased to catch the cranky professor smiling. The look that passed between them, like the earlier one, said they knew what each other was thinking. But this time, they were on different pages. Leah was thinking. Wouldn't you know it, nine women just turned their souls inside out for her, but it took a guy with a goddamn coach to really make an impression. She was thinking about how, in one short evening, she'd traveled from radical melodrama to flag-waving farce. Perversely, counterintuitively, unexpectedly, the party had made her feel proud to be a Wasserman woman. A Wasser-woman. Rachel was thinking that she should have left her marriage fourteen years ago when *she* was fifty. About fresh starts and how it shouldn't take a birthday to justify them. About terrible events that, if they don't destroy us, can help jump-start a new life.

The horse broke into a slow trot. Fiona called out, "Don't turn into a pumpkin! Clients at nine."

Shoshanna decided not to feel guilty about the evening's storybook ending. She leaned back, gazed up at the stars, and savored the open-air carriage ride through the streets of Greenwich Village. Her birthday wasn't over yet; wisteria was in the air, with intimations of the pleasures awaiting in the bedroom at home. As she drew in the scent and snuggled closer to Daniel, she caught in the trees arching overhead a glimpse of the Evil Eye smiling the devil's own smile.

Not so fast, Cinderella, he seemed to be saying. Not so fast.

seventeen

THEY MET IN THE HALL outside Chuck Schumer's office the last week in September. Leah was waiting to go in when out stepped Rachel, shaking hands with the senator. "Always good to see you, Mrs. Brent. Keep up the good work!"

After he left, the flabbergasted Leah managed a cool "*Quel* coincidence."

"Coincidences are God's way of remaining anonymous," Rachel said with a grin, and opened her sinewy little arms like French doors.

The axiom Leah knew to be one of Sam's favorites, the hug unfamiliar and entirely unexpected. "What are *you* doing here?" she blurted out. Whoops, wrong tone; wrong emphasis. Yet, why *was* Rachel on Leah's turf, chumming it up with the senator from New York? It made no sense.

"Tikkun olam. We're repairing the world." It was her first lobbying trip, she said. The NCJW—National Council of Jewish Women, Long Island Chapter—was trying to beat back one of those sneaky little amendments the right wing was always tacking onto legislation to erode abortion rights. "It's been twenty-five years since *Roe v. Wade* and those snakes are still pushing for parental consent and compulsory waiting periods. Now they're trying to outlaw late-term abortion even if a woman's life is at risk. Can you believe it?!"

Leah nodded mutely, still trying to reconcile the image of this fire-breather with her usually staid stepsister.

Rachel lowered her voice. "You know, before I had my five kids, I had two abortions, back when it was illegal and they did them with lye and coat hangers. Where were the pro-lifers when women were dying from back-alley abortions? Why aren't they pro-life when it comes to women's lives? Why aren't they marching on Congress to help babies who go to bed hungry and children who have no health care? I mothered five kids, Leah. No one's going to lecture *me* about family values."

Leah could only blink. Usually, no one dared lecture her about *any-thing*. But she couldn't bring herself to deflate her sister's righteous anger with a reprimand that was bound to sound arrogant. All she said was "Pro-lifers are people who think life begins at conception and ends at birth."

"That's Congressman Frank's line."

"Yes, it is." Leah, embarrassed that Rachel might think she was trying to pass it off as her own, quickly added, "Don't tell me Schumer's wavering."

"No, he's solid. We just want to make sure he stays that way. Every few months we give him new facts to beef up his arguments."

Leah gestured toward her group. "I came with friends from the magazine." Senator Schumer was not likely to mistake Leah's Schmendriks—she being the best dressed of the lot in her purple shades and black beret—for the NCW delegation, most of whom were decked out in pantsuits and real jewelry. Leah introduced Rachel to her friends as "my sister, Mrs. Jeremy Brent."

"Don't be ornery," said Rachel under her breath. "You know I'm getting divorced." She greeted the Schmendriks, then edged Leah away from her group. "I was thinking about you last week."

"What, pray tell, was the occasion?"

"Prayer, actually. Yom Kippur."

"Weren't you supposed to be cleansing your soul?"

"It was during the rinse cycle that I realized we ought to get together. Just talk."

"Say when."

Rachel looked at her. "How about today? I'm going back to my hotel to change into shorts. If you brought your workout gear, we could run together on the Mall."

"Not only don't I *own* workout gear, my dear Rachel, but I never, repeat *never*, work out. 'No pain, no pain' is my philosophy. Which is not to say I abjure fitness. I try to exercise discretion at least once a week. I jump to conclusions. Throw the bull. Play with words. Swim against the tide. On my best days, I run risks, lift spirits, run amok . . ."

"Okay, I get it. How about dinner, then?" Rachel buttoned her blazer.

"Not staying over."

"You could have dinner with me and still make the last shuttle."

"Shuttle's $202 one way. Can't afford it."

"You could stay over and take the early Metroliner," Rachel persisted, shaking her straight hair. "Share my hotel room. It's got two big beds and it's paid for already. Be my guest."

She was a world-class nudge, that's for sure. Probably desperate for company since the separation, or afraid to stay alone in a hotel. Most Stepford Wives don't even know how to pay a bar bill by themselves. Then again, Leah had no one to go home to either, so why was she playing so hard to get? She thought of the letter in her backpack—Leo had dated it "Labor Day." He was feeling better, he said. The new medication seemed to be working, his appetite was back and he'd gained a little weight. He'd struck up a friendship with a man down the hall, a former encyclopedia salesman. That night, after supper, they'd gone to a room called the Library, though it had only twenty books, and they'd played Bibliomancy. "It made me think of you," he'd written. "I miss you a lot. But the doctors say I should stay a while longer, maybe three or four months."

"What hotel?" asked Leah.

Her sister beamed. "The Mayflower. When you're done here—say 5:30—let's meet at the hotel bar. Dinner's on me 'cause it's my idea. Then we'll buy you a toothbrush and you can sleep in one of my T-shirts."

Bumped into her two minutes ago and already she was running Leah's life. "You mean I don't get a peignoir?"

"You can wear mine." Rachel disappeared down the hall, leaving Leah with her doubts. What in God's name would they talk about? God's name, maybe. Leah had a lot to say about masculine nomenclature in particular and patriarchal theology in general, but if she said a tenth of it, there'd be a fight for sure, and it could get a lot nastier than the brouhaha over the bris. Rachel took Judaism very seriously these days, and Leah would argue with a signpost—especially about religion and politics—so they were bound to be a combustible combination.

Oy, gevalt! What had she gotten herself into? It was hard enough navigating conversations with Shoshanna, who was whip smart. But Rachel was a total question mark. Could turn out to be a religious fanatic or one of those yentas who're out of their depth in a puddle. Except for some foggy Blue Spruce memories, and a few kernels Shoshanna had dropped over the years, Leah knew gornischt about her stepsister. And this was going to be a dinner à deux plus a sleepover, not a ninety-minute lunch.

An aide came out and beckoned them into the senator's office. Leah straightened her beret and, striding as forcefully as the hip would allow, led her constituents forward, looking for all the world like Che Guevara in a braid.

In the shimmering late-afternoon sunlight, with the leaves just beginning to give up their green, Rachel put on her running shoes and set her sights on the Washington Monument. She'd been to the Mall only twice before—a high school trip senior year, and a Soviet Jewry demonstration in the eighties. Leah must have camped out here hundreds of times, demonstrating against the Vietnam War, or for civil rights, or women's rights, or justice for the poor. She was always taking on problems that seemed to Rachel overwhelming and intractable. Leah should have run for office, Rachel thought. Chuck Schumer should have been waiting outside Senator Wasserman's office this afternoon, not vice versa.

Since Sam's letter had arrived last February, and Shoshanna started bugging her about "making the family whole," Rachel had often thought about Leah, but during the High Holy Days, her stepsister had become her obsession. Her rabbi had warned the congregation not to be easy on themselves this year. "A clear conscience is nothing but the sign of a bad memory," he'd said on Rosh Hashanah, and by Yom Kippur, Rachel had slogged through her spiritual ledger, found Leah's receivables the largest and longest overdue, and been moved to accept responsibility for her complicity in her stepsister's torments. On the Day of Atonement, twenty-two hours into her fast and with an audibly grinding stomach, she had stood up with the congregation and recited the confessional prayer in which Jews ask forgiveness for their collective failures, pounding her fist against her chest with each named transgression: "For the sin we have committed against You by malicious gossip; And for the sin we have committed against You by hating without cause; And for the sin we have committed against You by giving in to our hostile impulses . . . by exploiting the weak . . . by narrow-mindedness . . . by running to do evil . . . by fraud and falsehood." When the public recitation was over, Rachel had remained standing and silently confessed her personal iniquities. The sin she had committed by betraying her best friend, and the sin she had committed by lacking compassion. The sin she had committed by gloating over having Shoshanna all to herself. By helping to perpetuate the family fiction that erased Leah from their lives. By feeling jealous when Leah resurfaced, and hostile to her ever since (always careful not to let it show). By viewing Leah not as a sister but as a rival for Shoshanna's love. By being cold and unfeeling. By only pretending to be kind.

Sam used to say, "A conscience is what hurts when all your other parts feel good." At sundown on Yom Kippur 5760, corresponding to the secular year 1999, Rachel's conscience felt cleansed. She had denuded her soul and resolved that if she was ever going to change her life—and she *was*—she would have to redeem herself with Leah.

Later, back at the hotel, she would begin that journey.

Running helped her think. She hoped it would also help her outlive the disquieting statistic about the "marriage mortality benefit," the statisticians' fancy way of saying married women live longer than divorced women. This was no factoid, it was a big fat fact. While nearly 90 percent of wives made it to age sixty-five, only *60* percent of divorcées did. If the national average held, Rachel might have less than a year left. She couldn't bear the idea of dying. Silly as that sounded, she knew Margaret Mead had said something similar. "I can't *possibly* be dying," Mead protested, astonished to find herself at death's door. "Everyone dies," replied her nurse. "Yes," said Mead, "but this is different." Rachel couldn't bear the idea, because her life had not yet amounted to anything. She'd devoted her best efforts to raising her kids, but otherwise been a dilettante, a textbook case of arrested development, and she needed time to evolve into someone new, fifteen years at least, maybe twenty—time to go back to school, master Hebrew, Jewish history, the sacred canon. Time for serious Torah study. Maimonides wrote: "The words of Torah heal the soul, not the body." Rachel's body could take care of itself but her soul needed help.

Now, as her legs found their rhythm and the Mall relaxed its hold on her, she recalled something Leah had said at Shoshanna's birthday party—that a woman over fifty has earned the right to be herself. If so, Rachel Brent was fourteen years behind schedule. All this time, she'd been busy collecting and accumulating, as if filling a house were the same as fulfilling herself. She'd written checks to worthy charities and belonged to a synagogue and a couple of do-good Jewish organizations, but basically, she'd been cobbling a life out of clocks and mirrors, needlepoint pillows and lemon soufflés. Much as she loved her children and much as she excelled at the domestic arts and crafts, she knew now, may have known all along, that her *Good Housekeeping* world rested on a false foundation, a marriage of connivance. She'd opted for sex and security at the price of personal authenticity. Her self-swindle was stunning to her now. Since Blue Spruce, she'd been making the best of things no matter how bad, playing both the scam artist and the sucker; deluding herself that Esther had good reasons for sending her away, that Miss Cardwell chose her because she was special, that Jeremy was a good enough husband and their marriage was a fair pact. The deal was a quid pro quo. He'd made it possible for her to have financial comfort, social position, and children who would never languish in boarding school. She'd assumed the day-to-day family responsibilities, supplied the appropriately elegant environment and attractive feminine partner he needed to complete his image. Only after months of therapy and mountains of wet Kleenex did she understand that the deal she made with herself had replaced one massive fiction with another—Jeremy's lies with her own.

It took an extra rad of energy to run up the steps of the Lincoln Memorial. At the top, for no apparent reason other than having risen from below, she remembered a quote from Rabbi Nachman of Bratslav: "There must be a falling for a rising to take place." She was on her way up now; things were sorting themselves out.

Both women were in fine spirits when they hooked up at the Mayflower bar.

"Schumer's definitely against the ban," said Leah, munching on a pretzel. The rest of the evening might prove to be an endurance test, but she was going to go down eating.

"I should hope so," said Rachel. "I'd want my vote back if he betrayed us on this."

"Sounds like you've been pretty political."

"Heavens, no. Compared to you, what I do is nothing."

Good! She knew the difference. That would save a lot of time and palaver. "Shoshanna tells me you belong to a number of Jewish groups," said Leah.

"I guess I believe community service is the rent you pay for living on this earth."

"Is that a Jewish concept?" Might as well get the religion thing out of the way.

"Not *uniquely* Jewish," replied Rachel carefully. "But if you're a certain kind of Jew, repairing the world is compulsory."

"What kind's that—the kind who goes to shul?"

"Going to synagogue doesn't make me a Jew any more than going to a bookstore makes you an intellectual."

"What kind, then?" Leah licked the salt off a pretzel before she ate it.

"A Mitnagdic Jew, one who prefers study to dancing around the synagogue but who also believes, as the Talmud says, that the beginning and end of study is loving-kindness. The kind who thinks it important to act Jewishly in the world and not retreat into religious pneumaticism. As one of our sages put it. 'Torah is learning for the sake of doing; study is meaningless unless it leads to action.'"

Leah stared at her.

"White wine." said Rachel when the bartender asked; then, hearing Leah's "Vodka, rocks," wished she'd ordered Jack Daniel's.

"What does that mean—to 'act Jewishly'?" Leah wanted to know.

"To me it means *to actively pursue justice*." (Each word was as targeted as the numbers on a dartboard.) "That's why I came on this lobbying trip, for instance. Want to join us on tomorrow's rounds?"

"I teach a class tomorrow. Hungry minds, like hungry bellies, must be fed. Which reminds me, where are we having dinner?" She'd eaten nothing for lunch but an Almond Joy.

"I made reservations for the hotel restaurant. Hope that's okay." Rachel was sweating a little; she hadn't cooled down enough before her shower.

"I eat anywhere," said Leah.

A few beats of silence, awkward but not unbearable. Rachel played with her pearls, jiggling the two strands together, making them click and chatter like dice. She studied the liquor bottles lined up behind the bar, the shapeliest of them brands she'd never tried. Did anyone ever actually *drink* Galliano, she wondered, or do bars stock the jellybean of liqueurs because of its pretty bottle? She couldn't think of what to say next, until it occurred to her that she and Leah had something in common: no husbands.

"How are things with you these days?" she asked.

Leah swiveled on her bar stool. "My life is a round of inscrutable frivolity."

"I hear you've had a tough time lately."

"As the saying goes, 'You have to survive even if it kills you.'"

"That bad, huh? How's Leo?" She felt odd asking about Leo, having met him only twice. But it would have been odder not to.

"He's been at the sanatorium in Connecticut since March; probably have to stay through the end of the year. Believe it or not, they still call those places rest homes."

"I believe it. They call the U.S. War Department the Defense Department."

She was no dunce, thought Leah.

Not wanting to press further about Leo, Rachel stopped talking. Leah planted both elbows on the bar, nursed her drink, and stared straight ahead, unfazed by the conversational lull, which Rachel, who was bursting with things that needed saying, decided to fill. "Usually, I'm not this quiet," she began.

Leah shrugged. "Only a Jew has to *explain* silence."

"Actually, I'm quiet because I'm nervous. I have something to say but . . ."

"Just spit it out." Leah wasn't sure which was more annoying, the dish-detergent green of the crème de menthe or this tongue-tied woman reflected in the mirror behind the liquor bottles. What was her problem?

Rachel twirled the stem of her glass. Not being looked at made it easier to speak. "I know it's ridiculous; I mean it's years too late, but I want to say I'm *sorry*. I mean, I need you to know how sorry I am about how I treated you . . . what happened after Shoshanna was born. I never knew why Dad stopped seeing you. Doesn't matter anyway. We were friends; after he adopted me, we were *sisters*. It was up to me not to let you drop out of my life. I should have stayed in touch. I should have tracked you down. I'm sorry."

Leave it alone, thought Leah. Why rake things up? Her scars were thick as rope, the pain a dim memory. She was totally unprepared for this. She sucked up more vodka.

Rachel took her stillness as a sign to proceed. "I know nothing I say or do can ever make up for all that. But it's different now. I'm a new person, and I'm asking for a new friendship. Starting now." She gripped her glass to keep herself steady. "If not friendship, at least détente." She waited.

Leah's mouth, even with the vodka, felt dry. She circled the stirrer in her drink, cupped her glass, and stared into it as if the bottom contained a written message. Her distress was noticeable only in her hands, the silver rings—she still wore ten—clacking lightly against the glass. (Rachel remembered the young Shoshanna in her mimicry phase adopting the same affectation. Rachel had called them silver knuckles.)

"Détente," Leah croaked finally, relieved she could speak at all. She drank again, though her glass was empty except for melting ice. She reached into her satchel and fished out a pack of Gauloises. There was a lot of stage business associated with smoking, Rachel realized, rituals that kept the hands occupied. Leah tore off the cellophane, shook out a cigarette, tapped one end against the bar, snapped open her Zippo, and lit up. As an afterthought, she offered one to Rachel.

"Thanks, but I smoked my last behind the poolhouse when I was twelve."

Leah remembered the pool at Blue Spruce and Rachel's dagger dives. "I hated swimming."

Rachel reached for a bowl of peanuts and held it out. "You loved peanuts."

"Still do." She grabbed a handful.

"Let's go inside and feed you something more nourishing."

Mens sana in corpore sano," said Leah, while watching her sister sign the bar bill without anyone's help.

Rachel pushed off her stool and led the way to the restaurant. "That was my advice to Shoshanna, remember? 'A sound mind in a sound body.'"

"When did you study Latin?" Blue Spruce offered only French and Spanish. A person can't really know a person if her biography stopped when she was twelve, thought Leah.

"College."

"I'd like a table near a waiter," Leah deadpanned when the hostess came to seat them. Recalling the Barney Frank moment, she hastened to attribute the line to Henny Youngman. They were led to a corner booth, which pleased her; in case of ennui, she could look around the room.

"The steak sounds great, but I can only eat fish or dairy," said Rachel, studying her menu. She ordered monkfish.

"Monkfish?" said Leah, feigning surprise. "Too goyish. I'll have the flanken with kasha varnishkes." When the waiter looked blank, she gave her real order: roast beef, Yorkshire pudding, creamed spinach.

"Assume you want red with your beef," said Rachel, checking the wine list with assurance.

"Either's fine with me."

Rachel ordered a California Cabernet.

That was considerate of her—suggesting red when she was having fish. "How come not Carmel? Or Yardin."

"My kashrut stops with the noble grape. I can't stand kosher wine, except on Jewish holidays."

Rachel ordered the house salad, Leah the Classic Caesar.

"What's a Classic Caesar?" asked Rachel.

"It's when they serve you the salad, then stab you six times."

Rachel's laugh boomed through a body that seemed too small to have produced such a boiler-room bellow. "Just oil and vinegar for me," she told the waiter, then turned to Leah with a scampish grin. "If olive oil comes from olives, what does baby oil come from?"

Leah racked her brain for a comeback. "If vegetarians eat vegetables, what do humanitarians eat?"

"If humans evolved from monkeys and apes, why do we still have monkeys and apes?" said Rachel, the speed of her response suggesting this wasn't her first go at the game.

"Why are boxing rings square?" Leah countered after a few seconds.

Rachel shot back a fusillade: "How come it's a pair of pants, but only one bra? Why do we play at a recital and recite at a play? Why do they put Braille on drive-through bank machines?"

Though she rarely gave anyone else the last word, Leah threw up her hands and surrendered. She was having fun and, amazingly, not at anyone's expense. When the wine came, she raised her glass. "To conundrums!"

Rachel, hard-pressed to find something worth toasting, simply spoke what was on her mind: "To divorce!"

"Is yours final?" Leah asked, remembering her parents' drawn-out debacle.

"Not yet, but every negotiating session stiffens my spine. There's a reason why 80 percent of divorces are initiated by women: it's because 80 percent of men are pricks."

"Do you ever miss him?" Leah asked. "Prick" should have been her word, not Rachel's.

"The first couple of months, going home was like diving into an empty swimming pool, but the more I thought about my marriage, the easier it was to be single. When I confronted him about his skater girlfriend, he said he needed some fresh bread in his life. Can you believe it? I'm the size I was in high school; he's got love handles you can grab like a jug. I'm reading, studying, learning new things all the time; his whole life is his practice and the *Times* crossword. The man's been a crashing bore for the last thirty years and *I'm* the stale croissant? When I told him to get out, the last thing he said was 'You'll never find anyone like me again!' 'I should hope not!' I told him. How I took that man's shit all those years is a mystery."

Leah could tell Rachel wasn't used to saying "shit" either. The word was young and juicy in her mouth. "So, that was it? You told him to go and he went."

"Not exactly," said Rachel and, in that moment, decided to be honest with her sister—for the sake of détente. "He called a few days later, said we should go out to dinner, talk things over. There's nothing to talk about, I said. Then just listen, he said. We met in the city at this Chelsea brasserie he knows I love. I could tell he was in seduction mode—that's what he's best at, talking people into things. Only this time, I wasn't falling for it. He began every sentence with how much he appreciated me, but by the end of the paragraph, he was listing what he'd done for me, how generous he was, and how much I owed him."

"Guilt trip," put in Leah.

"Right. And when I didn't bite, he switched the bait."

"To which worm? 'Poor-me-I-can't-live-without-you.' Or 'This-is-your-last-chance-I'm-not-going-to-beg'?"

Rachel grinned. "The former. Which happens to be the truth. Without me, he can't live the life he's been living. Can't pretend to have the perfect family. Can't play the at-home host in the velvet smoking jacket with me pouring coffee for his guests. Or trundle me out for law school reunions or press interviews, or stick me in front of a camera in the slot marked Wife of Successful New York Lawyer."

Leah said, "Now that we're being straight with each other, the one time I met your former spouse, he seemed perfectly contemptible. Even smiling, he looked as if he'd just evicted a widow. Not that bright either, as I remember. Lots of chrome, but empty under the hood."

"That's where you're wrong. He's brilliant. And not just in his cases. He can convince anyone of anything." (Like Freddy, Leah thought; her own sorcerer.) "Me especially. He really knew how to get to me, through sex, the kids, my fear of abandonment. When all else failed, he played on my sympathy. Jeremy had a tough childhood, tougher than mine, 'cause he never had a Sam to rescue him. I saw his vulnerabilities—when it suited him, he let me see them—and I felt sorry for him. He's a colossal egotist, but no one has a better line."

"One nice thing about egotists," said Leah, "they don't talk about other people."

Rachel dug into her monkfish as if it were a T-bone. "He was sexy, I'll give him that."

"Who needs sexy at our age?" said Leah, puncturing a puff of Yorkshire pudding.

"You're probably right." Rachel realized she was agreeing with Leah just to be polite. What had happened to her other Yom Kippur vow—to stop saying things she didn't mean? It was a safe bet that a radical feminist was no prude, so why not level with Leah? "Truth is, I don't need sexy, but I do need sex." She leaned closer. "Even when we had nothing to say to each other, he was great in bed."

"I guess I lost interest in sex after menopause."

"Me, too. It's driving me up the wall—hot spells, mood swings, this terrible dryness . . ."

"Schtupping isn't your only option, you know," said Leah, expecting at last to fluster her. "There's lesbian love, Sapphic sex, whatever you want to call it."

Rachel drained her glass. "Been there, done that" (flash on Miss Cardwell). "It's not for me."

Leah couldn't believe this conversation, the plumping of her pruny sister. Had she completely misread the woman? "There's always masturbation; you might check out Betty Dodson's book," she said, attending to the salad croutons that kept falling off her fork. "*Sex for One.*"

"Cute title. But if Amazon doesn't sell it, I'm not about to waltz into my local book nook and order *Sex for One*. The neighbor ladies would be scandalized, though heaven knows they need it more than I do. I'm a confirmed onanist, but I'd bet half the women on the North Shore don't know how to *find* their clitoris, let alone pronounce it."

"Can you imagine a man going through life without ever finding his schlong?" Leah asked. "Which reminds me of a delicious Yiddish axiom: 'A cock makes a man a lover like a beard makes a goat a rabbi!'"

This was Rachel's chance to tell Leah her new life plan, but given how the evening was going so far, she was in no mood to get serious. She summoned a raunchy factoid: "Cock is the name of a deodorant in France."

"I must have missed that in *Le Monde*."

"And while I have your undivided attention, in Turkey, they sell biscuits called Bums, Sweden has a toilet paper named Krapp, and South African tuna fish is known as Grated Fanny."

"No wonder globalization isn't working," said Leah. "Some brands just don't travel well."

They leaned close together, their hair almost touching, and dissolved in girlish giggles, the sort unknown to Leah even as a girl. "Are you aware that laughter increases respiratory activity, muscular dynamism, and heart rate?" Rachel asked, while using the tine of her salad fork to dig out a piece of lettuce stuck between her teeth, a crude move, she knew, but since Leah was watching her do it, she added, "You have some spinach stuck in yours."

"Where?"

"Upper jaw; between the left canine and first bicuspid."

"What are you, a recovering orthodontist? Show me."

"Right *there*." Rachel stuck one of her fingernails between Leah's teeth and flicked out the green speck. "As I was saying, laughter stimulates the pituitary gland and releases endorphins, which are chemical cousins of heroin. Endorphins are what give me my runner's high." She ate a crouton off Leah's plate.

"Let me understand this: You have to jog to get stoned and *I* just have to sit here, let you clean my teeth, and jiggle my belly?"

"That's the whole idea. When Norman Cousins was fighting a degenerative spinal condition, he discovered that ten minutes laughing at a Marx Brothers movie gave him an hour of pain-free sleep. So I guess you and I are gonna conk out tonight like babies."

Maybe it was time to reconsider her prejudices, thought Leah, considering for the first time the possibility that grafting an observant Jew onto a sexual libertine could yield a rather engaging hybrid. At the moment, the names she once called her stepsister seeming utterly inapt. Fact fetishist? Tonight, Rachel's factoids had been fresh and amusing. Priggish? She'd owned up to at least one lesbian experience and was positively blasé about onanism. Stepford Wife? How submissive could she be if she'd thrown Jeremy out with swords aflame and seemed to be doing fine on her own? (Certainly no worse than Leah.) Maven of the meaningless? Bubble brain of the burbs? Not if she could translate a Latin axiom and use "pneumaticism" in a sentence.

T. H. Huxley once defined the demise of a theory as "the slaying of a beautiful hypothesis by an ugly fact." Leah's hypothesis—that Rachel was a dunce—dear to her all these years and buffed in periodic insult sessions, had been slaughtered tonight by the unassailable fact that this God-fearing, needlepointing Long Island housewife was also wry, witty, clever, randy, and damn good company.

She ordered a Boston cream pie, despite its being named for the city of Dena.

Rachel declined dessert. "I'd love a brownie, but it would replace every calorie I shed on the Mall." She asked the waiter for mint tea.

"How's the Mall holding up these days? I used to spend a lot of time there."

"That's what I figured. Actually, I'm going back tomorrow afternoon, to visit the Holocaust Museum. Would you believe sixteen million people have traipsed through that place since it opened in April 1993, 73 percent of them *not* Jewish. It's phenomenal. Have you ever been?"

Leah shook her head. She'd meant to go every time she was in D.C. but had been thwarted by the irrational, indefensible impression that the Holocaust was her father's "thing." During the war, Sam went to the White House with Rabbi Stephen Wise to beg Roosevelt to bomb the rail lines to Auschwitz. He lobbied Truman to support Israeli statehood so Holocaust survivors could find a home, fought to relax U.S. immigration quotas for Jewish refugees, and wrote about restitution, reparations, and Holocaust denial before others worked up the nerve. Sam was Elie Weisel before there was Elie Weisel. If the Holocaust was her father's issue, it couldn't be hers. Of course, she recognized the absurdity of this position; no one *owns* an issue, especially that one. Yet the feeling was so strong that whenever she saw a Holocaust movie or read the literature of catastrophe, her father loomed over the scene. It was always Sam's voice crying, "Never again."

"I guess I haven't felt ready to expose myself to all that pain," Leah replied. Her double meaning was not lost on her.

"Maybe Dad feels the same way," said Rachel, unaware that the analogy would grate. "What else would explain why he won't visit Yad Vashem, the Holocaust Museum in Jerusalem. I don't get it. The Shoah used to be his life."

Leah didn't get it either. But the subject was pissing her off, so naturally she tossed Sam on the griddle. "First of all, he's not *Dad* to me."

(She spat out the *D*.) "Second, he and I are incapable of having the same feelings about *anything*. I do things for my reasons, he does them for his. You want my guess about why he turned off on the Holocaust? Because he's an Israeli now and most Israelis have had it up to here with the Shoah. They don't want to look at pictures of emaciated inmates and sad piles of shoes. They're tired of the paradigm of Jew as Victim. Jew as Fighter is the new ideal for the new era. Sam went into the phone booth as Tevye and came out Ariel Sharon. Nowadays Jews want to identify with the IDF, the Mossad, the hot-diggedy helicopter pilot. Those old Holocaust survivors are dying off anyway. Let's just move on, shall we?"

"Leah, that's not fair!"

"You're damn right it's not. Sam once said God died in Auschwitz. Very poetic; also pure crap. God didn't die in Auschwitz, *Jews* died there. The death camps didn't kill *Judaism*, they killed *Jews*. But the average Israeli is in such a hurry to eradicate the idea of Jewish vulnerability that he'll detour around a heap of bodies to do it. Not only does he avert his gaze, he wants to pull a curtain over history, so the goyim shouldn't focus on that little ghetto boy in the cap cowering with his hands in the air. Hey, don't look at that scared little Yid. Check out the Sabra with the Uzi across his chest. When foreign dignitaries come a-calling in Jerusalem, I'll bet Sam is out there petitioning Barak to stop schlepping them through Yad Vashem, which Israeli prime ministers have been doing since the museum opened. God forbid Tony Blair should get the wrong idea about us!"

Listening to herself, Leah heard a fool ranting. She'd whipped herself into a frenzy over her father's views when she hadn't the foggiest idea of his actual position on anything. She always seemed to be arguing with Sam in her head. But now, having speculated on his reason for turning away from the Holocaust, she felt obliged to identify her own. It had to be self-preservation. She was unwilling to expose herself to that much brutality while her nerves were so frayed. A breakdown was not out of the question. That's why she hadn't gone to the museum during any of her previous trips to Washington. For fear of being saddened into madness.

Rachel was thoroughly confused. Were Leah and Sam on speaking terms, they'd undoubtedly agree on the basics: that Jews have suffered and anti-Semitism is a scourge, that Jewish identity should be embraced and Jews should fight back when oppressed. As for what to *do* about all that, they'd probably clash like tectonic plates. Sam's all-purpose solution was religious Zionism—the ingathering of the exiles and the practice of traditional Judaism. Leah's solution was to revitalize the Diaspora, make the whole world safe for Jews in every country, not just Israel, and pass down the radical heritage that sustained the Jewish people before there was a Jewish state and whenever God fell down on the job.

"I doubt Dad cares what Tony Blair thinks of us," said Rachel. "He's probably just trying to put the Shoah behind him."

"The Holocaust isn't the Monica Lewinsky scandal. You don't put mass murder behind you. You venerate its victims. You name its perpetrators. You remind the world of humanity's capacity for evil and you pledge to defeat the evildoers in every generation." From here, Leah launched a monologue on anti-Semitism that sounded like a tape from the Simon Wiesenthal Center played fast-forward. What surprised Rachel wasn't her sister's command of Jewish history—Leah was, after all, a scholar—but her visceral outrage as she sprinted through centuries of torture, sacrifice, siege, conquest, inquisition, pogroms, and death camps. Even more surprising was her strong identification with the victims. Until now, Rachel had assumed that because she'd strayed so far from Jewish observance, Leah would also be estranged from Jewish peoplehood, that her socialist universalism would demand that the Jews disappear as a national group in the interest of world harmony. Instead, Leah was obsessed with Jewish survival. Though critical of the Israeli government, especially its policies toward the Palestinians, she wasn't one of those extremists who expected the Jewish State to commit suicide for the sake of another people's self-determination. Leah was no Golda Meir; but neither was she Emma Goldman.

Decades of preconceptions dissipated in the reality of her sister's fervor and forced Rachel to entertain the idea that a person who violates the Sabbath, ignores Jewish holidays, opposes circumcision, and never goes to synagogue could, when all is said and done, be a good Jew. There were dozens of ways to be Jewish, and Rachel believed in a God who accepted them all. There was her way—egalitarian religious observance coupled with social action. Leah's way—against organized religion, but for radical politics and Jewish cultural identity. And Sam's way, which combined prayer, study, ritual, social action, and aliyah to the land of milk and honey. Rachel wondered where Shoshanna would fit on the spectrum.

When her dessert arrived, Leah bored her finger into the whipped cream, sucked it clean, then hacked off a big wedge of pie and shoveled it into her mouth. The custard curled around her teeth as she continued her tutorial. Rachel couldn't help thinking about Sam, with his fine manners, and how he'd have hated watching Leah eat. She didn't just ingest something—be it pie or life—she devoured it, chomping off chunks, chewing hard, then spewing it back into the world as the verbal equivalent of acid reflux.

Rachel was getting tired of Leah's lecture. "Let's not talk about anti-Semitism. We've risen from the ashes, we're flourishing, let's enjoy it. Was it Fitzgerald who said living well is the best revenge, or George Herbert, or Gerald Murphy?"

"Sam used that quote, too," said Leah. "Remember the TV interview when he said anti-Semitism could be cured by Jewish achievement and gentile familiarity with our wonderful ways. What bullshit. Jew-hating will always exist, even if we produce four Nobel Prize winners a year and an interfaith seminar in every community, because Jew-hating exists even where there are no Jews. Japan, for example. Or Poland. People need a group to despise, it's that simple. When blacks are unavailable, and sometimes when they are, Jews are the designated inferiors, and despite Rabbi Wasserman's wishful thinking, no amount of accomplishment or dialoguing can change that."

Sam was the third party at the table, had been all night, Rachel was tempted to point out, aware of how often Leah had referred to him, or defined her views in opposition to his. But that would only prolong the harangue, and more than anything else, Rachel wanted to close the subject. "You'll have to admit Jews are pretty comfortable here in America. We're only 2.5 percent of the population, but most of us are thriving."

"Don't be so sanguine," snapped Leah. "Swastikas still turn up on synagogue walls. And there are still places in this country where you can be ostracized if you don't string Christmas lights on your house in December or your hair looks like mine instead of yours." She reached over and tousled Rachel's bangs, which dropped back in place, straight as a fringe. "Jesus, Rachel, your parents must have been Louise Brooks and Alfred E. Newman."

"Is that *it*? Is the sermon over?" asked Rachel. Something was happening here. She'd picked spinach out of Leah's teeth. Leah had touched her hair.

"Not quite. Whenever I tell people it *can* happen here, they react the way you just did. Hey, we're doing great! Look how many of us are high up in government, on Wall Street, in the media! *Hell*-o?! Jews were just as highly placed among the elites of Berlin and Prague, and look what happened to *them*."

Rachel drank the last of her tea and set her cup on its saucer. She smiled at the animated woman in the straggly salt-and-pepper braid and the purple shades and the black turtleneck that had been stretched out of shape by too many impatient yanks over the head. "I have an idea," she said brightly. "What time's your class tomorrow?"

"Four."

"I could switch my Hill visits to the afternoon if you wanted to go to the museum with me in the morning. Then you could catch the one o'clock shuttle back."

"I told you, I can't afford a plane ticket."

"Let me spring for it. I'd be glad to."

"Thanks, but no."

"Why not? You're supposed to be a socialist—from each according to her ability, to each according to her need, right? Well, you need an airline ticket and Jeremy's money has given me the ability to pay for it." Rachel reached across the table to scrape up the last of Leah's Boston cream pie.

"You're sure about this?"

"Positive."

"Okay, then, but let's be clear: I'm only staying to help you squander the bastard's money."

On the way to the elevators, they stopped at the hotel's sundries shop and Leah bought herself a toothbrush. Despite their seven-inch, thirty-pound difference, she fit into one of Rachel's running shirts, a shapeless, faded schmatta that reminded her of Henry's apolitical T-shirt wardrobe. *I enjoyed talking to you*, it said. *My mind needed a rest.* No pejorative intended, but Leah thought it the perfect comment on this night.

Rachel, in her champagne silk nightgown, had surreptitiously watched Leah undress and now stood beside her at the big double sink, Mutt and Jeff brushing their teeth. "You really should wear a bra," she said. "Big boobs drag down the chest muscles."

"They also pull the wrinkles out of the face."

"Stop! I'm going to wet my pants."

Leah felt giddy. In the mirror she saw herself laughing through a mouthful of froth. Could she really be in a Washington hotel room, wearing nothing but her skivvies and a joke T-shirt and discussing her breasts with Rachel Brent? Or had she finally lost her mind? Mirror, mirror on the wall, am I my mother after all?

"This is the first time we've been together in the same bathroom in more than fifty years," said Rachel.

Leah spit into the basin and wiped her face with a washcloth. Leaving the cap off the toothpaste—what else is new?—she limped from the sink to the desk, extracted a book from her knapsack, and climbed into bed.

"That hip never did heal right, did it?" asked Rachel gently.

"Some things get a little warped with time." Leah could have been describing her misconceptions of Rachel, or Rachel's warped feelings about *her*, but both of them let the line pass. After a few yoga stretches, Rachel slipped under the covers and turned out her light. Lying on her back, perfectly still, she shut her eyes and recited the words of the Sh'ma.

Leah's lamp drew a yellow pool around her torso, a circle of light in a cave of shadows. As a small child, she'd said that prayer with Sam every night. Had Rachel been saying it all these years? Leah wondered if it might take as much strength of character and force of intellect to talk oneself *into* believing in God as to talk oneself out of it. She wondered if Rachel's faith in God had been more helpful to her than Leah's faith in herself had been to *her*. And if faith, not fate, had brought them together today. Though fueled by diametrically opposite belief systems, each was strongly committed to her ideology, and both of their ideologies had led them to the senator's door. They'd started at different points but ended up in the same place for the same purpose.

"I still can't get used to sleeping alone," Rachel murmured from her dark side. "Can you?"

"It's hard." That's all Leah would say. She thought of the letter in her backpack, Leo's letter telling her that he wouldn't be home for "at least another three or four months." She'd be sleeping alone at the turn of the new millennium.

"I'm beat." Rachel yawned. "But keep reading if you like; the light won't disturb me."

"Thanks," said Leah to the mound under the covers. She pulled the lamp toward her and opened her book against her tented knees.

"The average person falls asleep in seven minutes," Rachel added dreamily. "I can go shluffie in two."

That fluffy, cozy little word sent Leah back to her top bunk in Brooklyn. She could see a head of curly auburn hair poking through the door for the fifth time, Esther scolding, "Go shluffie, you noisy girls! You'll wake the baby!" though she had to know Leah and Rachel had been jabbering in their beds for hours, and Shoshanna, snuggled in a crib at their feet, could have slept through D-day.

A car horn blasted and waned on the street below the open hotel window. The mound moved. Rachel raised herself on one elbow. She had one more thought, something she'd felt when they were standing at the sink and wanted to put into words. "I'm glad we have Blue Spruce in common, Leah. Not every woman has a boot camp in her childhood. I think it was character-building, don't you?"

eighteen

NEITHER OF HER SISTERS had told Leah about Sam's impending visit, though it was five weeks away. Having witnessed her nonstop Sam-bashing in Washington, Rachel was more convinced than ever of the futility of a brokered peace, and while Shoshanna had every intention of mentioning it on March 8, then at the Seder, and again on her birthday, she'd never gotten around to it for lack of a practical plan, though cowardice may have had something to do with it, too. Now there was a chance their father might not come at all.

He'd called from Jerusalem on Halloween morning. Shoshanna remembered the date because she'd been preparing little bags of candy for the trick-or-treaters when the phone rang. He said a close friend's grandson had been killed by a Katuysha rocket while patrolling the Lebanese border, a wonderful young man, a chess partner of Sam's. The family was inconsolable, and as of now, he didn't feel he could leave, especially for something as selfish as an award ceremony.

"I'll play it by ear for the next few weeks and let you know one way or the other by E-mail," he'd said. "Give me your address."

"E-mail?"

"You heard right."

"You have *E-mail*, Daddy?"

"SamWass@Netvision.net.il." He spelled it slowly. "What's yours?"

Shoshanna swallowed a giggle. "Shishkebab@Juno.com. Since when are you wired? Last I knew, you didn't even own a computer."

"The boy who got killed—*alav ha'shalom*—he got me interested. He put me on the Internet. What's so strange? The year 2000 is around the corner, you know."

"You're almost ninety, Dad. People don't usually tackle new technologies at eighty-nine and a half." (She was having trouble with the Palm Pilot at fifty.)

"Nonsense. I'm always learning new things. This www is fantastic, mamaleh. Today I downloaded a sermon from a rabbi in Chicago and a d'var Torah from Chabad's Web site. I bookmarked the PLO Web site so I can keep track of their shenanigans. Every morning, after I lay tefillin, first thing I do is check my E-mail box."

"I'm impressed," she said.

"Don't be. It's easy as aleph bet. Now I need the whole family's E-mail addresses so I can stay in touch. Imagine what I'll save on stamps!"

Shoshanna promised to forward a family list. If she included Leah's address, maybe he'd take the hint.

Sam said he'd decide by Thanksgiving about the trip to the States.

Shoshanna begged him to come; everyone missed him.

Before they hung up, he wished her a happy Halloween.

Since then "Shishkebab" and "SamWass" had been corresponding almost daily about family news, the *Times*'s coverage of the Middle East (he read the paper on-line every day), stories in the English-language Internet edition of *Ha'aretz* (which he insisted was the most reliable record of events in Israel). Daniel forwarded scholarly articles he thought might interest Sam. Rachel broke the news about her divorce by E-mail, which made explaining it less of an ordeal. Tamara sent him a digital picture of Max in a baby-blue yarmulke. Jake, sitting in his dorm room in Boulder, Colorado, played chess with him. Rachel and Sam discussed the week's Torah portion, every parsha since the beginning of

November. The family was more connected to its patriarch than at any time in its history—except for Leah, who wouldn't have wasted her electricity on him anyway.

By Thanksgiving, he still hadn't made up his mind, and Shoshanna was annoyed. She'd planned to announce his visit when everyone was gathered around the turkey at Rachel's house, which would let Leah know he was coming without Shoshanna's having to take the repercussions alone. If the family atmosphere became half as warm as it had been by the end of the Seder, Shoshanna thought Leah might soften enough to want to repair the rift.

Rachel's decision to host the whole clan met resistance from her children and Shoshanna, who thought Thanksgiving dinner was too much to take on, given what she'd been through the last few months. Rachel had to convince them that cooking would be therapeutic and she'd like nothing more than to fuss over her family. A divorced friend, similarly concerned, warned that it would be hard for Rachel to sit at her own table with no husband, and maybe she ought to decide in advance who was going to carve the turkey. In fact, Jeremy had never been the carver; he hated the feel of grease on his hands. Carving was one of the many "head of household" roles that Rachel had taken upon herself years ago when he opted out of everything messy. Her whole married life, she'd been trying to match Norman Rockwell's *Saturday Evening Post* painting, the one with the quintessential American family saying grace over a golden turkey. But the Brents rarely made it to pecan pie without Jeremy spoiling the scene because something—the children's chatter, a lump in his gravy, too much food on the table at the same time—did not meet his approval. Holidays brought out the worst in him, probably for the same reason he was so resistant to Jewish rituals: he *wouldn't* do what his mother *couldn't* do. Since she couldn't get it together to keep the Sabbath or make a decent Thanksgiving meal (at best, she transferred a turkey TV dinner onto a plate), Jeremy refused to give himself to a celebratory Shabbat, or enjoy a real Thanksgiving. It would have betrayed his mother.

Rachel, on the other hand, was the impresario of holidays. Larding the calendar with sacrosanct dates gave shape to the sprawl of her year.

Though partial to Jewish haggim, she loved all holidays—secular, religious, and ethnic—loved their symbols, their special foods, and defining color schemes (it wouldn't be Hanukkah without blue, but who'd want a blue Valentine's Day?), and found the repetition of annual rituals reassuring and restorative. That a group of people doing the same thing on the same day had the power to bond them to one another and their history was deeply comforting to her. This was especially true of Thanksgiving, maybe because Esther had revered it as the quintessential American holiday and celebrated it so elaborately that she may as well have been a direct descendant of John Smith. Rachel loved Thanksgiving because it served as a bugle blast that summoned scattered family members to one table, and because beyond honoring the basic tradition of turkey and stuffing, the Wassermans, like most families, embellished the meal with flourishes that made the holiday theirs. "In *our* house, we *always* decorate with strings of cranberries," they'd say. "We always put bananas in our sweet potatoes." "We always go around the table—youngest to oldest—saying what we were most thankful for this year."

Rachel recognized these as passwords into a primal "we." People love Thanksgiving because it reminds them of who they are (or wish they were) and whom they belong to, she thought, and this year especially, she needed that reminder. Furthermore, this year she wanted to host the dinner because she had something important to tell everyone and she wanted to announce it on her own turf. By holding out the promise of an old-fashioned feast with the dishes that "we always" have for Thanksgiving (and by exploiting the family's concern for her emotional well-being), she'd been able to persuade the lot of them to come out to Long Island. For the first time in months, she was eager to cook. And for the first time ever, she was going to do everything her way, not Jeremy's. No more "making the best of it." Her new mantra was *Make it the best.*

So here they were again, same group around a different table, this time for the American Seder, Thanksgiving. As in the past, voices were raised (right now, Seth and Ezra were arguing about Steinbrenner's threat to move the Yankees from the Bronx), yet Rachel felt none of her usual anxiety, knowing that this was a garden-variety family tiff, not the prelude to a scene that would end with Jeremy slamming the door to his study or gunning down the driveway to one of his skating dates or testosterone tents, or wherever he went when he left home in a rage. What a contrast between Thanksgiving 1998—when he ruined the dinner because he found the knives too dull, the yams too sweet, and Tamara too critical of welfare reform—and Thanksgiving 1999, when people could speak their minds without causing an explosion at the other end of the table.

That was another interesting thing about holidays: they stuck in the mind more than other days. Since it's easier for people to remember where they were last July 4 than last July 24, they tend to use holidays as yardsticks for their personal progress. Last year, Rachel had an incipient ulcer. This year she was completely relaxed, even when an argument broke out two minutes after Shoshanna said, "Dad may be coming to the States at the end of the year to accept an award from Rodeph Tzedek. I'll know more in a day or two." December 31 would mark the synagogue's hundredth anniversary, she explained, and that night the congregation was going to honor Sam and two other former rabbis—the only ones still alive—with the Tzedek Prize for Distinguished Service to the Cause of Justice. Sam had served the longest by far, 1950 to 1980, and the trustees were so eager for him to be there to receive his plaque in person that they'd added the inducement of a paid ticket, round trip New York–Tel Aviv. Economy class but, as Sam put it, "That's not chopped liver." The event was a pretty big deal, since past honorees included Eleanor Roosevelt, Martin Luther King, Jr., Golda Meir, and Abraham Joshua Heschel. The synagogue had asked Sam to prepare an acceptance speech—fifteen or twenty minutes on a topic of his choice—to be delivered immediately following the regular Friday-night service.

"He wrote me a letter some months ago," said Shoshanna, choosing her words carefully (the letter tucked in the Filofax, lost on the highway, found under the underpass, never mentioned to Leah). "I was going to give you guys a heads-up about it, but then he called to say a young friend of his was killed and he might not come."

"I got the same letter," said Rachel, "back in February, I think." (Shoshanna wanted to kick her under the table.) "He must have had it Xeroxed. I remember he specifically said he wanted everyone to come to the ceremony—children, grandchildren, *and* great-grandchildren. I can't believe he's never even *met* Ruby, Pearl, and Max."

"Sounds like a vaudeville act—Ruby, Pearl, and Max," repeated Leah. "Who started this idea of naming girls after Sophie Tucker's backup singers and boys after the men our grandfathers took a schvitz with?"

Shoshanna recalled Leah's obsession with names. Some things never change.

"It's ridiculous, I know." Nellie laughed. "They're old people's names but it's an epidemic on the Upper West Side. At the twins' nursery school there's a Nathan, Harry, Molly, Bessie, Ben, and Gabe."

"Maybe it's cyclical," said Tamara, who had seven-month-old Maxie welded to her breast. "A hundred years from now they'll probably say, 'This is Shmuel and Sadie; we named them after Grandpa Sean and Grandma Stacey.'"

When the laughter subsided, Leah said in the most offhand way, "I got that letter, too." She didn't mention Sam's handwritten P.S.: *Please come, maideleh. It would mean so much to me.* Maideleh, yet! Suddenly she was his little girl.

Shoshanna was flabbergasted. She and Rachel looked at each other. Before either of them could ask why Leah hadn't mentioned the letter before, or whether she planned to go, Tamara said, "Hey! I just realized that's New Year's Eve! Grandpa can't expect us to celebrate Y2K at synagogue, can he?"

"He certainly can," said her mother.

Tamara slumped in her chair. "That's a downer."

"I think it's an upper, myself," said Rachel. "December 31 happens to fall on a Friday night, and where else would a Jew want to be on Erev Shabbat but in a beautiful synagogue like Rodeph Tzedek?" She reached for the cranberry sauce (which she'd made from scratch with orange zest and chopped walnuts, Esther's recipe).

Suddenly Sam was forgotten and the family was debating the relative merits of New Year's Eve and Shabbat or, as Rachel put it, the secular versus the sublime. Seth and Simon came to Tamara's defense with paeans to champagne and caviar, while Leah groused about the capitalist conspiracy that coerced people into spending big bucks on one minute of meaningless revelry.

"That Friday may be New Year's Eve to the rest of you, but to me it's the start of our day of rest."

Shoshanna waved her off. "Don't be disingenuous, Rache, it's a triple header this year, and you know it."

"Not for Jews, it isn't. The Fourth Commandment states, 'Remember the Sabbath day and keep it holy.' Nowhere does it say, Remember December 31. And, in case you haven't noticed, a *holy* day is several rungs above a *holi*day."

"We're not talking any old December 31 here, Mom," protested Simon. "We're on the cusp of something big. New year, new century, new millennium—even *you* have to admit that's pretty potent. Shabbat comes once a week. This combo comes once in a thousand years." As if to underscore Simon's point, Maxie put out a mega-burp.

"Hindus, Sufis, and Muslims will be watching the ball in Times Square just like the rest of us," said Seth, who rarely contributed to Wasserman debates unless he felt his wife needed him.

"I don't care who else is doing what else," replied Rachel impatiently. "Shabbat gives us something much more meaningful to celebrate—the wonder of creation and . . ."

"And a million prohibitions," interrupted Simon. "No using electricity, no carrying, no money, no driving, no phones. No life." (Except for the born-again Dalia, Rachel's children had given up Sabbath observance the minute they left home.)

"They're not prohibitions, dear, they're privileges. If you and Roy were to set aside one day a week when you weren't obsessed with the stock market and all your other daily endeavors, you might notice the wonders of God's world. Those peas and pearl onions, for instance. Pass them here and let's focus on how miraculous each one is."

"Perfection," said Daniel agreeably.

"One onion looks a little puckered to me," said Tamara. "And isn't that pea a tad pale?"

Rachel ignored her. "When I enter the weekly oasis of Shabbat, I experience pure time—nonutilitarian, nonproductive, transcendent time, a whole day of peace and tranquillity. One day out of every seven."

Speaks well, sounds weird, thought Leah.

"Cool," said Roy. A Jew raised ultra-reform, his idea of a Sabbath ritual was watching Saturday-morning cartoons.

"While I have the floor, I want to say something about this Y2K nonsense," Rachel persisted. "It's everywhere and it's infuriating. I resent it, but I can't escape it."

"Why would you want to?" asked Nelly.

"Because 2000 is not *my* millennium. According to the Jewish calendar, the year is 5760. I've got 240 years left until Y6K."

Suddenly Shoshanna understood that her sister Rachel was living in two time zones with two calendars, the secular one with holidays like Memorial Day and Thanksgiving printed in their appropriate squares, and the religious calendar listing Shabbat candle-lighting times, Rosh Hodesh, Hanukkah, Passover, Lag B'Omer, and Shemini Atzeret. And for Rachel, the Jewish calendar took precedence. While Shoshanna was beating herself up for her dependence on the Filofax, her sister, even more time-bound, was running her life by an ancient calendar while also observing her *personal* holy days, the dates that are as meaningful to each individual as any religious or national holiday, maybe even more so, because of their private resonances.

May 12, for instance, burned a hole in Shoshanna's and Rachel's calendar—it was the anniversary of Esther's death. August 30, the day Daniel's parents told him he was Jewish, never passed without his commenting on it, even decades after the fact. On the anniversary of Gideon's death, Rachel shut herself in her bedroom and stayed there until the yahrzeit candle flickered out. In future years, she would probably wake up angry every March 19, the day she found the condoms in Jeremy's drawer. And Leah would never feel the same about the ides of March; if only for a millisecond, she would revisit that lawyer's office every March 15 for the rest of her life. June 14 was an ordinary date in most people's calendars, but for Shoshanna her birthday had loomed like doomsday until she found a way to hang her future on it. Nor was she the first in her family to understand what a difference a date makes. Esther and Sam contrived a fake wedding anniversary, moving it back fourteen years to accommodate an immovable date—the year of Rachel's birth. Now the family was sitting around the table arguing about a date meaningful to millions around the globe, December 31, 1999.

Leah, gnawing on a drumstick, suddenly regretted opting out of past Thanksgivings, as she'd done on principle in deference to the Native Americans; her act of conscience had deprived her of years of crispy turkey legs and moist mushroom-cornbread stuffing while failing to advance the status of the Mohawk or Chippewa one whit. "I'm with Rachel on Y2K," Leah said, licking her fingers. "No one can accuse me of living by the Jewish calendar, yet I consider the fact that the world calculates temporal progress as the years since Christ's birth to be an insult to all non-Christians, not just to Jews. Cultural imperialism has always troubled me. But it's nothing compared to the heebie-jeebies I'm getting from the holy rollers who insist the End of Days is nigh."

"Ooh, that reminds me of an old joke," said Tamara. "God warns humanity that the End of Days is coming. In two weeks, the earth will be submerged in a flood worse than Noah's. So the Pope goes on TV and exhorts all Catholics to take confession, and the Protestant leaders urge their flocks to repent. And the Grand Rebbe tells the Jewish people, 'Nu, Yidden—we have fourteen days to learn to live underwater.'"

"Listen up, people," said Leah, stepping on Tamara's laugh. "This is no joke. The apocalyptic Christians say the conversion of the Jews is the only thing standing between them and the Second Coming. They're cooking up some pyro-terrorism to hasten the conflagration—the fire next time and all that . . ."

"Two-thirds of all Americans actually believe there's going to *be* a Second Coming. I heard it on PBS," said Rachel.

"Stop it, you two!" said Shoshanna, who'd poured more gravy on her stuffing than she'd meant to. "We're not talking about the apocalypse now, we're talking about Dad on December 31. With or without Y2K, the shul's centennial happens to fall on *that* Friday night and they're not going to substitute champagne for kiddush or "Auld Lang Syne" for "L'cha Dodi." They're going to have a regular Shabbat service and they're going to give our father a plaque, and if he decides to come to New York to receive it, I, for one, am going to be there."

A chorus of "Me, too's" rang out, even from Tamara, though not from Rachel or Leah.

"What's the problem, Rache? asked Shoshanna.

"Sorry. Wasn't listening. I'm a little strung out. Thanksgiving seems to have inspired my ex-husband to act like a turkey."

"Mother!" said Simon. "You promised!"

"No dirty linen, Simon, it's just that I found out yesterday your father wants the house. He's not going to live here, but he wants it anyway. I think I took it quite well under the circumstances. Managed to truss the bird and make the cornbread before repairing to my bed with a Valium."

"Mo-*ther!*"

"Just kidding about the Valium. Believe it or not, I'm happier than I've been in years." (Her sisters believed her; her children didn't want to.) "The few times your father deigned to honor us with his presence, he wasn't exactly a life-enhancing force at the dinner table. Usually had his cell phone in one hand and a double Dewar's in the other, and when he wasn't complaining about you kids or asking me to bone his fish, he sat there looking like the storm cloud everyone tries to ignore on a sunny day."

"We know, Mom," said Tamara, sounding both sympathetic and annoyed. "But let's not go there now, okay?"

Rachel arranged the vegetables on her plate—pea, onion, pea, onion, pea. A person could go crazy thinking about lost time and wasted years. She squashed a pea with the back of her fork. "Okey-dokey, where were we?"

351

"Sam's testimonial," said Daniel. "We're waiting to hear if you'll come."

"Of course I'll come," replied Rachel. "If Nelly and Ezra will put me up for the night." Shoshanna's daughter and son-in-law lived on Riverside Drive in the West Eighties; Rodeph Tzedek was on West End Avenue; Rachel could walk to shul from there.

"Sure, if you don't mind sleeping on the couch," said Nelly.

In the twang of the Motel 6 commercial, Ezra warbled, "We'll leave the light on for ya."

"I'll drive into town first thing Friday morning. Everyone's predicting the roads will be jammed. Don't want to get caught watching the sun go down from the middle of the Triborough Bridge."

Shoshanna thought about the logistics required by Rachel's Sabbath observance—having to know the precise minute when the sun sets at this latitude on the globe so she could do her chores and get where she's going before the witching hour; having to shop, cook, finish her workday, and race like a *Beat the Clock* contestant before she could reach that condition of perfect peace that made the frenzy worth the effort. Sam did the same. His February letter had said he'd be flying on Wednesday, December 29, so he got to New York before the Sabbath. On Thursday, the thirtieth, he was sure there'd be a mass exodus at Ben Gurion Airport, everyone wanting to get out at once, and Friday, of course, El Al didn't fly in the afternoon. (Here his letter digressed to explain that Israel's national airline had to ground itself on Fridays because the ultrareligious political parties effectively control Israel's commercial life and no pilot was going to tell the black hats exactly when the sun sets during a twelve-hour flight across seven time zones.)

Compared to an observant Jew's necessary fixation on time, Shoshanna began to see herself as laid-back. "I'll pick him up at JFK," she said. "Wednesday and Thursday he can stay in the Village with us; on Friday, we'll run him up to Cantor Levy's." The cantor was a widower with a two-bedroom apartment on the Upper West Side, also within walking distance of the shul. The two men hadn't seen each other since Sam made aliyah, but they'd shared Rodeph Tzedek's pulpit for years.

"I don't get why Sam moved to Israel in the first place," mused Roy. A month ago, he and Simon had celebrated their commitment ceremony—another personal holy date—and Rachel had given them her blessing. As an official member of the family, he felt entitled to ask.

"For heaven's sake, what better place for a rabbi to end his days than in Jerusalem?" Rachel helped herself to more sweet potatoes.

"I'm with Roy," said Shoshanna. "In New York, Daddy was a VIP. Over there he's just another rabbi, a Conservative rabbi, yet. The Orthodox don't even recognize his authority."

"Thirty-six percent of world Jewry live in Israel today," offered Rachel. "All of them can't be Orthodox. They *need* a rabbi like Dad."

"I'm not happy with a third of us being in one place," said Leah, who'd begun to pay closer attention to Rachel's factoids. "We're too tempting a target."

Simon brought the subject back to New Year's Eve. "What about you, Leah?"

"What *about* me?"

"Are you taking Grandpa up on his invitation?"

She astonished everyone when she shrugged and said, "Sure."

Shoshanna had one of her ping-pong reactions. Thrilled at first, then immediately apprehensive. The last time Sam had been in New York, Leah had shown up at his birthday party, then picked a fight with Rachel in her own house and spoiled everything. What if she were planning something similar for New Year's Eve?

"Why wouldn't I go? Haven't been to shul in thirty-five years. It'll be like cultural anthropology." The truth was, Sam's P.S. had piqued her interest.

"Great!" exclaimed Daniel before anyone could say something to change her mind. "Why don't you stay at our place Thursday night? We'll go to shul together on Friday. The city's closing down two square miles of midtown; it's bound to be a zoo."

"No, thanks. Sam'll still be there Thursday."

"So what?" said Shoshanna. "You'll see him at services; what's the difference if you see him the night before?"

"At services, I don't have to pass him on my way to the john."

"The man's nearly ninety. Isn't it time to give it up?"

"No, Shoshanna, it *isn't*," thundered Leah in her brook-no-backtalk voice. She leaned forward in her chair. "Hey, Roy, throw me a piece of bread. And pass the butter."

"There is no *butter*," said Rachel. "I don't mix meat and dairy, remember?"

"Oh, right. You learned that from our Father who art in Jerusalem, hallowèd be his name. Wasn't it something about not bathing a lamb in his mother's milk—or was it his daughter's blood?"

Embarrassed silence. Awkward kibitzing. Transparent discomfort with the lack of a real subject. Wassermans preferred their conversation to be about *subjects*. Shoshanna was noticing this, she realized, without rushing in to fix it. At the Seder, she'd been monitoring her control panel for fear her sister might malfunction. At her birthday dinner, she'd been fighting an internal meltdown. But tonight, she was simply enjoying the banana yams and her family's quirky company.

"Everybody! I have an announcement," Rachel's voice seemed uncannily powerful. "It's a pretty big thing and it's going to surprise you, and some of you might think it's a bad idea, but I hope you'll keep an open mind about it." Everyone turned toward her. She paused. Maybe that was the wrong way to begin. Too dramatic. Didn't have to telegraph the punch. Could have made a simple statement, the way she'd announce she was buying a poodle or changing her HMO.

"What sort of announcement?"

"We interrupt this program with a special bulletin . . ."

"Out with it."

"So?"

Rachel felt her confidence ebbing.

Old leather lungs came to her aid. "Pipe down and let the woman talk!"

Moved by Leah's intervention, Rachel decided to change course. She hooked her hair behind her ears as if tucking curtains in their tiebacks and said, "Before I share my news, I want to say something about Leah and me. Our relationship."

Leah cocked her head like a birder. Though the evening in D.C. had been a breakthrough and they'd talked on the phone a couple of times since, Leah considered the progress of their relationship tenuous and couldn't for the life of her imagine what Rachel was going to say. Neither could anyone else. The chunk of white meat in Shoshanna's mouth went down whole. She knew her sisters had run into each other in Washington, but neither had said much about the encounter and she hadn't pressed. Now she watched Rachel carefully fold her napkin in quarters and eighths, and remembered their mother doing exactly that with a wet washcloth years ago in Maine, folding it in that abstracted way that women fold laundry while thinking about the disappointments of their lives. Daniel leaned forward on his elbows. Tamara moved Max to her other breast. The others, though bewildered, sensed that something important was happening, so much so that Nelly hustled the twins into the den and put on a video so she and Ezra could concentrate without distraction.

"I want to talk about us, Leah, because today is Thanksgiving and our new relationship is one of the things I'm most grateful for this year."

"Well, thank you, Rachel; that's very nice." Leah sounded to herself like the woman in the flowered dress who stands at the church door accepting covered dishes for the potluck. "But maybe everyone else is less interested in our ups and downs than we are." She didn't mean to throw thumbtacks under her stepsister's tires, but she also didn't think she needed to hear what was coming.

Rachel was undeterred. "I want everyone to know we've reconnected after all these years. How happy I am about it. And I want to say it in my own way, if that's okay with you."

"Be my guest," said Leah. She realized she had nothing to fear but Rachel's humiliation. That she'd grown to like her stepsister didn't mean she had to protect her.

"My rabbi asked me to chant the Torah portion at services next Shabbat," Rachel began. (Leah wondered if this was a tangent or the main narrative.) "It's a big honor and I wanted to do a good job, so I started to prepare my cantilation several days ago, and when I looked up the portion—Genesis 33—I couldn't believe it. I felt God was sending me a message."

If there *was* a God, why would she take the time to concoct an epistolary riddle for Rachel was beyond Leah, but she said nothing.

Rachel unfolded the napkin and blotted her lips. "Genesis 33 is Jacob and Esau's reconciliation scene. The parallels between the two brothers and the two of us aren't exact, of course, but there are common themes. Jacob stole Esau's birthright and I stole yours. Not purposely, but I did end up replacing you in your father's house, if not in his heart, and I flourished because of it."

The only sound in the room was Maxie's suckling.

"After living apart for many years, Jacob sent his messengers to Esau, hoping to gain his favor and forgiveness. Esau told them he would meet Jacob halfway and he would have four hundred men with him. Jacob was terrified that his brother meant to harm him in retaliation for the past—as I have feared your retaliation, Leah. So he selected more than four hundred animals from his flocks and herds as a gift for Esau."

Leah shifted in her seat. "Now that you mention it, there were only 399. A sheep was missing," she said with her crookedest grin. "And the goats were long of tooth and short of milk."

Rachel allowed herself a smile, but forged ahead. "The night before they were to meet, Jacob had that famous dream where he wrestles with the angel, as I've wrestled with my conscience about having benefited from your misfortunes. Ironically, the Bible tells us, the angel wrenched Jacob's hip at its socket, and from then on, Jacob walked with a limp."

"I didn't have *enough* misfortunes? You had to give me your limp?" Leah sounded like Jackie Mason, but she was buying into the allegory.

"That brings me to the actual reunion. Jacob bowed low seven times as he approached his brother . . ." Rachel, watching Leah's expression, interrupted herself mid-sentence, closed her eyes, and raised her eyebrows dramatically. "I know, I know—I owe you seven curtsies."

Leah said, "Forget the curtsies. Sacrifice a ram and we'll call it even."

They were toying with each other as they'd done in Washington. Shoshanna felt excluded but relieved. Leah had brought out something she'd rarely seen in Rachel—whimsy.

"Rams make a mess. Besides, I've already sacrificed a turkey," Rachel said, holding up a half-eaten wing. "Now let me finish. Jacob bowed low. Esau ran to greet him. They embraced and kissed and they wept together."

"Weeping's not my thing," quipped Leah. "But maybe I could manage a little peck."

"Jacob pressed his gifts on Esau, but Esau refused them, insisting he had enough possessions."

"Hold it! Misquote! I never said that."

Shoshanna could see that Rachel was torn between rolling with the banter and giving vent to her deeper feelings. "Jacob insisted Esau accept his offerings because, he said, 'to see your face is like seeing the face of God, and you have received me favorably.'" Rachel sighed. "As you have received me, Leah."

Leah shrugged. "My God-face gets them every time."

"After Esau accepted Jacob's gifts, the brothers went their separate ways. If it were up to me, they'd have started fresh from there, but we can't change other people's endings, only our own. What's important, I think, is Esau's generosity, his willingness to forgive his brother, and the beauty of their reconciliation. You've been gracious in accepting my apology after all these years and I just wanted to say thank you." Rachel fingered her pearls.

There was a round of applause.

"Aw, pshaw," said Leah, feigning bashfulness. "Now, where do I find that cockamamie angel? I have a hipbone to pick with him."

Leah's irreverence, which often grated on Shoshanna, this time saved the day. Her humor had neutralized Rachel's intensity. It had also allowed Shoshanna to understand how her sisters might once have been friends.

"Okay, everyone," said Rachel. "Go hang out in the living room while I organize dessert. Simon's taking coffee orders. And don't anyone touch these dishes. I may not get the house but I get the housekeeper, and she's working tomorrow."

Simon kissed his mother, then dutifully called out, "Regular? Decaf? Hemlock? Who wants tea?"

Shoshanna wished they didn't have to leave the table. Tables were magical places, islands of transformation where small talk and politesse so often mushroomed into revelation. Who first discovered the table's marvelous effect on human interaction? she wondered. A couple of cave dwellers probably plopped a slab onto four piles of rocks, summoned the family to supper, and noticed in the middle of their behemoth stew how much easier it was to talk and eat when they had something to lean on. The important tables of Shoshanna's life appeared to her like four-legged friends carrying precious memories on their backs. The dining-room table at West End Avenue. The red-white-and-blue birthday party tables that helped persuade her she was a special little girl and, now, a well-loved fifty-year-old. The college cafeteria tables where she'd learned to argue. The table in the coffee shop where she and Daniel mainlined caffeine and fell in love. The outdoor table where he proposed. Lunch tables hammered by Leah's fists. Uncountable kitchen tables where the women in her life drank tea and steeped themselves in one another's lives. A lifetime of Seder tables and Thanksgiving tables, especially this one. She hated getting up from Rachel's dining table and missing out on whatever else might have transpired there had they stayed.

Coffee tables never had the same effect. In the living room, Shoshanna settled Max on the rug with a toy, hoping that eight months of vacuuming had sucked up every last speck of broken glass. Roy put on a CD—Ella Fitzgerald—though not loud enough to drown them out as he and Tamara, both avid skiers, compared notes on moguls. Nelly and Ezra, who'd reclaimed the twins from the den, snuggled with them on the couch, reading *Curious George*. Leah looked through Rachel's book-shelves, thumbing a Dumas novel, a biography of Colette, a volume of Steinsaltz's Talmud. Shoshanna wondered what she was thinking.

Cups and saucers and the carafe that would forever be associated with crashing mirrors were loaded on Simon's tray. Rachel followed behind him with her homemade pies—apple, pumpkin, pecan. "Who wants what?" she asked.

"None for me," moaned Tamara. "I'm still trying to get my body back."

"I know a great diet," said Nelly. "You can eat anything you want, but you have to eat it with naked fat people."

Tamara sighed. "My obstetrician told me, Thou shalt not weigh more than thy refrigerator, but I didn't listen."

Rachel offered her latest factoid, gleaned, of all places, from an issue of *Men's Health* she'd read on the checkout line: "The average American woman weighs 144 pounds and wears a size 12 or 14. That means three billion women on the planet don't look like supermodels, and only eight do. So tell me why you young people are so obsessed with your bodies."

"Look who's talking, Muscle Mom." Tamara grabbed her leftover tummy fat and turned to look at herself in Rachel's mirrors. "Hey, half your collection is gone. What happened?"

"Got tired of it," said her mother.

Tamara threw her a quizzical glance.

Coffee, a fire, music, children—Rachel felt the house had come out of a coma. But she couldn't remember the last time she'd felt the slightest interest in her collections. She had something better to do now, and with her loved ones gathered around, she was ready to tell them what it was.

"I have an announcement."

"Another one?" cried Nelly.

"Forty-two percent of Latvian-Americans hate guacamole," mimicked Leah.

Rachel rolled up the sleeves of her lime silk blouse. The room felt stuffy and close. She walked to a window and pushed it open. Evening had begun its slow crawl across the November sky. The air whispered winter. She took a deep breath, turned back toward her family, and said, "I've decided to go back to school."

The few remaining clocks in the room ticked audibly.

"Great, Mom," said Simon, not sure the bulletin was worthy of its introduction.

"Why would you want to do a thing like *that*?!" asked Tamara.

Shoshanna moved toward the window to catch the breeze. "What school?" she asked. "When?" She'd thought she was privy to everything in Rachel's life.

"Jewish Theological Seminary. Spring semester. I've been accepted to the rabbinical program."

Only the children continued moving normally; everyone else froze. Rachel imagined them trying to imagine her on the bimah. Counseling. Sermonizing. Raising her robed arms in the priestly blessing. She didn't care what they were thinking; her decision had nothing to do with them. It wasn't a reaction to her childhood or her husband. Finally, she could say without equivocation, she was doing what *she* wanted.

Daniel spoke first. "Mazel tov! What great news!" He crossed the room to embrace her. Dear Daniel. He'd always been in her corner.

"Yo, Rebbe Rachel!" said Roy, tossing an arm around Simon. "When you're ordained, would you marry us!"

Tamara, pretending to look grief-stricken, asked, "Can rabbis babysit?"

Shoshanna struggled past the lump in her throat, past her sense of having been left out, and said what was in her heart: "It's the perfect thing, Rachel. It's what you were meant to do."

"*Excuse* me," the raspy voice of reason weighed in. "Has it occurred to anyone that by the time she graduates, our esteemed sister will be sixty-seven years old and not what the average synagogue might call a compelling candidate?"

"Cut it out!" bristled Shoshanna. (Good grief! Had she actually told Leah to shut up?)

"It's okay, Shoshie; Leah's right." Rachel thrust her hands deep in the pockets of her flannel trousers. "There's a wonderful Yiddish saying: 'If you go to shul for ninety years, you'll be an old man.' Well, if I go to JTS for three years—or if I don't—I'll be an old woman. May as well be a rabbi at sixty-seven as a depressed divorcée with a needlepoint business. The pulpit doesn't interest me, anyway. I remember the toll it took on Dad. A rabbi needs stamina to hand-hold those macher trustees with their outsized egos. I might go into pastoral counseling. Teaching.

Maybe run a Jewish welfare agency. We'll see when the time comes. The point is, I'm going to be doing what I love and if I'm lucky enough to inherit Dad's longevity"—she grinned—"I might be able to do it for twenty years."

No one yearned to believe in fresh starts more than Shoshanna, but as she listened to Rachel, it dawned on her that her transmission lacked whatever gear put her sisters in overdrive. She would never change in the big ways; sharp turns and floored accelerators weren't her style. Much as she admired Rachel's spiritual zeal and Leah's political passion, Shoshanna's challenge was simply to accept that the woman she was, was the woman she would likely remain—intrepid, cautious, decent, and fundamentally content with her lot. She threw her arms around her sister. "Wait till Daddy finds out. He'll die happy when he hears one of his kids is following in his footsteps."

"Some kid," muttered Leah. Esau had forgiven Jacob, but not Isaac or the God who had let this happen. A one-night stand in a kittel had turned into a lifetime calling, the birth of a rabbinic dynasty, and though Leah knew Rachel was doing this out of a profound commitment, and not to fuck her over, the mere thought of the pleasure Rachel was about to give their father filled Leah with bitterness. At eighty-nine, Sam finally had an heir.

"He's gonna kvell," she said to Rachel, and without realizing how peculiar the gesture, Leah stuck out her paw and shook her sister's hand.

nineteen

LEAH WAS HOPING to grab a seat in the far corner of the sanctuary where a person could hear without being seen, but it was impossible to ignore Shoshanna insistently waving her forward to the front section roped off for the honorees' families. Damn! That close, Sam could eyeball her from the bimah, the last thing she wanted. She'd come to Rodeph Tzedek out of curiosity and a residual intellectual interest in his sermons, not to pay tribute. That he might have the satisfaction of seeing her there loomed as a major piss-off. Then again, her refusal to sit in the first row with her sisters and the gantza mishpocha would cause a big tzimmes and call attention to her anyway. So she shambled down the aisle and accepted the proffered seat, and the hugs and kisses she was beginning to get used to.

Hunkered down in her red shawl, she surveyed the sanctuary she hadn't laid eyes on in more than three decades. She'd taken the wrap as protection against the chill, but now its crimson seemed too Christmasy and shrill in contrast to the altar cloth, which wore its age with more dignity than Leah wore hers. Though its folds were threadbare, the velvet fabric cloaked the huge lectern like an elegant old bedspread, its nap, polished by a half century of sweaty palms, having assumed the patina of antique satin. The altar cloth's royal-blue color had faded to pewter, but the Magen David emblazoned on the side facing the congregation remained bright. Originally, Leah remembered, the Jewish star was mustard yellow. Until Esther pronounced it "depressing as rancid butter" and instructed Sam to bring the cloth home, where she'd embroidered over the six-pointed star with a heavy gold thread that, even now, shone like the braid on an officer's epaulets.

The last time Leah was here, she'd been in her twenties, camping at the Wassermans', and despite being a Secular Humanist Feminist Pagan, she'd gone to shul most Friday nights just to keep Shoshanna company. Esther, who lived in constant fear that the family secret would be exposed, and who probably considered Leah a ticking bomb, nonetheless always invited her to services; she was too nice not to. But once in the synagogue, she went through contortions to avoid having to introduce Leah to anyone, busied herself slicing hallah or pouring wine into paper cups at the Oneg Shabbat, or hightailed it home right after the last bar of "Yigdal." Finally, during Leah's fourth appearance at shul, when this stranger with the vaguely familiar face could no longer be finessed, Esther introduced her as "a cousin from Cleveland." *No! I'm his abandonded child from his secret first marriage!* Leah wanted to scream. But much as she'd have relished blowing Sam's cover, she couldn't bring herself to hurt Esther, who was clearly caught between a rock and a rabbi.

Now, more than thirty-five years later, she was amazed to find the Byzantine sanctuary deeply familiar to her: the Holy Ark, richly carved and gilded—one portal with the Lion of Judah, the other with the Psalmist's lyre. The Mizrach on the eastern wall, a hand-painted frieze of palm fronds, grapes, and flowers. The sculpted tablets of the law, surrounded by doves and surmounted by a crown. Twin bronze candelabra flanking the bimah, each tall as a tree. Along the side walls of the huge sanctuary, the arched windows with their brilliant biblical portraits in stained glass were darkened now by the night beyond. In the back, on the memorial wall, row after row of new nameplates had been added since she was last here, each punctuated by a tiny bulb to be illuminated on the person's yahrzeit date.

For all her criticism of Judaism's patriarchal bias, she had to admire the genius of its traditions. Remembering the dead so concretely gave each life a symbolic permanence. The plaques, like tiny gravestones, individualized human loss while affirming Jewish continuity, the implication being that on each person's yahrzeit date, other Jews would always care enough to light his or her bulb. As it is said, Those who live on in the minds of others never die. Leah believed that. How else to explain the fictional characters so vivid in her thoughts since childhood? To be remembered is to have mattered. Memory is the only immortality.

It took Leah some time to locate the name: "Esther Frank Wasserman. March 25, 1911–May 12, 1965."

A vision of Esther in the window seat with her embroidery on her lap had sewed itself into Leah's memory long ago. Now that image had a captioned platitude: *Like Mother like Daughter*, a comment, no doubt, on Rachel's having inherited her mother's needle skills. But add a question mark and it became a comment on Leah's anxiety about Dena's ultimate stamp on *her*. Leah had always suspected Sam of harboring a similar apprehension—that she might turn out to be as crazy as her mother—and wondered if he had abandoned her shortly after Shoshanna was born just to play it safe. God forbid his precious baby should fall under the spell of the wacky, wicked stepsister, who must have confirmed his fears when she showed up after fifteen years, a raging feminist—strident, militant, and raring for a fight. Like mother like daughter. She considered which of her many aptitudes she'd have passed along to a daughter of her own, a thought that was pleasantly diverting and rife with possibilities, until she reminded herself that she'd not only made a mess of her sons' upbringing but once had the chance to influence the young Shoshanna and had botched that as well.

The memory of her failures scooped and hollowed her, a curettage of regret. Nothing lasted. Nothing and no one had turned out as she'd hoped; Leo, the boys, the movement, her health, her life, all had fallen short. Layers of pride and arrogance peeled like old paint. Even her public legacy was in doubt. In the countdown to the new millennium, in this hundred-year-old sanctuary where the names of the dead were illuminated however ordinary their lives, Leah questioned whether the women of the Second Wave would be remembered at all, or if the lessons of modern feminism would prove to be less transferable than a mother's sewing skills. She stared at the memorial wall and envied Judaism its memory. After 3,500 years, Jews still practiced Judaism, while women, after a measly thirty-five, were forgetting feminism. We made a strategic error, she thought acidly. We should have called the movement a religion or a craft. Then future generations wouldn't feel they had to wipe the slate clean and start over, but would carry on the work of their predecessors as Rachel had done, taking the needle and thread from Esther, the tallit and Torah from Sam.

As if summoned by the thought of her needlework, Rachel arrived in a relic from her former life, a silver fox coat that matched her hair. She squeezed in beside Leah, who pressed her good hip against Shoshanna's to make room for her. "Aren't we a crowd!" Rachel said, and began counting the family. There were thirteen locals—herself, the Safers, Leah, Nelly and Ezra, and the twins; Tamara, Seth, and Maxie; and Simon and Roy (who been introducing himself as "Sam's grandson-in-law")—plus three who'd come from afar: Shoshanna's Jake, home from college for winter break, and Rachel's other two daughters, Zelda, the Seattle computer wunderkind who left behind angry colleagues predicting Y2K chaos, and Dalia, visiting from London without her husband and kids, which doubtless explained why she'd allowed herself to sit among men in a Conservative shul. Though the award ceremony was the ostensible reason for the tribe to gather in New York, there was a silent acknowledgement among them all that everyone had come to see Sam for what would probably be the last time.

The congregation hummed a niggun as the retired rabbis took their places in three high-backed chairs lined up on one side of the ark. On the other side sat the current rabbi—handsome, clean-shaven, mid-forties, wearing a black robe and a satin yarmulke; the cantor, a dark-haired woman in an embroidered Moroccan-style yarmulke, her long skirt and sleek boots peeking out beneath her robe; and the president of the shul, a pantsuited woman whose yarmulke had her name knitted into it in Hebrew: *Sarah.*

"See," Tamara whispered to Leah with a nod toward the bimah. "We've come a long way, baby."

"A long way, *maybe*," said Leah. "Women are still rare enough to notice, and the men up there still outnumber them two to one." She gave a snort of disapproval, upset that the younger generation could be satisfied with half measures, that they weren't taking up the cudgels. Thanks for the memories, they seemed to be saying, but all that marching and shouting, all those angry slogans and hippie clothes are passé or irrelevant. Everything's been solved, hasn't it? Eventually, Leah was sure, they would have to rediscover marching and shouting and create angry slogans of their own. It happened in forty-year cycles. Because they didn't listen, the next group would have to reinvent the wheel and build a movement from scratch, and then they would ask, as she was asking now, Why don't we ever learn? Why can't anything last? While mourning the willful amnesia of women, she realized that she was the wrong person to champion endurance. Nothing important in her life had lasted, even Leo, though his doctors said he was making progress and kept promising he'd be home soon. Now it was "maybe April," but Leah had begun to suspect it was maybe not. At century's end, all she had left was herself, a survivor like this synagogue. The difference was, she'd changed, while Rodeph Tzedek had stayed the same—same bimah, same altar cloth, same railing she'd stared at thirty-five years ago. It was an ironic paradox that, because they were unchanged, well-preserved artifacts could be reassuring in a transitory world; but they could also open old wounds. What Leah remembered most about this sacred space was being introduced here as a . . . Unwittingly, she spoke the words aloud, "a cousin from Cleveland."

"Shhhh!" hissed Rachel. "They're starting!"

The lamp hanging over the ark—the Eternal Light—always set off a song in Shoshanna's head and did so again tonight: "This little light of mine / I'm gonna let it shine." She'd survived her father's long services—four hours on an average Saturday morning—by losing herself in the sacredly meaningful Light, imagining patterns in its amber glass, counting the links in its three long chains, worrying that it might go out. That possibility had obsessed her for years, until Esther explained that the lamp's glow came not from a heavenly source but from an ordinary 60-watt bulb, replaced once a week by the maintenance crew.

Shoshanna could not fathom why the framers of the faith would make something as evanescent as a lightbulb, or in earlier times an oil lamp, the symbol of divine permanence. Rather than representing God's commitment to humanity, the Eternal Light seemed more appropriate as a symbol of humanity's commitment to God. Wasn't that why Jews were always kindling candles? White ones for Shabbat, the thick havdalah candle, the twenty-four-hour yahrzeit candle, multicolored skinny candles for Hanukkah. Light as spirit. Solace. Meaning. We're supposed to light candles to mark the transition from ordinary to sacred time, or to remember those who are no longer with us. But in fact, Shoshanna decided, human beings kindle light to imitate God. In the beginning, God said, "Let there be light!" And the chaos was swept away. Creation epitomized the imposition of order in a sequence deemed proper by God. Day One, light; Day Six, man and woman. The point was that God turned on the lights *before* we entered the room, knowing we could not function in darkness, and ever since, humanity (especially Shoshanna) had been trying to duplicate, in the fires of earthly invention, that divine act of beating back chaos with light. Not for nothing would a huge crystal ball descend in Times Square later tonight. Creation 2000: Happy New Year! Century! Millennium! Let there be light!

But the Eternal Light wasn't a flash in the pandemonium. It was always illuminated, in every synagogue in the world, except when enemies snuffed it out—and once, at Congregation Rodeph Tzedek, when Shoshanna broke it. The day after her mother died, she stormed the empty sanctuary, threw a prayer book at the hanging lamp, and, not content to crack its panels, struck it again and again until the glass came crashing down and only its metal casing was left swinging on its three long chains. Shoshanna was a teenager then. Rachel was a grown woman when she brought down the wall of mirrors. Both had been protesting the dying of the light.

The sight of her wizened father on the bimah reawakened

Shoshanna's eternal anxieties at a higher wattage. Sam's light would go out one of these days and she would have to make do with a yahrzeit candle. There, she was doing it again—thinking bad thoughts in the midst of a happy event, as if she could beat the Evil Eye to the punch. The Eye hadn't been around much lately, but she knew it would be back, would stalk her whenever pleasure mounted, business boomed, or her sisters took another step toward strength. And one of these days, it would prevail. Evil persists because it is so much more powerful than good, so much more patient and desperate and driven. No lover loves with the intensity that a hater hates. No act of kindness has ever been unleashed with the force and fervor of an act of cruelty. The Eye would wait it out, as much a captive of its character as Shoshanna was of hers. No matter how sweet her life might be, she would always feel the pall and sense that her tragedy was yet to come. That was the deal. Anxiety as the price of joy. Chaos coiled in wait. Happiness tempered by vigilance, love by fear of loss. God's trade-off. Take it or leave it.

She took it.

From the moment the service began, Rachel was lost in the liturgy, every chant as comforting and predictable as the beat of her pulse. Her life had been drastically altered, but the Hebrew prayers were the same and she knew them all; these psalms that she'd once thought belonged only to men like her father, they were her psalms, too. Rachel's kavannah was deep as it comes, but no amount of prayerful intentionality could have blotted out the flurry of activity on her left: Leah madly riffling through the siddur, reading things out of order, like someone diving into the middle of a novel, then jumping from the last chapter to the first. While the congregation sang "L'cha Dodi," Leah hopscotched from Hallel to Mincha to Shacharit, until she found on page 8 what she'd been looking for all along—the sentence she was now stabbing at with a be-ringed finger: *Blessed are thou O Lord our God, King of the universe, who has not created me a woman.*

"*Shehlo asani isha!* It's *still* here!" she whispered to Shoshanna, nearly levitating.

Since Rachel couldn't trust Shoshanna to defend Judaism, she plunged in, though people who talk during services were among her pet peeves. "These are *old* prayer books, Leah," she whispered. "The newer ones don't have this blessing. And even when it's in the text, most men don't say it. They thank God for creating them 'according to God's will,' the same prayer women say."

Leah, master of the instant rebuttal, was silenced by a glorious disturbance in the air, a fragrance of dizzying power and beauty. While stretching the crescent of her neck to propel her whisper, Rachel had exuded emanations of Joy, a scent so utterly, evocatively Esther's that one could only conclude she had worn the perfume to bring her mother into their midst. Leah closed her eyes. To hell with sexist blessings. She pulled her shawl around her and breathed in.

After the closing hymn, President Sarah straightened her knitted yarmulke and pulled a plaque from behind her chair. The first rabbi to receive the award was a pleasant-looking man who gave what Leah considered a lackluster, though mercifully short, acceptance speech. The second honoree, slightly older, with thick glasses and slurred consonants (perhaps the result of a stroke), spoke even more briefly. The president of the shul then called Rabbi Wasserman to the lectern and bestowed his award with appropriate superlatives. Left alone in the pulpit, Sam looked shrunken, his face like a gnome's topped by a white satin yarmulke and bottomed by a beard of white floss. His once imposing stature seemed compacted, as if he'd been hammered into the earth. The voice, however, was, as always, deep as a prophet's.

"Dear friends," he began. "A man pushing ninety doesn't sit in a plane for twelve hours with his knees to his chest unless there's a very good reason. This award is a very good reason. In fact, it's worth at least double the suffering, and I'll get to serve the other twelve hours next week on my return trip to Jerusalem." Like any seasoned public speaker, he acknowledged the congregation's titters by smiling up at the balcony and out to the back of the house as well as to the front rows, where his family—all except Leah—beamed back at him.

"Accepting this plaque, I join the ranks of such venerable prior honorees as Martin Luther King and Golda Meir. That means I must be famous. And as someone once said, the best thing about being famous is that when you bore people they think it's their fault."

Furtively he glanced at Leah. Their eyes met for a split second and quickly darted off, his to the balcony, hers to the darkness of closed lids. She inclined in the direction of her sister Rachel and breathed in Joy. He reached under the podium for a glass of water, then wiped his beard with the white handkerchief he kept, as always, with its four points up in the outside breast pocket of his jacket.

"I've been asked to speak about anything that's on my mind, and I hope you'll forgive me if, like a billion other people around the globe, what's on my mind tonight is New Year's Eve."

Shoshanna leaned across Leah's rounded bosom and sent Rachel a smirk that said, See!

"But before I go any further, I have a question for you, and since we're in shul, you have to tell the truth. How many of you believe in miracles?" Ten or twelve people tentatively raised their hands.

"Brave souls," he said. "Now, how many of you believe it's a miracle that the Jewish people has survived until the twenty-first century?"

Every hand flew up and the laughter rose like floodwaters.

"I meant this not to trick you but to prove that there's a Jewish way to think about everything. Though we are a small minority of the population in every country but Israel, we know how to sustain Jewish life while accommodating to the dominant culture. In that same sense, we needn't be afraid to acknowledge tonight's secular celebrations. We need only find a Jewish way to think about them.

"Preparing for this evening's talk, I consulted several Judaic sources to learn what might connect us Jewishly with New Year's Eve. And believe it or not, the answer is *midnight*."

Clever, thought Leah. She always admired a strong lead.

I'll never know how to do this, thought Rachel, trying to imagine her first sermon.

That'll show her, thought Shoshanna, remembering Rachel's disdain for New Year's Eve.

"Most Jews don't think of midnight as having any particular relevance to the Jewish view of time. For us, a day—an ordinary day, Shabbat, a holiday—begins and ends at sunset. Yet midnight occupies an important place in our tradition. What we often forget is, people in the ancient world went to bed at sunset, so when a text says someone rose *early*, it often means they rose at midnight. We're told that Abraham deployed against the four kings at midnight, the better to create confusion amid the sleeping enemy. God chose midnight on the fifteenth of the Hebrew month of Nissan to go forth among the Egyptians and inflict the tenth plague, and 3,500 years later, not only do we hold our Seder on the fifteenth of Nissan, but we must finish eating the ritual foods—matzoh, bitter herbs, the Passover offering, and the afikoman—before the clock strikes midnight, since that was when God broke the last manacle of our bondage. The Hebrews' status changed and Israel was born as a free people at midnight.

"But there's more: Samson gets up at midnight and pulls down the gateposts of Gaza. Ruth lies at the feet of Boaz at midnight, and when you realize that their union led to the birth of David, and the Messiah is to emerge from the Davidic line, it's clear that what happened in Boaz's bed was more than a romantic matter. Psalm 119 proclaims, 'I arise at midnight to praise You for Your just decrees.' The 'I' in this case is assumed to be David, also known as the Psalmist. A midrash in the Pesikta de Rav Kahana posits that David placed his harp at an open window so it would catch the midnight wind and awaken him to sing God's praises. That harp may have been the world's first alarm clock." (Sam paused while laughter skipped like lambs through the crowd—or so it seemed to Rachel, who'd been studying the Song of Songs.)

"At midnight on the Saturday before Rosh Hashanah—*our* New Year's Eve—we say selihot, the penitential service. On Shavuot, when we celebrate the giving of the Torah at Sinai, we look for a crack in the sky at midnight, because that's when the heavens are said to open to accept our prayers."

Leah, riveted to the railing in front of her, listened to Sam's disembodied words and thought, Cracks in the sky! Superstition! Bubbemeisehs! She marveled at what lasts.

"Since the singer Madonna became enamored of the Zohar, Jewish mysticism has attracted a number of celebrity admirers, so please forgive me if I count myself on the cutting edge for citing this thirteenth-century document as my main source this evening. It happens I agree with Gershom Scholem that 'Kabbalah is nonsense; but the *study* of Kabbalah is scholarship.'" (Murmurs from the cognoscenti.) "If you study the major work of Kabbalistic Judaism, the Zohar, you will find three reasons for designating midnight as the ideal time for the pious to awaken and study Torah: First, because human beings are thought to be more vulnerable at midnight, which makes our prayers more open and sincere. Second, because the midnight hour is said to exert a beneficent influence, both on those who study and on those in the upper worlds. And third, because most people are asleep at midnight and, presumably, God has less to do and can better concentrate on our entreaties. I'll admit that this theory falters on the fact that midnight in Israel is five in the afternoon in New York and God, like the rest of you, is probably stuck in traffic."

Shul was starting to feel like New Year's Eve in a comedy club, and Rachel could only assume Sam had planned it that way. He knew many people had come to services out of obligation—they'd much prefer to be partying—and he was rewarding them with entertainment. She'd forgotten what an ingratiating speaker her father was, how deftly he nudged his flock deeper into the thickets of Jewish theology. They were in his thrall now. By conditioning them to expect a laugh every few paragraphs, he'd commanded their attention. When her day came, Rachel resolved to do the same.

"What I want to leave you with tonight is a ritual meant specifically for the midnight hour. The Zohar describes it as a two-part ceremony, the first being lamentations commemorating the exile of the Shekhinah from the Holy Temple in Jerusalem; the second, a plea for her return. I needn't remind you that the Shekhinah embodies the female presence of God. Incidentally"—he gestured toward the cantor and president— "it hasn't escaped my notice that we have a strong female presence right here at Rodeph Tzedek."

Leah was not charmed, certain that beneath his benign wisecrack lay a malignant disregard for women's equality. In the seventies and eighties, Sam hadn't opposed the ordination of women or the counting of women in the minyan or the right of women to have an aliyah, but he hadn't actively advocated for these advances either. Given his prominence, he could have been a frontline asset. At best he was noncombatant, seemingly unconvinced that sexism was a sin or women's causes worth his time. That was yet another item on Leah's bill of particulars, her endless indictment.

Her sisters, on the other hand, felt nothing but loving admiration for their father. Shoshanna was wishing she could relive her childhood. Why hadn't she spent more time with him? Why hadn't she learned from him instead of mimicking Leah and battling him at every turn? Rachel, with an eye on her future career, was even more regretful. Had she apprenticed herself to Sam from the moment she became his daughter, he could have been her teacher and given her s'micha.

"Many texts, notably the Babylonian Talmud, assert that the Shekhinah travels with the Jewish people, even in exile. Gershom Scholem wrote: 'The exile of the Shekhinah is not a metaphor, it is a genuine symbol of the "broken" state of things in the realm of divine potentialities.'" Sam paused for emphasis. "The Kabbalists' midnight ritual is meant to realize those divine potentialities, to reunite the Shekhinah with God and bring about our ultimate redemption. The two-part ceremony has a name: Tikkun Hatsot. In Hebrew, *tikkun* means repair or mend, and *hatsot* is the word for midnight. As you well know, we Jews do our major repairs during the ten days between Rosh Hashanah and Yom Kippur; that's when we give strict account of our deeds and commit to mend our weaknesses. The gentiles do pretty much the same thing on December 31, only they call it a New Year's resolution, and they put it into effect at midnight. What I'm suggesting is, Tikkun Hatsot, with its dual emphasis on redemption *and* the midnight hour, is the perfect Jewish link to the secular New Year's Eve. Obviously, then, it is entirely appropriate for a Jew to respond in a special way to this special evening, the Shabbat that ushers in a new year, century, and millennium."

Obviously, thought Rachel, bursting with daughterly pride. While acknowledging what was on everyone's mind, Sam had woven a literate and commanding discourse that proved Jews had as much right to celebrate the midnight hour as anyone else.

Leah had been listening not as a daughter but as an intellectual who grudgingly appreciated the speaker's oratorical gifts. Which made the shock of Sam's next statement all the more stunning.

"According to the followers of Isaac Luria, the charismatic visionary who lived in Safed in the sixteenth century, Tikkun Hatsot's two parts are called Tikkun Rachel and Tikkun Leah. Rachel and Leah, of course, are the names of two of our four matriarchs. Remarkably enough, from my perspective, they're also the names of two of my three daughters."

Leah flinched. Her eyes flew up from the railing. *Three?* Had he said *three* daughters? What the fuck was he doing? She glimpsed him taking out the white handkerchief and wiping his forehead, then nailed her gaze back to the railing, dimly aware that her sisters, on either side of her, had each grasped one of her hands.

"Tikkun Rachel symbolizes the Shekhinah in exile, while Tikkun Leah addresses her redemption and consolation. These concepts are not anachronistic. Exile is a contemporary condition, and redemption and consolation are timeless yearnings." Looking down at the first row, Sam found Shoshanna's and Rachel's faces, upturned and luminous, but only the top of Leah's brown-gray head, her braid running down her back like a stripe. "So tonight, let me suggest that we do as our ancestors did in Safed. At the stroke of midnight, wherever we are, with whatever text our hearts dictate, let us take a moment to search for a crack in the sky and send up our prayers for the return of those who are in exile, consolation for those who suffer, and the redemption of our sad, sweet world.

"For now, dear friends, I thank you for giving me the opportunity to serve this congregation for more than thirty years and for honoring me tonight with this cherished award."

Three daughters. *Three.* Just a number: ordinary, unremarkable, except when it's joined to that particular noun and Sam Wasserman is the person speaking it from the pulpit. Then it's a revelation, the admission of a colossal lie. People who knew the rabbi from the old days knew him as the father of Rachel and Shoshanna, two daughters. But tonight, he had stood before an overflow crowd in a sacred space, before the Torah and whoever might be left of flock and friends, and obliquely confessed that his uncannily familiar guest of years ago, the young woman who'd attended synagogue with Esther and Shoshanna, was *not* a cousin from Cleveland but a daughter. His.

After Sam received his standing ovation, the congregation, including the Wasserman family, proceeded to the social hall for the Oneg Shabbat, everyone but the three daughters, who remained squashed together on the bench, still holding hands. When the sanctuary emptied out and they were alone beneath the domed ceiling, Rachel and Shoshanna released their grip and Leah collapsed onto her knees, only to feel her hunched-over body encircled by her sisters' arms, their kisses in her hair, and flooding through her body a disquieting vulnerability that she was beginning to understand was the correlate of love.

Shoshanna rubbed her back. "How does a piece of sponge cake sound?" she asked, indirectly approaching the question of Leah's next move.

"Tasteless."

Rachel grinned. "Are you up for the reception? Seeing Dad?"

Not if it meant she had to talk to him. She certainly wasn't going to knight him for admitting the truth. Besides, she'd want to know more, and three daughters was probably the best he could offer. She ought to go home now, while she at least had that. Yet the idea of spending midnight alone in the Shtarka-Barca was unthinkable.

"I don't think so," she answered. "Not yet."

Rachel rubbed her eyes. "Well, I've got to make a pit stop, anyway. My mascara's runny."

"Me, too," said Shoshanna. "Come on, Leah, you should wash your face."

In the women's room, Rachel and Shoshanna repaired their makeup. "Tikkun Maybelline," joked Leah, who had only to splash cold water on her eyes and repair from within.

"I hope there's some honey cake left," said Rachel. "I hate sponge."

Shoshanna linked her arm through Leah's and started for the social hall. "Maybe they'll have Ring Dings."

"You guys go ahead. I need a smoke."

Her sisters exchanged glances. "Okay," said Rachel. "But promise you won't leave?"

"Promise," said Leah, though she knew she might break it.

In deference to the Sabbath observers hanging around in front of the shul, she walked a couple of blocks away and lit up under a street-lamp. Why had she come in the first place? Did she think she was just going to sneak in, give a listen, and go home—eintz, tzvei, drei? The problem was, she didn't think. But now that she was outside and freezing her ass off, it seemed a good idea to keep going, head over to Central Park West and hop a train back to Brooklyn. A flashback to the weirdo on the platform slowed her down. But the idea of returning to Rodeph Tzedek was almost as unpleasant. Why subject herself to curious questions from a bunch of strangers, worse yet, their pity, or the agony of waiting for something more substantive from Sam and getting nothing? He probably thought all it took for Leah to send him back to Israel with a smile was some intellectual razzle-dazzle and a quickie acknowledgment of paternity. Well, he could take his "three daughters" and his phony "maideleh" and shove it.

West End Avenue, too, was virtually unchanged, its dowager apartment buildings having held out against those ubiquitous white brick eyesores that were all over town. Arched canopies still stretched from entry to curb. Uniformed doormen still stood guard as they had thirty-five years ago, when she'd strolled the avenue en route to shul, chatting with Esther and Shoshanna and ignoring Sam. If she didn't cave then, why do it now? She started walking toward the subway.

What *had* changed was her tolerance for the cold. Despite many layers and her woolen shawl, she shivered as she turned east into a block of brownstones. Their tall Victorian windows revealed scenes of domestic delight: a couple in a book-lined parlor, a crowded New Year's Eve party awash in helium balloons, a young family gathered around a

TV set tuned to the revelry in Times Square. Leah stopped in the middle of the block and stamped out the Gauloise beneath her shoe. How could she run out on her sisters? Amazingly, she seemed to matter to them. They cared about her. And she'd promised to come back. Two blocks from the green globes of the subway entrance, she turned and retraced her steps to Rodeph Tzedek.

Back in the building, she sought a warm radiator and some privacy before rejoining Rachel and Shoshanna in the social hall. The main floor was full of stragglers from the Oneg Shabbat, so she climbed the stairs, hoping to take refuge in one of the meeting rooms, all of which proved to be locked. Up another flight, the Hebrew school, dark but for an illuminated EXIT sign at either end of the corridor whose classroom doors were also locked, except the last—a kindergarten, just the place to brood on a life that had gone sour from the start. A radiator grill stretched the length of the windows but was stone cold. She stood with her back to it, as if at a dead hearth. In the blueshine of the streetlamps, she could make out tiny tables and chairs. Stunted easels. Lilliputian pots and pans and dishes. Midget cars and trucks. Shelves filled with Lego blocks and Lincoln Logs. Dainty dolls with staring eyes. Even the shadows were smaller than life. As a girl, she'd never known a room like this, a room dedicated to the cared-for child.

There was a yellow bean-bag chair near the toy shelves. Dena once had a similar pouf, bigger though, and barf green, and Leah remembered being curled up in it reading *Great Expectations* the night her mother announced she'd never see Sam again. Though she hadn't thought of this for years, she remembered picking and pulling at the bean bag's frayed seams until she'd torn a hole wide enough for its filling to escape. The pellets had poured out like grain from a silo, peas from a calabash. Furious, her mother demanded she pick up every gobbet with her fingers. No broom and dustpan. No scoop or vacuum. Just her fingers. That was how she'd spent her first night as a fatherless child, on her hands and knees harvesting plastic pellets.

This yellow bag, though pint-sized, was fully packed and surprisingly comfortable. Leaning back in it, Leah noticed a poster tacked to a bulletin board that listed children's names down one side in block letters (clearly a teacher's hand)—Jonathan, Stacy, Noah, Judy, Adam, Robert—and across the top, two columns headed: "If I were a fruit or vegetable, I would be a ———" and "If I were an animal, I would be a ———." All the blanks had been filled in. Noah would be a banana and a dinosaur. Stacy, a carrot and bunny. Adam, green bean/zebra. Judy, mango/lion. (Brava, Judy!) Leah wasn't sure if her vegetable should be an artichoke or a prickly pear, her animal an armadillo or a porcupine.

Mascara refreshed, Shoshanna and Rachel rushed to the social hall, where they found their father in the center of a knot of admirers. Rather than interrupt the adulation he was so clearly enjoying, they hung back and occupied themselves greeting the occasional familiar face, drinking kiddush wine from plastic cups, and eating cake, two slices each, honey and sponge. When Sam caught sight of them, his face brightened, then fell as he looked beyond them and saw no one else. "Where's Leah?"

"Outside, having a cigarette." Oops, thought Rachel, the minute she said it. Sam wouldn't approve of smoking on Shabbat, though he'd probably expect it of Leah.

"Are you sure she didn't leave?"

"She promised not to." Shoshanna was getting annoyed. He hadn't even given them the chance to congratulate him.

"I have to find her. She doesn't believe in promises."

"I'm sure she'll be back," said Rachel, grasping his sleeve.

He pulled away. The two women started after him.

"Please!" he said. "Stay here." They backed off and watched him hurry through the door.

He checked the front of the shul and the side alley where the Hebrew-school kids put up the succah every year. He searched all the rooms on the main floor. Unable to use the elevator on the Sabbath, he took to the stairs, slowly. On the second floor, he tried the library. Rabbi's study. Cantor's study. Small chapel. Meeting rooms. All locked, his memories stored within—of bar and bat mitzvah classes, prenuptial consultations, Men's Club and Sisterhood meetings. Of conversion classes, poetry readings, Israeli dance nights, Torah study groups, Jewish film festivals, the lifeblood of the synagogue he'd presided over for thirty years. But no Leah.

He began to doubt she was in the building, but climbed the last flight anyway. Breathless, he made his way along the Hebrew school's murky corridor, peering through the chicken-wired glass inset in each door. *Please let her be here,* he silently allowed himself, though he knew it a wasted prayer. Either she was or she wasn't; it was too late for wishing.

In the gloom of the last classroom, he made out the red swathe of her shawl. A bloodied angel, collapsed on a yellow bean-bag chair.

The clack of the latch startled Leah. Her father appeared in the doorway like a painting in a frame. "Just leaving," she stammered, and hoisted herself up.

"Maideleh, no!" His body blocked the door. "Listen to me."

"Heard you already."

"This you haven't heard."

"Gotta go. Downstairs. Shoshe. Rachel." Her timorousness was barely recognizable to her, though it bore a fleeting resemblance to the fear she'd felt with Leo, a fear of her own compassion. Where were her pronouns, her prepositions?

"Ten minutes, that's all I'm asking." He came toward her, an apparition, a slivery penumbra. His beard and his white satin yarmulke shone preternaturally in the azure air. Watching him stroke his beard as one might pet an old dog to calm its jitters, she realized he was more frightened than she. They hadn't been alone together since the mid-sixties, when she showed up at West End Avenue and he took her into his study and tried to welcome her back. That night, she'd stared at the floor. Now she wanted to look at him. Before she could listen, she needed to see his face.

"Turn on the lights," she said.

"I can't. It's Shabbos."

"I can." She made a move toward the wall switch.

He covered it with his hand. "You're not a Shabbos goy, you're a Jew."

"Never Jew enough for you."

Their eyes locked. With a frail hand, he gestured toward one of the small wooden chairs. "Sit," he whispered. "Please."

She sat, then felt too small, too low down; hemmed in by too many small objects. She folded her arms defiantly. Stooped as he was, he looked like a giant amid the diminutive furniture. He spoke quickly, as if time was running out.

"Last Yom Kippur, I took an accounting of my soul, a heshbon nefesh . . ."

(Another accountant. Rachel, and now Sam.)

". . . and I decided that if I was still alive at the turn of the year, I'd fly here for Rodeph's centennial, and while I was here, I would . . ." He coughed, reached for the white handkerchief, and blew his nose. ". . . tell you this . . . this terrible thing I've carried too long inside."

December in an unheated classroom, yet Leah was sweating. She shrugged off the shawl, letting it drape over the back of the little chair and onto the floor. Sam returned his handkerchief to its pocket, points up, then turned to the window, as if what he was about to say was unsuitable for a kindergarten classroom and had to be sent out into the night.

"Downstairs, I told the congregation I have three daughters. That's all they need to know, but not you, tateleh. You need to know everything."

The air bristled between them. Leah inhaled subatomic puffs, afraid the sound of her breathing might drown her father's voice. She looked at his still-broad back silhouetted against the light of the streetlamps outside. His shoulders hunched, then fell. Her hands were clammy and wanted something in him. A basket of dreidls on a shelf within reach. She ran her fingers through the dozens of tiny four-sided tops made of plastic, ceramic, metal, painted wood, even a lead dreidl, an antique from her era. She scooped up a handful and trickled them back in the basket. Their clatter drew her father's attention (hearing still sharp). Leah knew why he was frowning. Hanukkah had been over for weeks, yet the dreidls were still out, in full view of the children. Were Rabbi Wasserman still running the place, he'd have reprimanded the teacher in the words of Ecclesiastes:

"To every thing there is a season, and a time for every activity under heaven." A holiday must not spill beyond its time lest it lose its specialness, its place in God's plan. The time for dreidls was Hanukkah, not New Year's Eve. Sam used to scold Dena when she insisted on eating matzoh the day before Passover, or when she balked at dismantling the succah at the end of Succot, or kept humming "Avinu Malkeinu" weeks after Yom Kippur. "There's a time to keep and a time to throw away." When she answered, "Time-schmime," he'd growl, "A time for silence and a time for speech."

Tonight, it seemed, was a time for speech.

He approached the little table where Leah sat with her basket of dreidls and stood close by, looking down at her. "I want to tell you about your mother . . ."

"You can't tell me anything I don't know," she snapped. "I was there."

"You don't know why I left. Just let me talk."

She grabbed a carved wooden dreidl and fingered its letters: Nunn, gimmel, hei, shin—the Hebrew acronym for *A great miracle happened there*. There, not here. To the Maccabees, not the Wassermans. But now the miracle was Sam, standing before her, finally willing to explain. She would shut up and listen.

"You know your mother was unbalanced, but I doubt you remember what really sent her off her rails. It was Shoshanna. When she was born, Dena started smoking three packs a day. Chopped off all her hair." (The year of the crew cut. Her mother's shorn head had frightened her.) "I guess Shoshanna represented the permanence of my new family," he went on. "I'd moved on, but Dena's life had stalled. The conservatory rejected her. She had no concert bookings. The last straw was when you asked to spend the summer with me and my new family. Dena said I'd put you under a spell. I'd used my new baby and your old school pal to steal your affections, and she was going to steal you back."

Leah picked out another dreidl with the letter pai in the place of the shin. Pai for po: *A great miracle happened here*. An Israeli dreidl. She spun. It landed on the pai.

With the opalescent light behind him, Sam's eyes disappeared into their dark hollows, panda sockets in a lunar face. He bent down to smooth the red yarn hair of a Raggedy Ann doll propped in a miniature stroller. Might he be regretting the dolls he'd never given Leah, the childhood she'd been denied? Or was he thinking of his red-haired Shoshanna, the kid who'd been so easy to love? He was talking more slowly now—about Dena conniving to take Leah away from him, cutting short his visits, sabotaging him with the school. "I found ways around her, though, and we spent some wonderful weekends together, you and I. Remember?"

Leah had no lines in this scene. It was Sam's monologue and he would have to deliver it without the sounding board of her recriminations or the trampoline of her resistance. Still, with a list of grievances as long as her life, it took every bit of self-control to keep her tongue lashed down.

He sighed. "Well, *I* remember those weekends. We had great times. And I remember how they were stopped for good. It was 1950, April. The school sent out a notice that they'd be closed during July and August and your mother and I were arguing about where you would spend the summer. I wanted you for either month, but the *whole* month, not just weekends. Esther and I were moving to Manhattan that June. No more squeezing between the double-decker and the crib; our new place had a room for Shoshanna and a bigger one for you and Rachel. We'd bought you some nice twin beds. Pink beds." (By the time Leah made it to West End Avenue, Shoshanna was sleeping in a four-poster and the beds had been painted white.) "We wanted you for a month so you'd get used to the apartment and start feeling at home in the city. It's what *you* wanted that drove your mother crazy. You wanted to spend the whole summer with us. You asked Dena's permission, remember? That's when all hell broke loose."

Leah drilled the point of the Israeli dreidl into her flesh. He didn't know the half of it, how Dena had dragged her by her braid across the floor, cheek bleeding, the hair nearly ripped off her scalp.

Suddenly a coughing jag caved Sam's chest and sent him stumbling over a tyke bike. Pity for her father wasn't in Leah's repertoire, yet she rushed to the sink, pulled two Dixie cups from the dispenser, and filled them with water. She left her cup untouched on the table before her. He drained his in a single gulp, but the cough started up again. To steady himself, he planted his knuckles on the little table, a move that sent Leah's cup and the basket careening to the floor, the water splashing his wingtips. She scooped up the dreidls while he hurried to fetch a roll of paper towels and bent to wipe his shoes. His hand brushed her arm, a touch that scalded through her long-sleeved shirt; their first physical contact in fifty years and it was accidental, motivated by her father's fastidiousness. It made her wonder what he'd have been like to live with. Those four months when she'd stayed with the Wassermans in her twenties, he'd picked up after her with a silent grimace. But could he have survived the barnyard hygiene of her teen years? Beyond her sloppiness, could he have tolerated her politics—who she was and what mattered to her? Would he have helped her get an abortion back when it was illegal? Let her move in with her boyfriends? Approved of her books and essays? What would he make of her passion for Yiddish literature and Borscht Belt jokes? Her renegade Judaism, the church of cholent and chopped liver? Her criticism of Israeli policy?

Maybe it was just as well they'd split when she was twelve.

He sat in the tiny chair across from her and patted the tabletop to be sure it was dry before leaning his elbows on it. She noticed with a stab of regret that his widow's peak, that brooding black arrow, had thinned to a colorless wisp. "Your mother accused me of bribing you with the new apartment. But all I was offering was a normal life. To punish me," he reminded Leah, as if she hadn't lived through it, "she moved you to Boston and cut me off completely."

"How could you let her do that!?" Leah shouted, before she could stop herself. *"How could you let her get away with it?"* Though she hadn't meant to speak, that was, after all, the question she'd been asking her whole life.

He leaned closer to Leah across the table. Very softly, as if someone might be listening in the corridor, he said, "I let her get away with it because she threatened to go to the police, and the chairman of the board of this shul, and the head of the rabbinical association, and the editors of *The New York Times* and all the Jewish papers, and tell them I'd been . . . that I was . . ." He coughed into his handkerchief, then stuffed it back into his breast pocket without rearranging the points. ". . . molesting you. Sexually," he added. "She was going to tell everyone she'd found me in your bed. Doing terrible things."

Leah tried to read his face. It was cadaverous, his skin papery, the whites of his eyes webbed in red. She made a tear down one side of her empty Dixie cup, then another and another, the petals of a paper tulip.

"They were awful, horrible lies! But she could say whatever she liked. She had nothing to lose. I had everything to lose, and I lost. You, maideleh. *I lost you.*" He said he'd considered calling Dena's bluff. He would tough it out, explain everything to Esther, fight for custody no matter what it cost. Then he realized that even if he won, he would lose. No matter how vehemently he denied the charges, or if he was completely exonerated in court, people would always look at him—and at Leah—and wonder.

"It was the fifties, don't forget. No one ever heard of child sexual abuse back then, I mean, the stories were so rare, you'd damn well believe one if you heard it. Especially from a rabbi's wife. Who could make up something that despicable? Even if, by some miracle, I'd gotten custody, I could never have cleared my name. A rabbi testifying about sex with his daughter? Impossible! In the act of denying everything, I'd have to use those hateful words and that's all anyone would remember. The scandal would ruin us all. We'd be shamed. No one would trust me with their children. No one would hire me. How would I support my family? How could you be happy with me after that? I'd have destroyed your life."

He wept silently, pulled the sodden handkerchief out, dabbed at his cheeks, and stuffed it back, this time in a pants pocket. The mighty had fallen. From the spiffy, four-pointed schooner, white sails above his breast pocket, to the depths of his trousers.

Leah turned away in time to catch the moon dipping below the rooftop of the building across the street. On the fifth floor she thought she saw a woman with shiny black hair dangling a child out the window. She knew better than Sam what her mother was capable of. He was right to be afraid.

"That's why you left me . . . why you stopped coming." She feathered her cheek with the fringe of her braid. "But you knew she was crazy! How could you leave me alone with her?"

"Better a neurotic mother, I thought, than a father who's a national disgrace."

"Neurotic?" Leah felt herself harden again. "Try psychotic. Psychopathic. Paranoid schizophrenic! You left me with a maniac. Talk tachlis, Sam: she almost *killed* me."

His lips seized at each other with dry, parched sounds. He spoke slowly. "I thought she'd be okay if I stayed away. She seemed to want you so much. I thought she was only crazy because of me."

Leah twirled her braid. "What about child support?" It was her last unanswered question. "Dena was desperate for money. We were poor."

"I sent a check every month."

"She said she got nothing."

"Not true! Every month I sent a check."

"You were a deadbeat. Why not just admit it? Too late to make a difference anyway."

"I swear it, Leah! She returned my envelopes unopened."

"So you just gave up? Without even trying to find out if I was okay?"

"Every day I thought of you. Every day I wanted to call. But I was afraid to set her off."

"You could have kept trying until I picked up the phone. Until she wasn't home. You could have driven two hundred miles and checked things out. Met me surreptitiously after school. Slipped twenty bucks into my bookbag. Kidnapped me. Something!"

"I should have. I was scared, Leah. But I should have . . . Oh *God*, I should have." He was sobbing now, not even trying to control himself. He folded his arms on the little table and dropped his head into their nest. The sight of his creased and withered neck, that slash of mortal flesh between hairline and shirt collar, seemed suddenly too naked to be seen.

Leah had uttered those same words lately, wished she'd done something or said something . . . Leo, Freddy, Henry, the pot of tea she should have made. Are there sadder words than "should have" once you know you can't?

There were children's drawings tacked to the cork board behind her, pictures of mommies and daddies, girls and boys; stick figures with big heads and hair like Leah's, curly as a telephone wire; cat and doglike creatures, a bird in a cage, and a blob that might have been a gerbil. Above the drawings stretched a banner headline: THIS IS MY FAMILY. That's what everyone wants to say, she thought, as she filled in the last blank in hers.

"Why didn't you tell me this when I first came back? I lived in your apartment for four months. You never even tried to explain."

He looked morbidly tired. "By then, it was too late. You were seething. And I was sure it would sound as if I'd given you up to save my reputation. I didn't think I could explain what it was like back then, how trapped I was, why I knew I would lose you anyway. Esther, too . . ."

With great effort, he rose from the little chair and began pacing. "I never told her about Dena's real threat. I just said she'd threatened to hurt you if I tried to stay in touch. But Esther knew something was wrong. She understood human behavior. She kept asking, 'Why are you letting Dena do this? How could you let Leah go? What really happened?' Her harping was constant at first, but after a while it stopped." Sam was back at the window, searching the opaque sky. "She must have known it was killing me."

Tea and mandelbroit appeared before Leah's eyes, Esther's welcome; Esther moving her into Rachel's room without a moment's hesitation, running interference for her with Sam, defending her, bringing her to synagogue despite the risk. Sam's wife knew something was wrong and, in her own way, tried to fix it.

Without meaning to deflect from his sins or diminish her suffering, he wanted Leah to know that he suffered, too. His heart had always had one empty chamber. He was despicable in his own eyes. "Abandonment is a terrible sin," he said. "I missed your whole life. I never met my own grandsons. I did this to my own child. But I never stopped loving you, bubbeleh, not one day." He slumped against the windowsill, an old man in a white yarmulke, sobbing into his hands.

"You could have told Esther," Leah said, chilled now, as she raised the shawl to her shoulders.

"She'd have thought me a monster. And I was. What I did was monstrous."

Monster. From the Latin "to warn." Was there a warning here? Was he making this up, trying to cleanse his conscience by Judgment Day? Was his grief a charade? Maybe, but her gut said *believe*. She didn't know her father, but she knew Dena: one breech, one intercepted phone call, and her mother would have gone massively meshugah and everything would have come to pass exactly as Sam predicted. Though Leah had trouble imagining a more crazed childhood than the one she'd had, as they say in Yiddish, "Things are never so bad that they can't get worse." She used to think that having a father under any circumstances was better than not having one at all. Now she wasn't sure. Maybe Sam was a cowardly bastard, or maybe he'd loved her best by letting her go. Either way, the next move was hers. She could keep fighting and risk losing him altogether, or give up and lay claim to whatever fathering the man had left to give. Though surrender was not her style, she found her answer in Ecclesiastes: "A time to tear and a time to mend." She received her father's penance.

As the crowd at the Oneg Shabbat dwindled, Rachel and Shoshanna, sloshed on kosher wine, speculated, worried, and waited. When Sam and Leah finally came downstairs, his red eyes told one story, her Cheshire cat smile another, and those contradictory clues were all that was forthcoming from either of them. Sam was surrounded by the remaining well-wishers. Leah, after being pounced upon by her sisters, made it clear that they were not to probe. "We talked" was all she would say. What transpired between Leah and her father on New Year's Eve was the one family secret that would outlast them all.

After another ten minutes, Sam, yawning discreetly, said he was ready to call it a night.

"It's still early," protested Rachel.

"Not if you're on Jerusalem time."

The president of the shul shook his hand. "You were marvelous, Rabbi Wasserman. Come back soon."

"Only on the *Concorde*," said the old man.

Four remained. Three sisters, one husband, standing in front of a hundred-year-old synagogue, watching in silence as Rabbi Sam Wasserman loped up the block, taking the old year with him. Shoshanna wished she could hold on to the moment, this image of her brilliant, complicated father growing smaller in the distance, belying his once huge presence in the world. His life had virtually paralleled the twentieth century. He'd seen the dray horse give way to the moon shot, the quill pen to the computer, and the unimaginable become reality in the cinders of Auschwitz and Hiroshima. The century was his, for better or worse. He'd fought in one war and against another. Witnessed the Jews nearly annihilated, then reborn in a land of their own. Counseled, blessed, bar and bat mitzva-hed, married or buried thousands of congregants. Met nine presidents. Endured a cavalcade of liars—McCarthy, Nixon, Westmoreland, Ollie North, Bill Clinton (and himself). He'd had two wives and three daughters, who were trying now, in the century's closing hour, to imagine how they would feel when their father was gone.

acknowledgments

WITH GRATITUDE TO: Phyllis Wender, my literary agent and treasured friend. Peter Bricklebank, a wise and patient teacher. Blu Greenberg, Judaic scholar, mentor, and lamed vavnik. The MacDowell Colony of the Arts for its bucolic solitude in the hills of New Hampshire and the solicitude of its caring staff. The Mercantile Library, whose quiet work space in midtown Manhattan offered a constant oasis of calm. And above all, to my beloved husband, Bert, who believed even when I did not and who tolerated my long hours at the computer beyond the call of devotion or duty. My daughters, Abigail and Robin, who brought a fine critical intelligence to their several readings of the manuscript. And my son, David, whose faith and enthusiasm always fuels my efforts.

a note about the author

LETTY COTTIN POGREBIN is the author of eight books of nonfiction, most recently *Getting Over Getting Older*, a memoir. Her essays and articles have appeared in a variety of periodicals including *The New York Times*, *The Washington Post*, *The Nation*, *Ms.*, *Moment*, and *Tikkun* magazines. A past president of the Author's Guild, she lectures widely on feminism, Jewish issues, and the Israeli-Palestinian conflict. *Three Daughters* is her first novel.